Enchanting Winds

Debra I hope you find great delight in seeing your direct influence in this book. Thank you for your wonderful suggestions! HAPPY READING !! Fondly, Mary

MARY HAYES

Mary Hayes
Winter Park, FL

Editing: Kristen Tame
Cover Design: Mary Hayes and Kristen Tame
Back Cover Original Watercolor: Armen Silverbach
Interior Graphics: Mary Hayes and Kristen Tame
Interior Design: Judi Fennell at www.formatting4U.com

First edition 2023
ISBN 979-8-218-29580-6

Dedication

I dedicate this, my first novel, to Silmar - a faithful friend beyond words and my spirit's truest twin. You have laughed beside me, cried along with me, guided me wisely, and deeply enriched the journey of my life for almost 50 years. Thank you with all my heart for being an inspiring and illuminating example of compassion, wisdom, and love. Thank you for being you!

PORT SAINT SMITH

A little town with a lot of heart.

Prologue
Friday, November 25
Maddie

Why am I so restless tonight? Maddie wondered as she paced through the spacious bedroom in the coastal rental home. *The storm hasn't let up all day, which may be adding to my mood*, she realized. *Yet, I don't think this uneasiness has anything to do with that or with the fact that I've been so incredibly unproductive. I've honestly enjoyed an excuse to be lazy, giving me even more reason to relax.*

However, I definitely haven't been this unsettled since arriving at the Cape. In fact, I've felt more content and peaceful here than I have for a very long time. For the past several hours, though, I've had an anxiousness that doesn't necessarily feel bad - it's more like an eagerness or expectation that something good is about to happen. But I can't imagine what.

The *rat-a-tat-tat* of rain continued falling heavily on the metal roof as it had since before dawn, and Maddie welcomed a day without plans. During her much-awaited getaway, she'd already seen many wonderful sights, savored delicious meals, become friendly with several of the locals, and purchased original gifts to take back home. Thus, on this rainy morning, she'd decided to do her own imitation of her elder cat, Miss Priss. True to her intention, Maddie curled up in bed and lingered much later than usual. She then stretched idly and gazed at length with contentment and curiosity out the window. Yet, by mid-afternoon, an unrecognizable yearning began to rise within her.

I'm not nervous or even agitated, she recognized. *No, this seems more like anticipation—similar to the excitement I have when my birthday's coming up, but I'm not exactly sure what to expect. So, what is this I'm sensing? And what could possibly happen on this stay-in-alone, stormy night?*

Maddie reflected on these thoughts and her three decades of life as she ambled down the stairs. So much was going well - her job as a college career counselor was fulfilling, her health was strong and vital, and she enjoyed the company of several close friends and a devoted cat companion. Romance, however, was still missing, and Maddie was doing her best to accept that, or at least, she was trying.

The week away from her daily routine had already been far better than she'd imagined. Most surprising was the number of signs and coincidences that had led her to this remarkable home. And the captivating wind, which had first invited her to the Cape, continued to engage and enthrall her.

Now, after enjoying a simple, delicious supper, Maddie wandered into the small study. She loved this cozy room with its large and varied book selection, the stylish yet comfortable furnishings, and the impressive hearth. Approaching the dwindling fire, she added three sturdy logs and decided to spend the rest of the evening there, enjoying the golden-red blaze in hopes that would calm her restlessness.

The loveseat across from the hearth had become her favorite place to sit. So, Maddie eased herself down with effortless grace, curled her legs up to one side, and wrapped a soft quilt around herself. She then breathed in the woodsy smell of the fire and adjusted to the softer light. After many hours of silence, she began to realize that her senses were heightened, and her awareness was notably more acute.

Ah, Maddie thought, leaning back with a sigh, *what more could I possibly want in this moment? I can't imagine what would make this evening even more special.*

Suddenly, as though in response to her thoughts, a presence became evident in the room. Not a sound was heard nor a word spoken. Yet, Maddie knew she was no longer alone. This presence, *his* presence, which had been unfamiliar to her until recently, was becoming quite irresistible now.

Could he be an angel? she wondered breathlessly. But Maddie sensed this probably wasn't true because he didn't feel either elusive or ethereal. And her response to him was so intensely visceral. *Perhaps,* she further considered, *he's someone that I've known before that has since passed away. I don't think so, though, because his essence is entirely unrecognizable. So, who could he be?*

Everything within Maddie grew still. She did not flinch or move. Not from fear but out of her fascination and desire to know him even more. She wanted to understand all she could about him. Thus, Maddie allowed herself to bask in his palpable proximity and the evident connection between them that was nearly intoxicating.

In those exact moments, Maddie realized that this intriguing encounter must have been the source of her anxiety and anticipation. And she finally dared to be with him fully, allowing her doubts and concerns to fall away. In that togetherness, she felt utterly seen, completely understood, and entirely accepted. That extraordinary sense of connection was what she had been seeking and what she now welcomed and willingly embraced. Yet, in the soft, flickering light, Maddie knew that if she turned to look, no one would be seen.

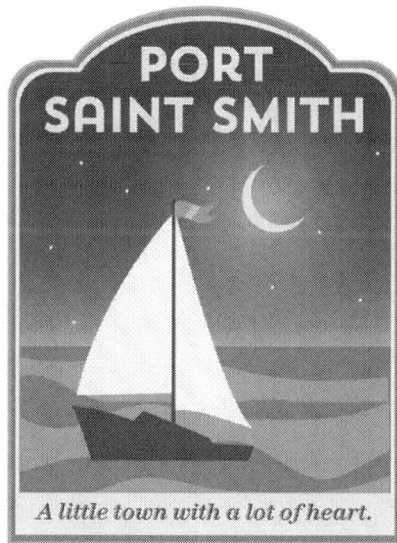

PORT
SAINT SMITH

A little town with a lot of heart.

Six Days Earlier…

SATURDAY, NOVEMBER 19

Chapter 1
Maddie

Madeline Anise Stuart bounded down the front steps of her brownstone apartment shortly after 9 a.m. The sun shined brightly overhead on this crisp, cool November day, and Maddie, as she had been called since childhood, cherished the vibrancy of autumn in the Northeast. Turning left outside the building, she walked briskly toward Market Square, noticing so much along the way—the brilliant colors of the fall leaves, children playing joyfully in the park, and a young couple, oblivious to it all, entranced only with one another.

The city, just a few hours from the coast of Massachusetts, was alive with activity that served to increase her excitement. Maddie appreciated the convenience of living close to the city center, where she could take care of her errands efficiently.

As she made her way through the streets, the highlights of her lovely, auburn hair shimmered in the sun. She was a natural beauty with clear green eyes and a warm, sincere smile. Never one to spend time endlessly primping, Maddie chose minimal makeup and preferred comfortable and classic clothing. Today, she wore a sage-colored turtleneck, a brown corduroy skirt, a vintage cropped jacket, and low-heeled boots. A crimson woven scarf tied loosely around her neck moved gracefully with the rhythm of her purposeful stride.

Maddie enjoyed seeing the many shop windows adorned with autumn decorations.

Not that long ago, she remembered, *during one of my biking excursions, these same places were decorated for the 4th of July. And it was after that bike ride that I had the most unforgettable experience…*

The temperatures had been high during Maddie's July ride through the city. Yet the constant movement kept her cool. After she came to a stop in front of her apartment building, however, heat and fatigue caught up with her. Lingering for a while to simply catch her breath, Maddie noticed just how still the air was. Little, if any, wind was apparent, and the trees around her remained motionless. Suddenly, as though out of nowhere, a small but intense gust of wind kicked up, swirling entirely around her. Maddie was transfixed, watching in disbelief as it encircled her once again. Next, as though coming from the wind itself, she heard a distinct male voice say, *"Come to the coast. Come to Cape Cod. Come and find me here."*

What an enchanting experience that was, Maddie thought reflectively. *Even now, four months later, I can't help but wonder if my fatigue, combined with the intense summer heat, had caused that phenomenon. But I really do believe I heard the wind whispering to me. I'm so glad I went ahead and started planning my trip to the Cape that same afternoon because the day after tomorrow, I'll be on my way! I'm so excited but also a bit nervous. Many times in the past, I have doubted my intuition and used only my intellect to make decisions. However, I'm committed going forward to living differently. I will acknowledge the signs along the way and do my best to trust my inner wisdom. And as far as this unexpected adventure is concerned, my gut sense says that I must go and go soon!*

Traveling alone during Thanksgiving week is so unusual for me. Typically, I would spend this time with family or friends, but I feel so strongly that this is the way it needs to be. I do enjoy traveling with my friends or a boyfriend when I have one. But I'm also comfortable by myself exploring new places and meeting new people without the pressure of any other expectations.

I'm looking forward to bundling up and taking a couple of bike rides, perusing a bookstore, and enjoying the local fare at a nice cafe or two. But, of course, those are not my actual incentives for going to the Cape, Maddie admitted to herself with a smile. *Right now, though, I need to focus on what I'm doing in town and save the wistful daydreaming for later.*

Upon reaching Market Square, Maddie knew exactly where to go and what needed to be done. She walked efficiently in and out of shops, picking up this, dropping off that, and making a few small purchases for the week ahead. Morning quickly transitioned into afternoon as each of the items on her "to-do" list was checked off. Then, satisfied with her accomplishments, Maddie picked up a light lunch and sat down at a picnic table in a nearby park. This welcome reprieve from the day's full agenda gave her an opportunity to think a little more about her pending plans, including the fact that she'd never felt strongly inclined to visit Cape Cod in the past. She had always regarded this popular vacation destination as a place either for the wealthy elite or weary, sunburned tourists. Considering she was neither, she'd never made the three-hour drive east. However, after that auspicious summer day, when the whispering wind encircled and entranced her, the thought of visiting the Cape became not just a fanciful idea but a true longing. Little else had been on her mind, for she was unable to dismiss the mysterious invitation or the intense feelings already imprinted upon her heart. And Maddie could not help but wonder who had called her to the Cape and if she would indeed be able to find him there.

So, as the days grew cooler and the departure date closer, the sense of intrigue intensified. Maddie often laughed, remembering the words of her good friend and neighbor Stephen, who had teased her playfully about her vacation. "I predict the drive time to the Cape may take much longer than your GPS indicates," he'd quipped. "You're so over the moon with excitement that I'm guessing the distance from that lunar location was not factored in."

Still, Maddie had never completely confided in Stephen about her apprehensions regarding her lack of specific travel plans. Usually, the organizational aspects of any previous trips received extensive consideration, followed by scheduled reservations.

Am I really going to be so bold as to drive to the Cape and trust that I'll instinctively know where to stay? she worried. *Perhaps I'm being a bit of a romantic fool who's read too many fairy tales. Honestly, though, there is no telling what might happen. And, since I don't know where I'm going or who I'm actually looking for, I haven't even made rental reservations - which is entirely unlike me. What if I get there and can't find somewhere reasonable to stay? After all, this is Thanksgiving week, which brings up yet another concern. What if I get lonely on Thanksgiving Day, surrounded by unfamiliar people in an unknown place? That would be terrible.*

Maddie knew that courage and conviction would be required to follow through on her decision. And although doubts still nagged her, she was committed to taking the more adventurous route rather than staying anchored to the safe but predictable patterns of her life. Fortunately, several past experiences had served to remind her of the rewards that can result when she followed through on her instincts. So, although her mind could not fully comprehend the lack of a secured itinerary, she was determined to be intuitively guided toward a remarkable getaway.

Once she finished her meal, Maddie gathered her purchases and began heading back home. Only one important task remained to be done before leaving on Monday morning. That task, however, was going to be difficult because saying goodbye to her cat at such an advanced age was getting harder every time. Luckily, Miss Priss would be in the best of care with Stephen, and they would have each other for company.

After walking several blocks, Maddie turned the corner on her street. As she began ascending the building steps, a strong gust of wind caught the loose end of her scarf and twirled it around her shoulder. Simultaneously, a deep, compelling voice whispered, *"We are meant to be together. I await your arrival."*

Maddie caught her breath and thought … *again?! I'm hearing this voice on the wind again?* The same enveloping chills spread throughout her body as she paused to stay present with the sensation as long as possible. *Yet why*, she wondered, *does his voice seem so welcoming, almost like a sense of home? I am not sure, but I certainly want to know.*

Now, with more conviction than ever, Maddie was determined to find out who was beckoning her to the Cape. Tomorrow afternoon, she would deliver Miss Priss into the hands of her trusted, albeit indulgent, caregiver. Then, on Monday, she would leave behind her cat, her concerns, and her daily life to drive east with a decaf latte and a heart full of hope.

Chapter 2
Tink

The parlor in Mrs. Theresa Isabelle Kendleton's home was very dark—much more so than any other room in her historic Cape Cod home. Grief gripped the old woman's heart with no mercy. She felt, therefore, this cheerless room was the perfect place to sit on such a beautiful autumn afternoon. Like a New England fog rolling in from the sea, death had once again blanketed her life, shrouding another day and everything around her.

Slumping over in her formal chair, Mrs. Kendleton knew many in the quaint town of Port Saint Smith were also feeling a sense of shock and sadness over the death of such a special man. She sincerely hoped, though, that no one else was feeling as desolate as she was. For, in her eighty-six years on earth, she'd known true friendship, the sacred honor of being a mother, and the immense joy of one true love. But few had touched her heart in quite the same way as this man had.

'Tink,' as she was fondly called, was considered to be the town's cherished sage. Many of the locals, at various points in their lives, had relied on her wise counsel, boundless compassion, uncanny insights, and sweet sense of humor. This long-time resident's typically delightful presence was as valued in the community as that of the rising sun.

However, who was there for Tink as she endured another significant loss? Where was the solace and support she so desperately needed in

13

these lonely hours? Only her loved ones in spirit, who had passed before, seemed present to her now. Yet, regardless of how faithful and loving they remained, their ability to comfort her was understandably limited. Bless and surround her they could. But not one of them could bring her a restorative cup of hot tea or a handkerchief to dry her eyes. So, in her deep despair, Tink still felt unbearably alone. Grief—that most unwelcome of guests—had come to stay and was not about to take its leave. Thus, this characteristically spry and upbeat woman remained unable to feel happy or grateful, even during this week of Thanksgiving.

Tink recognized, though, the importance of embracing her sorrow. For she well knew from past experiences that ignoring or denying that exhausting emotion would never diminish or destroy it. And so, she committed to staying with the uncomfortable presence of her pain so it could, in time, subside. She also reflected on the wise words of her late mother:

> "Better succumb today to sorrow
> so that hope and joy
> will return on the morrow."

The small lamp on the antique end table next to Tink's chair offered the only light in the otherwise dark room. The single bulb shined dimly onto numerous silver frames below. With tear-filled eyes, the grieving woman gazed at the array of familiar images. She saw there the faces of her deceased loved ones - those dear souls whom she could no longer hold in her arms or kiss on their sweet faces.

Tink's focus went first to the faded photograph of her parents, a devoted couple whose gentle presence she often sensed close to her. The respect and kindness they'd shown to each other through the years had created an unfailing foundation of love for the whole family. And this foundation is what supported them through the heartbreak of Constantine's death, her youngest sister who passed at the age of six. Her sweet image was displayed in the frame next to their parents.

The remainder of the frames featured Tink's immediate family. Her gregarious late husband, Grant Edward Kendleton, III, occupied much of the little table. Among her personal favorites of this handsome man was a youthful shot of him standing proudly in front of the first plane he'd ever piloted. She also cherished the double oval frame behind curved glass. On the left, a shy kiss was documented, showing their early courtship, and on the right was a regal, black-and-white formal taken on their wedding day. But undoubtedly, the most treasured photographs were the two placed closest to her. One depicted Grant standing in their garden, tenderly holding the tiny hand of Noah, their son and only child. And it was a precious image of Noah smiling with innocent delight on his third birthday, which was to be his last.

Tink always made a conscious effort to remember the happier times. And she firmly believed that inner peace and even joy would undoubtedly return. But, in her desolation, she could not begin to fathom how or when that might occur. Since this recent death, the heavy days and weeks had dragged on mercilessly. Yet, deep in the core of her belly, Tink had an uncanny sense that something extraordinary was about to happen. Was this a premonition? She'd had several in her lifetime, and this particularly positive foreshadowing had the same uncanny feeling as many she'd experienced before. And although she was unclear what exactly might come to pass, Tink chose not to question it. For she was certain whatever it was would help bless and uplift her. She clung, therefore, to that hope as though finally seeing the first tiny sliver of dawn piercing through the blackest of nights.

Shifting her thoughts away from the deceased family photographs, Tink thought next about her sister and only living relative, Martha Louise. For many years, Tink had braced herself for the inevitable death of her oldest sibling. This was not a gut sense she'd had but merely common sense, for her sister was more than six years her senior. Surprisingly though, doddering and near ancient Martha Louise lived on, and the two sisters still enjoyed seeing each other on occasion. While visits were infrequent due to their age and the distance between their homes, they made up for this with phone calls, letters, and sincere affection.

Abruptly, the old grandfather clock in the hallway chimed, startling Tink back into the present moment. She tightened her grip on the richly bound book she'd been holding in her gnarled hands. Still, within those pages, she would not find compassionate words of comfort for the bereaved. Nor would she read poetic prose promising a celebratory reunion with the deceased in the great beyond. For here was the journal of her dear friend who had just passed, which he had affectionately bequeathed to her in the final hours of his life. This most personal of presents was something she had never expected to receive. And now her hope was that by carefully studying his written words, she would better understand this dear man's life and the love he had so earnestly yearned for.

Under no circumstances had Tink considered, let alone prepared herself for, the death of this man. She'd assumed her own passing would occur long before his since he had been young enough to be her child. And in truth, he had become like a cherished son to her.

So why, she often questioned, *was he the first to die? Why was this good man taken so soon from this transitory world? Didn't he have so much more to offer through his work and charities? And didn't he, of all people, deserve to find lasting love?* The grief-stricken woman continued to struggle every day with these unanswerable questions.

Every word in his handwritten book had been read and reread since it came into her possession in early July. Here, on each page, he had modestly, yet accurately, recorded in detail his many accomplishments, personal triumphs, and plans for the future. He wrote with honor about his work, as well as his goals for the Spirit of Sailing Foundation. And he described with humble gratitude the sense of fulfillment he felt being a committed philanthropist and visionary for his beloved community of Port Saint Smith.

But many of the pages and passages also revealed his frustrations regarding the delays with his home's renovation. Materials were taking longer than promised to arrive, and his commitment to meticulous craftsmanship was something he was not willing to compromise. Thus, he worked long hours into the night with resolute determination toward a deadline that was idealistic, even for a man of his notable abilities and ambition.

Beyond that, though, Tink was most astonished by an entry that had nothing to do with the goals he'd set for his business, the S.O.S. Foundation, or the transformation of his home. In the privacy of this journal, he had written candidly about his desire to share his life with a loving sweetheart. This did not surprise Tink. But what she could not fathom was his firm belief that her much-anticipated arrival was imminent.

How could that be true? the elderly woman wondered. I don't understand. Yet his drive to create a home well suited for his beloved mandated a sense of urgency to complete the renovation in a timely manner.

For over two decades, Nicolas Paramonos had been Tink's neighbor, close friend, and loyal confidant. On a chilly winter day, he had moved into the sizable and stately home next door. Tink had watched curiously from her kitchen window in admiration as he willingly helped the moving crew carry boxes and furniture inside. His athleticism and convivial personality were most evident as he joked easily with the hired movers. Then Tink experienced for herself his immense kindness ʃwhen she hurried over with a plate of freshly baked cookies for everyone. Sincerely touched by her gesture and the amazing taste of her cookies, Nic thanked her repeatedly in his rich and comforting voice. And through his eyes and actions that day, Tink began to glimpse the warmth and depth of this great man's soul.

That initial meeting marked the beginning of their long and meaningful friendship. Soon, they began speaking nearly every day and enjoying one another's company for hours at a time. On a lovely summer's eve, they would often meet in Nic's garden to share in nature's magnificent symphony of sight, smell, and sound. Then, on a cold winter's night, they would typically gather in Tink's kitchen, indulging in hot chowder, homemade biscuits, and fresh fruit pie. But the holidays at the Kendleton home were almost always the most memorable. At each gathering, Nic would be the honored guest sitting at the other end of the long table—laughing, sharing stories, and enjoying the celebratory feast. And afterward, he would stay and help his close friend and hostess clean up in a way that only true family would.

Tink felt, therefore, that she'd known him so well and, in most ways, she had. Still, she was deeply puzzled by the mysterious love he'd mentioned in his journal. *Who could she be? Had he already met her or just felt her so strongly in his soul? And either way, why had he not shared this promising news with her? Or,* as Tink secretly feared, *were these actually the confused writings of a fever-induced man?* Not likely. But, the thought alone caused her entire body to shutter.

I long to receive more insights regarding Nic's anticipated love, Tink desired silently. *He was always such an expressive and honest com-municator. But then, perhaps I am just a wee bit biased,* she acknowledged with a faint smile. *Still, I do find comfort in thinking about him, glancing over at his home next door, and reading this journal. And for that, I can be truly thankful. So, on this Saturday before Thanksgiving, I will express my gratitude for the rare privilege of reading his heartfelt chronology from the last few weeks of his life.*

She then lifted the book closer to her weary eyes, opened to the page dated July 2, and began to reread the entry written just two days before his tragic death.

Chapter 3
Nic's Journal

Thursday, July 2... 6:20 a.m.

Last night, I dreamed I owned a sailboat named Forever.

In the dream, I was on the boat alone at sea. A massive storm developed, but I was completely unaware. Only as the dreamer-observer could I see the intense squall approaching.

For most of the day, the boat and I had been pleasantly adrift as I worked relentlessly on the interior renovations. I wanted everything to be perfect for my beloved, and I was driven to complete the changes before her arrival. As in my awakened state, I felt certain she would soon be here.

Even as a seasoned sailor, the storm's ferocity caught me completely off guard. I rushed on deck and watched the fierce winds blow and the violent sea attack Forever *like a small toy boat. Mistakenly, I believed I still had time to decide what to do. But I was wrong. For at that moment, the boom swung wide, knocking me hard and toppling me into the frigid ocean.*

The water was unfathomably dark, cold, and turbulent. I struggled to breathe. Like the grasp of an angry beast, I was pulled even deeper into the ocean's depths. Helpless and alone, I watched as my boat vanished quickly from sight. And

18

although I sensed that Forever *would survive the storm, I feared I would not.*

I faded in and out of consciousness and began to accept the fact that I was dying. Just as I started to fully surrender to death, a luminous presence appeared. The lovely figure floated just above the waves—like an angel, wholly untouched by the raging sea. Her eyes were kind, and her sweet smile comforting. And even amidst the ominous clouds, her auburn hair glistened as though the sun was still shining brightly.

With all my heart, I knew she was the beloved I had been preparing for, the one I had so eagerly awaited. Her presence brought me peace, and her essence radiated such love. As she drew closer and closer, I was hopeful that she would save me. But just as she reached out to grasp my hand, I sank below the surface, and I drowned.

I am so shaken by this dream and struggling to make sense of it. I can't believe I died before we were together. Was this a foreshadowing of what may come? Or am I just reading too much into this?

Either way, I don't have time now to dwell on it. The renovation of the house is nearly complete, and I must push on. Because I still strongly sense that my love will be here soon.

I definitely don't feel like my usual self, however. My body feels sluggish and off, and my normal strength and stamina are bewilderingly absent. I often feel faint and exhausted, yet I can't sleep, which is frustrating since this is slowing down my progress considerably. I really should find time to talk to Tink. I'm sure she could offer insights about my dream and also suggest a remedy that might help me feel better. Besides, we haven't spent enough time together lately since I've been so preoccupied with the house. Maybe I'll stop by before the week's end and have a good chat with her. I miss her and hope she knows that.

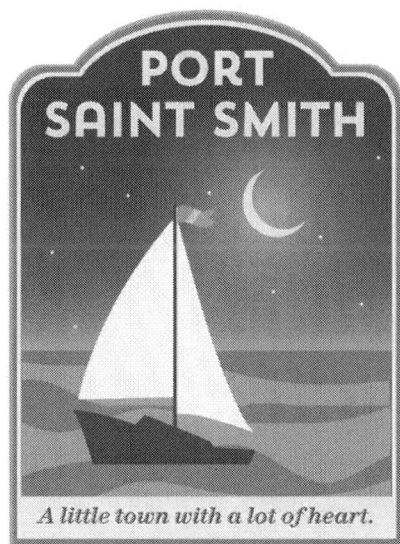

PORT
SAINT SMITH

A little town with a lot of heart.

SUNDAY,
NOVEMBER 20

Chapter 4
Maddie

The suitcases by the door let Miss Priss know that change was afoot. She did not like change - she never had. Maintaining her happiness was paramount. And to ensure this, a predictable sense of order was essential. With routine came the steadfast assurance that life centered entirely around her, as well it should. Any disruption in her small universe, as indicated by the travel bags, was not at all welcome.

Sasha had been Miss Priss's given name, but curiously, she wasn't called that much anymore. And she shared her home with a kind and good person named Madeline Anise Stuart, who, curiously, also wasn't called that either, as she preferred to be called Maddie instead.

Miss Priss had always encouraged Maddie - required her, actually- to pet, feed, love, and consistently adore her. And typically, she would oblige. But this normally obedient woman had been acting rather odd lately. She'd been unusually preoccupied and noticeably happier. Apparently, this inexplicable activity and increased giddiness had nothing to do with Miss Priss. Thus, the full-figured feline, a beautiful white Persian, could be found sulking in the brownstone apartment's large bay window.

On the sidewalk right below, most unaware, Maddie stood catching her breath. Although there was a real chill in the air, she was quite hot, having just returned from an extensive early morning bike ride through

23

the city. Plans and concerns about her trip had slipped away, however, as she'd immersed herself in the pleasing sights on a lovely Sunday outing. As expected, riding through the beautiful parks and near the many bustling cafes in Market Square had brought her back to center and calm.

Bike riding was an activity Maddie had always enjoyed on her own. Although she'd considered joining a cycling club, the idea did not appeal to her private, sensitive nature. Nor had asking a friend to join her for such a lengthy ride ever been successful. Even once, early in their friendship, she'd mentioned the idea to Stephen. His response had been quick and direct. "Thanks for the invite, Maddie, but I'll definitely pass. I tend to avoid sports, especially if they require tight-fitting outfits. I'm comfortable right here in my apartment. If ever I do get a bit restless, I walk to the coffee shop and back or simply stand at the window and watch others toil and train. That's enough of a workout for me," he'd added with a laugh. "You go right ahead, however, with your strenuous excursions, and when you get back, you can tell me all about it." True to his word, Stephen was always a willing listener - attentive and inquisitive regarding her cycling escapades and other aspects of her life.

Now, as Maddie prepared to carry her bike upstairs, she considered bringing it on the trip. *I'd better not*, she quickly decided. *My bike is getting pretty worn out, although I've done my best to maintain it. But the gears alone are practically antique. Still, bike riding would be a great way to explore Cape Cod. I assume there will be rental places in most of the towns, and I'll look into that once I get settled.*

I would sure love to take Miss Priss with me also, Maddie acknowledged. *Sadly, though, just like my bike, she is really starting to show her age. I've noticed she plays a lot less and sleeps a lot more. Plus, riding in the car is a nearly unforgivable experience for her. So, I know she'll be much better off staying here, quite literally, in the lap of luxury.*

With Miss Priss in mind, Maddie looked up in the direction of her apartment. There, in the window, was the reassuring sight of her beautiful cat napping in the midday sun. They had shared almost fourteen great years together, and Maddie was deeply grateful for her remarkable companionship. How would she ever bear the heartbreak when this precocious yet precious cat passed? Maddie couldn't begin to imagine and certainly did not want to think about it today.

Recognizing that her slumbering feline needed to be delivered to Stephen's fairly soon, Maddie turned her attention back to her bike. As she did, a cool gust of wind swept quickly around her, caressing her skin ever so lightly. She remained still and receptive until, like the previous experiences, the wind departed as swiftly as it had arrived.

With renewed vigor, Maddie carried her bike up the two flights of stairs. At the landing near the front of Stephen's door, she paused momentarily. *How lucky I am to have such a good friend living this close! Stephen was the first to greet me*, Maddie remembered fondly recalling the day she moved into the building. With a car full of possessions parked on the street below and holding her anxious cat in a carrier, she stood at the door of her new apartment, fumbling with the unfamiliar keys.

"Well, hello there!" a voice had called from across the hall. Maddie turned to see a handsome man, about forty years old, leaning against the frame of his open doorway. "I believe that fate has brought a true beauty to my building—how very exciting! And look, she even brought her lovely owner with her!"

Chapter 5
Elizabeth

Elizabeth Harden Moreau sipped slowly on her coffee as she caught up with morning correspondence. Her damp, blonde hair was wrapped in a towel, and a thick cotton robe was cinched snugly around her narrow waist. Elizabeth's clear blue eyes remained focused on the efforts in front of her, grateful that little else was demanding her attention.

She'd thoroughly enjoyed the easy pace of a quiet morning at home. The only other activity scheduled for the day was attending a matinee performance at the local theater. Elizabeth knew that this small yet earnest production would not compare to the many extraordinary shows she'd seen on Broadway. Still, the citizens of Port Saint Smith loved their arts and eagerly poured themselves into every event, exhibit, and production. And as an active board member, she'd been able to watch a few of the rehearsals and expected this performance to be most heartwarming.

However, once her phone signaled an incoming text, Elizabeth feared that the relaxed rhythm of the day was about to come to an end. Reluctantly, she set down her coffee and glanced over at her phone. The short message left little choice but for her to go into the office, go soon. After releasing a long sigh of resignation, she rose and walked into her large dressing room. There, she selected a russet-colored sweater set, a deep brown pencil skirt, and stiletto heels. She decided that dressing now for the theater would be easier than coming back home to change after attending to this business matter.

"I don't understand why this can't wait until tomorrow," Elizabeth muttered aloud. But her objection was not heard - not by a person, a pet, or even a plant. For she lived alone and had for many years. Elizabeth's reasoning was that a demanding work schedule and her spontaneous travel whims precluded her from sharing a home with any other living being. Thus, her spacious townhouse, complete with amenities such as building maintenance and yard care, provided the freedom that suited her best.

As a seasoned real estate professional, Elizabeth believed her consistent work ethic, rather than luck and good timing, had been the key to her success. She put in long hours and usually worked on weekends. Because along with the commitment to her career came a salary allowing for guilt-free indulgences that helped make it all worthwhile. She loved shopping trips along the narrow side streets of Paris and traveling on to Tuscany to visit her good friends Lucas and Stella. When she remained in the States, Elizabeth indulged herself in restorative getaways near the Berkshire Mountains or extended weekends in New York. Her trips to the Big Apple were usually scheduled to coordinate with gala events at the museum and opening nights on Broadway.

Elizabeth, who had remained single for all of her 45 years, was content. After relocating to Cape Cod from New York, she'd found a near-perfect balance to her life in the charming seaside town of Port Saint Smith. She exercised regularly, shared meals and coffee with friends and colleagues, and enjoyed serving on the theater's board of directors. Although Elizabeth welcomed romance, she realized that fulfillment for her would not come in the form of caring for a husband, a hound dog, and even hydrangeas.

While completing her preparations to leave, Elizabeth did her best to avoid agitation. She was determined not to let this unexpected text impact her good mood. Still, she was concerned because this request was just one more conflicting directive received from her boss in the last few months.

Walters Real Estate and Investment, Elizabeth's place of employment, was located in an impressive building on Center Street in the heart of town. Larry Walters, the sole owner-broker and attorney-at-law, had established the company two decades earlier. During those years, Larry had become a highly respected and dedicated citizen in the

27

community. Many looked to him for legal assistance, as well as help with their real estate dealings. He was trusted and revered by the citizens of Port Saint Smith.

But, since mid-summer, much had changed. The company's primary investment partner, a successful builder-contractor, had died unexpectedly, leaving behind numerous jobs on the docket, a thriving charitable foundation, a complex trust and estate, and an unimaginable void. This loss had been felt in every aspect of Larry's life - both professionally and, more importantly, personally. For this prominent partner, Nicolas Paramonos, had also been his best friend.

In the nearly nine years of her employment, Elizabeth had come to know Larry Walters well. She could almost always anticipate his patterns of behavior, business choices, and personal preferences. However, just weeks after Nic's passing, Larry's erratic actions and odd requests began. He was like a different man. Usually quick-witted and ambitious, Larry was now sullen and unmotivated. Conversations with Elizabeth and his other staff members were shaky and uncertain. And he often withdrew to the safe confines of his plush office to avoid making any decisions.

Elizabeth realized Larry was grieving deeply, but she also wondered if something else was bothering him. He was unresponsive in many ways, including with his phone, which had always been of the utmost importance. In the days before Nic's death, Larry could be seen texting and talking throughout the day. Yet, Elizabeth had recently witnessed his hands actually shaking when a text message arrived. What could he be afraid of? Was there something he was avoiding? She dared not ask but continued to make note of this and his other uncharacteristic behaviors.

As a result, Elizabeth had stepped up to assume considerably more responsibilities at the office, which she managed with her usual efficiency and effectiveness. Occasionally, her typically calm demeanor was challenged, but she still kept her composure and remained committed to her work, even though her outlook was now peppered with growing apprehension.

Interestingly, Larry had initially been reluctant to hire this off-islander, stating that she was obviously overqualified for the position. Elizabeth hailed from Manhattan, where she'd been both a successful real estate agent and a sought-after interior designer in that world-renowned city. She was accustomed to much more lucrative and prestigious work. Still, she managed to convince Larry to give her a chance to prove herself with the promise that if, after a one-month trial, he was not satisfied with her efforts, she would take her leave without argument. The month passed quickly, and Larry easily recognized her contributions and appreciated the respectful and effective working relationship that was already evolving. And soon, he was relying on Elizabeth's expertise and keen business sense in almost every area of his company.

Not only was Elizabeth a competent employee, but she also took particular pride in her appearance. Standing 5' 11", she was a strikingly beautiful blonde with cropped short hair, stylishly dressed in her usual attire - tailored blouses, fitted skirts, and fashionable shoes. While the other residents in Port Saint Smith tended to wear more relaxed clothing, they had come to admire this commanding woman.

Presently, with no time left to dawdle, Elizabeth selected a small, color-coordinated clutch and placed her center-seat ticket inside. She drove the short distance to the office, unlocked and entered the large real estate building. Immediately, she noticed how very quiet it was. No one had been expected to work today - the Sunday before Thanksgiving - nor had she planned to come in until receiving the unusual request earlier today. Besides the sharp clicking of her high-heeled shoes on the hardwood floors, the only audible sound was the low, symphonic buzz of the various machines running the business.

Elizabeth knew she would have to work quickly to be on time for the performance. Arriving late would be unacceptable . Fortunately, there were no other demands or distractions, and her desk was precisely how she'd left it the afternoon before - tidy and well-organized. Thus, she was able to immediately set about accomplishing the task.

The real estate branch of Larry's company represented many lovely homes on the Cape. *So, why rent this one?* she could not help but question. *Especially in light of the fact that just two days earlier, Larry and I discussed this very property and decided to close it up for the winter. Why, then, was Larry having her prepare a rental agreement? And why did he need it done today? What could have happened to change his mind so unexpectedly?*

Nonetheless, Elizabeth dutifully prepared and printed the rental forms and placed them neatly in a packet in the center of her boss's desk. Next, she notified Larry in a brief text that this task was now complete.

Satisfied with her efforts, Elizabeth smoothed a wrinkle in her skirt and strode confidently toward the door. With a slight toss of her hair and the turn of the key, she locked and left the building. As she started up her car, another thought crossed her mind.

I wonder if Tink is going to be in attendance today? She's also such an ardent supporter of the theater, and I believe this uplifting performance would do her grieving heart much good. Nic's death stunned all of us, but perhaps none quite as much as Larry and our good friend, Tink. I do hope to see her. But either way, Elizabeth determined, *I have every intention of immersing myself in the entertaining show. Then, tomorrow morning, I will accomplish Larry's other bewildering request for that property.*

Chapter 6
Tink

With quivering hands, Mrs. Tink Kendleton gripped the treasured book and held it tightly to her chest. She wiped the tears from her eyes, recognizing the necessity to avoid self-pity and find a way to live again. She'd been missing out on so much, including the opening weekend at the theater, an activity that always brought her joy.

Life must eventually go on, she affirmed. *If I sit in this chair another day, I could turn into one of those grumpy, old ladies no one likes to be around, rather than the spirited senior that I truly am.*

No matter how often she reread Nic's journal, Tink realized she might never grasp the full meaning of his words. Yet, she yearned, more than anything, to understand who the woman was that Nic wrote about so openly on these pages. Who was this great love he had been preparing his home for? And why did he believe she would be joining him there soon? The inquisitive woman did not have the answers but decided nevertheless to set the journal aside in order to rest her weary mind.

Nic told me more than once, Tink recalled, *that I was the wisest person he'd ever met. But I definitely don't feel like that person right now. In the past, I've been able to flow with notable ease through life's many hardships. But this current wave of grief has hit me hard, and I feel so adrift in this intense storm of sorrow. I'm humbled to admit the extent to which this grief has robbed me of my vitality. I feel like the ancient*

31

Raggedy Ann Doll slumping over in my attic. Still, I am determined to do something worthwhile with this new day.

Resolutely, Tink placed the journal on the small table beside her. She then pressed her wrinkled hands firmly on the arms of the formal chair and slowly pushed herself up to standing. Wobbling just a bit, she cautiously steadied her stocky frame because even the slight gesture of rising required much effort. She was sure; however, her weariness and weaknesses were due more to this current emotional state than to her advanced age.

The widow of Mr. Grant Edward Kendleton, III, had several good options for activities due to her busy personal life, as well as the commitment she'd made to many of the local civic and volunteer organizations.

I know it's too late to attend the theater, so maybe I'll do a wee bit of gardening. My yard could certainly use some attention before winter arrives with all its frosty glory. Tink loved working in her backyard amongst the beautiful flowers, seasonal vegetables, winding jasmine, and interweaving grapevines. Yet, more often than not, she could be seen stomping about in her bright-colored boots at the community garden. There, right along with the other volunteers, she would be seeding, weeding, and harvesting, appreciative of the fact that all the wonderful, organic fruits and vegetables would be donated to local families in need.

Tink also spent a significant amount of time volunteering with the Port Saint Smith Women's Guild. She attended weekly meetings, made crafts and cookies to raise funds for their local causes, served in various leadership positions, including past president, and oversaw the annual rummage sale. However, the hoity-toity luncheons, where she was expected to dress in pearls and finery, were among her least favorite, especially now when she struggled to find joy in every day.

But by far, this active elder's favorite charitable endeavors always began in her kitchen. For Tink loved to bake, and her award-winning desserts were coveted county-wide. Pies and tarts, cakes and cookies, muffins and scones—she made them all exquisitely. In her dining room, a large custom-made cabinet showcased the many baking trophies she'd won throughout the years. And at philanthropic auctions, her baked goods always brought the highest bids. Her appreciative friends and neighbors continued to be astonished at how Tink's annual holiday tray of treats could possibly be better than the year before.

Even so, Tink reserved her most earnest efforts in the kitchen for the excited recipients who never thanked her with proper etiquette or handwritten notes on monogrammed stationery. Nor did they pay any heed to her weight, age, or outfits. Instead, these friends simply delighted in her warm personality while eagerly gobbling up her delicious goodies. With tails-a-wagging and noses-a-twitching, Tink always knew that her nutritious and delicious canine cookies would be winners at the Homes for Hounds Rescue Center.

Located on the edge of town, the rescue center had become an important part of Tink's life, and her considerable volunteer contributions were nearly legendary. The appreciative pooches within their confined cages always demonstrated how cherished her companionship and cookies really were.

Perhaps I will bake for my darling doggies today, Tink considered. *That always cheers me up. But, first, I'm going to let some light into this dreary room, which, in and of itself, should do me good.*

Slowly, the octogenarian shook the stiffness from her legs as she walked toward the window, feeling a small sense of purpose rising within. She smiled, noting the slightest spring in her step, and recalled a recent conversation with her sister.

A well-meaning but considerably less optimistic woman, Martha Louise often scolded her younger sibling, saying, "You've got to remember, Theresa Isabelle, you're NO SPRING CHICKEN! All this do-gooding and hopping to and fro will surely wear you out!" To Tink, though, the mere thought of hopping around like a lively spring chicken brought her a welcome moment of merriment.

"Martha Louise," she'd responded, "You are so right! I am by no means a spring chicken. However, you must realize how much I enjoy all my activities. I thrive on the sweetness of giving and am filled with happiness when I help others. So, I would much rather spend my time doing that which I *can* rather than focus on that which I *cannot*. Please know, dearest Martha Louise, that this feeble, old bird you call your sister," Tink had continued, stating with great mirth, "intends to keep peeping and persisting throughout the remaining days of her life!"

Remembering this now, Tink began pulling open the heavy drapes to let the sunlight in at last.

Chapter 7
Larry

Finely diced Porcelain garlic and Hen-of-the-Woods mushrooms simmered in a large skillet on the chef-inspired stove. Larry Walters relished the ritual of cooking—the shopping, chopping, sautéing, and most importantly, the eating. For him, preparing meals was not merely a hobby but a near-perfect escape. And creating culinary masterpieces was one of his favorite ways to relax from the stresses of everyday life. But very little time had been spent in the kitchen of late due to his overwhelming feelings of loss. Lethargy had set in where excitement and exploration had once reigned. Most of his cooking gadgets remained unattended, like children's toys long since forgotten in a sandbox.

Sailing had been Larry's other passionate pursuit. When he wasn't working, Larry would almost always be in his kitchen cooking or off to sea sailing. But this maritime enthusiast had not been aboard his boat in over four months. Going anywhere near the marina was simply too painful since all he could remember were the many great adventures he shared with his sailing mate, Nic. Nic was dead now, and Larry was constantly confronted with, yet desperately trying to avoid, the intense feelings around this irrefutable fact.

Nic Paramonos and Larry first became acquainted through their mutual business interests. Each man was an entrepreneur and visionary in his own right: Larry - a successful realtor, developer, and attorney; Nic

- a highly respected builder-contractor and philanthropist. Additionally, they shared a strong commitment to helping manage the growth in their Port Saint Smith community. Like nearly all the other residents, they wanted to preserve the town's innate charm and the integrity of the environment.

For years, they worked together on a vast range of projects, establishing a partnership built, quite literally, on the firm foundation of honor, respect, and trust. Yet, it was on a sailboat at sea where their true friendship flourished.

During one of their initial business meetings, Larry had casually mentioned an interest in learning to sail. Nic, a lifelong sailor and avid sportsman, took this as an invitation to share his expertise. Lessons began within the week, and these tutorials quickly gave way to pleasurable day-long excursions.

Nic had always freely shared sailing lessons and his love of the sea with anyone who showed interest. Many of his Port Saint Smith friends would join him on deck to learn how best to use the tiller or how to observe and, thus, optimize the direction and force of the wind. But Larry was the one who became his most accomplished student, as well as his very best friend.

After just five months of instructions, Larry purchased his own impressive boat. For a man who liked to live life large, the majestic 37-foot sloop was perfect. Whenever possible, the two men would leave behind the world of work and spend the day navigating the waters of Cape Cod Bay on a sailboat aptly named *The Great Getaway*. Laughter, good food, and camaraderie were as plentiful as the rolling ocean waves. Soon enough, the mates recognized the prosperity of their friendship accruing - a treasure far greater than bank accounts and profit lines.

Being on the water felt inherently natural for both Larry and Nic, which they credited to the fact that each hailed from seafaring ancestry. Lawrence Rolf Walters's forbearers had been Scandinavian, as evident by his ruddy complexion, sand-colored hair, and formidable stature. Although once a physically fit man, Larry had become increasingly indifferent to the growing paunch in his mid-section. With good-natured wit, he would often boast to Nic that he was by far the more fit and ruggedly handsome of the two. The inaccuracy of this statement was most evident and became an amusing point of contention.

Nicolas Demetre Paramonos was of Greek descent. Although

considerably shorter than Larry, the tanned and trim man could easily surpass his counterpart in strength. On job sites, this builder effortlessly scaled scaffolding and climbed along rooftops to closely inspect every detail. And even before his full workday began, Nic would typically rise early and ride his bike through the picturesque coastal towns neighboring Port Saint Smith.

In regard to romance, both men shared the title of "Eligible bachelor." Larry remained reluctant to trust love again following a painful divorce. He declined all party or dinner invitations that were intended to set him up with yet another promising woman, and he refused to consider the idea of online dating.

Nic, on the other hand, yearned for the sweetness of a lasting love and believed strongly that one day he'd share his life with a beautifully kind and caring woman. But finding that love had eluded him, and, in his final days of life, the desire had only become more urgent.

Thus, without romantic commitments, Larry and Nic had ample opportunity to navigate the spectacular waters off the shore of Port Saint Smith. However, that changed abruptly in the months leading up to summer when Nic became fixated on completing an extensive renovation of his home. Days would pass without any communication as the near perfectionist focused solely on his singular goal. Even their mutual friend, Tink, confided in Larry one day that Nic's preoccupation with this project was unprecedented.

Thinking back, Larry would become deeply distressed about Nic's sudden change in behavior. Should he, as his closest friend, have tried to stop him or at least encouraged him to slow down? Could the tragedy of his untimely passing have been prevented? With unending remorse, Larry had not been able to find a resolution to his guilt. Thus, in the presence of such tumultuous emotions and the absence of Nic's good company, Larry spent most of his leisure time now watching television or sleeping. A loyal sports fan, hours would pass as he lay distracted by the Red Socks, the Patriots, and the Bruins.

Luckily, Larry had never fallen into the unfortunate dining habits of many a single man. He did not gorge on chips from oversized bags or eat frozen food formed in plastic microwave trays. Nor did he order super-sized meals at drive-thru windows to be consumed with little awareness. Instead, the partaking of meals for him still remained important, even if he dined alone on a single burger seared on the stovetop.

Upon waking earlier that day, Larry had felt a rare burst of energy and inspiration. So, he'd gone to the market to buy fresh ingredients and purchase, among other things, a tasty regional Massachusetts blue cheese and a tart, crimson cranberry relish. Both would be added to his current creation - an omelet topped with sautéed asparagus.

The smell of the melting cheese and simmering vegetables was tantalizing, and Larry was quite hungry. Still, he restricted his tasting to only seasoning the food properly and no more. For he was always willing to wait to eat until the ingredients melded together into a savory symphony of flavors.

Before long, Larry was gathering the makings of a single table setting - silverware, cloth napkin, placemat, and a glass of sparkling water. Then, with the plated meal in hand, he walked onto the extensive back porch and looked out over the bay. This, he thought, is what life is meant to be—savoring finer moments and devouring wicked good food.

Reveling briefly in a deep sense of satisfaction, Larry's near-hallowed experience was abruptly interrupted by the sound of his phone receiving a text.

I'll check that message later, he grumbled to himself. *It will have to wait until I'm done eating.*

Still, Larry could not help but feel agitated receiving a message on his private phone. Only three people had ever been given that number. The first was his sister in Colorado, who never texted but called instead and only then on special occasions, such as his birthday and holidays. The second was his office manager, Elizabeth Moreau, who preferred texting and did so often. But he'd already received notification from her stating that the rental paperwork was complete and she'd be unavailable for several hours while attending the matinee performance at the theater. That left only Nic, his deceased best friend.

As Larry struggled with this realization, a strong wind rustled through the trees surrounding the porch.

That message can't possibly be from him, Larry muttered, hanging his head in disbelief. *And yet, how can I explain the other two texts I received earlier this morning?*

Chapter 8
Maddie

After returning to her apartment following the long bike ride, Maddie tended to a few last-minute chores. She would be gone for a week. So, bills were paid, plants watered, and the cat's toys, food, and bowls gathered to be taken to Stephen's apartment across the hall. In the remaining time before delivering her cat into his care, Maddie picked up Miss Priss for a cuddle as memories of her first encounter with this good friend came to mind again.

Maddie could still hear Stephen's friendly hello as she stood, struggling to hold the cat carrier and fiddle with the unfamiliar lock and keys.

Exhausted from the move but excited about settling into her new place, Maddie had held firmly to the carrier for fear that, if it were set down, loud meowing or even howling would ensue. And that was not how she wanted to be introduced to the other tenants on the floor.

From across the way, she heard a friendly hello and a comment about the cat's beauty. Maddie turned to see who was speaking and saw a man close to her age standing at an open door. He was of average height and build and quite nice-looking. Yet, his ruffled sandy blonde hair and relaxed demeanor seemed in direct contrast to his designer attire.

"Allow me to introduce myself," he said, walking toward her. "I'm Stephen Thomas Taylor, and I'm honored to meet you both," he offered with a slight bow. Then, peering toward the carrier, Stephen asked, "What, may I ask, is the name of this wondrous creature?"

"Her name is Sasha," Maddie replied.

"Well, that's certainly a lovely name," he stated honestly. "But I may be inclined to call her Miss Priss instead. Unless, of course, you object. Because I'm guessing from her appearance that she is highly sensitive, incredibly discerning, and perhaps prone to being a bit fickle? Am I right?"

Before she could answer, however, he continued, "Please don't take offense because I'm sure she's also a most worthy companion."

Maddie smiled and laughed in astonishment at this man's bold yet astute observations. *How refreshing*, she'd thought, *to meet someone who shares their opinions so freely.*

"And you," Stephen inquired, looking up, "the caring owner of this fabulous feline, what is your name."

Hesitant at first to answer for fear he might assign her a nickname as well, she replied, "I'm Madeline Stuart, but I prefer to be called Maddie."

"Now," he said cheerfully in reply, "that name suits you perfectly. And, although you're a great beauty yourself, I doubt you're affected by your good looks like this kitty cat is. In fact, I sense that you are a truly kind person and very humble by nature, almost to a fault. Oh, do forgive me, Maddie," he pressed on. "I usually have pretty keen instincts when it comes to understanding people. In fact, I wouldn't be the least surprised if you and I became friends. But right now, apparently, there is work to be done. So, I'm going to stop prattling on and lend you a hand. That is if you'll allow me."

"Really?" Maddie asked in disbelief.

"Certainly. I'd be glad to help bring up some of your things. I can be trusted with small lamps or tiny, potted plants. Although, I'll be useless with anything large or heavy. Being strong," he admitted while attempting to flex a nearly unperceivable bicep, "is clearly *not* one of my strengths."

Maddie willingly accepted Stephen's assistance. She was exhausted from weeks of planning, packing, and repeatedly consoling her cat. So, together, they managed to bring her entire car full of possessions upstairs and into the apartment even before the professional movers arrived with

39

the furniture and larger boxes. And Maddie found Stephen's company to be immensely enjoyable, without a moment lacking in laughter.

Following the successful move-in, Stephen invited Maddie to join him that evening for Chinese takeout.

"Would you allow me to treat you to a nice, warm meal tonight?" he requested. "You couldn't possibly want to cook, and I would welcome the company of both you and Miss Priss. But please, do not worry, Ms. Maddie Stuart; the only object of my affection will be your cat. Of this, I can assure you."

Appreciative of the offer and too tired to say no, she readily agreed and thanked him for his kindness.

"Of course, you're very welcome. Why don't you go freshen up and attend to whatever else you need to and then come over in about an hour? That will give me sufficient time to order our dinner and purchase a few tasty treats for Her Highness."

"That's so nice of you!" Maddie replied. "Can I bring anything?"

"Certainly not. You are my guests, and I will be honored to entertain you both."

After a restorative bath and a small bit of obligatory unpacking, Maddie walked across the hall and rang Stephen's doorbell with a worrisome cat in her arms. The host, now wearing even more formal attire, answered immediately and invited them inside.

"Well, hello, Ms. Maddie and Miss Priss. Do come in."

Stepping into the foyer, Maddie was speechless. Unsure of what she had expected, nothing prepared her for what she saw. Every room featured such elegant décor that she felt as though she'd entered a European chateau. Each wall was covered with lush wallpaper, beautiful tapestries, and ornately framed original paintings. Stunning sculptures were displayed on antique furniture pieces. And atop the polished hardwood floors were richly woven wool carpets.

"I've decided tonight to forgo the formal dining room," he announced affably. "We'll eat instead in the living room, which is where I eat most of my meals anyway. Please follow me."

Maddie did her best not to gawk as Stephen led them past the dining room, which was indescribably formal. They soon entered the living room, and Maddie noted that this room was by no means informal. Stephen directed her to sit on one of the two plush wingback chairs as he seated himself across from her on a sofa. Between them was an inlaid wooden coffee table covered with impressive art and architectural books, silver candlestick holders, crystal goblets, and linen napkins that matched the two placemats he'd already set. The only incongruent items on the table were the red and white paper cartons filled with their aromatic Chinese dinners.

"Make nothing of it," Stephen gestured to her, waving his arms around the room. "I was an only child, and obviously, my mother loved to shop. She was an art collector, and I was lucky enough to end up with nearly everything. I realize it looks rather pretentious. But I promise you, I am not."

The evening proceeded in a most enjoyable and relaxed way. While they dined on delicious food and talked about their lives and interests, Miss Priss sat contentedly next to Stephen on a silk throw. Her new admirer's attention, coupled with the decadent treats he fed her, enchanted the Persian cat. And thus began their weekly ritual of memorable Sunday night meals.

Grateful for that initial encounter and Stephen's faithful friendship, Maddie brought her thoughts back to the present. Soon, she would be taking her cat over to the most devoted caregiver imaginable, and Stephen would undoubtedly be eagerly awaiting their arrival. He was always glad to welcome this royal guest into his home whenever Maddie worked late or traveled to attend conferences for her job.

When the time came to walk across the hall to deliver Miss Priss, Maddie inquired of her cat if she wanted to go get fancy treats at Stephen's home. In response, Miss Priss yawned slowly, stretched leisurely, and, with the slightest flick of her tail, moved with an aloof air toward the door.

After hearing the knock, Stephen greeted them warmly, saying, "I've been looking forward to seeing you both all day!" He immediately reached for the cat, who quickly settled into his adoring arms. "Miss Priss and I will be just fine together, won't we, precious?" he asked, seeking assurance from the oblivious feline. "Please don't worry, Maddie. I'll take the best care of her like I always do."

"Thank you, Stephen," Maddie replied softly. "I'm not worried about her. But I am feeling a little anxious," she admitted.

"I sensed something might be bothering you. Do you want to talk about it? You know you can tell me anything."

"I guess I'm concerned about the trip. I mean, who does this? Who

41

hears a voice on the wind and follows it all the way to the coast? Am I crazy for doing this? What are your feelings about it, Stephen? Because you're the only one who knows why I'm really going to the Cape," Maddie stated sheepishly.

When she first shared her travel plans with Stephen back in August, he'd questioned her directly. "I thought you'd always avoided the Cape. And now you're planning to go there during the off-season when the weather is cold and the beaches are empty? And you're going *alone* during Thanksgiving week? No one will be there except the locals, a few weathered fishermen, and the snack-seeking seagulls. That doesn't sound like much fun, Maddie. Is there something you're *not* telling me about this little getaway?" he'd teased playfully.

Maddie had been scared to admit the actual reason she was going. Did she dare mention the whispering wind's invitation and risk alienating her good friend? She could instead just say she needed quality time alone and some good old-fashioned R & R. But, having such a close friend, she recognized, was a true gift. Besides, she truly wanted to tell him everything. So, she revealed to him how the wind had completely encircled and enthralled her and then invited her to the Cape.

Stephen's response that day had been unusually quiet. He nodded silently and then went into the kitchen with the excuse of filling their water glasses, leaving Maddie unsure what his actual thoughts were.

Explaining to her professional colleagues about going away during the Thanksgiving holiday had been considerably easier. The college where Maddie worked as a career counselor was closed for the week, so vacations were to be expected. But, sharing the precise reason *why* she was going to the Cape had been quite another matter. Upon announcing her plans, several of her co-workers asked particularly pointed questions: "Do you know how cold it's going to be on the coast? What if a 'nor'easter' kicks up? Is anyone going with you? Are you meeting someone there? Or will you be *alone* on Thanksgiving?"

For fear of being ridiculed, Maddie had simply replied, "My plans are to read, rest, and do a little sightseeing." Her answer had been honest while still not revealing the complete reason for her journey. Fortunately, her co-workers had accepted her simple explanation without pushing back. But Maddie's ultimate motivation for going was to find out who had invited her to the Cape. And Stephen was the only one she'd trusted with that incredible information.

Now, on the day before departure, Maddie hoped that Stephen would offer her some words of support or reassurance regarding her decision. Stephen's answer amazed her. In a quiet tone, he said, "Ever since I've known you, Maddie, you've been very sensible and, at times, even predictable. But today, I am unreservedly commending you for following through on something this unusual. And I want you to know that I totally believe you. I'm certain that you did hear a voice, and you owe it to yourself to not only explore that but also to be proud of yourself for doing so.

"How many people," he continued, "have extraordinary experiences and never dare to believe them or follow through? Not many, I would guess. So go to the Cape, my brave friend, knowing that you have my full support and encouragement. Because you never know where that might lead."

"Oh, Stephen, thank you so much."

Quickly, though, Stephen returned to his more typical mannerisms, asserting, "Regardless of what happens to you, however, I plan to enjoy every minute here with 'our cat.' Miss Priss and I will be snug as bugs together while you are out facing the cold in the coastal hither lands. So, run along, and get to bed early so you're well rested for this intriguing adventure!"

Immensely grateful for his reassurance, Maddie thanked Stephen again and said goodbye. She then blew a tender kiss to her sleeping cat and walked back toward her apartment.

Stephen watched as she crossed the hallway and added, "I will await your reports about the wonders of your trip and, more importantly, about the whisperings of the wind…"

Chapter 9
Tink

Tink Kendleton tugged hard on the drapes' thick, braided cords, revealing a brilliant autumn afternoon. Since moving into this house decades earlier as a young bride, the large windows had rarely been covered during the day. For Tink always enjoyed the flood of light coming into the room, as well as the lovely view of the neighborhood. But, for the past several months, the intense brightness had been too much of a contrast to her darkened mood. Plus, seeing the vacant house next door was simply too painful of a reminder of Nic's absence. So, the drapes had remained tightly closed day after day. But now, with a determination to get on with her life, Tink was ready, at last, to allow more light into her heart and home.

As the old woman began looking out onto Windswept Way, she felt enormously comforted. The stunning trees lining the street glimmered with gold, russet, orange, and red. As she watched in fascination, a soft breeze joyfully tickled their colorful leaves, many of which danced down the sidewalk and across her lawn. Tink was also delighted to see that many of her neighbor's homes were decorated for the season. Porches were filled with dried corn stalks, bales of hay, and carved pumpkins, while the doors featured festive fall wreaths and Indian corn.

Looking directly across the street, Tink thought about the Lerner family, who had moved in three years earlier. Devoted parents, Sarah and Benjamin, often played in the front yard with their two young children,

Clara and Josh, while Bailey, the family's lovable golden retriever, romped about. Tink was always glad to see this young family and frequently gifted the children homemade cookies and other goodies, which invariably solicited gigantic grins and grateful giggles.

This family had been good to her as well. Following Nic's death, Tink had been quite touched by the considerate sympathy card brought over by Sarah and Benjamin. And the children each made colored pictures for her that depicted their lofty idea of heaven. Filled with clouds and angels and dogs of all sizes, the drawings still graced the front of her refrigerator.

Tink's good friend of over fifteen years, Shirley Lund, lived to the right of the Lerners. *Through the years,* Tink reflected thoughtfully, as she looked over at Shirley's modest but well-kept home, *I've watched my dear friend shake off the heaviness of death and disappointment swifter than almost anyone I know. With childlike innocence, she remembers the reassuring truth of what awaits the deceased on the other side, and thus, she quickly returns to her usual positive self. Had it not been for her supportive and devoted help during and after the memorial service, I'm not sure I would have made it through the day.*

Yet, Tink recognized whimsically, *my elderly friend Shirley is no spring chicken either. Just like me, she hops all over town doing good deeds, and I'm certain she is healthier and happier for having done so.*

Indeed, the two civic-minded seniors dedicated a great many hours each week to several local charities. Both were active founding members of the Port Saint Smith Women's Guild. Weekly meetings and numerous philanthropic events kept them busy year-round. Shirley also volunteered several days a week at the Chamber of Commerce. There, the retired schoolteacher enjoyed welcoming visitors as much as Tink loved delivering tasty treats to her neighbors, friends, and the raucous rescue dogs.

I'm genuinely happy that Shirley has such perfect plans for Thanksgiving, Tink acknowledged. *Even though I would have loved her to be here for dinner, she will be hosting her own little celebration for her visiting house guest, her cousin. But my greatest disappointment comes from the fact that another important guest will be absent from my Thanksgiving table—someone who has not missed a holiday feast in my home since the year he moved in next door so long ago.*

With this in mind, Tink felt a familiar heaviness begin to settle into her chest. She didn't want to sink into a place of deep despair again, especially since she'd promised herself to do something useful with the remainder of the day. So, with determined effort, she forced back a tear, sighed resolutely, and deliberately glanced past Nic's empty house towards the home of Charlie Kelly just on the other side.

Tink couldn't quite see Charlie's house from inside her own, but she could easily picture the old fella whistling contentedly in the garden. Most likely, he'd be kneeling on the ground with gloved hands digging in the dirt, extracting all unwelcome weeds.

What a dramatic testimony to his change in attitude my friend Charlie has had since his wife's death, Tink recognized. *During her life, Charlie had always begrudged Genevieve's dedication to her garden. He couldn't understand, nor did he want to, its importance to her. But that same patch of verdant soil now proved to be his saving grace. More than once, Charlie has confided in me that there, in her beloved garden, he always feels the closest to his late wife. And I can understand his reasoning because whenever a small, red plane flies overhead, I'm sure my handsome late husband, Grant, is sending messages of love.*

Charlie, a truly reserved man, had at last found purpose in his own backyard. This small piece of land was providing the opportunity for him to give back to those who'd offered such kind support during the desolation of his grief. Every day throughout harvest season, he worked tirelessly gathering, quite literally, the fruits of his labor. Then, in the early morning hours, often long before dawn, the quiet man would pull a rusted red wagon down the sidewalk. Without fanfare or need for recognition, he would anonymously stop at all of the nearby porches. Then, as each neighbor opened their front doors, they would find a paper sack filled with fresh herbs, organic fruits, and vegetables, alongside beautiful flowers arranged in a plain, glass jelly jar.

Tink had known Charlie Kelly long before his back was stooped, and his eyes were clouded. She clearly understood and respected his need for solitude. But the promise of homemade pie would almost always bring him around on a Saturday night. There, in her cheerful kitchen, they would sit for hours talking about the challenges and successes of their respective gardens. They also spoke of the struggle at certain times - carrying on in life without their loved ones - all the while consuming nearly half a pie filled with seasonal berries and fruits.

"Does it really matter," Tink would often ask him emphatically, wiping crumbs from her mouth, "if we indulge a wee bit extra from time to time at our advanced ages?" Without so much as a word, Charlie would silently nod in agreement and extend his empty plate in hopes of receiving another piece of her award-winning pastry.

Tink felt grateful they had become good friends. And she was immensely pleased Charlie was planning to come for Thanksgiving dinner—a tradition that started after he became a widower.

I was glad to offer support to Charlie through many of his dark days of grief, she thought. *And, at this point, his ongoing friendship is a cornerstone of strength for me. Still, his friendship will never replace the endearing relationship I had with--,* and pausing mid-thought, Tink found herself looking directly at the deserted house beside her own. Although the property continued to be beautifully maintained both inside and out, the emptiness of the house seemed to mirror and mock the void she'd felt since Nic's unexpected passing.

What a pity, she murmured, shaking her head—*and what a shame that Nic didn't have the chance to experience the love he so desired in the very place he worked relentlessly to prepare for her.*

"Oh, dear. Oh, no," Tink said aloud in exasperation. *There I go again, thinking about him, and I simply must stop! From this time on, whenever I look out the window, I vow to shift my focus to the sights that please and uplift me because I refuse to miss out on the happiness of the holiday season. So, even if his home remains unadorned without wreaths, pumpkins, or the usual tree with trimmings, I plan to look at that which is bright and gay along Windswept Way.*

Interestingly, though, amidst my own worries and woes, I still have the faintest sense that something special might happen. Like a brilliant ray of sunshine cutting through a stormy sky, I feel that good is on the horizon. I'm not sure what that may be, but I'm going to keep looking out the window with hope and expectation.

Then, as though in response to her resolution, Tink watched as Bailey came bounding out of the house across the street, followed by the Lerner family of four. Soon, the playful dog was running in giddy circles around the children as they jumped and frolicked in a pile of autumn leaves in their front yard.

"How perfect!" Tink declared aloud with a clap of her hands. *I am certain that for every tear shed and every moment spent in sorrow, there will always be a balance of blessings whenever I am willing to see it.*

47

Mary Hayes

However, as for me, in this moment, I am going directly into the kitchen to begin baking.

The idea of mixing bowls, measuring cups, spatulas, and spoons pleased the seasoned baker immensely. As she walked out of the parlor, her pace quickened in anticipation of the pleasure of purpose and pie.

But first things first! Tink decreed, *while the oven heats up, I'm going to enjoy a large glass of coffee milk and a pumpkin muffin or two. 'Tis a rare day or mood,* she mused, *that can take away my appetite for sweets!*

Chapter 10
Larry

More than anything, Larry just wanted to sit and enjoy his home-cooked meal. Preferring to dine outside, he'd positioned himself on the back porch so he could watch the shifting colors of the sky reflected in the bay below. So much was shifting in his own life that this seemed fitting. Additionally, a robust wind rushed through the nearby trees, serving to accentuate that fact. Still, Larry was thankful not to be confined inside.

Attempting to set aside all other thoughts, he took the first full bite of his omelet. The taste exceeded even his own high expectations. And although he was quite hungry, he intentionally ate slowly. He wanted to savor this meal and the rest of what he hoped would be a quiet, uneventful afternoon. His endeavor to focus singularly on his dining failed, however, after he heard yet another text notification on his personal phone.

Technological devices had long since been an essential part of Larry's life. As a business owner, he knew he could ill afford to be out of touch with his clients and associates for any length of time. As a rule, therefore, his phones, computers, and iPad were always close at hand. The only exceptions he made were during food preparation and sailing. He dared not risk the splatter of grease, sprinkle of spices, or splash of saltwater on these invaluable tools of his trade. Nor was he one to speak on the phone or text while eating, and he encouraged others, including Nic, to do the same.

"I've always felt it was advantageous to focus fully on the dining experience," Larry would tell his friend and sailing mate. "The intention is to savor the food, the surroundings, and any guests with whom we may be sharing the meal. Attentiveness will unquestionably increase our appreciation for the diverse aromas, textures, and tastes of the various foods, making the meal that much more satisfying. Furthermore," he would continue explaining, "I recommend celebrating the cleaning-up aspect of the cooking as well. The pots and pans, knives, and cutting boards require extraordinary care, like so many of our other valued possessions. Not only is this beneficial for their longevity, but it also guarantees they'll be ready for the next great culinary adventure!"

At one time, this gourmet enthusiast had given real consideration to the idea of selling his business and opening a restaurant. However, after carefully assessing the risks, as well as the demanding hours, Larry decided Walters Real Estate and Investment Firm was right where he belonged.

Larry pushed away from the table when only a sprig of fresh rosemary remained on the plate. He'd finished his meal but without nearly as much satisfaction as he'd desired since the sound of the phone had jarred him back into a state of distress. Carrying everything back inside, he still chose to ignore the text message, opting instead to systematically transform his kitchen from a chaotic workspace into an immaculately clean room. This reflected yet another aspect of Larry's fastidious cooking regimen and one he hoped would help restore not only a sense of order but perhaps also a sense of peace.

Upon completion of that task, Larry allowed himself one more tasty indulgence. In lieu of a traditional whiskey or cognac, he crafted instead his acclaimed Apricot Fizz Appetif. Some years earlier, Larry had randomly decided to try mixing apricot juice with sparkling water and a generous spritzing of fresh lime. In doing so, he inadvertently created a popular after-dinner drink well-loved by his dinner guests, friends, and staff members. "Cheers!" Larry would boisterously proclaim on many occasions, raising his glass in a toast. Following the first sip of this effervescent drink and resounding words of praise, he would often playfully add, "This is such an ingenious concoction, even if I do say so myself!"

But on this day, without friends or reason to celebrate, Larry simply held his drink in one hand and turned off the kitchen light with the other. Never one to hurry anywhere, he ambled over to the living room, picking up his private phone along the way. Still aware that he was continuing to neglect the text, the nervous man sat down on the sofa, set his beverage beside him on a table, and began fidgeting anxiously with the cushions. In doing so, he noticed one of them was much more worn than the others due to the fact that his large frame had, quite literally, left a sizable impression.

This couch was where Larry preferred to relax after a full day's work and on the weekends. He would usually lay at one end watching sports or dozing off - a habit that earned him the nickname 'Slouch on the Couch,' which was eventually shortened to 'Slouch.' On a stormy afternoon, when a planned day of sailing for the two mates had been canceled, Nic had stopped by for an impromptu visit and could not help but comment on Larry's hesitation to rise and greet him.

"Ladies and gentlemen, may I have your attention, please," Nic announced in a deep, mock broadcaster's voice to no one at all except Larry. "What we have here is a perfect example of the lethargic human male, more commonly known as the 'slouch.' For just like a sloth needs a tree, a slouch must have his couch."

At first, Larry had grimaced at this statement. Then, reluctantly, he began to smile in recognition of this astute observation, which Nic had presented in such a witty way. Because while most everyone in their community considered Larry to be a highly disciplined and hard-working businessman, he could also be exceedingly lazy.

The nickname 'Slouch' had stuck. And while not another person called Larry that, Nic nearly always did unless they were signing legal documents or in the presence of prominent clients. And it was this particular nickname in two recent texts that had unnerved Larry. Could those messages have really come from his deceased friend? That was unthinkable. And yet, what other possible explanation could there be?

The first message had arrived the day before, and Larry had dismissed it as a fluke.

Hey Slouch...
It's me checking in.
I'll need your help with
my house soon.
Will get back to you.
Thanks, mate!
N

Although disturbing, Larry assumed it was just an old message resurfacing for reasons unknown.

Nic probably sent it during the renovation and wanted me to come by and lend a hand. There's no telling why it's showing up now, but I've got plenty else to think about today.

So, with little hesitancy, Larry disregarded the odd request, placed his phone in his briefcase, and drove to the office to begin the workday. Out of sight, out of mind was Larry's go-to motto when wanting to avoid uncomfortable thoughts or feelings. Still, it had stirred within him an uneasiness and the painful reminder that Nic's recent death had created such uncertainty and imbalance in his life.

Then, upon waking this day, Larry had received another text - this one nearly impossible to ignore.

Good morning, Slouch.
I really need your help with the house today.
Please have rental docs prepared asap.
Also, make sure a new woman's bike
is delivered tomorrow before noon.
Thanks,
N
P.S. Yes, mate, it's really me!

So distressed by the message, Larry had thrown his phone down on the couch and paced back and forth, unable to ease his mind.

This cannot be happening, he repeated again and again inwardly like a frantic mantra. *These messages cannot be coming from Nic. There's no way he could be texting me.*

But Larry could not resolve the conflict within nor find a plausible reason for these messages. So, against his better judgment and without offering any explanation at all, he'd texted his office manager and delegated the tasks to her. He instructed Elizabeth to prepare rental paperwork immediately for the Paramonos home, as well as make sure a new women's bike was delivered to that address by noon the next day. Larry also fervently hoped she would not question these two odd requests.

Throughout the rest of the day, Larry had tried his best to go on as if nothing out of the ordinary had happened. Now, however, as he sat on the couch, he could no longer avoid the obvious. This most recent message was in need of his attention, and he doubted seriously it was from either Elizabeth or his sister. Reluctantly, his eyes gazed at the screen, but the reading was hard since his large hands were trembling.

> **Slouch…**
> **Thanks for asking Elizabeth**
> **to prepare the paperwork and**
> **have the bike delivered.**
> **Please list my house**
> **for immediate rental tomorrow morning**
> **with the Chamber of Commerce.**
> **Much appreciated.**
> **N**

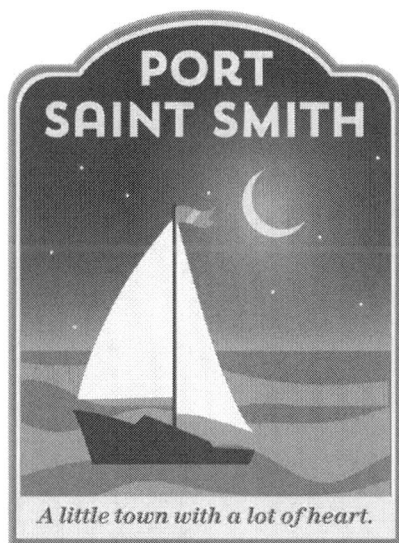

PORT SAINT SMITH

A little town with a lot of heart.

MONDAY, NOVEMBER 21

Chapter 11
Maddie

Maddie woke abruptly at 2 a.m., startled by a dream—so vivid and real that she spent several dazed moments glancing around her bedroom to make sure she had not yet left the city. In the dream, she'd already arrived at her vacation destination and was leisurely sipping a cappuccino at a café. Although the temperature outside was chilly, the stillness of the air and the abundance of sunshine helped keep her warm.

As she listened to the serene sound of a nearby fountain, she suddenly felt a strong presence behind her. Maddie waited to hear a voice, but instead, she heard nothing. And although there was silence, the feeling of someone being there still lingered. She had met very few people since arriving in the quaint seaside town. But no one uttered her name. So, Maddie turned around to say hello. However, all she noticed was a fluttering cluster of autumn leaves carried on a gentle breeze that then tenderly caressed the side of her cheek.

Maddie sat up in bed in the darkened room, strongly sensing that her dream might be a foretelling of something, or even someone, to come. Still, she had no idea who this was. The essence was similar to that of her late Grandmother Anise, whom she often felt close by. Yet, this presence differed greatly in that it was distinctly masculine and ever so alluring.

Who could he have been? Maddie wondered. *And could there be a connection to the voice I heard on the wind inviting me to the Cape and the essence that has now appeared in my dream? Perhaps so,* she pondered. *And what about that sweet touch on my face?* Maddie thought with a shudder. She continued to consider all of this as she got out of bed and went downstairs to the kitchen to prepare herself a cup of chamomile tea.

Before long, she was sipping on the warm beverage and opening her journal to write. There, she recorded all of the details of the dream. She also allowed other words to spill out onto the pages about her apprehensions regarding the trip. Why hadn't she at least created an itinerary—loose or otherwise, she wrote, to optimize her vacation? That and other concerns were candidly conveyed from pen to paper. Still, Maddie chose not to succumb to worrisome thoughts in the final hours before leaving. She also greatly appreciated the fact that the journaling process alone had helped ease many of her worries. She concluded the entry by writing her intention for the vacation.

> *I would love this time away to be filled with moments of adventure, relaxation, and perhaps even unexpected enchanting experiences.*

The honesty of the writing and the warmth of the herbal tea helped calm Maddie enough that she was able to return to bed and fall back to sleep for a few more restful hours. Then, as the first streaks of light peeked through the window, she realized her doubts had dissipated along with the darkness of the night. With the dawn had come a renewed sense of optimism and exhilaration. And in the final stages of preparing to leave, Maddie entered these happier thoughts and feelings in her journal.

> *I'm leaving very soon for Cape Cod!! And these written words barely begin to express my excitement! In addition to my intention for this trip, I also hope to see clear signs along the way to help guide me in the most inspired direction. I trust that will happen, and I'm ready to go.*

Maddie then tucked her journal inside the suitcase and noted that the book was almost full. A new one would be needed soon. Next, she wheeled it over to the front door, stepped outside, and walked down the steps to her car.

The day was clear and bright as she headed east toward the rising sun. And because of her early departure, there was little traffic on the roads. With each passing mile, the eager traveler was keenly aware of how her joy was increasing as her day-to-day life drifted further and further behind. The three-hour distance between her home and the Cape passed quickly, and soon, Maddie was driving across the Sagamore Bridge.

Deciding to stop for a brief respite to stretch her legs, she looked for a good place to pull over. Maddie wanted to take in the natural beauty and also decide in which direction to drive next. Once she saw a small playground surrounded by trees, she turned in and parked the car. Several children scampered cheerfully about on the various swings and slides while their parents remained faithfully attentive. And just beyond this happy scene was a trail leading into the small, wooded area. That seemed like a perfect place to explore, so Maddie began walking toward the inviting path.

The solitude amidst the grandeur felt wonderful, and the crunch of the forest floor beneath her feet was grounding. Slowly, she meandered along the way, appreciating the outstanding beauty, especially an exquisite cluster of golden birch standing erect amidst the enormous oaks that were showing off their own brilliant fall colors. Striking shards of light pierced through the thick canopy above while a wistful wind danced among the branches. In response, the autumn foliage swayed in unison as a few renegade leaves fluttered to the ground.

In the seclusion of the woods, Maddie felt lighthearted and carefree. She breathed in deeply, smelling not only the rich, musky scent of the earth but also the slight tinge of salty air from the nearby sea. Like the falling leaves, she instinctively began to twirl in circles, enjoying the sensation of spinning. Concerned, however, that she might get a bit dizzy, Maddie stopped after one last turn, better able now to see the forest in all its glory.

The spontaneous twirling felt wonderful. Yet, after Maddie came to a stop, she realized her sense of direction was askew. Because of that, though, she noticed a little sign tucked within a thick patch of underbrush. The words were still legible, although green moss covered the rest of the small wooden placard.

Port Saint Smith - 23 miles

How remarkable, Maddie thought in amazement. *Apparently, a playful approach is good for me. Because otherwise, I would have never noticed that sign had I only walked straight forward on the trail. And ironically, just two weeks ago, I spoke all three of those exact words to Stephen. Could that be a coincidence? I doubt it. In fact, I'm wondering if that is, quite literally, the sign I was hoping for.*

"My maternal grandmother, Anise Margaret Smith, and I were extremely close," Maddie had shared with Stephen recently. "And although she died several years ago, I still miss her and think of her often."

"I understand that," Stephen had stated candidly.

"Grandma Anise understood me like no one else and invariably found ways to demonstrate her love and support for me. And to be honest," Maddie admitted cautiously, "I believe she still does."

This conversation had taken place during one of their Sunday evening take-out meals at Stephen's apartment. Maddie had confided in him how often she felt her grandmother's presence. And, true to character, Stephen's reply had been candid and direct.

"That makes perfect sense to me," he concurred. "I believe that our deceased loved ones are around frequently. And why wouldn't they? We're so gosh darn lovable!"

Stephen's quick-witted yet affirming response helped Maddie relax.

"But truthfully," Stephen continued, "they must also see how much we struggle in their absence. Think about it - there they are in that perfect place called heaven or paradise or the light. And we are the ones left behind on our own, feeling all of the heartbreak, pain, loss, and sorrow. They know we miss them and that life gets hard at times without them. So, I imagine they do come around to help give us the support and encouragement we need. Doesn't that make sense to you?"

"Yes, it does make sense, and I think you're absolutely right," Maddie readily responded.

"Aren't I almost always right?" he laughed in jest.

"Good point," Maddie replied with a laugh and then asked, "Do you also think that they send us signs and messages?"

"Most definitely and probably more often than we realize. We simply need to be attentive, as well as willing to override the fears that stand in the way of our beliefs. I know some people see butterflies and rainbows, while others find pennies or hearts from heaven. But that's not how I get my messages," he stated strongly. "Do you remember me telling you how much my mother loved to shop?"

"Yes, I do."

"Well, I can almost always sense her around me when I go shopping, especially if I'm buying clothing. And I swear I have the best luck finding just the right fitting shirts or pants, and they'll also be on sale at ridiculously good prices. Oh, how my dear mother loved a bargain! I know it is her guiding me, and I imagine she still finds great pleasure in helping from behind the scenes. Which is, admitted, pretty amazing!"

"It sure is," Maddie agreed.

"But that's enough about my extravagant mother. Tell me more about Grandma Anise. I don't think you've mentioned her to me before."

"Alright," Maddie replied reflectively. "Grandma Anise was so loving, patient, and ever-present with me. Until her sickness really set in and she could barely see or write, I could go to her anytime for advice and receive the most compassionate and wise counsel. I never felt judged or ridiculed by her because, to me, she was like a saint. I actually told her that once near the end of her life. And her response was astonishing. In a raspy whisper and with the slightest twinkle in her eyes, Grandma promised to always be there for me, even after death. Her words that day brought me such comfort, and they still do. And, true to her promise, I know she continues to send me support, as well as signs of direction, love, and reassurance. I have often thought of her as my own saint - Saint Anise Smith - my port in the storm."

Recalling the details of this recent conversation, Maddie stood transfixed on the woodsy path, staring at the little mossy marker.

How amazing, Maddie murmured, *that all three of those words about my Grandmother are right here. Port Saint Smith. I have chills on my arms. And, although I know I may be biased, the name of that location has such a great feel. So, I'm going to take this as a literal sign from my sweet Grandma, trusting that she is guiding me today.*

With confidence and excitement, Maddie began her walk out of the woods. She was eager to find her way to the nearby town of Port Saint Smith and what adventures might await her there.

Chapter 12
Elizabeth

Elizabeth's eyes teared up as she turned into the entrance of the abandoned estate. Rarely did she succumb to such sentimental feelings, so this explicit display of emotion surprised her. But the play she'd attended yesterday afternoon at the theater had apparently stirred within her a strong sense of nostalgia. Plus, it was, after all, Thanksgiving week. So, instead of going directly into work after her first cup of coffee, she'd driven in the exact opposite direction.

Maybe I shouldn't be doing this, Elizabeth debated with herself. *I have a full agenda at the office, not to mention that bewildering task Larry has asked me to take care of before noon. But the bike shop doesn't open until 9 a.m., and I've already texted Larry to say I won't be in until that delivery is made. So, I really do have time to actually wander right down memory lane. I need to trust my heart more often to lead the way, and that is precisely what I'm doing right now.*

The quiet roar of the engine seemed too loud for this place. Thus, Elizabeth quickly parked her car just inside the bent iron gates. She slipped off her high-heeled shoes and stepped out onto the worn gravel driveway. The chance to walk barefooted in reverent silence was welcome, as was hearing the faint whisper of the wind through the trees blended with the sound of the waves striking the stone wall that surrounded the property.

Elizabeth had intended to come here more often after her move to Port Saint Smith. But she'd made excuses to herself not to drive the pleasant twenty-five-minute journey into the country. In truth, though, she feared being at the property would be more heart-wrenching than joyous. Because she had yet to face that unspeakable sorrow.

Few on the island of Cape Cod were familiar with this estate, *Beauté Par La Mer*. And those who were had heard varying stories about its past. No one, however, was aware of Elizabeth's personal connection to this once-majestic place. She'd always planned to share that with at least a few people - certainly Larry and Nic and perhaps even Tink. But Elizabeth was by nature a truly private woman, and the timing to tell anyone had never felt entirely right.

How could she speak about such a vulnerable subject and share the stories of her profoundly personal childhood without appearing weak or visibly shaken? Regardless of the fact that Elizabeth had been powerless at the time to change the outcome, that did not stop her from feeling tremendous guilt and shame. Thus, the secret had remained hers and hers alone.

Now, as Elizabeth walked slowly toward the house, the cool, rounded stones of the drive felt soothing under her feet. She'd always adored this long, regal entrance with the enormous beech trees lining the way. To her, as a young girl, they'd felt like two rows of friendly giants gladly greeting her. Today, however, the trees looked more like tired sentries weary from neglect and lack of duty.

Elizabeth continued on until the impressive building came into view. As if frozen in time, little had changed since she'd stayed here as a child. There were obvious signs of decay, yet the bones of the building that had once been the proud residence of her Grand-Papa appeared sturdy and strong.

The idyllic days and nights spent at this seaside estate had been enchanting. Each summer, her family of modest means would journey from their distant town, nearly a day's drive away, and visit her grandfather for at least two weeks. No doubt, the adults could clearly see the signs of his aging and his inability to maintain the property on his own. Yet, to innocent Elizabeth, the beloved man and his home spoke of fairy tales, castles, and dreams.

Grand-Papa, who she thought of as a mighty king, was kind-hearted and generous. He'd always indulged Elizabeth and her brother, David, giving them almost anything they ever wanted. Unlike the rules in their own home, here, the children were allowed, even encouraged, to jump on beds, run up and down halls, and holler out to the sea from the second-story balconies. The days filled with grand adventures inside and outside this great manor would forever be cherished in her heart.

But, upon her grandfather's death, the impoverished family had been unable to fund the many repairs. Nor could they begin to pay the staggering property taxes. Night and day, for nearly a year, her parents tried in earnest to find a solution. But their efforts were in vain. That did not stop their eight-year-old daughter, however, from incessantly begging her parents to save Grand-Papa's home. Elizabeth was far too young to understand how hard they'd tried and how impossible it was for them to maintain the family's property.

Therefore, Elizabeth vowed to herself early on never to be so poor that she would be unable to save anything that meant as much to her as *Beauté Par La Mer*. She used her pain as a driving force to fuel success, and, in return, her career flourished. But the lavish apartment, luxury sports car, and extensive travels were never the incentive. She just refused to be financially powerless ever again over her own fate and future.

Through the years, Elizabeth had done her best to avoid feeling anger or resentment toward her parents. She'd loved them dearly but still felt conflicted about their failure to fight hard enough to preserve their heritage. Yet, in denying those feelings, she'd also become removed from the wider range of other emotions. And she'd feared that seeing *Beauté Par la Mer* would expose a myriad of unfamiliar and unwelcome feelings. So, she'd only visited twice since relocating to this portside town.

Now, however, Elizabeth no longer wished to hold back the strong tide of emotions. She was ready to feel and face them all. And to her great relief, the most predominant one was hope. And that hope was also giving her great courage.

Remarkably, the magnificent twenty-acre property had never been purchased since the families' misfortune decades earlier. The estate, she understood, was in the care of a distant relative—one she had never met. Elizabeth often wondered why no change had ever come to this property - for the view of the sea alone was breathtaking. Numerous developers had set their sights on buying *Beauté Par La Mer* with the intention to demolish the building, parceling the land into minute plats, and turn it into yet another exclusive, gated community. But none of their plans ever came to fruition, as if thwarted for reasons unknown. Rumors even began to spread that the place had been cursed. But Elizabeth knew otherwise. She was certain the land and home were instinctively waiting for the rightful owner. Her gut sense told her that it had been spared for a purpose far greater than greed. What that purpose was, though, had eluded her until just the week before. And now, she knew with great certainty, this was the time to take action.

As a valued and respected employee at Walters Real Estate and Investment Firm, Elizabeth had considered more than once speaking with Larry and Nic about investing in and restoring *Beauté Par La Mer* to its original glory. But the two men always seemed to be immersed in work projects or offshore sailing. Then, fatefully, Nic had died, leaving everyone in shock. Their worlds had changed, and perhaps no one's more than Larry's. So, any thoughts of a sale and, thus, saving the estate quickly fell away, or at least that is what Elizabeth had assumed.

Presently, on this misty morning, the vulnerable businesswoman stood breathlessly in front of the mansion. As she gazed at the striking silhouette contrasted by the backdrop of the sea, Elizabeth could easily envision the transformative renovation. Her heart swelled with excitement and the realization that this cherished place could possibly be brought back to life. Incredibly, seven nights earlier, she'd had a profoundly realistic dream that gave rise to this inspiration. Or, as she surmised, it was actually a vision presented to her while sleeping. Either way, Elizabeth knew that the magnitude of such a comprehensive plan was far beyond her own creative abilities. And she sensed Nic was behind this brilliant idea. Still, she was baffled how that could be true since they'd never discussed *Beauté Par La Mer* while he was alive.

The originality of the concept, she realized, definitely had the distinct signature of the gifted builder and good friend, Nicolas Paramonos. Nic had always been admired, respected, and critically acclaimed for his masterful and meticulous designs. And in the dream, every detail had been specifically revealed - from the landscape layout to the extensive, historic restoration. Even specifics about coordinating with regional resources to raise the substantial funds for such a massive undertaking were included. Nothing had been overlooked or omitted. The most remarkable aspect of that entire dream was the fact that her grandfather's estate and the S.O.S. Foundation would be joined in such a collaborative and ingenious way.

Elizabeth continued to wonder, though, how Nic, dwelling now in spirit, had come to realize her history with *Beauté Par la Mer*. And how was he able to create such an amazing concept and then present it to her in such a precise way? These facts Elizabeth could not fathom. Nevertheless, upon awakening that day, she had walked directly to her computer to document every specific detail with immeasurable joy. Since then, she'd reread the document often, and every time came away even more convinced that the idea was both sound and achievable.

The Spirit of Sailing (S.O.S.) Foundation, Elizabeth knew, had been solely envisioned and established by Nic, an avid, lifelong sailor. He wanted to share his love of the sea and sailing with those not afforded the same opportunities. Consequently, he'd started the sailing camps for inner-city youth five years earlier. All expenses for the children, including transportation, two healthy meals, and comprehensive sailing lessons on both land and sea, were provided by the foundation. Initially, Nic had funded everything with his own inheritance. Then, after two seasons with a proven track record, corporations, individuals, and two government grants began to cover the majority of the costs. Additionally, the popularity and success of the sailing camps continued to expand each summer despite two considerable limitations - operating in the town's small yet active port and insufficient dedicated office space to run such a dynamic organization.

Following the founder's death mid-summer, many in the community became involved to prevent the camps from being canceled. Elizabeth quickly volunteered to take over the role of operational director through the remainder of the season. And, because of that position, she came to better appreciate the profound significance the camps had on the young sailors and their families, as well as on the citizens of Port Saint Smith.

Standing now in front of Grand-Papa's house, Elizabeth could clearly foresee this oceanfront property becoming an ideal setting for the foundation's sailing camps, classrooms, business offices, dining hall, kitchen, and other year-round activities. Still, she wondered if the once-impressive building even wanted to be saved. Did it have the strength to withstand the rigorous renovation that would be required? Or would it prefer being laid to rest—leveled and removed, with only the precious memories of the past remaining?

Without a spoken word, the faithful granddaughter posed the

important question to the home itself. What did it wish for its future? Within seconds after her inquiry, an exquisite ray of light broke through the mist, shining directly on the facade of the building. Like the resilient spirit of her grandfather, who had weathered many challenging storms—fighting in the frontlines of the war, the early death of his dear wife, and impending poverty - the mansion assured her it was indeed ready and truly willing. And in that moment, Elizabeth knew with certainty that she must find a way to convince Larry and then the community to do their part in bringing this inspired vision into reality.

Feeling a new level of excitement and commitment, Elizabeth turned and began the walk back down the gravel driveway. But, before going to the bike shop, she decided to stop by her house first.

I want to get the photograph of me seated on top of Grand-papa's shoulders as he stands proudly in front of his home. I'm finally ready to share my history with my friends and this community about this special place.

As Elizabeth passed between the two sentry rows of trees, she noticed that they were standing taller now and swaying ever so slightly as a pleasing breeze moved amongst their leaves and branches.

Chapter 13
Maddie

The drive to Cape Cod had taken little more than three hours. And Maddie had stopped only once to walk in the woods and reflect on her next direction. That one stop, however, provided both restorative time in nature, as well as the precise guidepost needed to point her toward the beautiful seaside town of Port Saint Smith.

As soon as she arrived in town, Maddie decided to visit the Chamber of Commerce, which was easy to find due to its central location. The attractive historic building, old but well cared for, featured a classic Cape Cod symmetrical design, weathered cedar shingles, and a steep roof to block the strong sea winds.

Maddie immediately felt a sense of welcome as she walked up the three steps leading to the front door. She tugged at the cold brass handle, and the thick wooden door opened readily. Then, upon entering, Maddie heard a melodic sound overhead as small chimes announced her arrival.

The room was warm and inviting, and a crackling fire cast an amber glow on the wide-planked pinewood floors. Looking to the left, Maddie saw vintage wallpaper providing the perfect backdrop for historical images of sailors, maps, and boats. A montage of faded black and white photographs covered two of the other walls, telling a far greater story about the town's history than any guidebook or travel magazine ever could. The fourth wall, behind her, featured a large bulletin board filled with colorful posters and flyers announcing numerous local events and activities.

"I'm sorry I won't be able to attend Thanksgiving dinnah this year. Will your sistah be coming?" a voice inquired.

Sister? Maddie wondered, looking around to determine who was talking, but no one else appeared to be in the room.

Then again, she heard an older woman's voice saying, "I undahstand. We're all getting oldah, and travel can be a challenge. I still hope yah sistah will have a good Thanksgiving, even if she's on her own. I'm surah glad to be staying herah in town and entertaining my cousin."

Maddie soon realized there was a partitioned wall in the back of the room obstructing the speaker from view. Most likely, this was a phone conversation, of which only half could be heard.

Since she had not been greeted yet, Maddie proceeded to have a good look around. She stepped closer to the corkboard featuring the regional offerings. There were cranberry bog tours, whale-watching excursions, and lavender farms to visit. For the upcoming holidays, there was a tour of historic homes and a traditional theatrical production being presented. Other happenings and classes were also posted promoting an impressive range of topics - historical lectures about Port Saint Smith and the Cape, yoga, tai chi, and micro gardening, scheduled to begin in the new year.

"Thank you so much, Tink, for your well wishes!" the voice continued. "I'm surah we will have a wondahful time togethah."

Another pause was followed by, "Well, even if our Thanksgiving celebrations are small, we have plenty to be thankful for, like this cherished friendship of ours."

Maddie was not trying to eavesdrop. Still, she could not help but be privy to this sweet exchange of words and the heartfelt acknowledgment of enduring friendship. But in hearing this, she also was reminded how little consideration had been given to her own Thanksgiving plans. She hoped that something promising would show up, but worrying about it today was of no use.

"Well, I'd bettah let ya go," the voice rang out. "I think I heard the chimes jangling, which means I may have a visitah. Keep warm, old friend, and I'm surah we'll talk soon enough. Tootle-loo!"

As soon as the conversation ended, Maddie saw an elderly woman curiously peeking out from behind the partitioned wall. Upon confirming that a visitor had indeed arrived, she then stepped fully into view.

"Good mahning!" the woman cheerfully said, walking over towards Maddie. "I thought someone may have come in. Welcome to the Port Saint Smith Chambah of Commerce!"

"Good morning," Maddie replied, pleased to be greeted so enthusiastically and by someone who was clearly from the area.

"I'll tell yah, the frost is on the pumpkin today. I think it may be coldah than yesterday. Plus, I noticed the wind picked up just minutes before yah came in. I hope you're warming up in hefah alright. I lit the fire just in case someone did come in."

"Yes, I'm quite comfortable. Thank you."

"Would yah like a hot cup of cawfee or some cocoa?" she asked.

"No, thank you," Maddie answered graciously, trying hard to conceal her anxiousness to find a place to stay. For she didn't want anything to delay that, not even a tempting cup of cocoa. Once that was settled, she could relax, and the adventure could officially begin.

"Alrighty then. But if yah change yah mind, just let me know. Okee dokee?"

"Yes, I will," Maddie agreed with a tiny giggle because she couldn't remember how long it had been since she'd actually heard someone say, "okee dokee."

"Well, I'm guessing yah didn't come in simply to chitter chatter. So, let's start over with a friendly introduction, shall we? My name is Shirley Lund, and I'm a volunteer herah at the Chambah. It's a pleasure to meet yah."

"It's nice to meet you too, Shirley. My name is Madeline Stuart, but most everyone calls me Maddie."

"I'm glad to meet yah, Maddie. Now, how can I be of help?"

"Well, I just arrived in town and was hoping to stay for the week. I don't have any reservations yet though, so I was wondering if you might be able to help me find a nice place to stay?"

"I most certainly can help yah with that," she replied excitedly, glad to have something to do and someone to assist. "And let me say I had a wonderful student years ago named Maddie. She was sweet and bright— much like you, I imagine."

Maddie lowered her glance modestly, unaccustomed to such a personal compliment, especially from someone she'd just met.

"I taught school for over forty years. I loved the classroom and most of the students, too," Shirley offered with a laugh. "What about you - do yah work?"

"Yes, in fact, I also work in education, but not in the classroom. I am a career counselor at a small, private college."

"I'm surah that is very rewarding, just like teaching was for me. But I like being retired now, although I stay very busy with activities herah at the Chambah and with the local women's guild. You may have even heard me talking on the phone with my neighbah, Tink Kendleton. She's another active woman in our community. But, fah goodness' sakes," Shirley said unexpectedly as her hands fluttered up in exasperation, "I'm prattling on about me and not listening enough to you. I'll be glad to help yah find lodging. But, please tell me first, what brings yah to Port Saint Smith? Is there a special reason you've come to our little-known town?"

For a moment, Maddie was speechless because she was not sure how to respond. How could she ever explain that the wind had invited her here?

Chapter 14
Tink

The brightness of her kitchen and the warmth of homemade food had definitely helped Tink avoid feelings of melancholy the afternoon before. She'd mindfully distracted herself by making and then indulging in a hearty bowl of lentil soup and two pumpkin walnut muffins smeared with spicy pumpkin butter. She'd also baked a batch of her original Cape Cod cranberry cowboy cookies - an original recipe and everyone's favorite.

By nightfall, though, Tink had felt her advanced age and the unwelcome heaviness of sorrow. Exhausted, she'd collapsed listlessly, crumpled over on the edge of her bed. Grief had once again returned, and she'd had to summon every bit of willpower to avoid thinking about Nic or rereading passages in his journal.

But, for Tink, one worrisome thought persisted - why hadn't Nic come to her by now or at least sent some sign of reassurance? All her loved ones on the other side had found significant ways to let her know they were fine and would continue to be a supportive presence in her life. Why, then, had her dearest of friends not yet reached out in some confirming way?

Her concerns, however, were not truly about Nic's well-being. For she held firm to the understanding that he was fine and, most likely, enjoying sweet reunions with his own loved ones in spirit. But she still yearned for a meaningful sign for herself - a message that would put her heart and mind at ease as to the endurance of their friendship and his lasting presence and support.

For Tink thoroughly believed in the afterlife and the idea that all souls go to a place where only good abides. She openly shared these views with her friends and neighbors during their own difficult times of grief and despair. Having experienced so much loss in her own life — grandparents, parents, siblings, her spouse, and even her only child— Tink well knew the comfort these insights could bring.

"Not one of us will live a perfect life," she would compassionately explain. "And some of us live far less saintly lives than others," she'd add with a touch of whimsy. "Yet, in the presence of the Divine, that brilliant source of unconditional love, I feel strongly that pain, suffering, and all our human shortcomings will be gone. Once the body has completed its earthly purpose, the pure soul goes on to glory. And I can't tell you," she would say reassuringly, "how many times I've heard that well-intended but inaccurate statement, 'May they rest in peace.' If heaven really is the paradise we imagine it to be, then anything less than peace clearly makes no sense. Nor does the concept of sleeping or resting make much sense, either. Since there are no more physical restrictions or requirements, the departed loved ones are free to move about, celebrate, and continue having meaningful connections with family, friends, and even their beloved pets. I feel certain they are not only peaceful but also experiencing unimaginable contentment and joy. So, for goodness' sake, why would they want to take a nap?"

Likewise, Tink had given much thought to the specific location of heaven. Was it somewhere way up there in the distant sky? Was it so far away that the deceased could only look down in observation like faint stars in a foreign galaxy?

"I think not," Tink would boldly say. "I believe departed souls are just on the other side of this seen and known realm, no further away than a whisper. And I assure you also," she would add, while often providing a consoling hug or a plate of warm cookies, "that, before long, they will find a way to let you know they're close and doing well. You may suddenly hear that special song or receive a sign from a winged messenger - be it a ladybug, butterfly, or bird. Or you may find hearts in unusual places or other significant tokens of love. They may also present themselves in a visitation dream so real that you'll actually experience the beauty of meaningful union. And, best of all, you may start to sense them close by—softly saying hello or gently touching your hand, shoulder, or cheek. I am as sure of this," Tink would conclude while patting her ample tummy, "as I am of my love for sweets."

But, the night before, as Tink lay in bed, feeling profoundly sad, she continued to worry why Nic had not communicated with her at all. Months had passed since his death, and still nothing. Yet, she had been the one to hold his hand in the final moments of his life. So why was he not offering her the love and comfort now as her old hands shook and her weary spirit tried in vain to rest?

Is my grief so great, Tink feared, *that I cannot sense him? Am I so consumed with doubt that I cannot hear him? And are my eyes so filled with tears that I cannot see the signs?*

With no answers to those questions, Tink turned off the light and pulled a blanket around her, hoping that sleep would bring her the respite she sorely needed. Fortunately, at last, she was afforded deep rest. And she awakened early - just minutes before 5 a.m., a most familiar time.

This was the precise time when Nic had always left his home to go for an invigorating bike ride in the cool morning air. He loved watching the sunrise from various locations throughout the county. And, quite often, while he was gone, his next-door neighbor and gifted baker behaved much like a mischievous, elderly elf slipping out of her house and leaving freshly baked cookies, muffins, or scones at his back door. Upon returning from his ride and finding the homemade treats, Nic would always blow a kiss of gratitude in the direction of her kitchen window. But never once did he catch her watching with pure delight through the holes of the lacey curtains.

Then, later, during the dark of night, Nic would return the empty plate to Tink's back porch. It would always be accompanied by a note of thanks written on his personalized monogrammed stationery with his classic signature, "Love, N." Inside the envelope would also be a tiny treasure found somewhere along his journey, such as a brilliant autumn leaf, a tiny double acorn, or a unique seashell. Yet, never once did they speak about this playful game of give and take. Instead, they remained secretive and silent, enjoying the endearing antics like two children passing playful notes in a classroom.

At this point, without Nic's presence in her life or the motivation to rise early and deliver homemade treats, Tink invariably struggled to find a reason to get out of bed. The giving game had been so enjoyable that now the morning offered only the same loneliness as the day before. Thus, in the darkness of this early Monday morning, Tink had wanted nothing more than to go back to sleep. Mercifully, she did, and in the realm between wakefulness and rest, Nic at last appeared to her.

A gentle breeze was ruffling his dark, wavy hair, and he smiled in such a way that Tink knew, even in this slumbering state, this was not a typical dream but a true visitation. This was the meaningful connection she had longed for and sorely needed. And in the purest place that transcends ordinary understanding, Nic spoke silent words that her heart could clearly hear.

"My dearest friend, Tink, please forgive me for not coming to you sooner. In the light, there is no time, and I have been blessed to reunite with many precious souls like my parents, our family dog, and the close friend I lost in college. For this, I am infinitely grateful.

"But trust me when I say I have thought of you endlessly. And, from now on, I promise I will send signs often. In fact, on this day, I am sending a very special messenger who could not have come any sooner due to the season of the year. Watch for this bright, flighted friend, and know he brings you my love and comfort. As well, this bird signals the beginning of the fulfillment of my hopes and dreams right next door.

"My devotion to you, Tink, in appreciation for your steadfast love and friendship, far exceeds anything I could ever express. Now, awaken good lady, and find joy in this and every day. And never doubt my love for you again." Then, without another word, Nic was gone.

With her head still on the pillow, happy tears rolled down Tink's wrinkled cheeks. She slowly sat up with more hope than she'd felt in a very long time and greeted the day with a sweet smile and a thankful heart.

Chapter 15
Larry

Larry was already feeling agitated even though he'd only been awake a few minutes. The recent text messages were troubling him greatly. Nevertheless, he did not want to be distracted from his usual work routine. So, despite being physically and emotionally exhausted, he rose early, showered, dressed, and promptly left the house. He stopped briefly at the local coffee shop and then pulled into the parking lot at the stately building of Walters Real Estate and Investment Firm.

As the business owner, Larry preferred to be the first to arrive. He took great pleasure in switching on the lights and watching his office come to life. He was quite proud of his accomplishments and would often stand at the entrance, admiring the little kingdom he had created.

But this day was different. He barely managed to flick on the lights and shuffle to the back. And though the door to his private office was typically left open, today, he firmly closed it behind him. The office manager, Elizabeth, was not due in for at least another hour, and the rest of the staff had the week off for the Thanksgiving holiday. Alone and deeply shaken, Larry was relieved no one would witness him in his present state.

Four brass sailboats held a place of honor on the polished wooden surface of his desk. After sitting down, Larry instinctively grasped one of the little boats in his large hand in an effort to calm himself. This was a habit he'd started several months earlier. As he fiddled with the boat, Larry recalled many of the fond memories these four objects represented. Although small in size, the nautical tokens of appreciation signified a tremendous amount of time, effort, resources, as well as office space dedicated in support of the S.O.S. Foundation. He recognized those had been some of the most fulfilling days in his entire life. Turning the boat over, Larry read the inscription on the back once more:

Larry Walters
In gratitude for your contribution
to the Spirit of Sailing Foundation.

During a time when confusion was common, and reality seemed to be slipping away, Larry was thankful to be holding something this solid and tangible. Still, he continued to agonize over what needed to be done next. What would become of the foundation now that Nic was no longer alive? This concern mattered greatly and would need to be addressed very soon. But the current task at hand felt even more daunting. Yet, this task was minuscule by comparison. All Larry needed to do was call the Chamber of Commerce and list a property for rent. He'd done this countless times before. However, the home being listed was not simply another ordinary home on the Cape. Nor was the request to do so even comprehensible.

As the legal representative and executor of Nicolas Paramonos' estate, Larry had the authority to change the status of this home. Additionally, he was the only one privy to the contents of the will, including the inexplicable modifications made just two weeks before his passing. Nic had trusted his best friend and business partner completely, not only because of their many years of shared history but also because of Larry's business ethics, professional background, and education in law.

After graduating near the top of his class from a prestigious law school, Larry was immediately hired by a sizable firm specializing in land acquisitions and property management. He proved himself readily to be a top-notch professional. But, as a bright young man, Larry quickly realized that buying, developing, selling, and renting real estate was much more creative and potentially profitable than his current position. Why not do this for himself, he'd reasoned, rather than for someone else? So, after only three years with his employer, Larry gave notice and opened his own fledgling company. Excellent timing, along with decisive thinking and good, old-fashioned hard work, converged in such a way that his business became very successful in a relatively short amount of time. And soon, Larry was enjoying the benefits of a lucrative and rewarding career.

Due to his background in law, Larry chose to handle the majority of his own personal legal transactions and those of a few select clients. He did not hesitate, therefore, when Nic had asked him to be the executor of his estate—a request he considered to be an honor, especially since his best friend had no living family.

As an infant, Nicolas had been adopted by an older couple who'd tried for years but had been unable to conceive. Their prayers were answered after reaching out to a Greek adoption agency. Once they brought their cherished infant home, they faithfully thanked God every day for sending them the "most precious boy."

Raised as an only child by parents of considerable means, Nic experienced a life of great privilege. Private schools, international travel, endless sailing, and competitive cycling were an integral part of his upbringing. Yet, his parents, who were well respected for their philanthropic work, impressed upon him the importance of always giving back. Mr. and Mrs. Demetrius Paramonos contributed in extensive ways to their community. And the example they had set for their son was so indelibly imprinted upon him that many Port Saint Smith citizens felt he had even surpassed his parents' extraordinary generosity.

Upon their death, Nic had been left a sizable fortune. Yet, despite his affluence, he still welcomed the challenges and rewards of his profession. Licensed as a general contractor, he continued to build, in all regards, a strong name for himself in and around Cape Cod. He was frequently awarded for his innovative designs and exceptional execution of his projects.

In town, however, Nic was just as revered for his kindness and commitment to the community as he was for his quality craftsmanship. Offering his gifts of service and fortune always brought him tremendous fulfillment, and among his more notable contributions was the singular check he'd written to fund the city's new library. Nic also oversaw the renovation of the historic playhouse, refusing to accept any payment for either his labor or the materials.

Thus, when Nic began his own charitable foundation, nearly every business owner and resident of Port Saint Smith was willing to help bring this remarkable idea into fruition. Not long after he presented the idea to his friends and colleagues, did the first summer camp take place. Then, with each passing year, the Spirit of Sailing Foundation camps became even more successful, thanks to the tireless volunteer efforts and considerable contributions. And the real triumph of these summer programs surpassed everyone's expectations, including Nic's.

What happy times those were, Larry recalled, as he continued fidgeting with the miniature brass boat. But, when his best friend had first mentioned the idea of the camps and his commitment to serving the inner-city youth, Larry had not been at all supportive. "You must consider the risk of liabilities," he'd argued. "And isn't this endeavor far too grand for our sleepy, little town?" Fortunately, Nic had not been dissuaded by Larry's fears and skepticism. For this visionary's dreams, passion, and drive were far too great to be dismissed, and thus, he was not going to be discouraged from establishing the foundation.

"Watch, my friend," Nic had told Larry early on, "as this charity becomes something very meaningful for all of us. I feel certain that the community of Port Saint Smith will rally around in ways we have never witnessed before. Much like the original conception of a new building, I can foresee the plans coming together long before the ground is broken by the first strike of a shovel. And believe me, in time, you will understand this too, mate. Of this, I am most certain."

Now, Larry could clearly understand the truth in his business partner's words. Not only were they accurate - they were also prophetic. For, despite Nic's tragic death in the midst of summer, the camps had proceeded to run smoothly, thanks to the community's devoted and unwavering commitment to the fallen founder. Two of Nic's former sailing students willingly stepped into his role as instructor. And the unlikely pair of Tink and Elizabeth created a highly effective team overseeing all other aspects of the camps. The gregarious elder organized the volunteers while the proficient administrator handled the registration, daily schedule of activities, and purchasing necessary supplies and meals for the children. Side by side, this duo successfully managed the camps, although neither of them had previously been involved prior to Nic's passing. At the graduation, every one of the volunteers and administrative staff took great pride in watching the young sailors navigate their boats around the harbor as their families and friends cheered loudly from the docks and nearby shore.

I don't know what will become of the sailing camps now, Larry fretted as this concern tossed about in his mind like a helpless boat succumbing to turbulent waters. *Although Nic's recently altered will still allocates the majority of his assets to fund the foundation for years to come, without him at the helm, who could possibly be a capable captain to replace him? Who could guide the foundation through the demanding waters of change? And how would this person be identified, let alone trained, when I can barely manage my own daily affairs?*

I know for sure it won't be me, he muttered nervously. *But for the program to survive, a new director will need to be found and soon. And for pity's sake, the organization doesn't even have a proper facility to work out of besides needing a qualified leader. I know I can't let the foundation fail, but I also can't foresee a positive outcome from my own dismal place of despair.*

Frustrated, sad, and scared, Larry accepted this was yet another unimaginable consequence of his best friend's demise. What aspect of his life had not been upended by this devastating blow? Was there nowhere he could hide from the destructive impact of Nic's death?

Lost in his doubts and worries, Larry was startled when he heard a light knock on his office door.

"Yes?" he asked gruffly.

The door opened slightly, and Elizabeth offered a tentative hello.

"Good morning, Larry," she said softly.

"Morning," he managed to say without looking directly at her.

"I was just wondering," she asked, "since no one else is coming in today if we could talk for a few moments."

"I suppose so," he agreed reluctantly. "What do you want to talk about?"

Chapter 16
Maddie

When Maddie initially arrived in the town of Port Saint Smith, the decision of where to go first had been an easy one. Certainly, she would have enjoyed strolling down Center Street, meandering through the bookstore, visiting a few gift shops, and dining at one of the tempting cafes. But she felt strongly that finding a place to stay needed to be her first priority.

There will be plenty of time this week, she thought, *to explore the area - not only the delightful downtown but also the parks, port, and nearby beaches.*

So, as soon as she saw the Chamber of Commerce, Maddie decided that would be the perfect place to begin. Perhaps someone there, she'd hoped, would be able to assist her with lodging recommendations, if not also a reservation.

Standing now inside the Chamber of Commerce, the enthusiastic volunteer, Shirley, was eager to help Maddie and was asking what exactly had brought her to Port Saint Smith.

How can I answer that question? Maddie pondered. For she wasn't inclined to say that the wind had invited her to the Cape or that her deceased Grandmother had shown her a sign in the woods pointing towards this town.

If I did mention either, she feared, *Shirley might look at me differently. Of course, she may be more open to those truths than I realize.*

I think many people actually are. But either way, I'm not going to risk finding out today.

Thus, Maddie opted to be a little vague in her reply while still remaining honest.

"The idea to visit the Cape," she explained, "came to me this past summer, and I've been very excited ever since. So, when I arrived in Port Saint Smith and saw just how quaint the town was, I thought that stopping by the Chamber of Commerce could be helpful."

"How very clevah of yah!" Shirley exclaimed. "The Chambah is such a terrific resource, and this part of Cape Cod has so much to offah—boats and beaches, meadows and woods, festivals and fairs, exceptional restaurants and, if I do say so, plenniah darn nice people! I'm not kidding about that, eithah. Almost everyone in this town is friendly. Of course, I may be a bit biased," she admitted with a chuckle, "but you'll see for yahself; I'm quite surah!"

Maddie smiled in acknowledgment of Shirley's assurance and continued listening attentively.

"The funny thing is most people have heard of Nantucket and Mathah's Vineyard, so that's wherah they tend to go on vacation. But don't get me wrong. Those are fine destinations. Howevah, since so few folks have heard of Port Saint Smith," she boasted proudly, "our quaint town remains serene and peaceful and not overrun with t-shirt stands or knick-knack shops."

Then, Shirley added in a near whisper, "And we don't really mind that eithah. So… if a charming, portside town, with invigorating ocean breezes, is what yah looking for, you've arrived at the right destination."

"That sounds perfect," Maddie replied, especially intrigued by the promise of invigorating breezes.

"Excellent! Now, how long do yah plan to stay? For the night? A week? A month? Forevah?"

"No," Maddie laughed, "I don't think I'll be here that long, as much as I might be tempted! I plan to leave on Sunday since I'll be going back to work next Monday."

"Well, I'm glad yah have the entire holiday week off. I believe those who serve in education really need their vacations. I know I surah did! And you're looking for somewhere to stay, is that correct?"

"Yes, that's right. If you could help me with that, I'd be very thankful."

"Yah betcha! I can show yah a wide range of excellent recommendations. And, if I may I ask… ah yah traveling alone or with someone else?"

"It's just me," Maddie responded quietly.

"That's fine, dear," Shirley assured her. "Many of us in town are on our own. I live by myself. And Tink, my neighbor who I was talking to when you came in, has been a widow for many years. The nice old guy who lives on our street, too, Charlie, is a recent widower. Now that I think of it, even our attractive, always-put-togethah businesswoman from New York City, Elizabeth Moreau, is single. So, you'll be in good company. Now, why don't you follow me to the back office, and I'll show yah what we have that might be of interest to you. Okee dokee?"

"Okee dokee," Maddie found herself repeating with a suppressed giggle.

Shirley led the way to the area behind the partitioned wall, where there was a pocket-sized workspace featuring an ancient wooden desk and two antiquated metal filing cabinets. Maddie watched as Shirley made an effort to clear an area on the desk's crowded surface by pushing aside an old black rotary phone, bulky tape dispenser, stapler, scissors, and several baskets overflowing with files.

"Now then - let's take a look at 'The Book,' as we affectionately call it at the Chambah," the volunteer said as an enormous volume came thumping down in the empty area.

'The Book' proved to be a worn and tattered three-ring binder stuffed to capacity with colored brochures, dog-eared magazines, paper-clipped flyers, and yellowed newspaper clippings. Maddie was bemused by this outdated approach to organization. The computer-driven college where she worked had been streamlined for decades, as had most other working institutions. So, this nostalgic step back in time was a fitting reminder of an earlier era when the business world was not so dependent on technology.

"I realize, Maddie, that 'The Book' looks quite daunting," Shirley said, "but we have so many wonderful places to choose from. Take as long as yah want to look through this, and I hope you'll find something that really suits yah fancy. I'll get busy over herah with one of the filing cabinets, which I've been meaning to de-clutter. Then, once you've decided, that is, if yah do find something yah like, we'll have you settled in as quick as a wink. How does that sound?"

"That sounds great. Thank you again so much."

As Maddie began her search, she noticed that amidst the clippings, brochures, and torn scraps of paper were tabbed dividers with alphabetized headings such as Beachfront, Bed and Breakfast, Private Homes, Condominiums, etcetera.

Speaking over her shoulder while rifling through the tightly packed forest green folders, Shirley soon inquired, "Do yah want to stay at the beach? Or at one of our lovely B and Bs with a delicious breakfast and a view of the garden? What did yah have in mind?"

"Well, I… um," Maddie said hesitantly. For not only had she resisted the urge to make a reservation, she hadn't even envisioned what her stay would look like. She wanted every aspect of the journey to feel as inspired as the initial invitation on the wind. But, because of that, she was once again at a loss for words, unable to answer Shirley's question.

Fortunately, the big black phone began to ring loudly at that very moment.

"Oh, bothah!" Shirley exclaimed. "Right when we're getting started, wouldn't yah know, a call comes in. Forgive me, please, but I do need to pick this up since I'm the only one working today."

"That's alright," Maddie replied, feeling relieved. "Would you like me to step away while you speak?"

"No, that's not necessary. Yah can stay right there and keep looking. I'll just stretch that long cord ovah here out of yah way," she explained, reaching for the phone and giving the tangled, black cord a mighty tug. Then, cheerfully she said, "Good mahning! The Port Saint Smith Chambah of Commerce. This is Shirley Lund. How may I help you?"

A silence followed as Shirley listened to the caller speak.

"Well, hello, Larry! What can I do for yah today?" she asked.

Maddie could hear the slightly muffled sound of a voice on the other end of the line but stayed focused on looking through 'The Book.'

"Of course, Larry! I'll just get a pen and paper to write down all the details. And, yes, I do understand. Yah need this home listed immediately."

Chapter 17
Tink

The bright red bird fluttered anxiously outside the kitchen window. He was not trying to see his handsome reflection in the glass but instead was trying to get the attention of the lady of the house. She, however, was preparing to bake for the Thanksgiving week ahead. And so, on this brisk Monday morning, Tink did not notice the earnest cardinal whose singular mission was to deliver a reassuring message of love.

Tink had been in the kitchen for more than an hour and was moving about with happy vigor. Nic's profound visitation dream and his promise had left her feeling elated. Nothing was going to hold her back now from honoring and enjoying Thanksgiving and, hopefully, the entire holiday season.

After gathering and pre-measuring a plethora of ingredients, Tink sat down at her cheery checker-covered table to partake in a snack. The experienced baker understood how ambitious the endeavor ahead would be, and thus, she hoped that a pumpkin walnut muffin along with a coffee milk would give her the strength needed. With her thoughts on the baking and her back to the window, she gave no notice to the excited bird hopping feverishly about on the windowsill.

For nearly half an hour, Tink enjoyed her refreshments and a brief respite. *I'd better get on with the baking, though,* she decided, *or I may still be sitting here at lunchtime.* Glancing down at the empty plate, devoid even of crumbs, she noticed the important book next to it, which she had placed there earlier in the morning. But the grief-weary woman still hoped to keep her promise to resist reading Nic's words until she consistently stood on stronger emotional ground.

For the past few months, Tink's personal foundation had been weak and wobbly, and she dared not risk throwing herself off balance again. Fortunately, the early morning's profound dream had helped stabilize her. And Tink knew now for certain that Nic was not only fine but would be sending her comforting signs to look forward to. She hadn't felt this hopeful since his death. Still, she wasn't entirely certain that his journal would remain closed throughout the day.

Tap, tap, tap came the sound of the eager cardinal pecking at the window above the sink. Certainly, she would look up this time since his other attempts had failed to get her attention. Yet, Tink continued to linger at the table, oblivious still to his presence. So, when the repetitive tapping did not work any better than the hopping up and down, the bird, in defeat, flew away.

I really must get something in the oven, Tink determined with a loud clap of her hands. *I'd like to have time to bake at least one or two batches of cookies. But first, my dear doggies will need more holiday treats. Why should only my two-legged friends have a plentiful cornucopia of food? Those precious four-legged pooches also deserve to share in the bounty of this Thanksgiving holiday.*

Intending to visit the Homes for Hounds Rescue Center on Tuesday, this faithful volunteer planned to bring at least twice the number of canine cookies that each dog normally received throughout the year. With that in mind, Tink pushed herself away from the table, gathered her plate and glass, and walked over to the sink. Standing still momentarily, she noticed a slight breeze gently twirling the tiniest red feather just above the windowsill.

"Well, my goodness," she declared aloud. "What a delightful sight!" *I wonder if that little feather has anything to do with Nic's promise to me? He knows how much I love finding feathers, and this one is my favorite color, red.*

Then, in that moment, Tink recalled a memorable conversation that had occurred during the past spring with Nic. They'd been sitting at her kitchen table talking and eating rhubarb pie when a petite bird began hovering just outside.

"Oh, look, Nic," Tink had exclaimed, "the first hummingbird of the year has arrived. My late husband must be sending me a messenger of love. Each spring, when this red-throated bird shows up outside my window, I believe it's a symbol of his enduring devotion to me. Isn't that amazing?"

"Yes, it really is!" Nic had agreed, turning in his chair to have a better view.

"On the morning after Grant died, I noticed a hummingbird outside that same window," she explained. "I was standing at the sink, listlessly rinsing a drinking glass when a gorgeous little bird appeared in front of me with its bright colors and the famed red throat. I swear it was looking directly into my eyes, and I wanted to believe that was Grant's way of telling me he was fine—flying strong like that little bird. Then the most amazing thing happened! As though in response to my thought, the agile bird flew up into the air and made a looping pattern," she said enthusiastically while sweeping her arm in a circle to illustrate the loop. "Then it came right back to me, hovered just a moment longer before flying off. I was absolutely certain then it was Grant's way of saying, 'I'm doing well, darling. There is no need to worry about me.' Because as you know, my husband was a talented pilot, and his favorite maneuver was doing loop-de-loops mid-air. And I do realize this may all sound a bit crazy to you. But that is what I believe."

"No, I don't think that's crazy at all," Nic replied honestly. "In fact, I think that was an ingenious way for Grant to let you know he was fine."

"Thank you for believing me, Nic. I may be seeing birds at my window, but that doesn't mean I have 'bats in my belfry,'" she proclaimed with an outrageous laugh. "And now, every spring since then, when the cold of winter has passed, a red-throated hummingbird faithfully comes to visit me. What a beautiful bird it is, and you know how fond I am of the color red!"

"Oh, is that a fact?" Nic asked in jest. "I thought it was just a coincidence that in this room alone, the color red is seen nearly everywhere. Your apron is red, the checkered tablecloth is white and red, the salt and pepper shakers are—you guessed it—red. And, of course, the old rooster timer is red, and well... should I continue?"

"No," Tink replied with a giggle. "I think you've made your point."

87

As the laughter subsided, the widow added, "When the weather gets cooler, unfortunately, the bird stops coming due to their migration pattern. So, many months pass without a winged visitor. But I wait and trust it will come again, and that's why I'm so thrilled you're here to witness my first, sweet messenger of the year."

"I'm honored to share this special moment with you," Nic said sincerely.

"When I die, Nic," Tink offered thoughtfully, "I wonder what sign of reassurance I will send to you. Of course, it's unlikely I'll pass before you since I am only forty years your senior," she added whimsically. "But, if by chance I do, maybe I'll send you red sailboats since you are my favorite sailor. That, of course, may prove to be difficult, seeing as you don't live near the water. I'd better give this a little more consideration," she concluded while putting a sizable bite of pie in her mouth.

"And I would like to assure you, Tink," Nic responded, reaching out to hold her aged hand, "if I happen to die first, I promise to send you a clear message also. I'm not sure yet what that might be, but you can be certain it'll be the color red!"

"Thank you, dear Nic. I would welcome having any sign from you. But for now, there's certainly no need to worry about that. You eat well, except when I force sweets upon you, you exercise faithfully, and you are a vibrant young man. Besides, we have much more pressing matters to decide on at the moment, such as how big our next slice of pie should be!"

I could never have imagined Nic would precede me in death. But, amazingly, I now know he will find a way to keep his word by sending me a red sign, Tink thought, as a warm feeling of comfort swelled in her chest. *And I'm excited to see what other surprises may be coming.*

With even more hope in her heart, Tink quickly set the oven to the proper temperature and turned her full attention to the current projects. Focused and determined, she began to mix and mold the dough into various-sized bone shapes. The next hour passed in a pleasant flurry of activity as she moved with purposeful precision between the counter and the oven and back again. Before long, the room smelled of oats and peanut butter as the stacks of nutritious dog treats grew higher and higher.

While the four batches of cookies were cooling, Tink decided to wash the bowls, spoons, and baking sheets in preparation for the next go-round. Elbow deep in suds, she glanced out the window. In doing so, she could not help but look at Nic's vacant home. The newly renovated house, intended to be shared with his beloved, felt like it was still waiting - but for what? Or, better yet, for whom?

Until this past summer, the proximity of Nic's home, as well as the owner, had been a constant source of solace. She loved seeing him riding out at dawn on his bike, driving off to work, and coming back home again. And whenever Nic noticed her in the window, he would always wave hello across the expanse between their yards and then blow her a little kiss.

"My fondness for you, dear Tink," he'd once told her, "is carried on the wind, like the fragrance of night jasmine in mid-summer." Softly laughing, Tink had teased him about being a true romantic and definitely in need of a sweetheart. Hopefully," the wise sage had continued, "your beloved will be the kind of woman who will cherish your endearing ways and tender whispers on the wind."

Seeing Nic's empty residence every day now was so hard. Yet, Tink was grateful it was not for sale or falling into disrepair. She was relieved that his home was still being cared for exactly as it had been during his lifetime. But the reason why that was true was not fully known to her.

Following Nic's funeral, Larry, who remained in a state of shock, had asked to speak privately with Tink. He needed to tell someone, and Tink had always been the most trustworthy of friends. Besides, she would soon be witnessing the very evidence of what he was about to tell her. So, in a secluded place, Larry had confided in her that Nic had changed his will just two weeks before his death. In a new part of the will, he had allocated funds for the sustained upkeep of his residence. "In the unlikely event that my death predates the arrival of my life's mate," Larry had quoted in a whisper to the old woman, "my house, yard, and garden are to be maintained as they were prior to my passing."

At the time, when this extraordinary information had been revealed, she and Larry had exchanged troubled glances, for neither could find a plausible reason for this modification. As hard as Nic worked on refurbishing his house, she had been shocked that he'd made such unusual provisions shortly before his untimely death. And ever since, Tink had often wished she'd asked Larry for more information regarding those changes to his will. But, in such a blurred state of sorrow, questioning Larry any further had not seemed appropriate.

So, as stipulated, the two primary caretakers, who had helped maintain this home for years, remained on. Maria, the housekeeper, continued her rigorous cleaning routine on the inside even when her eyes were clouded with tears. And Henry, a respectful Southern gentleman, worked diligently on the exterior of the premises. Twice a week, he would come rumbling up the driveway in his truck with as much commitment as ever. Without reservation, he would tend to the needs in the yard and see to any necessary repairs. But unlike Maria, Henry had the satisfaction of at least seeing the extension of life with his efforts, especially in the garden which he and Nic had meticulously designed together. The owner's death had not diminished the beauty of the land. Nor had the passing of this employer and valued friend deterred either of the devoted caregivers from their dedication to his estate.

As Tink completed the task of washing the dishes, a swift flash of red caught her attention outside the window. She immediately became distracted from her chores, looking curiously at the motion not far away. But instead of a floating feather this time, she watched a small, red sports car pull up next door. Elizabeth Moreau had arrived with her usual swift, signature style. This dependable businesswoman had been appointed property manager of the homestead. For even though Elizabeth's boss, Larry Walters, was Nic's best friend and executor of the estate, he had returned only once to this home, and that was solely in order to hand over all aspects of the care to Elizabeth. From then on, she oversaw the efforts of Maria and Henry and addressed any concerns or needs that arose. Because of that, Elizabeth would stop by periodically. Thus, today's arrival did not seem out of the ordinary.

But just then, without warning, Tink started to feel very weak. The day's busy activities, coupled with months of sadness, had noticeably caused a drop in her stamina. So, she shuffled slowly across the room and plopped down on a chair at the kitchen table. Dismayed by how different everything felt now, her little remaining "get up and go" seemed to have gone, along with any remaining willpower. Without restraint, Tink opened Nic's journal, hoping it might give her an energy boost. And there, she purposefully chose a specific passage, knowing it always made her smile. For Nic had clearly documented his appreciation of Elizabeth and her considerable contributions to his home's renovation. Without regard to the promise made earlier, Tink began to read as the red bird returned, flapping and fluttering fervently right outside the window.

Chapter 18
Nic's Journal

Tuesday, April 12… 8:00 p.m.

I believe I have an excellent understanding of what exactly needs to be done to the house. However, all of the remodeling will have to be accomplished during my off-hours, and I estimate that will take about 2-3 months, which may be challenging since I'm already extremely busy with work. But I'm really looking forward to the changes. Because once that is complete, I sense my home will be ready to welcome the love I have so eagerly awaited.

Being a bachelor and builder for so long, I can confidently say this house is comfortable and well-constructed. Nevertheless, it obviously lacks a sense of style and what a woman needs to feel truly at home- the exception being the small study. That room, with its attractive, functioning hearth and my father's and my own book collection, exudes a true sense of comfort and warmth. I am completely committed to doing whatever it takes to make the rest of my home an inviting and most welcoming place for her. And the time to begin is right now.

I went over to Tink's a few days ago to ask for suggestions about making my place more "female-friendly." She laughed so hard I thought the apron around her waist might come off.

Apparently, she hasn't made any interior changes to her own home in "a few decades." My dear, humble friend went on to say she'd be the last person to ask about paint colors, comforters, closet needs, and bathroom sizes. However, if I wanted to make a proper scone or an award-winning pie, she would definitely be my "go-to gal." Of course, I then offered to sample some of her baked goods, just in case I did decide to master any of those particular skills. Sensing my ulterior motive, yet being such a generous and good-humored person, she produced the most amazing "samples" for my consideration should there be even "an ounce or a quarter teaspoon of sincerity in my inquiry." We had a good laugh and, although nothing came to light regarding the decorating advice I sought, our visit was a delight, as is she!

The next day, however, after returning from my morning cycling, I found at my backdoor not only a plate of fresh blueberry scones but also two notes from Tink. The first one contained typed instructions for making those exact scones with these words hand-written at the top—"Nic, this is my prize-winning scone recipe for your first baking tutorial. If, by chance, this ends up in a kitchen drawer without a smudge of flour or smear of butter on it, don't worry. I will always be glad to provide you with baked goodies, regardless of your success in mastering the skill of baking. With love, Tink."

The other note illustrated again just how thoughtful Tink really is. She had taken to heart my request for design help and came up with a great idea. Her message read, "Nic, I have an idea regarding your need for interior design help. Why not speak to Elizabeth Moreau, that clever gal who works at Larry's office? Word has it, she did some kind of interior design work in New York City, and I feel quite certain she'll know a thing or two about what makes a woman happy. Perhaps she could assist you. Hope so! Much love, Tink." And, as per usual, she was absolutely right!

I went by Larry's office that afternoon and had a most engaging conversation with Elizabeth. She offered to stop after work and share a few pointers. But, before even seeing my place, she enlightened me that there are three important things almost every woman needs in her home:

1. *A private place for solitude and quiet reflection*
2. *A wonderful view of the garden—preferably from the kitchen and the bedroom*
3. *Ample closet space*

Later that day, Elizabeth came by and was exceptionally generous with her time and expertise. As soon as she arrived, I suggested we walk through the garden first before it got dark. She was genuinely enthralled with the beautiful layout and said only one thing was missing - a swing on the back porch from which to admire such a magnificent view. I love the idea and would never have considered it on my own. I will make sure Henry and I hang one up right away.

Then we walked through every room where she made helpful suggestions and willingly explained the thought behind each recommendation. Her reasoning was so sound that I plan to incorporate nearly everything we discussed. I have since created a list - outlined on the next page - of what needs to be accomplished. According to Elizabeth, if I make these changes, nearly any woman would be ecstatic to live in this home.

When I walked her out that night, I told Elizabeth what a natural talent she has for interior design. She softly smiled and said, "I might even have an award or two in my closet that validates your opinion." That "clever city gal," as Tink calls her, is also such a valued employee at Larry's office. And, although I've seen her often and spoken with her at length a few times over the years, I know so little about her. I wouldn't be at all surprised if she has an intriguing past. But either way, Larry is certainly fortunate to have someone with her creativity and capability working at his firm. I plan to remind him of that the next time we go sailing.

And now...

The Renovation To-Do List:

1. *Refinish hardwood floors*
2. *Convert 3rd bedroom into primary bathroom and large walk-in closet*

3. *Expand back porch and add a sturdy swing*
4. *Make the study "her special place" by adding a hand-sewn quilt, throw pillows, etc. - Elizabeth said this room should definitely be hers due to the intimate size and the fireplace*
5. *New paint, drapes/blinds, sheets/towels, and decor in the main bedroom, bath, living room, and kitchen.*

Elizabeth offered to assist with all of the decorative elements, saying that gives her "a good excuse to go shopping." With my approval, she'll select the most "divine" necessities and accessories. Then, she'll have everything delivered within the month. However, she won't accept any payment for her efforts, which is exceptional. So, I intend to find a meaningful way to repay her kindness. Perhaps there will be some way I can offer her my insights, expertise, and maybe even some of my treasure for a cause that touches her heart like this gesture has touched mine. And I'm certain in time, I will know exactly what that is.

Chapter 19
Maddie

The office space in the back of the Chamber of Commerce was very small. So small, in fact, that Maddie could not help but overhear the phone conversation Shirley was having even though the volunteer was trying to speak in a hushed voice. Still, Maddie did her best to remain focused on her immediate priority - finding a place to stay. The search began by looking through the extensive selection of offerings laid before her in the voluminous 'Book.'

Maddie opened first to the section labeled "Beach" and could easily imagine the restorative benefits of being close to the ocean. There, she could go on walks every day, enjoying the salty air and the rhythmic sound of the waves as the gulls and terns swirled and swooped in the sky above. She realized, however, that those walks would probably be quite short due to the cold temperatures outside. *I think I'll just plan to bundle up one day and go for a very long walk. Or maybe I could rent a bike to ride to the beach, which would be great!*

Confident about her decision to stay somewhere other than the beach, Maddie turned next to the section labeled "Bed and Breakfast." The large, overstuffed pockets were filled with gorgeous, full-color brochures promising charming inns with picturesque grounds, splendid accommodations, and a gourmet breakfast.

The idea of staying in a tranquil home setting appealed to Maddie.

The Bed and Breakfast would certainly provide a beautiful bedroom, lovely property with great views, and, most likely, a cozy room with a fireplace to sit and read. Plus, many of the B & Bs were close enough to the center of town that she could walk to restaurants, shops, and central park. But Maddie didn't like the idea of feeling obligated to speak with the hosts or the other guests every day. Since so much of her workday was spent talking to students and staff, having a quieter week felt like a much better fit. *But I do hope to get to know a few of the "kind-hearted locals" Shirley's been talking about. So, I guess I'd better keep looking,* Maddie decided with a shrug.

"Larry, I haven't turned the computah on yet," Shirley stated quietly. "So, I'll be writing everything down by hand. But don't yah worry. Aftah we hang up, I promise to entah the information into the system immediately. Go ahead now. I've got my pen and papah ready, so tell me what you want the ad to say," she instructed the caller.

"Fah rent," Shirley repeated back slowly while carefully writing each word. "Classic Cape Cod home in a quiet, residential neighborhood within walking distance to chahming downtown Port Saint Smith. Two large bedrooms, two baths. Newly renovated, hardwood floors, expansive eat-in kitchen, comfy study with library, and log burning fireplace. Second-floor owner's bedroom features a full spa bath. Large back porch with a swing overlooking a private garden."

Despite her attempt to be respectful, Maddie found herself listening as Shirley spoke so emphatically about every detail pertaining to this new listing. The rental home sounded ideal, especially as she refined her list of desired features.

Then, rather abruptly, Shirley excused herself from the conversation, saying, "Larry, would you hold on fah a moment, please? There is a lovely young lady herah, and I don't want her to think she's been fahgotten. I'll be right back."

Covering the speaker of the phone, Shirley turned toward her visitor and asked, "How's it going, Maddie? Have you found anything that suits your fancy?"

"Not yet," Maddie said, smiling softly, "but I am getting some good ideas."

"Wondahful!" Shirley responded enthusiastically. "And I'm surah grateful fah your patience."

"I don't mind," Maddie replied, "I'm not in a hurry."

"Thank yah. I don't think this call will take much longah," Shirley explained as she uncovered the phone.

"Sorry for the delay, Larry. What's that? I certainly do undahstand that you need this listed immediately. So, tell me, what exactly are the terms? Will this rental be available by the year, by the month? MmHmm, I see. No minimum stay required. I've got that. And would yah please give me the address?"

Shirley carefully repeated back the house number and street name. After realizing what had been written, however, she exclaimed, "Wait a minute, Larry! Ah yah talking about the Paramonos house? I didn't realize that was going to be rented," she declared in surprise. "But, I suppose, why not? It's a pity for that lovely home just to be sitting empty."

At that point, Maddie completely abandoned her search. The home they were speaking about sounded so perfect. Still, she could not imagine the cost to stay there could possibly fit within her single-working-girl's-vacation budget.

As if in answer to her unspoken concerns, Shirley inquired next, "Alrighty then, I need to ask about the rent. Hello? Hello, Larry?! Are you still therah? Oh, good, I can hear yah now. Ok, I can hold on while yah check that incoming text message."

While waiting, Shirley immediately proclaimed to Maddie, "What surprising news! One of the homes in my neighborhood is being listed fah rent, and I'll tell you what—it's gorgeous! I know that for a fact because I saw the house right before the renovations were finished. The owner did almost all of the work himself, and when I told him just how beautiful the craftsmanship was, his response was so humble. I could clearly see, once again, that this man, my friend, was the true salt of the earth."

Maddie immediately got goosebumps on her arms. For this was another phrase her Grandmother Anise would often say in regard to her. "I firmly believe, Madeline, that everyone has special abilities and their own unique worth. But you, my dear granddaughter, are an absolute treasure to me and the very salt of the earth."

Unaware of her visitor's reaction, Shirley continued speaking, "I had a chance to ask my neighbor what had motivated him to make such significant changes to his home. He looked me directly in the eyes and said, 'This has been a labor of love and a labor for love.' I was so touched by his heartfelt words that I doubt I will evah fahget them. Oh, excuse me, Maddie, my caller is back on the line.

"Larry, I've been having the nicest conversation with my visitah. She arrived in town today, and this is her first time visiting Port Saint Smith. Isn't that nice? What's that? Yes, I am ready to write down the rental price. Go ahead. I'm listening. What? I'm sorry, what did yah say? Did I hear yah correctly? Are yah surah about that? Well, okee dokee," she added, committing the price and the contact information to paper as the conversation concluded.

"Yah betcha, Larry. I'll get right on this, and if I have any other questions, I'll call yah right back. Happy Thanksgiving!"

After placing the phone back on the base, Shirley mumbled aloud while making a few additional notes. Then, she spoke candidly to Maddie, "Well, I'll be dahned! This is such a wondahful home, and it's being offahed at the most reasonable price. Plus, what the advertisement does not state is the fact that beyond the walls of the private garden is the Piney Grove Trail. That is a paved nature trail that leads through a wooded area all the way to the shore. It's a vigorous walk or pleasant bike ride to the ocean that only the locals know about. Except now, yah're in on the secret, too," she added with an impish smile. "Maybe yah would considah staying at this place? Unless, of course, you've found something bettah."

"No, I haven't found anything yet," Maddie admitted.

"Well, I think yah might really love this place. I wouldn't be surprised if it actually suited yah perfectly! Even the name is chahming— *La Maison Enchantée*—the Enchanted House."

Chapter 20
Tink

Tink Kendleton forced herself away from the kitchen table just after reading a short excerpt from Nic's journal. She knew better than to sit too long, or grief, that most unwelcome visitor, would likely come knocking again. She rose, therefore, walked over to the sink, and resumed the task of cleaning the baking pans. In doing so, Tink noticed more movement outside the window as a small truck pulled into the driveway next door. The familiar logo on the vehicle was recognizable, yet she was certain the driver must only be turning around. Without a resident in the home, there was no need for his products or services. But, to Tink's surprise, the truck pulled up behind Elizabeth's car and came to a stop. And because of that, so did all of the activity in the baker's kitchen. Tink did not move from her perch in the window as she watched Jimmy, the owner of the local cycle shop, carefully unload a brand-new woman's bike. Attached to the handlebar was an attractive Nantucket Basket, along with several sales tags fluttering in the wind.

Elizabeth, who had arrived earlier, returned from having a look about in the garden and greeted Jimmy warmly. Apparently, the property manager had been expecting him. *That health-conscious Ms. Moreau must be taking delivery of the bike here for her own personal use*, Tink surmised. *But why have it delivered to this house when her own home wasn't much further away? And would it even fit into that tiny sports car of hers?* Tink's thoughts and theories were soon abandoned as she watched the bicycle wheeled further up the drive and securely placed inside the garden shed.

"Well, goodness gracious!" Tink said aloud as soap suds flew. "Why would they put a new bike in there? Oh, fiddlesticks, here I am talking aloud like a silly ol' coot." *Still, I would like to know,* she murmured. *I'll just have to ask Elizabeth the next time I see her. In the meantime, I'd better pay attention to my baking, or those canine cookies will quickly become canine crispers. I don't want them to be too crunchy, even if my precious doggie friends at the rescue center wouldn't complain.*

Hearing the insistent buzz of the rooster timer, Tink dashed across the room. *Best I put my nosey-nose in front of the oven window rather than the kitchen window in order to check on those treats. Oh, not a minute too soon,* she confirmed, quickly removing both trays.

With expertise, she slid a smooth spatula under each hot, bone-shaped cookie and placed it alongside the others on the cooling racks. Next, with the warm baking sheets still in her mitted hands, Tink carried them back to the sink to be rinsed. Once there, however, the inquisitive woman struggled with the urge to peer outside again. *I can only imagine what my sister Martha Louise would say if she saw me right now. She would undoubtedly call me a 'busybody' who needs to mind her own business! Yet, how can I not look? These baking sheets need cleaning, and there just happens to be a window right in front of me. Plus, I may be lucky enough to see another red feather on the windowsill.*

Remembering Nic's promise to send signs more often, Tink was eager to receive any of his additional messages. Even the thought of seeing another red feather caused an unexpected tear to slide down her cheek. Then another tear followed and fell *plop*, right into the sink. Tink quickly brushed the unwelcome tears away, then rinsed and dried her hands. Without seeing the reassuring sign she desired, she quickly turned away from her chores and decided a snack might be the best diversion to avoid feeling any more disappointment.

Tink so eagerly wanted to believe the red feather was a sign from Nic, yet it didn't quite feel like enough reassurance from him. They'd been so close, and seeing the feather earlier had been wonderful. But if her late husband, Grant, could send a hummingbird each spring, why hadn't her dearest of friends sent something almost as meaningful? For the feather could have just been a coincidence, and the thought of him failing her hurt too much to even consider. So, Tink reached deeply into her reservoir of strength and decided to wait and trust, although doing so was going to be extremely hard.

Hoping that a snack would calm and distract her, the elder woman made a small cucumber sandwich and ate that, along with a sliced red Honeycrisp apple smeared with almond butter. Although the canine phase of baking was now complete, she didn't want to linger any longer at the table, and for good reason - the sooner she began the next phase of the baking, the better. For, by doing so, she would most likely avoid the possibility of sorrow slipping in again surreptitiously.

The plan for the second phase of baking included four batches of people cookies: Tink's well-loved Cape Cod Cookies with Cranberries to be given as Thanksgiving gifts for her neighbors. Therefore, she ate without delay and soon made her way back to the sink to finish up the washing.

With her head down and her thoughts focused on gathering the ingredients for the cowboy cookies, Tink did not notice when the cardinal landed once again on the windowsill. After a few more failed attempts at hopping up and down, he began pecking instantly on the glass.

Startled, Tink looked up and exclaimed aloud, "Well, glory be! Is that you making all that noise, you handsome red cardinal? Have you come to say hello?"

In response to her questions, the red bird jubilantly flapped his wings.

Tink smiled broadly and continued inquiring, "Are you the special messenger Nic promised to send? And was it you that left a red feather earlier as a calling card for me?"

Immediately, the bird rose into the air as though lifted by an unexpected breeze and flew effortlessly around twice in a circular motion. The winged courier then returned to the sill, landing exactly where the red feather had been seen earlier that morning.

Tink was nearly overcome with happiness, and her eyes once again filled with tears. *As delighted as I was to notice the little red feather before, seeing this beautiful cardinal now really helps validate Nic's promise to send an ambassador of affection to me today. And, of course, I realize that this winter bird could not have come any sooner since cardinals don't arrive on the Cape until fall or later. This certainly helps*

Mary Hayes

explain the delay in receiving this special messenger from him. And as hard as it was not to lose hope, I'm glad I had a little reserve left.

Tink continued to watch in awe as the bird lifted one last time in circular flight and then flew out of sight. Whispering next in a soft voice, Tink confessed, "Nic, I should have never doubted you. However, grief is a cruel companion. But, I know, without a doubt, that you are fine - like all those that I have loved on the other side. And as hard as it is for me to admit, your timing is exquisite. Because I will always remember that you sent me the very first cardinal of the season and that he arrived during Thanksgiving week. Forever, will I be grateful to you for that, as well as our ever-enduring friendship."

Chapter 21
Elizabeth

Elizabeth Moreau was a truly courageous woman. Those who knew her well would often comment on her apparent fearlessness. "I wouldn't dare to do half of what you do, amica mia," her Italian friend Luca would chide. "Yet, it is I who has always prided myself on the belief that I am so brave!" Many other friends and work associates would also admire Elizabeth's outstanding accomplishments, which she typically took in stride.

But Elizabeth was not fearless. Like everyone else, she had her doubts and concerns. However, she'd made a strong commitment to herself to not allow any apprehensions to stand in the way of her making important decisions. She refused to be immobilized by fear.

As a young girl, Elizabeth had watched her family become overwhelmed and defeated by doubt and worry. Early on, therefore, she instinctively developed a process for working through her fears. The two-step technique prevented her from running or hiding in the face of adversity. Instead, she would use this reliable approach and almost instantaneously be assured of inspired direction.

For the process to work, Elizabeth would write down all of the facts and fears pertaining to any given situation. She would then ask a few simple, singular questions regarding any possible action she was considering.

"Is it wise for me to...," she would begin. "Is it wise for me to become more involved with the S.O.S. Foundation? Is it wise for me to seek Larry's support soon?" Immediately, her body would signal a distinct gut sense, allowing her to quickly ascertain an answer. In an effective and efficient way, the wisest option would be revealed—one that would appease both her mind and her heart. And thus, Elizabeth was able to proceed with clarity and confidence.

Throughout her life, Elizabeth had experienced remarkable results by using this trusted tool. Yet, few had ever witnessed her using this dependable strategy that inevitably guided her through the dark clouds of doubt. They only saw the results in outward bravery, watching as she succeeded in nearly every effort, including interior design, real estate, and remarkably enduring friendships.

So, after driving away from the chateau on this Monday morning, Elizabeth had stopped back home briefly. Sitting at her writing desk, she quickly worked through the two-step technique and, within moments, was rewarded with clear direction. Next, she retrieved her most treasured photograph from a hidden drawer within Grand-Papa's French Escritoire—a very old black-and-white image featuring herself as a young girl in pigtails and overalls. With an enormous smile on her face, innocent Elizabeth sat on the shoulders of her beloved Grand-Papa, standing proudly in front of his majestic home, *Beauté Par la Mer*.

Whenever Elizabeth looked at this photograph, she was flooded with the joys and happy memories of her childhood. She could once again hear the comforting sound of the waves and smell the salty air delivered by uplifting breezes as she and her brother scampered about the gardens and expansive grounds.

After walking the property earlier, Elizabeth could easily envision the extraordinary possibilities that had been revealed to her in a dream. And she felt certain that the time to act was now. This grown-up granddaughter wanted nothing more than to restore her Grand-Papa's home to its original glory and, in doing so, provide an idyllic location for the Spirit of Sailing Foundation.

For years, Elizabeth had served as an active board member of the Port Saint Smith theater. And the idea to completely restore the regal, old building had been solely hers. After receiving the initial go-ahead from the other board members, she had single-handedly planned and directed the successful fundraising, oversaw every aspect of the renovation, and then hosted the themed gala event on the grand reopening night. Everyone in town saluted her determination and ensuing success. Thus, she considered how much more she would be willing to do when it involved her own family's legacy?

The first person Elizabeth needed to speak to, she realized, was going to be Larry. For he was Nic Paramonos' only business partner, steadfast sailing mate, and best friend. Additionally, as the sole executor of Nic's estate, Larry was responsible for allocating the substantial S.O.S. Foundation funds. So, while Larry's direct involvement was not absolutely necessary, Elizabeth could not imagine the project moving forward without this man's blessings or, preferably, his willing participation.

Convincing Larry to listen, however, let alone commit his support, could prove to be very difficult. He was already reputed to be a cautious and judicious businessman, especially when it came to financial decisions. And perhaps more than anyone else, Elizabeth knew that Larry had not been faring well following Nic's death. Since that tragedy, her boss had become more distant and unpredictable, continuing to retreat further into his office and a world of discouragement and disheartenment. Lately, when he did interact with Elizabeth either in words or via text, he'd given her contradictory directions, which was most unlike the consistent and predictable man she'd been working closely with for nearly nine years. Thus, overlooking his increasingly erratic behavior was becoming more difficult with each passing day.

Why, for example, had Larry asked her to order a new women's bike for Nic's home when, just two days before, they'd discussed and decided to close the property for winter? This, and other uncharacteristic behaviors, created concern about his overall well-being and ability to think rationally.

Fortunately, Elizabeth found comfort in the fact that the original idea for ensuring the future of the S.O.S. Foundation had not been her own. And the more she considered the possibilities, the more she realized the brilliance of the plan. The entire concept, including every notable detail, felt as though it was being propelled forward by a mighty wind that was creating momentum and dynamically leading the way.

Steeled with the strength of conviction, Elizabeth took care of Larry's remaining unusual request for the new rental listing. She met up with Jimmy and oversaw the placement of a new women's bike in the garden shed. Then, she drove directly to the office, and when she arrived at Walters Real Estate and Investment Firm, Larry was the only one in the building.

What a perfect chance to speak with him privately, she'd thought, hoping distractions and interruptions would be minimal since this was a holiday week.

Over the years, Elizabeth's contribution to the business had been so well-established that Larry always listened to and typically deferred to her many good ideas. Yet, due to the sensitivity of this particular subject, the simple task of addressing him made Elizabeth nervous. She hadn't felt this vulnerable since her childhood. So, when she'd approached his office door, Elizabeth drew courage from a lesson learned from her friends in theater, both locally and on Broadway. "Regardless of what is presented before you, breathe deeply, darling," they would instruct her, "put on a brave smile, and then go out and show them what you've got!"

Still, Elizabeth's knock on Larry's office door had been intentionally soft so as not to startle the already edgy man. After Larry offered a gruff response, Elizabeth entered gingerly and asked to speak with him. To her relief, he had agreed to talk, although with evident reluctance.

Maybe he wonders if I want a pay raise, Elizabeth considered. *Or even worse, he might be afraid I want to address his absentee management during these past few months. Fortunately for him, however, I have no intention of mentioning either of those two subjects. My only desire is to discuss the future of the Spirit of Sailing Foundation and how to save it along with Grand-Papa's estate.* So, when Larry had asked what Elizabeth wanted to talk about, she'd simply replied, "About the little S.O.S. sailboat in your hand."

The astute yet slightly anxious woman spoke slowly and quietly, carefully choosing each word. She did not intend to mention Nic's name either. For, more than once, she'd seen the big man shutter upon simply hearing the sound of his deceased best friend's name.

"Thank you for taking the time to speak with me today, Larry," she began. "First, though, I want to assure you that both of your requests have been handled. And you found the completed rental paperwork on your desk, right?"

"Yes," he replied, awkwardly adding, "I, uh, realize yesterday was, uh, meant to be your day off. So,… uh… thanks for taking care of that."

"I was going to the theater anyway, so stopping here was not really a problem. The bike was just delivered, and while I was there, I went ahead and did a thorough walk-through of the property. Everything looks fine. Maria has done an exceptional job keeping up, and I've already texted the request to her that fresh linens and towels be in place by noon. As for the outside," she added with a broad smile, "Henry is truly a master gardener. I'm convinced he could take any patch of soil and bring it to life with exceptional beauty and vibrancy. And regardless of the fact that this is off-season, the garden is still a veritable work of art. The rest of the yard looks great also."

"Thank you again, Elizabeth. That's very helpful. But," he continued hesitantly, "can you give me ten minutes before we start to talk? I have an important phone call that I need to make first."

"Certainly. I'll get some coffee and take care of a few things at my desk," she replied.

Elizabeth left Larry's office and made herself a strong cup of coffee. Then, the statuesque woman stood looking over the expansive room. Every associate's workstation, except her own, was adorned with personal memorabilia and photographs of little babies, weddings, graduations, and other meaningful family events. By contrast, her desk, although well organized, was devoid of any sentimental items or images. Elizabeth did not have children, a sweetheart, or even a plant on display. As she contemplated this, Elizabeth realized that she now hoped, after this crucial conversation, that would change. She welcomed the opportunity to share the story of her history, as well as the photographs of her past on the Cape.

About fifteen minutes later, Elizabeth returned to Larry's office. She brought with her the black and white photograph tucked inside a small notebook. Before she could say anything, however, Larry began talking as though already in mid-conversation.

"Nothing seems to make sense anymore," he muttered. "Just look at this little boat," he stated, holding up the miniature commemorative gift. "Nic worked so hard, so selflessly, to establish the sailing camps. And for what? So his dreams would fall apart in his absence? And I realize, of course, Elizabeth, that you, Tink, and the other volunteers worked so hard to keep the programs going this past summer. But what will happen next year? How can the camps keep going? Don't even bother answering those questions. I don't want to talk about it. Anyway, forgive my ramblings. What was it you wanted to discuss?"

Standing straight in front of him, Elizabeth paused for just a moment, preparing to speak. Her efforts were interrupted once more, though, when Larry's cell phone began to ring. Quickly identifying the number, he said with noted exasperation, "I'm sorry, Elizabeth, but I need to take this call. I spoke to Shirley at the Chamber just moments ago, and she must have forgotten to write something down. Just wait here, if you would please.."

"Larry Walters," he answered curtly, still fidgeting with the little boat. "Yes, Shirley, I do remember your telling me you had a visitor there this morning," he repeated impatiently. "What? Are you serious? She's interested in seeing the new listing? I can't believe it," he said incredulously. And after another pause, he replied, "Yes, it's available today and could be rented through Sunday."

Elizabeth watched as Larry almost collapsed in front of her. Only his hefty arms and elbows seemed to be propping him up.

"Sure, we can show her the house this morning," he continued. "I'll ask Elizabeth to meet her there, in what, thirty minutes? Fine, then... bye."

After Larry hung up, an uncomfortable silence filled the room. Still, Elizabeth waited until he spoke.

"I don't know what to say," he mumbled aloud, visibly shaken. "Apparently, someone is already interested in renting Nic's home. How can that be possible?" Elizabeth offered no answer to his question. "I apologize, Elizabeth, but do you mind driving back over there and showing this woman around? I just can't go there, at least not yet."

"Of course," Elizabeth responded politely and with noted compassion in her voice. She also managed to hide her disappointment in delaying such an important conversation again.

"Thanks," he stated weakly, "and Elizabeth, I'm well aware that you've been carrying more than your share of responsibility around here, and I'm really grateful. We can talk later if you still want to. I plan to be in the office for the remainder of the day unless I go out for lunch."

"I would like to speak with you today, if possible. In the meantime, would you please have a look at this?" Carefully, she pulled out the old photograph and placed it on his desk. "See if you can guess where this photograph was taken and who that little girl is." Not waiting for his response, Elizabeth turned and walked out of the room, crossing her fingers at her heart.

Chapter 22
Maddie

As she walked away from the Port Saint Smith Chamber of Commerce, Maddie looked behind once more. There, in the doorway, she saw the endearing sight of Shirley Lund waving goodbye to her. Thanks to this helpful volunteer, Maddie was on her way to view a possible rental property that had just been put on the market. Although she had considered a wide array of choices for the week's lodging, nothing had seemed quite right. But this new listing offered so many of Maddie's desired features, and the timing of the call felt more than uncanny. It felt serendipitous. Plus, according to Shirley, who had seen this home shortly before the renovations were completed, it was a dream location - a home deserving of the name *La Maison Enchantée.*

However, before leaving the Chamber of Commerce, Shirley had insisted on making Maddie a map to help her not only find the home's precise location but also other points of interest in town.

"Forget about using your GPS," Shirley had insisted. "This will get you right there. And I will also highlight in yellow where we locals go to shop, eat, and sightsee when our own relatives and friends come to visit. Then," she'd continued eagerly, "with a green markah, I'll indicate the prettiest route to and around my neighbahhood, including the many wondahful places to walk or ride a bike. And, of course, included will be the Piney Grove Trail that I mentioned to yah earlier. In fact, one of our prominent citizens, who was a former champion cyclist, used to ride all around this beautiful area very early in the morning. I betcha yah can't get that kind of information from your GPS, can yah?"

After taking a sheet of paper from the old copier and clearing a bit more space on the desk, the former schoolteacher cheerfully began creating a comprehensive layout of the area. Included on the diagram were a smattering of seasonal suggestions and enough local landmarks to ensure that this newcomer to the area could find almost anything. For Shirley's mission was to make sure Maddie had the most enjoyable holiday week imaginable in Port Saint Smith.

Maddie looked on with sincere gratitude as Shirley contently drew with focused determination and delight. Many years had passed since she'd been given a hand-drawn map. As a youngster, Grandma Anise had also insisted on making her maps even if she was only walking a few blocks to visit a friend. With much consideration, her grandmother would draw the route on a piece of stationary so Maddie could not possibly get lost. Now, as a grown woman, she found it easy to appreciate the sincere intentions behind these earnest gestures, especially in light of a conversation she'd had with her grandmother way back when. One day, after receiving yet another custom map, Maddie had innocently asked the elder why she'd made such a fuss over something so simple and perhaps even unnecessary. Her grandmother had softly replied:

"Maddie, I would like you to write down these five letters on this piece of paper. H E A R T. And Maddie willingly complied.

"Please tell me what that spells."

"That spells heart!" she answered quickly.

"You are correct. Next, cover the first two letters with your hand and tell me what *that* spells." Maddie did as requested and, with surprise, replied, "It spells art!"

"You're right again. As you can see, the word art is contained right there within the word heart. So, when someone feels inspired to create something special—whether it's a painting, a puppet show, a dance performance, or a seemingly insignificant, hand-drawn map—love is made visible. This small gesture," Grandma Anise had said, handing the directions to Madeline, "is one of the little ways I can show you just how much I love you."

After receiving Shirley's heartfelt custom creation, Maddie offered her sincere thanks. Yet, what Maddie treasured most about the map was not so much the beneficial directions or even the local suggestions but rather the childlike rendering of the house centered in the middle of the map. There, Shirley had drawn a lovely front yard sprinkled with colorful, fallen autumn leaves. A short walkway cutting right through the middle of the lawn led up to the front door of the most charming house. Weathered shingles enhanced the facade, and a slightly crooked chimney completed the roofline. Swirling trails of smoke rose up out of the chimney, merging with the wind above to form a delicate heart in the sky.

"I love this part the most," Maddie had said, pointing to the gossamer heart above the house. Shirley smiled, replying, "I just drew what I foresaw, which is a lot of love there for you."

Not long after, Maddie waved goodbye to Shirley. With the map and a few brochures in hand, she walked to her car. However, doubts soon began to arise as she drove away from the Chamber of Commerce because the rental property sounded too good to be true. The other listings all had photographs, affording her a better sense of the place. But this home had no images at all since it had just been listed. That concern, coupled with the reasonable rental rate, caused Maddie to worry even more. Although the fee fit comfortably within her budget, it seemed suspiciously low, considering the location and the upgraded features.

Maybe Shirley misheard what was being said on the phone, Maddie considered. *Yet, she wrote everything down so meticulously. Well, this is another part of the adventure, I guess. And Shirley promised that, if for any reason I'm not happy, she'll help me find another place to stay.*

Then Maddie giggled, recalling Stephen's warning about finding a rental place in an unfamiliar town during Thanksgiving week. "Be careful, my friend," he'd cautioned her. "The Cape may still be quite expensive, even during off-season. If the property advertises quaint and charming, for example, that may just be clever wording for cramped and antiquated. Best you see it for yourself before signing anything."

I still have a little extra time, though, Maddie thought, *before meeting the rental agent at 11 a.m. So, I think I'll drive around and get a sense of the area.*

As Maddie continued down Center Street, she passed several small businesses and intriguing shops. *I will definitely come back to the downtown area soon. The bookstore looks so inviting, as does the café and bakery. And the park across the street is very beautiful. But I'll just have to wait for now. And then, after I get settled in, I'll have plenty of time to explore everything.*

Maddie referenced the hand-drawn map after the third intersection and decided to turn right toward the sea. She drove mindfully down the narrow street, admiring the evidence of the mid-cape region's long history. Ancient cemeteries, crowded with rugged, gray tombstones, were folded in amongst the gentle hills. Notable buildings dating back to the 1600s displayed plaques identifying their status on the National Register of Historic Places. And the perimeter of most properties was defined by weathered stone walls covered with complex weavings of trailing vines and long-established plants.

Despite the cold, Maddie rolled down the window and was instantly greeted by the salty smell of ocean air, which felt ever so invigorating. And soon, the harbor came into view, featuring an impressive entrance marked by an arched sign that read *Welcome to Port Saint Smith*. The two large columns supporting the immense sign were entirely covered by colorful buoys and other intriguing nautical items.

Maddie pulled in, parked the car, and stepped out into the bright sunlight. For just a few moments, she wanted nothing else but to experience this idyllic port setting. How clearly she could envision this picturesque scene on a souvenir postcard or on the cover of a well-respected travel magazine. To her left was a small shack, which, according to a myriad of wind-battered posters, offered bait, boating supplies, snacks, and ice-cold drinks. In front of her was a wide and well-marked boat ramp, allowing ease of entrance into the sea. And, to the right, were two long docks reaching far out toward the horizon. Fishing and sailing boats, along with other vessels of all sizes, lined the docks, safely tethered to their slips.

Mesmerized, Maddie focused on the sounds of the port - the clanking cacophony of ropes striking against the sailboat masts as the gulls cawed and cried overhead. She also watched the reflection of each bobbing boat brilliantly mirrored in the rippling waters below. With conscious intention, she began breathing in unison with the lapping waves, gratefully integrating with the tranquility of the sea. She then noticed a breeze swiftly moving across the water, sweeping up over the docks and swirling around her. It brushed against the skin of her bare face and ungloved hands, causing Maddie to shiver in response. Yet, she knew that her reaction was not so much from the cold but from the intense feeling of being so fully embraced by the wind.

Maddie then realized that in order to arrive at the property on time, she would need to get going. So, she turned away from the harbor, appreciating the fact that the wind continued to playfully linger around her. And she carried with her the pleasant sense of the port's peacefulness.

Driving back toward town, Maddie watched in fascination as the names of the various streets she passed transitioned from Lighthouse Lane and Captain's Row to Queen Anne's Lace and Willow Bend Road. *How very different from where I live,* she realized. *The roads where I live have much less appealing names than these. Plus, I have to ride pretty far away from the city to be out of the shadows of tall buildings and away from the crowded streets. But here, there is so much natural beauty left to enjoy.*

After referencing the map one more time, and within a few minutes, Maddie entered Shirley's neighborhood. She turned onto Windswept Way and was immediately captivated by the stunning canopy of limbs and leaves created by the massive oaks, sycamores, maples, and elms. The effect elicited a gracious feeling of welcome serenity.

Neatly edged sidewalks lined both sides of the road, and Maddie could easily picture a family riding their bikes together or an elderly couple walking hand-in-hand on a lovely late afternoon. The houses were neither small nor large, yet the overall effect was quite stately. Each residence seemed to be well maintained, and Maddie noted that the yards were designed with the natural landscape being the primary focal point rather than the house itself.

She was also pleased to see the festive decorations in celebration of the autumn season. Nearly every porch was adorned with bountiful fall displays. Pumpkins of all sizes cascaded down steps, bales of hay stood stacked and guarded by friendly scarecrows, wheelbarrows burgeoned with gold and russet-colored chrysanthemums, while Indian corn and dried foliage wreaths enhanced the doors.

As the house numbers got closer, Maddie concentrated on locating the property to ensure her timely arrival. But when she saw the exact address, her neck muscles tightened, and her hands gripped the steering wheel in concern.

There must be a mistake, she concluded. *Although the address matches the one Shirley gave me, this home is far from the whimsical one she sketched into the center of the map.* For here was a classic, two-story Cape Cod home with an elegant doorway, a straight and striking roofline and chimney, and meticulously groomed grounds. She had been told to

113

expect something special by the earnest volunteer. Yet, she could not have imagined anything this splendid.

Maddie was perplexed. *Is this the right house?* she wondered. *Could this really be it?* Stunned, she sat watching as a small cluster of colorful leaves swirled across the front lawn as she delighted in the innocent antics of the autumn breeze. Without further hesitation, Maddie pulled into the driveway, acknowledging her sense of excitement and the hope that this was indeed the right house.

Chapter 23
Shirley

Well, isn't that just remahkable? Shirley mused, sitting in front of the hearth. The Port Saint Smith Chamber of Commerce was quiet now, and the contented volunteer was enjoying the warmth of the fire as well as a tasty cup of hot chocolate. Less than an hour earlier, she'd been wondering what to do—because something always needed to be cleaned or organized. But, like most everyone else in town, Shirley was feeling distracted by the upcoming holiday. So, when Maddie walked in needing to find a place to stay, Shirley had leaped at the opportunity to assist her.

Of course, I was so glad to help her, Shirley murmured with a smile. *I always feel the most fulfilled when my work here is not only administrative but when I'm also able to give personal assistance. And who would have evah guessed such an ideal rental would become available at that exact moment? Not me, that's for surah! Plus, I happen to know that particular place could be such a dreamy home for her to stay in. And I can just imagine the surprise on her fair face when she sees it for the first time!*

Quite pleased with herself, the volunteer decided to sit for just a little longer. The cocoa was soothing, as was the sound of the crackling fire and the creaking of the rocking chair against the old pine floor.

The homes in my neighborhood are laid out so thoughtfully. And mine is by no means the grandest of them, Shirley acknowledged. *But it*

115

suits me perfectly. I'm able to keep up with the tiny gahden, the weathered cedah shingles, and almost all the maintenance myself. But Nic's house... now that really is something above and beyond the rest. That clevah buildah put so much love and effort into the renovation that I really hope Maddie loves it. I can't imagine why she wouldn't.

Maybe I'll give Tink a call, Shirley deliberated. *I'm mighty tempted, but I don't want to be considered a gossip. Still, I wondah if my good friend will notice when the sweet visitah arrives to look at the house next door? I could simply ask Tink to be on the lookout for Maddie. Oh, I'd bettah not. I don't want to intervene. So, I'm just going to sit right herah, sip my drink, and be content with my own little world.* And with that, Shirley sighed deeply and inhaled the rich, blended scent of chocolate and burning logs.

However, just a few minutes later, the associate's thoughts drifted back to her neighborhood. *I had no idea Nic's house was to be listed for rent, let alone for such a pittance. Certainly, Larry knows the true value since real estate is his business. And I was very careful to repeat the information back to him twice to make surah I had the correct amount. I would have even asked him again, but I could tell he was in no mood to chat.*

My heart really goes out to Larry, though. He's been so lost since Nic died, which is undahstandable. We all miss that wondahful man. But the decision to rent his house for the same rate as a modest motel room is kinda hard for me to figure out.

If Maddie does decide to stay there, I know Elizabeth will make surah everything is in perfect ordah. She's a top professional and a right good gal. I would trust her with just about anything. She could run a successful business, no doubt, if she were of such a mind. And everyone would thank her for doing such a dahn good job. Oh, golly gee, my thoughts are wandering all over the place. While there's still a lull herah at the Chambah, I'd bettah think about the plans for my cousin's pending Thanksgiving visit. I'm certain she and I will enjoy our time together as we have in the past. But, truthfully, everything is already planned, purchased, and put in place for her stay. So maybe, for a change, I'll just sit here and relax.

Shirley then settled into the stillness of the room surrounding her. Soothed by the gentle glow of the fire, she soon shifted into a calm state of being. And perhaps because the reds, oranges, and yellows of the

116

flames reminded her of the colors of a particular twilight sky, unexpected memories of a recent summer night floated to the surface of her consciousness.

She and Tink had been sitting on the back porch of Tink's home, staring at the empty house of their deceased neighbor next door. In their hazed state of grief and exhaustion, the funeral felt as though it had occurred days before instead of earlier that same morning. The last of the guests had finally gone, and the two elders had little strength left to even talk to one another.

Following Nic's death, Tink had not hesitated to host the memorial reception in her spacious home. And nearly every able-bodied resident in town had attended the service and the reception that followed. Shirley had insisted on helping her dear friend with every aspect of the gathering. She arrived early to help with the cleaning and cooking and then laid the table with a generous spread of cheeses, appetizers, fruits, vegetables, and desserts. She also made a point to greet everyone as they arrived, guiding them to sign the guestbook. And, more than once during the reception, Shirley encouraged Tink to get off her feet.

Everything had gone beautifully, and for the citizens of the Port Saint Smith Community, Nic's funeral was everything they needed. Stories were shared about his and his family's legacy. Tears were shed, and the shock of his sudden passing was candidly discussed as copious amounts of food and drink were consumed. And when at last the two elderly women were alone, like two weary rag dolls, they sat out back watching as darkness consumed the twilight sky.

Shirley was the first to speak as she glanced across the way. "Isn't it amazing that Nic told both of us that he was motivated to renovate his home for the arrival of his beloved? What do you suppose will happen to the house now? Because I can't imagine anyone else living there, not aftah knowing what his deepest desire really was."

Tink, however, was too sad and exhausted to respond. She merely shook her head in uncertainty. Then, both women sat for some time in silent concern. For who else could possibly live there and genuinely appreciate his heartfelt efforts?

Presently, Shirley rocked a little more in the chair and took another sip of cocoa. As she did, a warm sensation began to fill her. But, this was not the result of her proximity to the fire, nor due to the consumption of the now lukewarm beverage. Instead, Shirley noticed a pleasant feeling rising within her as she envisioned the sweet, new visitor staying in Nic's home. She no longer feared that Maddie would return to the Chamber, wanting a more suitable place to stay. Because the volunteer had a strong sense, an inner knowing really, that *La Maison Enchantée* would be ideal for Maddie in ways even beyond her own imaginings.

I've done my best since the funeral to avoid thinking about what might become of Nic's lovely residence, Shirley recognized. *That has not been an easy accomplishment, especially for someone as curious as myself. But surprisingly, I can foresee Maddie being very content there, almost as though she already belongs. I even believe Nic would be pleased if he knew she was staying in his home.*

Maybe I will go ahead and make that call, Shirley decided. *Because Tink could not only be on the lookout for Maddie but also help make surah all goes well for her there.* And with no more deliberation, Shirley set down her drink and stood up. Hurrying to the back office, she picked up the phone and dialed her dear friend's number.

Chapter 24
Larry

I can't stay at the office another minute, Larry declared, pounding his fist on the desk. *I need to go for a walk and get some fresh air. At least when I'm outside, I don't feel quite as upset as I do inside.*

Elizabeth had left a few minutes earlier to meet the potential renter at Nic's house, and Larry felt more unsettled than ever. He couldn't begin to process the significance of that possible transaction. Nor could he fathom the reason why his office manager had asked him to look at some old photograph. Why would she want him to guess who those two people were? That kind of sentimental silliness was not typical for her, a rather reserved and cool-headed woman. Couldn't she see he was in no mood for guessing games? These thoughts and others swirled around the anxious man's mind as he prepared to leave the office. He hoped that walking through town would help him regain enough composure to carry on a coherent conversation when she returned.

Instinctively, Larry reached for his phone—a long-established habit. But, remembering the inconceivable text messages he had recently received, he shuddered and debated whether or not the nuisance of a device could be left behind. After all, this was a holiday week, and business was quieter than usual. And Larry wanted to believe he could just go for a nice walk, get a bite to eat, and return to the office without missing any critical calls. This would also guarantee the avoidance of another upsetting text. But he feared missing an important call or message from a client. So, the responsible business owner overruled the troubled individual, and, with a heavy sigh, he slipped the phone into his pocket and walked toward the door.

The cool air outside felt wonderful, and Larry was relieved to have a distraction from the uncomfortable circumstances in his life. So profound was his confusion that he walked without conscious consideration of his direction. He turned right outside the building and then again at the first corner. In order to avoid the busier area of town, he continued south a few blocks and soon found himself standing at the entrance of Freeman's Nursery. This was a place of business he often frequented. For Larry greatly enjoyed making improvements to the landscaping at his home. He also understood the value of curb appeal and, thus, had used Henry Freeman's superior design and installation services through the years - not only at his residence but also at his numerous investment properties.

As he stepped inside, Larry was greeted warmly by the proprietor himself. Henry, along with his equally talented wife and co-owner, Ella, hailed from Alabama. They had come to the Cape long ago to help care for her ailing father and found the area suitable to their liking. So they stayed on and became well woven into the fabric of the town's beloved citizens.

"Good to see you, Larry," the elderly gentleman said in a slow, southern drawl. Removing his rugged hand from the gardener's glove, he wiped it clean on the towel hanging from his bibbed overalls and extended it to Larry.

"Good afternoon, Henry," Larry replied with a handshake and a strained smile. For as much as he cared for the Freemans, he was not inclined to have a conversation with them or anyone else today. And he hoped Henry, a most perceptive man, would recognize that.

"If you need any help, my friend, let me know. Otherwise, I'm sure you'll be just fine moseying around on your own."

Larry nodded in silent appreciation and proceeded down the center aisle. He had no idea what had motivated him to come in today and was relieved that no explanation had been required.

He ambled slowly amidst the various trees and shrubs, but nothing held any interest to him, including his usual favorites - the Winterberry Holly nor the Norfolk Island Pines. So, he continued on and eventually

ended up in the back of the store. There, in front of him, was a large display cooler filled with fresh-cut flowers and numerous autumn arrangements.

I can't remember the last time I bought anyone flowers, Larry muttered to himself. *Mother's been gone for years, and she was always so pleased when I brought her 'pretty posies.' But those days are behind me now. And I haven't been on a date either since, well,* he paused, struggling to remember, *since the one fiasco of a blind date following my divorce. Then, there was the time I made the mistake of giving Elizabeth Moreau a plant to commemorate her five years with the firm. I have never seen anyone so displeased receiving a present.*

When Larry had proudly presented Elizabeth with the impressive plant, complete with a large decorative bow, she'd offered him a polite thank you, followed by a cordial written note. But word soon filtered back to him from other staff members that she objected to the additional responsibility of having to keep a plant alive. To her, that felt more like work than a reward. Ever since, Larry made a point to only give her inanimate gifts such as imported scarves, restaurant certificates, or tickets to the neighboring town's theatrical productions.

Still, the large man felt drawn to open the glass door of the cooler. Without understanding why, he reached inside, selected an arrangement, and began walking back toward the checkout counter.

Henry, who was pushing a cart filled with autumn-colored chrysanthemums, passed him and commented, "Looks like you found something real pretty there."

"Uh, yes, I suppose so," Larry replied, trying to hide his own bewilder-ment.

"We only sell that cornucopia-shaped basket at Thanksgiving, but it's always an annual favorite. I imagine you'll make someone mighty happy with those flowers," he continued. "My sweetheart and better half will take good care of you at the register. And I sure wish you a good Thanksgiving, Larry. One that is filled with blessings."

Larry acknowledged Henry's sincere greeting with a mumbled response, "Same to you." He didn't want to think about Thanksgiving or any other holiday. Still, he could not help but wonder why he was making this holiday-themed purchase.

Larry placed the cornucopia on the counter and settled up with Ella. Like her husband, she was gracious in greeting him and wishing him well. Larry did his best to respond, then quickly left the store. Despite the genuine pleasantness of the Freemans, he felt even worse. Here were two of the kindest people in the community, and he'd barely been able to speak to them. Hopefully, of all people, they would not judge him. For hadn't they been the ones to generously donate all of the flowers and plants for Nic's funeral without anyone asking? And wasn't it Henry who had given such an eloquent speech at the memorial service of their mutual friend? Larry knew this devoted gardener continued to care for Nic's property with as much pride and devotion as he had before the owner's death. So, undoubtedly, Henry and Ella must be feeling the pain of this loss, as well. Yet, despite their optimistic demeanor, Larry recognized that they must also have times when their personal suffering feels almost unbearable.

Presently, though, Larry felt too entangled in his own grief to offer words of comfort or support to anyone else. He just hoped his friends and other fellow citizens would make allowances for his sorrowful short-comings.

With a heavy heart and a sizable floral arrangement, the distraught man walked in the direction of Center Street. As he got closer, he decided to turn down the alleyway behind the businesses that lined the busy main road. His longing now, even more than before, was to steer clear of as many cheerful holiday shoppers and townsfolk as possible. He just wanted to eat lunch at his usual restaurant in order to gain some sense of normalcy. When he stepped through the back entrance of Robertson's Gourmet Deli, however, he saw an immense crowd and decided to head right back outside.

His next choice was the Boulangerie Bakery. Their food was also delicious. Due to their brighter and more trendy environment, though, Larry typically ordered his meal to take back to his office. But that was a place he still wanted to avoid. Fortunately, he managed to find a small table in the corner, and before being seated, he carefully placed his floral purchase on the opposite chair for safekeeping.

Soon enough, a friendly, young server in a crisp, white pinafore came over to take his order. Larry decided on the daily special—a crockpot of French onion soup, along with a side salad and fresh, buttery croissant. He also ordered a large chocolate frappe and a cruller to go since lately he'd been most cavalier about his calories. *What was the point anyway*, he'd reasoned.

While he waited to be served, Larry glanced around the room at the collection of framed images on the walls. There were no photographs of famous people featuring broad smiles and sweeping signatures, nor were there artistic renderings of lighthouses on a misty morning or Adirondack chairs lined up on the beach at sunset. Instead, he saw photographs of the bakery-sponsored youth softball team, as well as weary but proud, competitive runners just beyond the finish line, receiving their sponsored T-shirts and fresh bagels from this business's owners. There were also several photos of the bakery's popular parade float, participating in the annual winter holiday festival. The Boulangerie Bakery was known for its whimsical entries, usually featuring a gigantic pastry item - a donut, scone, or croissant, rolling down Center Street on four tiny wheels.

Pleasantly distracted, Larry turned his attention next to the large photograph directly above his table. A posed and appreciative man was speaking to a large crowd gathered at the port. He was presenting the proprietors of this establishment, along with many other business owners and community leaders, commemorative brass sailboats in gratitude for their generous support of the S.O.S. sailing camps. Larry suddenly felt nauseous and wanted nothing more than to bolt right out the door. Had his order not already been placed, he most likely would have left. Of all the seats in the restaurant, how had he ended up just below the picture of Nic Paramonos?

Feelings of grief and frustration quickly flooded back as Larry struggled to maintain his composure. All he'd wanted was to forget his troubles for an hour or more. But, once again, he felt emotionally lost at sea without his sailing mate to help. For Nic had been more than just a hang-out buddy and a business partner. He'd been Larry's only confidant and trusted friend, the one person he would talk openly with about his fears and feelings. And Nic consistently offered him wise counsel and clear guidance as naturally as a gentle wind catching the sail of a boat and helping guide it in a better direction.

Always a sympathetic listener, Larry had come to lean on Nic for his sensible advice on nearly every topic. Nic had informed him on financial and business matters, as well as any challenging staffing situations. He'd also helped him through his divorce and had been a steady source of comfort following the death of his parents.

But, at this time, overwhelmed with sorrow and frightened by the inexplicable text messages, Larry had no one else to turn to. For the only person he'd allowed himself to be vulnerable with was now buried in the rolling hills of the Port Saint Smith cemetery.

Fortunately, the cold, frothy drink arrived, followed by his lunch. So, Larry gratefully shifted his focus to the food in front of him. As an amateur chef, he usually gave himself over to the full experience of seeing, smelling, and fully enjoying his meals. And by doing so today, his goal was to suppress the intense feelings that had resurfaced at a most inopportune time.

The soup was hot and seasoned to his liking. he warm croissant, served with two generous pats of real butter, had just the right amount of flake and crunch. And the salad was topped with such an exceptional raspberry dressing that Larry was motivated to ask the owners for the recipe, perhaps on a return visit.

Eating slowly and deliberately, he felt somewhat revived. The emotional reprieve had been most welcome. He settled the bill and started to reach for the cornucopia arrangement when he decided to take just a brief look at his phone before walking back to the office. Regret rocked him instantly; however, when he read the new text, he began to panic. Because if he avoided this current request, Larry realized that the texting would persist until he did. So, he sent a brief message to Elizabeth, conveying the instructions, and then quickly put his phone away. Barely able to think, Larry left the restaurant, worried if he would even have the strength to make it through the rest of the day.

Chapter 25
Maddie

Although she was still hesitant, Maddie pulled into the driveway of the rental home. The house appeared to be empty. But she couldn't be sure, and there was no visibly posted "for rent" sign. She feared this could be the wrong address. And since the real estate agent scheduled to meet her was not due for a few more minutes, the inquisitive traveler decided to have a look around with the hopes she was not trespassing. Thus, Maddie got out of the car with Shirley's map in hand and looked at the property with admiration.

The home was a traditional Cape Cod design with its historical roots in the colonial era. Two dormers below the roof line and two windows on either side of the front door created an inherent sense of balance. Cedar shingles and black shutters also served to distinguish it from other architectural styles.

As she studied the attractive details of the residence, a delicate breeze fluttered the map in her hands. Maddie instinctively clutched it tighter, for she appreciated the significance and sincerity that went into creating this customized traveler guide. The wind responded with a knowing embrace that spun slowly and only once around her and then retreated again.

Due to the appealing characteristics of the house, Maddie could not help but wonder why the rent was so reasonable. She worried there could have been a miscommunication and that the rate quoted was per night rather than for an entire six-night stay.

Well, I'm here now, Maddie resolved with an accepting shrug. *So, at least I'll have a chance to see inside one of the lovely homes in the area. Then, if I have to, I'll go back to look for a more affordable place to stay— maybe something named the Cape Budget Inn. That would definitely give Stephen something to tease me about,* she thought in good humor.

In the time remaining, Maddie decided to take a glimpse at the backyard. On her way there, she noted a small shed on the right where tools and potting soil were most likely stored. On the left, she saw a magnificent garden featuring tall, custom trellises richly woven with climbing morning roses. Small stone pathways meandered through ivy, ferns, and other mature flower beds. Multi-colored hydrangeas, along with drooping sunflowers, now shadows of their former summer glory, still commanded attention. And although this was a cold autumn day, Maddie could easily envision the magnificence of this garden during the seasons of the year when the various plants were in full bloom. This alone gave credence to the home's name, *La Maison Enchantée.*

Although tempted to meander along the inviting footpaths, Maddie felt it wouldn't be appropriate without the accompaniment of the agent or the homeowner. *But, what a gorgeous rental,* she thought. *If I am able to stay here, I will definitely be spending in the garden and on that inviting porch swing, even if I have to get all bundled up.*

Excited, Maddie turned to go back toward the front of the home to wait there. In doing so, however, she saw that the house next door had a large window facing in her direction. She also noticed that the curtains in that window were quickly pulled closed, but not before seeing a startled, elderly woman's face.

Just then, the roar of a car engine could be heard approaching. Maddie turned to see a sports car pulling up in the driveway and coming to a quick stop. An attractive woman soon emerged, and with a welcoming smile, she walked directly towards her.

"Hello, my name is Elizabeth Moreau. I'm with Walters Real Estate and Investment Firm, and I'm guessing you're here to see the property. Is that correct?"

"Yes, that's right. I'm Madeline Stuart. But please call me Maddie."

"I'm glad to meet you, Maddie. I trust you haven't been waiting long?"

"No, I haven't. I just got here a few minutes ago and decided to have a little look around back."

"Good for you! Even without the abundance of bright colors, isn't the garden lovely?" Elizabeth asked. "Henry Freeman, a very dear man, and the town's most trusted master gardener, is to be credited for that work of art. He and the owner came up with the initial design. Ever since then, Henry has been the faithful caregiver, tending to the upkeep and never failing to produce more beauty than ever before.

"As for me," Elizabeth confided, "I have no talent when it comes to caring for plants. But I am an avid admirer, and this garden truly is a showpiece. Even today, when the cold has snapped much of its vitality, there is still plenty to admire. Just listen, for a moment, as the wind rustles amidst the brittle foliage, creating the most captivating sound. Forgive me, though, as I realize you must want to see the inside of the house. So let's go in where it's warm, and you can see if it suits you, okay?"

"Yes, that sounds great," Maddie replied, then hesitantly said, "I do one question first, though…"

"Of course, ask me anything, and I'll do my very best to answer."

"My plans are to stay tonight through Sunday morning, and I would like to confirm the rental price for that length of time," she stated.

"That's understandable," Elizabeth replied as she opened the folder in her hands. She then showed Maddie the paperwork. "This is what the entire fee would be through Sunday noon, including taxes, etc. Is that what you were quoted?"

"Yes, it is," Maddie responded with evident surprise. "The rate just seems, so um, reasonable compared to the other properties I considered."

"You are right about that. But the owner of our company was very clear about the price. So, if you like the house and decide to stay, you'll definitely be getting an exceptional rate, especially on the Cape!"

The two women then walked toward the front and up the steps. Elizabeth unlocked the door, and as they entered the foyer, she explained, "Just so you know, I stopped by earlier today for a full walk-through. The housekeeper was also here to freshen up, put out new towels, and make up the beds with the most amazing, natural fiber sheets one could ever imagine. Why don't you go ahead and have a look around? In fact, you may want to start with the upstairs—the main suite alone is a dream! While you're doing that, I'll be in the kitchen taking inventory. This listing came up quite unexpectedly, so there wasn't time to stock the basics, such as paper towels, coffee, tea, etcetera. I will tend to that immediately if you do decide to stay."

Maddie agreed to Elizabeth's suggestion and ascended the wide, polished, wooden stairs which led to a sizable landing. The two bedrooms were separated, one on either side and each with its own bathroom. Glancing first to her right, Maddie saw that the guest bedroom was sizable and very attractive. However, when she walked into the main bedroom with its adjoining bath, she felt as though she'd stepped into a luxury suite at a five-star hotel. The room was decorated in rich colors, stylish fabric, and classic furniture. A sizable alcove with an expansive bay window provided a sweet nook for reading, writing, or simply looking out onto the garden below. And the bathroom featured an enormous sunken tub with a block-glass window, which let in an immense amount of natural light.

As she returned downstairs and wandered through the first floor, Maddie could barely believe the beauty of the home. There was a stately but not stuffy dining room, as well as a cozy study with a loveseat, a sizable library, and a handsome hearth. After seeing those two rooms, she continued down the hall to the only place remaining to be seen—the kitchen. This large and bright room appeared to have all the necessary amenities, including an eat-in dining area. But what was most extraordinary was the wall of windows overlooking the garden. From any perspective, one could look outside, enjoying the truly lovely view.

Elizabeth was busy writing at the repurposed wooden kitchen table when she heard Maddie come in. "That didn't take long," the agent commented. "And I'm guessing, by your expression, that you're pleased with the accommodations?"

"Yes, I am. This home is amazing! My actual preference would be to move in, but seeing as this is only a vacation, I would definitely like to rent it for the week."

"Excellent. I'm so glad that you like it here. Now," Elizabeth stated, shuffling the papers in front of her, "if I may, I would like to ask you a couple of simple questions—just a few formalities. Why don't you have a seat?"

Maddie agreed, and after joining Elizabeth at the table, the rental agent proceeded. "Shirley Lund provided me with your basic contact information only—your name and cell number. However, I do need to inquire if you are traveling by yourself or if will you be joined by anyone else?

"No, I'm traveling alone."

"Bravo! I often travel alone, and I do rather enjoy the company of one," Elizabeth stated with an air of confidence. "I can rise early or sleep in late—whatever is my preference. And I can move about at any pace that suits me. No one will tease me for being lazy, spending too much money, or having too much fun!"

Maddie laughed and said, " I understand that!

"Right?! Now, my second question concerns pets. Did you happen to bring any feathery or fluffy friends with you?"

"No, I left my cat back in the city with a trusted friend who, I'm afraid," Maddie confessed in a moment of honesty, "will spoil her beyond recognition."

"What a lucky cat! We all need spoiling from time to time, don't we?"

"Yes! We sure do."

"Well, then, this is my plan—to spoil you a little bit myself while you're here on vacation. But first, I must go back to the office to finalize this paperwork, which will need to be signed. I will also pick up the necessities for the house and would like to bring you a gourmet meal to eat at your leisure while you unpack and get settled in. We have a wonderful deli in town with the most divine soups, snacks, appetizers, and entrees. If you've ever had soup in France, sushi in Japan, or chocolate in Belgium, then you'll appreciate the fact that this shop's offerings are on par with those world-renowned destinations. In fact, many residents of Martha's Vineyard and Nantucket travel by boat to shop there. So, would that be acceptable if I brought you a few tasty offerings from Robertson's Deli?"

The thought of a delicious meal delivered to her after a day of traveling sounded wonderful. Because Maddie wanted nothing more than to enjoy a quiet night in this special place, preferably sitting by the fire. Nevertheless, she declined.

"That is very thoughtful of you," Maddie replied, "and although I don't plan to eat out today, I'll just make do with the snacks that I brought."

"Nonsense," Elizabeth insisted with a dismissive wave of her hand, "You save those little nibbles for another time. I'll be at the market anyway and would be delighted to treat you to a delicious first meal. Besides, that gives me a chance to do more shopping. You wouldn't want to deny me that pleasure, would you?"

"Well, if you put it like that," Maddie agreed with a soft smile, "how could I possibly say no?"

"Exactly! This is your first night in town, and I'd like you to feel the true Port Saint Smith spirit of kindness. When I moved here from New York City, I was astonished by the good deeds extended to me. Most everyone went out of their way to be welcoming and helpful. So, please let me extend that same kindness to you."

"Alright. And thank you, Elizabeth. That's very kind of you."

"My pleasure, Maddie. I'll be on my way now and will probably return in about an hour or two, depending on how busy the stores are since this is, after all, Thanksgiving week. That should give you an opportunity to bring your luggage in and start enjoying yourself."

The accommodating businesswoman was soon gone, and for a few moments, Maddie simply stared out the picturesque windows. She was impressed by the beauty, and also by the good fortune that continued to prevail. And she found comfort in watching the evidence of a light breeze dancing and playing in the garden.

Chapter 26
Tink

Tink was enthralled with the arrival of the red bird and the fact that Nic had kept his word. Without hesitation, she paused momentarily from her dishwashing to watch the clever cardinal's circular maneuvers in the sky, followed by brief stopovers on the narrow runway of the kitchen windowsill. Upon landing, he often looked up at her as if to ask, "You see me now, don't you?!" With immense joy, she replied, "I do see you, my handsome winged messenger, and I am overjoyed!"

When the cardinal came to yet another stop along the sill, Tink noticed, just beyond him, an unfamiliar car pulling into the adjoining driveway. Soon, an attractive young woman got out and stood looking around.

She must be lost, Tink reasoned, *since she keeps referencing that piece of paper in her hand. Yet, she doesn't really seem upset, just bewildered*, Tink observed as a strong breeze rustled the paper in her hands. Instinctively, the young woman clutched it tighter and then began walking toward the back of the house. All activity in the kitchen came to an immediate halt as the once-busy baker looked on with unbridled curiosity. The visitor stood in obvious admiration when the backyard came into view. *Who could blame her?* Tink mused, for she also found great pleasure in looking at and walking through that exceptional garden. *Perhaps the young lady isn't lost at all, because a lost person would not be so interested in seeing anything behind the house. Maybe,* Tink considered next, *she's studying landscape architecture at the state college, and the professor suggested his students come by to take note of such a masterful design. I could be entirely wrong, but I can't think of any other reason why she would be there.*

Surprisingly, though, Tink found comfort in the visitor's gentle presence and continued to be intrigue. She moved about with such grace as the sun accented the highlights of her auburn hair. When Tink finally managed to catch a glimpse of her face, she was taken aback by her natural beauty. Still, the old woman could not help but wonder who this stranger was.

Keeping a watchful eye on Nic's house had become second nature to Tink Kendleton. They had grown so close over the years, and she cherished this man who had become like a son to her. So quite naturally, Tink became familiar with his daily routine, as well as his comings and goings.

However, when the lights had gone out for good following his death in July, there had been little left to observe but the same two steadfast caregivers arriving to perform their usual tasks. Yet, Tink could readily perceive, by the slightest slouch in their shoulders and the slower pace of their steps, that neither one found the same feeling of fulfillment in performing their duties without the presence of their appreciative employer and friend.

Earlier that morning, Elizabeth Moreau had also arrived, followed shortly by Jimmy Johnson, who was apparently making a delivery from his store. The woman's bicycle, complete with a spiffy Nantucket basket, had been wheeled up the drive and placed inside the shed. All of this sudden and unexpected activity was very bewildering to Tink.

Then, the distracted elder realized, while peering out and pondering, that she'd been unabashedly staring out the window. For fear of being seen, she quickly reached for each side of the lace curtains and pulled them closed. At that very moment, however, the young woman happened to turn and look right in her direction.

Oh dear, oh my, Tink muttered aloud, backing away from the window. *I've done it now. I'm afraid I've been caught shamelessly gawking! Fortunately, Nic never took offense to my insatiable curiosity. But I must remember that others might consider that type of behavior quite rude.*

To avoid any further risk, Tink began busying herself with the present day's task. She let out a deep and intentionally slow sigh and started moving the canine cookies onto cooling racks. In doing so, though, she noticed that her hands were trembling.

Thank goodness these baked treats are for the dogs and don't require much precision. With all this excitement, I'll be lucky to get them off the baking sheets without dropping or breaking them into tiny bits.

One by one, she gingerly placed the cooled cookies into a large container to be delivered to the Homes for Hounds Rescue Center. This type of volunteer effort had long been a favorite of hers, and she could easily focus on the giddy reception anticipated, complete with wagging tails as the dogs delighted in their holiday goodies. Even so, Tink was not successful in avoiding thoughts about the unprecedented events happening next door.

Sometime later, the familiar roar of Elizabeth's car could be heard pulling into the driveway again. With no more discipline than a child told not to eat an ice cream cone in their hand, Tink immediately abandoned her work and returned to the window. But, this time, the clever woman found a way to peek through the larger holes in the lace so as not to be detected. By doing so, she managed to see her friend get out of the sports car and approach the young woman in a familiar manner. The encounter appeared to have been planned, and after a brief chat, Elizabeth escorted her to the front door, and they both disappeared inside.

Why didn't I bake for my human friends this morning, as well? Tink murmured. *I could have easily made a few pumpkin scones or my popular Cape Cod cranberry cookies. Then, I'd have a reason to go say hello and find out what's going on. Understandably, though, I was focused on the dear doggies since the rest of this week will be devoted to my Thanksgiving preparations. Still, if I had any kind of non-canine offerings ready, I could go over there because almost no one can resist my hot out-of-the oven-baked treats, not even that figure-conscious beauty, Elizabeth.*

That's settled, Tink decided with a clap of her hands. *I'll just make a little something right now in case I do have a chance to go by later.* Without hesitation, she eagerly pushed aside the other ingredients and made room for her new itinerary.

I'd better go poke around the pantry to see what I can find for this spontaneous endeavor. I'm sure I can put something together in a jiffy, she decided. *Because if there is one thing I am good at, it's improvising in the kitchen.*

With much excitement, Tink scurried across the room toward the large pantry. She passed through the laundry room first, picking up a step stool along the way. Once inside the sizable storeroom, the elderly woman cautiously climbed up to have a better look around. There were jars and cans, boxes and bags, tins and trays—all filled with an amazing array of ingredients. The pantry also housed tall stacks of plates, baskets, bowls, and other serving ware for her various inspired creations.

But, as she considered the choices, Tink heard the phone ringing in the other room.

Fiddlesticks, she mumbled aloud from atop the ladder. *I obviously can't answer that now. I can only hope that if it's important, they'll call back.*

Without becoming further distracted, Tink continued her search. And, when she felt satisfied with the selection, she stepped down, replaced the ladder, and returned to the kitchen clutching a small basket filled with fanciful fixings. Adding a pinch of this and a cup of that, the mixing had swiftly begun in her large, red Fiestaware bowl. Soon enough, a sheet of desirable drop cookies went into the oven, with the rooster timer set for fourteen minutes.

While the cookies were baking, Tink tidied up her appearance. Once the timer sounded, the hot baking sheet was pulled from the oven, and six of the best-looking cookies were placed on an attractive plate. Tink covered the plate with a red and white checked napkin, slipped on a practical pair of shoes, and walked right out the kitchen door.

However, just as she began to descend the back steps, she saw Elizabeth backing out and driving away. *Oh, goodness gracious!* Tink bemoaned, "If only I'd started those cookies sooner!"

Nevertheless, she noted, the other car remained in the driveway. Apparently, the visitor—most likely not a landscape architect student—remained inside the home. *I can't go over now, though, without Elizabeth being present. Because whoever she is, she has no idea who I am. And I'd have no reason to show up unannounced other than the fact that I'm just so darn inquisitive.*

Feeling disheartened, Tink returned inside and plopped down at the table.

Maybe I'll just eat one of these cookies to lessen my disappointment.

As she began munching halfheartedly, Tink noticed Nic's journal lying close by and remembered the dream she'd had just before waking.

Nic promised to send a sign today, and sure enough, that handsome cardinal came hopping and chirping at my window. But perhaps the bird is also a messenger notifying me about other changes coming. Besides, didn't Nic say, as well, that I would soon start seeing the fulfillment of his hopes and dreams right next door? I wonder if the young woman has anything to do with that promise? Tink felt immediately comforted by that idea, and she continued to ponder the thought as another big bite of cookie disappeared into her mouth.

Chapter 27
Elizabeth

I like her, Elizabeth thought, as she pulled out of the driveway onto Windswept Way. *I'm grateful for that since I have such special ties to Nic's home. After all, I was the one to suggest the name*—La Maison Enchantée. *Nic had struggled with several ideas, all of them a bit too masculine. But knowing he wanted to appeal more to the feminine, this name came to me without effort. And once I suggested it to him, he smiled and told me it was perfect.*

His love and devotion, I well know, are infused in every room of that lovely home, in every piece of wood, and in the very fabric and fiber he chose for the renovation. Therefore, I would hope that anyone fortunate enough to stay there would not only be respectful but also truly appreciative. And I sense that Maddie will be both, if not even more.

Nicolas Paramonos and Elizabeth had first become acquainted at her place of employment, Walters Real Estate and Investment Firm. As Larry's business partner, Nic usually came by several times a week. And because she was the office manager, he and Elizabeth would typically discuss scheduling and other aspects of the business. Gradually, a casual friendship formed. Then, after Tink informed him of Elizabeth's background, Nic sought her design suggestions for the renovations of his home. Elizabeth readily agreed to help, and, in doing so, they began to forge an even closer friendship.

For this astute and creative woman, working with such an honest and imaginative man had been a pure delight. Nic proved to be an appreciative and cooperative collaborator. As a developer and builder, Nic had focused primarily on the structural aspects of the job while deferring nearly all of the interior design decisions to Elizabeth. Side by side, they worked for many months as professionals and companionable peers.

Remembering this now, Elizabeth smiled in acknowledgment of Nic's uncompromising good taste. And she reflected on the idea that if Maddie truly felt enveloped by the comfort and beauty of this home, they had succeeded. For Nic's deepest desire was for his place to be a sanctuary for his beloved. But this recollection caused the smile on her face to subside due to the sorrowful realization that his most profound wish had not been realized in his abbreviated lifetime.

As memories continued to come to mind, her luxury car wound through the beautiful streets of Port Saint Smith. Elizabeth navigated with agility around each curve and every rotary. Pure performance and precision were her intentions both in driving and in life. This, along with thrilling adventures and elevated moments of elegance, was the balance she sought.

In little time, Elizabeth arrived back at her office. Upon entering the building, though, she realized no one else was there. Although her boss's car was parked outside, Elizabeth reasoned that Larry must have gone out for a walk or for lunch. *Good for him,* she thought. *A walk on such a perfectly beautiful autumn day will most likely do him great good.*

Elizabeth went directly to her computer and add the necessary updates to the rental agreement. Next, she texted Larry to update him on the status of the Paramonos property and inform him she would be shopping for the necessary essentials. She then gathered her coat, the updated paperwork, and a new cup of coffee before leaving the office.

The file with the rental forms was placed securely in her car. But Elizabeth also welcomed the chance to stretch her legs on such a gorgeous day. And since the downtown area of Port Saint Smith was quite small, all of today's errands could be done on foot with ease and enjoyment.

Thus, she walked briskly past the library, post office, a busy café, and a few independent shops before arriving at Robertson's Gourmet Deli. Theodore Robertson, one of the two proprietors, noticed her instantly amidst the other holiday shoppers and made an effort to accommodate her quickly. Even though he would never admit it, Elizabeth had become one of Theo's favorite customers due in part to her frequent purchases. But, more importantly, he genuinely appreciated her discerning taste, her honest admiration of the shop's distinct product lines, and their unwavering commitment to excellent standards.

To be fully prepared, Elizabeth had composed a concise shopping list of necessities, hoping to avoid any additional temptation in stocking the new rental property. Her full intention was to adhere to this plan until startling instructions advised her otherwise. To her great bewilderment, a text message from Larry arrived just then, insisting she "go overboard in all ways for this renter." And although stunned, Elizabeth replied with an enthusiastic affirmative.

Undoubtedly, Elizabeth mused, *Larry asked the right person to surpass the basic shopping requirements. I consider myself an expert in the field of shopping, and with a bit more practice, I may become that much more proficient,* she thought, laughing aloud. *Besides, I'm honored to do even more for Maddie Stuart. She seems like a kind person and one who I believe will truly enjoy the extra efforts and indulgences.*

Now, with Larry's permission, as well as his unexpected encouragement, Elizabeth began looking intently at the display cases filled with delicious delicacies. Her boss's unusual request, however, continued to nag at her. For the typical protocol at his firm had always been to only pamper a few returning clients who stayed at the most upscale rentals. And here was yet another odd directive from Larry, so out of character for the man she'd worked with for nearly a decade. Nevertheless, Elizabeth proceeded like the true professional she'd always been.

Theo soon offered her excellent advice regarding an enticing array of offerings, and Elizabeth settled on a roasted pumpkin soup, walnut and pear salad, and a generous portion of their renowned sweet potato casserole for Maddie's meal. She made that purchase and a few others, thanked Theo profusely, and exited the shop. Elizabeth's next stop was the grocery store to buy the household supplies for the property. Yet, as she passed the Boulangerie Bakery en route, she felt the strong urge to go in. *Because,* she reasoned, *no meal is complete without a generous side of freshly baked bread.*

Upon entering, Elizabeth saw that this retailer was also extremely busy, which afforded her the opportunity to take in all the heavenly scents and extensive selection. When the time came to order, though, Elizabeth was still undecided. She wasn't familiar with Maddie's preferences since they had only just met. So, she requested a plentiful sampling of breads, pastries, and desserts. And as she was leaving the bakery, Elizabeth felt quite pleased with her choices.

Next, the essential items to stock the new rental were gathered at the local grocery. Due to anticipated crowds in this small store, Elizabeth didn't attempt to push a carriage. Instead, she chose a handbasket that she efficiently filled with coffees, teas, and various sweeteners and creamers. Additionally, she found pleasure in gathering a lovely assortment of soaps, toiletries, and other items, including a jar of lavender bath salts topped with the fragrant purple blossoms recently harvested from a neighboring organic farm.

Each aisle offered her a chance to select another special treat or treasure for Maddie. But, when Elizabeth turned onto the juice and beverage aisle, she was pleasantly surprised in recalling a precious memory from the preceding summer.

Nic had been a competent and inspiring leader for the S.O.S. Foundation and the successful summer programs. But no one else had been trained to oversee the camps. Thus, upon his death, like so many other citizens of Port Saint Smith, Elizabeth immediately volunteered to help. And one of the tasks that she assumed was as unfamiliar to her as sailing itself. Because in her entire life, this independent, single woman had never given much consideration to what children liked to drink or eat. Yet, there she was every week in this very same store, buying carrots, apples, miniature pizzas, chips, cookies, and countless individual boxes of fruit juice. To Elizabeth's great surprise, this task, more than any other she'd agreed to, became one of her very favorites. After a full morning of lessons on the water, she delighted in watching the hungry, young sailors telling triumphant tales about their escapades on the "high seas" while slurping their drinks and devouring their meals. Although this executive woman had never witnessed such a cacophony of gulping, gobbling, and giggling, it truly brought her unexpected delight and satisfaction.

Elizabeth tried her best to imagine what the upcoming summer would be like for the foundation without an official camp director. With ample time to plan, prepare, and delegate the responsibilities of the staff and volunteers, the camps could definitely continue. And she secretly hoped that one of her tasks would still be to provide the meals and snacks for the hungry children.

Before any of those details could be carefully considered, though, Elizabeth knew that the first priority was to announce and promote the S.O.S. Foundation fundraising efforts. She fervently hoped that Larry would support this enormous endeavor. Yet, if he would not or could not, Elizabeth knew with certainty that she would take this on regardless. For she firmly believed that the foundation deserved not only to be saved but also to be brilliantly transformed so as to ensure many years of successful service.

I am willing to work harder than I ever have in my life, Elizabeth affirmed as she stood in front of the multi-colored juice boxes. *I will also seek the assistance of our community because, without their commitment and contributions, this vision would be impossible to attain. I intend to honor the calling of my heart with the hope that every idea and each decision will be truly inspired, assisted perhaps by the S.O.S. founder himself, who undoubtedly revealed this remarkable vision to me in a dream. And at night, I will wish upon the stars and listen to the wind whistling through the trees.*

With an even stronger sense of purpose, Elizabeth purchased the items selected. She then went outside, arms burgeoning with bags of bread, bisque, bath soaps, and other sundries. The day was bright, and Elizabeth paused momentarily to enjoy the warmth of the sun before beginning her invigorating walk back to the office. Soon, she became aware of a constant breeze accompanying her along the way.

After loading everything into the car, Elizabeth peeked into the building and saw that Larry was not yet back. Before returning to the Paramonos residence, though, she decided to make one more purchase with the hopes that it would help Maddie feel that much more welcome. She got into the car, therefore, and drove through the town's side streets, arriving next at Freeman's Nursery.

Elizabeth entered one of her other favorite establishments and immediately sought help rather than looking around on her own. As usual, Ella Freeman was happy to assist and accompanied Elizabeth to the display cooler in the back. There, Elizabeth found an impressive bouquet with fall flowers, autumn-colored leaves, and fresh fruit cascading out of a cornucopia-shaped basket. She opted for this rather than a more modest arrangement because that was precisely what she'd been asked to do—indulge the renter at *La Maison Enchantée.*

"I wouldn't mind having an arrangement this exquisite myself," Elizabeth remarked as they walked back together toward the counter. "That would certainly bring some Thanksgiving festivity to my home."

"Yes," Ella responded, "This beautiful horn-of-plenty is just brimming with autumn splendor."

"How right you are, Ella. But I live alone and don't expect any company this year. So, I feel this would be too excessive to buy for myself."

The women laughed and then were joined by Ella's husband, Henry.

"Happy Thanksgiving, Elizabeth," he offered joyfully.

"Happy Thanksgiving, Henry," she responded in kind.

"You know, we're both always glad to see you. And that sure is a mighty good-lookin' bouquet you've chosen. In fact, Larry Walters was in here just a little while ago, and I believe that he bought a similar arrangement."

Ella quickly gave her husband a sideways glance as a way of reminding him that one customer's purchase was never to be discussed with another customer.

"I figure, though," Henry stated after awkwardly clearing his throat, "that's not really mine to say. So, I, uh, hope that the recipient of your fine bouquet - whether it's for you or someone else - will enjoy it in bountiful good health and gratitude."

"I hope so too," Elizabeth replied politely, carefully avoiding any reference to his earlier comment.

"Now, you take good care of yourself. And we both wish you a blessed Thanksgiving."

"I hope you also have a most enjoyable Thanksgiving with your family," Elizabeth said as she reflected on the sincerity of this couple's gracious ways.

She then left the nursery, and as she placed the arrangement carefully on the passenger seat of her small car, Elizabeth couldn't help but be curious about who the recipient of Larry's floral purchase might be.

Maybe he's started to date someone, she considered, getting into the car. *He's been so sullen, though, that I can't imagine that's a real possibility. Perhaps he bought them for himself with the hopes that they*

141

would cheer him up. But, my history with Larry has shown that he isn't exactly a fresh flower kind of guy. Well, regardless, Elizabeth decided, driving away, *that is yet another unusual behavior on his part. But, at least this one shows more promise than many of his others. And, as Henry Freeman wisely stated, who those flowers are for isn't any of my business. Either way, I'm glad to know he bought them because I'm sure they will make someone very happy.*

With a car full of goodies and the happy satisfaction of getting to share them with the special new guest, Elizabeth drove directly toward Windswept Way. She felt inspired and excited by her new direction and the positive impact it would have on the community. And somehow, the timing of Maddie's arrival seemed as though it might also be part of the plan.

Chapter 28
Maddie

How astonishing, Maddie thought as she carried her suitcase up the stately wooden staircase. *I feel as though my day-to-day life in the city is quickly receding like the ebb of an immense ocean wave, and a new surge of goodness is abundantly flowing toward me. And this has all occurred with remarkably little effort on my part. I'm so amazed and thankful.*

Maddie reached the second-floor landing of the rental home, and as she did, her cell phone began ringing downstairs. Although reluctant to answer, she realized it could be important since the real estate agent might be calling to ask her additional questions or to confirm information. So, Maddie left her suitcase outside the main bedroom and quickly returned to the first floor. Upon seeing who the caller was, she answered eagerly.

"Hello there!"

"Hello, my favorite traveler," the animated male voice replied. "Miss Priss and I are calling to make sure you're okay. We were just concerned that in all the flurry of excitement, you may have unwittingly headed west toward the mountains instead of east toward the sea. But, by the sound of your voice, I'm guessing that our worries were unwarranted."

"Oh, Stephen, I didn't drive west. You're so ridiculous!" Maddie said playfully. "In fact, I'll have you know, at this very moment, I'm bringing my luggage upstairs into a luxurious vacation property on the Cape."

"Okay, so let me guess. You've checked into a historic Bed and

Breakfast, and they've tucked you away in the corner of an old, musty attic. Am I right?"

"You're not even close," Maddie replied with feigned arrogance. "What if I told you that I've rented an entire gorgeous, yet surprisingly affordable, house for the entire week?

"Then I'd say my good friend Maddie's happy holiday dreams are already well underway."

"Yes, I believe they really are. I'm staying in a charming little town named Port Saint Smith with cafes, a bakery, a bookstore, and other cute shops. The town also has a working port, beautiful parks, bike paths, and beaches. Finding this particular home in such a wonderful community has in and of itself been remarkable -- something I'm pretty sure is more than just coincidence. Oh! And the realtor, Elizabeth, insisted upon bringing me dinner tonight as a welcoming gesture. I feel so pampered already. But I can't talk too long because she'll be returning any minute with the food along with the keys and paperwork for me to sign. Please tell me, though, how are you both doing?"

"Well, first, let me say how happy I am that everything is going so well for you. It all sounds amazing! And we're doing great. I'm indulging Miss Priss as best I can to take her mind off the fact that you're far, far away traipsing around the Cape in search of the wind. I do have a question for you, however, which is one of the reasons I called. Have you ever seen one of those fancy strollers, um, I think they're called pet prams or something like that?"

"Yes, I've seen them. Why do you ask?"

"I was thinking about buying one and taking this fabulous, fluffy feline for walks in the park. Would I actually do that, Mr. non-athletic, you may be wondering? Yes, because I believe that Miss Priss needs a considerably wider circle of admirers. With her exceptional beauty, the world will be better off for having seen more of her, in my humble opinion. So... what do you think? Do you like the idea? Or are you concerned that the very sight or sound of a dog might send her over the edge?"

"I love the idea," Maddie answered brightly. "I've never tried taking her out like that myself. But whenever we go to the veterinarian's office, she's usually quite calm. Even if there are barking dogs in the waiting area, she's always quiet and seems to feel safe inside her carrier. But Stephen, I am the one with a question for you now. Would you please explain why you, the same guy that loathes *any* form of physical exertion, is suddenly willing to go for walks in the park?" she asked with noted sarcasm.

"I admit, it's bewildering, isn't it? What a contradiction I can be! The truth is, I miss her when I'm away. Take this morning, for example, when I went to get my coffee. I felt terribly guilty knowing poor Miss Priss had been left all alone in the apartment. So, I thought, why not venture out together? She could accompany me to the coffee shop, and then, if all goes well, we would continue on for a few blocks into the park. Who knows… we may even make a few friends along the way."

"I love your idea! Allow me a moment, though, to get over the sheer shock of it all! Still, I guess this shows just how much you adore "our" little kitty cat!"

"That's right. I'll admit it," he said, laughing raucously. "Love can make a fool out of all of us, can't it?"

"It sure can," she agreed, thinking about her own folly in following the voice of the wind to the Cape.

"I simply hope that this picky pussy cat will find our little outings to be amusing. I warn you, though, that if her Highness hisses or howls hysterically, the stroller will immediately be returned."

"I understand that and give you credit for even trying. Definitely keep me posted, okay?"

"I certainly will. And now that I have your permission, I'll probably buy it today because adventure awaits. I have one more quick question before we say goodbye. Is there anything else you want to tell me, such as," he paused for dramatic effect, "have there been any significant winds to speak of on your journey yet?"

"As a matter of fact, the answer is yes. After I crossed the Sagamore Bridge to the Cape, I went for a little walk along a wooded path. Had it not been for a delightful breeze causing the autumn leaves to dance and spin, I may not have twirled around myself. But because I did, I noticed a tiny sign pointing toward Port Saint Smith, which inspired me to come here. And, since I arrived in town, everything has lined up so beautifully. I feel welcomed by the kindness shown to me and excited about staying in this lovely home. The only part I'm kind of nervous about is the woman living next door. I've seen her staring out the window at me at least twice.

"When I first arrived at this property, I walked around back to look at the garden, which is gorgeous, by the way. I could see her peeking out the window then, so she quickly pulled the curtains closed with her shaky, old hands. After Elizabeth arrived, she and I went inside so I could view the house and decide if I wanted to rent it. I loved it right away! So, after a brief discussion, she left to finalize the paperwork and pick up a few necessary supplies. At that point, I went back to the car for my luggage. And I'm pretty sure the old woman was peering out again, but this time from behind the lace curtains because I noticed shadowy movements more than once."

"Oh, Maddie, I was afraid something like this might happen. Obviously, your windswept fairytale must have some kind of a wicked witch! Promise me, you'll be very careful! I want you to live until the happily-ever-after ending of your story."

"Stephen, you really do have such a flair for the dramatic! I'm sure she is quite harmless - probably a shut-in or a senior citizen with nothing better to do than stare out the window at strangers. But, I may mention this to Elizabeth and see if she knows anything about her."

"You must!" he insisted. "Otherwise, I'll be a nervous wreck worrying about you. I'm glad that your rental agent is returning soon. Please report this to her immediately. But, for now, Miss Perfect Pussycat and I need to let you go so I can buy the pet pram. We are eager to take it out for a test ride. Be careful, Maddie, and we hope you have great fun in everything you're doing!"

"Thank you, Stephen. That means a lot to me. And I hope that the pet pram will be a great success. And thanks for calling. I'm sure we'll talk again soon. Bye for now."

"Tata, sweetie."

Maddie smiled and tucked the phone in the back pocket of her pants. She then paused for a moment to breathe in the goodness. And, with even more joy, she all but skipped back up the stairs.

Chapter 29
Larry

Larry barely noticed the loading ramps, dented doorways, and dingy rubbish bins as he shuffled through the back alleyways. He desperately wanted to avoid the holiday shoppers on the sidewalks of Center Street, so he chose, once again, to walk in the alley behind the stores. He was grateful to have been left alone in the restaurant, and the meal had been satisfying. So, for a few short minutes, he'd been able to put aside his overwhelming concerns. But, as soon as he checked his phone, he was immediately jolted back into his tumultuous life.

Although unnerved, he still dutifully sent a text message to Elizabeth relaying the outlandish directive. For Larry knew that ignoring the text would only result in additional messages appearing until he finally conceded. And the instructions had been so succinct that he did not need to reread the words to remember what had been written.

Slouch,
As I'd always hoped,
she has arrived and will be staying
at *La Maison Enchantée.*
Please ask Elizabeth
to go overboard
in all ways

for this renter.
Fresh fruits, cheeses, hors d'oeuvres,
soups, croissants, chocolates,
candles, bath items, etc.
Thanks, mate!
I'm counting on you.
N

Every text received in the past few days had been more specific and distressing than the previous. And the dismay Larry felt after reading this latest message was palpable. But he didn't bother to understand it or ignore it. He didn't have the strength anymore. He simply followed the orders which were in direct conflict with the company's well-established rental policy. He also avoided any thoughts about who "she" could possibly be. Doing that, he feared, would be defined as sheer madness.

Thus, Larry lumbered back toward his office like a reluctant child about to get in trouble. He dreaded what awaited him there—most likely a challenging conversation with Elizabeth, who must, at this point, be ready for a plausible explanation regarding his controversial directions. And what imaginable justifications could be given without admitting that these ideas weren't even his own? How could Larry possibly explain to her what he couldn't begin to understand himself?

As Larry's anxiety increased, the idea of just going home instead of returning to the office became a real consideration. He could feign sickness, a belly ache perhaps, blaming it on the pungent, onion soup. Or, he could claim to have a migraine brought on by stress. That was certainly believable! But the prudent businessman decided otherwise. For Larry realized that he could ill afford to lose the trust of this loyal and essential employee who had, until now, unquestionably gone along with his outlandish requests. Nor did he want to disappoint Elizabeth, who rarely asked for anything, including something as simple as a conversation. She deserved better from him, which during these days seemed almost impossible.

Fortunately, he thought, *Elizabeth has continued to handle all of this with her usual professionalism and efficiency. She's acted as though nothing I've asked her to do is out of the ordinary. Yet, what else could I have done? Don't I owe it to Nic to follow through on his wishes, even if they are coming from a man so recently laid to rest?*

When Elizabeth asked to speak with me, I was fiddling with one of the commemorative sailboats Nic presented at the end of sailing camp. Without a doubt, I was amongst those recipients featured in the photograph at the restaurant. And Elizabeth said that's what she wanted to talk about. Well, to the best of my knowledge, she doesn't collect miniature sailboats, nor have I ever seen her show interest in learning to sail. So, I'm guessing the connection must be with Nic and the effect his death is having upon my work or, more accurately stated, the lack thereof. Perhaps the time has come for her to insist on explanations for all my odd requests. And I don't blame her!

Larry found himself mulling over plausible answers to offer Elizabeth. First, she must question his decision to list Nic's house right after they'd discussed closing it up for the winter. Next, she must wonder why he'd asked that a new bike, specifically a woman's, be purchased and placed at the home. That alone was unprecedented. Renters were always provided with a comprehensive packet upon arrival, which included a list of local recommendations such as restaurants, beaches, boating locations, and several reputable bike rental shops. But never would a bicycle be provided—let alone a brand new one. Then, the most recent request that she go 'overboard shopping' continued to contradict Walters Real Estate and Investment Firm's own policy. Larry's long-standing position on rental procedures had been unwavering for years: the property was to be immaculate, the basic staples supplied, and nothing more.

"I have no interest," Larry would remind his staff, " competing with other lodgings on the Cape, like the more indulgent Bed and Breakfasts. We will not be providing wine and cheese happy hours or fanciful teas and chocolates on the bedside at night. There are plenty of specialty shops and stores in Port Saint Smith where visitors can buy whatever indulgences they desire. Our only obligation is to provide safe, clean, and quality accommodations."

So, how can I justify asking her to shop extravagantly for this property? he fretted. *Honestly, I'd simply like to tell her the truth and go so far as to show her the text messages. That would be a huge relief! But, if I took that risk, my valued associate may understandably conclude that her boss has come completely unraveled. And perhaps I have.*

Fortunately, the door was still locked when Larry arrived back at the stately building that bore his name. Relieved to be alone, he presumed that Elizabeth had not yet returned from shopping and finalizing the paperwork with the new renter. And who was she - this visitor, this interloper - that his best friend insisted on giving an unfathomably reduced rental rate, providing a new bicycle, and then indulging with expensive chocolates, gourmet food, and lavish welcome gifts? Just the thought of someone else staying in Nic's home was deeply disturbing. And none of it, absolutely none of it, made any sense to the disheartened and increasingly distraught man.

Putting aside all of those thoughts, however, Larry focused instead on where to put the cornucopia floral arrangement. He considered various places. But instinct told him precisely where they belonged. And so he complied and stood back with hopes they would be well received, even though history indicated otherwise. Yet, when he'd made this purchase, Larry had no agenda other than to follow his gut that clearly signaled this was the right thing to do. And lately, he hadn't felt that sure about almost anything else in his life.

Larry stared briefly at the flowers before returning to his private office. There, he felt increasingly comforted, surrounded by the familiarity of this refined setting. His oversized leather office chair not only supported his weight but also his stature as the company owner. The mahogany desk and matching bookcases elicited a sense of tradition and style that pleased him immensely. And here, in the confines of this safe space, he was the king of his destiny... or at least he had been until recently.

Looking up at the antique brass clock, Larry guessed that Elizabeth might not return for another half an hour or more. So, to avoid fixating on his anxiety and the pending conversation, he turned his attention instead to the photograph Elizabeth had handed him. The old black and white image portrayed two people—a proud older man standing in front of an impressive estate with a young girl on his shoulders. *Could they be relatives?* Larry considered. *How odd, though,* he thought, *since Elizabeth has never been one to show off personal photographs, not even those from her trips abroad. In fact, she's always remained exceptionally private about her life outside of work.*

Larry respected her for that and had never pressed her for more details. Now, however, he realized just how little he knew about this significant employee. She had no spouse, no children, and no pets. Of this, he was certain. And most likely, she didn't have any plants at home either. But, Elizabeth's life, prior to moving to Port Saint Smith, was mostly a mystery to him. He knew she had lived in New York, experienced a successful career in both real estate and interior design, and traveled extensively. But none of these facts helped explain the old photo that was now turned face down on his desk.

Weary beyond words, Larry did not want to think anymore. So, he leaned back in his chair, closed his eyes, and wished he were at home napping on the couch and living up to his nickname, Slouch. But just the thought of that nickname caused his body to flinch.

How could Nic know what was going on, let alone communicate through my phone? How many texts has he already sent in the last few days? And how many more will there be? The written words feel like his, and yet, how on earth, or I guess in heaven or wherever he is, can that be possible?

The room remained so quiet that the ticking of the clock seemed unfathomably loud. Larry became even more agitated and started to fidget with the sailboat again.

When is Elizabeth going to get back? How much longer do I have to wait? Maybe listening to music will help fill this empty space that seems to be closing in on me. With that thought in mind, he reached for the phone, which had been silenced at the restaurant. But, in turning it over, he saw that yet another text had arrived. With no more ability to resist, his thick finger pressed the small icon, and he read aloud.

I know this is hard, Slouch.
You're the best friend
any guy could ever have.
But don't worry.
You'll be home on that couch
napping again
before long.
N

The vulnerable man, alone and afraid, put his head down on his desk and did something he hadn't done in years. He cried.

Chapter 30
Elizabeth

Elizabeth felt giddy as she concluded the shopping and drove back to meet Maddie. Just weeks ago, her life had felt so ordinary. As a successful professional, she lived in a nice home in a lovely little town. She had a fulfilling job, dear friends, and many true pleasures in life. She was content. There was little to complain about but also little to look forward to. And to this dynamic woman, contentment felt dangerously close to complacency, which would never be acceptable.

Filled with pure *joie de vivre* and an immense longing to be helpful, Elizabeth knew that more must be done with her life. She wanted and needed to make a difference. But was she ready for such an intense undertaking like the one that had been revealed to her in a dream? And was she right in believing that Nic was responsible for that brilliant idea?

Elizabeth was shocked at how much Nic's death had impacted her. He'd been such a dedicated athlete—cycling through town, sailing out of the port, or occasionally playing racquetball with Larry. And on the job, he was often teased for outpacing the younger workers. No one, therefore, could have guessed that he would die so young.

When word got out about his tragic passing, the entire town was in a collective state of shock. Elizabeth managed to control her emotions throughout the well-attended funeral and reception held at Tink's home. But immediately following those two events, she went home and

152

collapsed in bed for a full day and a half. Nic had become a dear friend, and Elizabeth allowed the deep torrent of sorrow to run through her like a rapid, raging river. And in those moments of grief, she realized that her sadness was not only due to her good friend's death but also in acknowledgment of the gnawing emptiness that had been welling up inside, demanding her attention.

Nic had left an indelible mark with his constant outpouring of good deeds. He'd donated generously to several causes, remodeled the dated theater at no cost to the town, and willingly helped the ladies of the Port Saint Smith Guild whenever the need arose. But, most significantly, he had solely envisioned and started the Spirit of Sailing summer camps, which had already inspired and improved many lives. And he had done it all with boundless passion, drive, and true humility.

Elizabeth also yearned to leave a lasting legacy. Since living in town, she had volunteered to help with clothing drives and raffle events. And she had served for many years on the theater board, where she helped raise substantial funds for costumes, props, and the entire renovation. But, until she personally witnessed the joyful triumph in the children during the summer camps, nothing had really compelled her to do more. But that moving experience, coupled with the visionary dream involving *Beauté Par la Mer*, had awakened within her such a purpose that she could focus on little else.

She instinctively believed that this could be the grand project in which to dedicate her time and talents. This could be the legacy that bore her unique stamp, insured her family's history, and safeguarded the future of the S.O.S. Foundation.

I've been much more aware, she realized as she approached Nic's home once again*, that I haven't felt inclined to travel lately. Nor have I been looking to strike up a new romance. But I do long for a mission that could transform lives in this precious community. I want to commit to an accomplishment that will transcend my everyday existence, and somehow, today feels like it could be the start of that.*

When I walked the regal grounds of Grand-Papa's estate this morning, I was reminded of all the happiness I experienced there as a little girl. Now, I can easily imagine other children playing there and sailing in the waters nearby. What a joy that would be to see and help bring to fruition. And I strongly sense that inspiration will guide the process all along the way. The dream already showed me how the funds

153

could be secured. And I don't think it was a coincidence that Nic and I grew so close during the renovation. We trusted each other, and now I think he trusts me with this extraordinary opportunity. And I don't want to disappoint him or myself.

Elizabeth was soon steering her car into the driveway and ringing the bell. Upon opening the door and seeing her arms filled with bags, Maddie exclaimed, "WOW! I'm guessing that your shopping trip was successful!"

"Yes, it most certainly was!" Elizabeth exclaimed with excitement. "Do you mind if I go ahead and put this all away in the kitchen and supply closet?"

"Not at all," Maddie answered, opening the door even wider. "Can I help you carry anything?"

"No, I've got it. But thank you for asking," Elizabeth replied assuredly as she walked directly toward the kitchen. Maddie followed behind, watching as she expertly stocked the shelves with the coffees, teas, sweeteners, and more. Next, the real estate agent began setting out an amazing array of edible offerings on the large wooden table.

Quite stunned, Maddie asked, "Is this all for me?"

"Absolutely," Elizabeth answered enthusiastically. "This is your holiday week in Port Saint Smith, and we want to ensure that it begins with great gusto! Plus, if truth be told, I was a bit indecisive about what to get you, which I promise doesn't happen very often. So, I simply bought you a small smorgasbord of almost everything, which I hope you will truly enjoy!"

"I'm sure I will," Maddie acknowledged, still in awe.

"Robertson's Deli was featuring a Roasted Pumpkin Soup with a cranberry walnut side salad that sounded divine. I would have asked for a tasting, but they were just brimming with customers. But I doubt it will disappoint. I purchased that meal and then asked my friend, Theo, the co-owner, to include a few extra surprises for you as well. Then, I went to the bakery, where I was utterly perplexed by the variety of amazing choices. Fortunately, the sales clerk was most accommodating, and she suggested a sampling of their best sellers, which I readily agreed to. So, you'll find freshly made French bread, pastries, tarts, and other fine treats.

"I don't even know how to thank you," Maddie said, perplexed. "From the look of this, I think you're trying to make me feel more spoiled than my cat!"

"Perhaps you're right," Elizabeth agreed with a wide smile. "But you must remember, Maddie, this is your getaway, and calories never count on vacations."

"Well, that's a relief to know," she giggled.

"I adhere to that philosophy whenever I travel. So, eat up and enjoy! There should be plenty here to tide you over tonight and, hopefully, well into tomorrow. *Bon appétit, m'amie!*

"Now, if you'll excuse me, I'm going back out to the car to get something else," Elizabeth announced as she swished out of the room with the same air of enjoyment as someone leaving Bergdorf's after an extravagant shopping spree in New York.

Elizabeth returned momentarily with a huge box. From this, she lifted out a woven cornucopia-shaped basket filled with lush autumn-colored fruits and flowers. The arrangement was carefully placed in the center of the large table, and not until the display was complete did Elizabeth turn to see Maddie's expression.

"Elizabeth," Maddie stated, obviously moved by the sight, "That's one of the prettiest arrangements I've ever seen in my life. It's so beautiful!"

"I'm truly glad that you're pleased!! I thought it was exquisite myself. Our company's policy has always been to go above and beyond for our clients. Admittedly, though," Elizabeth admitted as she pointed toward the bountiful spread of food and flowers, "this is more than our typical protocol. However, Maddie Stuart, you are the first honored guest to stay at *La Maison Enchantée*. And that alone makes this a special occasion!"

As those words were spoken, Elizabeth unexpectedly felt as though she were the steward of the home, speaking directly on behalf of the owner. She sensed that Nic would be very pleased to welcome Maddie here - if only he could. With this thought came powerful chills that ran across Elizabeth's shoulders, down her back and even along her arms. Her eyes began to tear up, and she quickly turned away, fearing Maddie might see her reaction. Then, excusing herself, she said, "I have a few more household supplies to put away. Let me attend to that, and then we can discuss more of the logistics regarding your stay."

"Of course, go ahead," Maddie replied, still shocked by the extraordinary outpouring of generosity.

Elizabeth then walked through the house, thoughtfully placing each item in an appropriate place. She found a welcome distraction in doing so, especially as she arranged luxurious bath items in the primary bath and set a cloisonné jewelry tray on the nightstand in the bedroom. As she continued to move about upstairs, Elizabeth noticed the wind rustling the leaves of the trees just outside the second-floor windows. Watching this was calming and allowed her to assume a more composed state of being.

Returning downstairs minutes later, Elizabeth then produced a large manila envelope and a set of keys.

"Why don't we go sit in the front room to finalize everything?" she suggested. "It's so lovely there."

Maddie agreed, and they soon entered the cozy confines of the small study. Elizabeth seated herself in the plush armchair while Maddie sat on the loveseat across from her.

"I'd like you to know that is a working fireplace," Elizabeth explained, looking in the direction of the hearth. "The logs are there for your use. And, if you need more, simply text or call me, and I'll have additional bundles delivered to the house at no charge."

"Thank you so much. I definitely plan to enjoy the fireplace while I'm here."

"Excellent. Also, as I mentioned earlier," Elizabeth said in a quieter tone of voice, " this house has never been rented before. It was a private residence until quite recently. I tell you this because I've done my best to anticipate everything you'll need, including a few extra indulgences. But, if I've overlooked anything, please let me know immediately, alright?"

"Yes, I will. You've done so much for me already that it's hard to imagine you've overlooked anything.

"Well, since this rental came up so suddenly, there wasn't as much time to coordinate everything."

"I understand. And what I love already about this home is the fact that it still has such a distinctly personal and inviting feeling. After I brought my luggage in, I looked briefly at some of the beautiful books in this room, like the sailing books."

"Yes, you'll find an exceptional collection of books in this study. The owner was an avid reader, sailor, and cyclist. Oh, that reminds me— did I mention that there is a bicycle here for your use?"

"Is there really?" Maddie asked in surprise. "That's amazing! I was hoping to ride this week but guessed I'd have to rent one at a local bike shop."

"That won't be necessary. Just this morning, a new woman's bicycle was delivered and placed in the garden shed."

"That's great! I really enjoy cycling and I'm sure I will use it during my stay."

Elizabeth was still bewildered by Larry's request that a women's bike be delivered. Yet, seeing Maddie's enthusiastic response made her realize just how perfect that actually was. *But how could Larry have known?* she wondered. *The house hadn't even been listed when the delivery was made.* Without time for more consideration, the conversation continued.

"Well, Maddie, it's there for your use anytime."

"Fantastic! This home feels as though it was made for me," Maddie said sincerely.

"That makes me so happy to hear! Quite a lot of planning and effort went into the renovation this past spring. In fact, the owner asked for my input on many aspects of the modifications due to my experience as an interior designer in New York."

"I imagine that was a fun project for you."

"It really was great fun and so rewarding. We worked really well together," she noted wistfully. "And what's most interesting is that his singular wish was for a woman to feel fully embraced and at home here. Honestly, I believe he accomplished his goal."

"From what I've seen so far, I think he did, too," Maddie concurred, looking around the room with true appreciation.

Once again, Elizabeth had to hide her feelings as memories of working alongside Nic rushed to the surface. She had done everything possible to support his heartfelt intention to prepare this home for his beloved. If only he could have met someone special like Maddie, perhaps that fateful outcome could have been altered. But, she would never know, so there was no point dwelling on that thought.

Elizabeth shifted in the chair and pulled the rental agreement from the packet, saying, "Let's complete the formalities so you can begin to fully enjoy this lovely place."

The seasoned real estate agent adeptly guided Maddie through the various procedures—rental agreement, deposit fees, signatures, etc. Once complete, the packet was still brimming with items that Elizabeth went on to explain.

"I won't go through all of this with you today, but this envelope is filled with so much helpful information, such as brochures and flyers listing upcoming events and holiday activities. There are also recommendations for shopping, restaurants, and interesting historical places to visit. Additionally, you will find a map of the many wonderful local trails, including the stunning Piney Grove Trail, which happens to run right behind this property. The code to unlock the back gate is here, and you can simply step through the arched doorway and out onto the trail. Then, you could either walk or ride the bike down to the shore in probably 25 minutes or less. How ideal is that?"

"I don't think it could be much better," Maddie answered her, smiling broadly.

"I agree. Now, I have one more thing to bring to your attention before I leave," Elizabeth remarked. "Here is a printed list of important phone numbers. The first number is mine—both the office number as well as my personal cell. Next, you'll find Larry Walters's cell number; he is the owner of our company. But, I would encourage you to contact me first, if you would please. Feel free to call any time, day or night, even if it's late. I really won't mind. And, if for any reason you can't get a hold of either Larry or me, I suggest that you reach out to the elderly woman who lives next door. I'm sure she would be willing to help you if she can."

"Do you mean the woman that lives in that direction?" Maddie asked, pointing toward the house where she'd seen the curtains moving.

"Yes, precisely," Elizabeth responded. "Her name is Theresa Kendleton, but she goes by Tink. Her number is third on the list."

"Ok," Maddie replied. "I may have seen her a little while ago looking out the window."

"Yes, you probably did!" Elizabeth confirmed with a sweet laugh. "That wouldn't surprise me at all. Tink is as inquisitive as a child and just as delightful, too! I personally find her to be one of the most precious people that I've ever met. And I don't know what this town would do without her. No doubt, she was curious about what was happening over here. So, I plan to go by and give her an update on the home's rental status after I leave here with you. When I tell her what a perfect fit this all seems to be, I'm certain she'll welcome you with great kindness. And, if you're lucky," Elizabeth added with a wink, "she may bring you some of her homemade baked goods. I assure you that no one can bake like she can! If I lived next door, keeping this slim figure would be absolutely impossible!

"Speaking of food and eating, though, you're probably getting hungry, so unless you have any other questions, I think I'll be heading out now.

"No, I'm good."

"Well, I've thoroughly enjoyed meeting you, Maddie."

"And I've enjoyed meeting you too, Elizabeth," Maddie remarked, rising to walk her to the door.

"I hope your holiday week in Port Saint Smith will be everything you want and even more!" the realtor cooed as she stepped outside.

"Thank you so much. And really, thank you again for everything! Happy Thanksgiving!"

"Happy Thanksgiving to you, too!"

Maddie closed the door and quickly realized just how hungry she was. Leaving the information packet open on the loveseat, she walked directly toward the kitchen to have a delicious meal.

Chapter 31
Tink

"Eee-liiiIz-a-beethh," Tink called out in a sing-songy voice, "I have something special for yoooouu!" The melodious message drifted across the driveways, aided by a soft autumn breeze.

As soon as the old woman had seen Elizabeth leaving the house next door for the second time, she rushed outside, precariously carrying a plate of homemade cookies.

"Hello, Tink," Elizabeth said as the two women met on the lawn between the properties. "I was just coming over to speak with you."

"Were you really?" Tink replied in surprise. "Well, how nice! I'm always glad to see you. But I certainly hope you weren't planning to come to my front door. After everything we went through this past summer, we're good friends now. And my friends all know to come around back to the kitchen door. Because that is most likely where I'll be—baking, cooking, or having a little something to eat," she added with a chuckle.

"So that's settled then. I'll make sure to come to your back door from now on. And I thank you sincerely, Tink, for the honor of your friendship. I am a better person for having known you," she affirmed.

"I feel exactly the same way," Tink agreed with a pleasant smile.

"Do you happen to have a few minutes to talk?" Elizabeth inquired. "I'd like to update you about what's happening at Nic's home."

"Yes, I have time," Tink replied eagerly, "I did happen to notice that something was going on over there," she stated with a slight tinge of guilt since she'd been watching as much activity as possible from her kitchen window.

"Well, as of today, the home is being rented. Maria and I have made sure that everything is ready, and I've done my best to anticipate the guest's needs."

"I'm sure you have," Tink acknowledged.

"And I'd like you to know that the person staying in the house is named Maddie Stuart. She will be there through the remainder of the week. I'd guess that she's about thirty or so. And, in my opinion, she's very pretty and has the most enviable auburn hair. But, more importantly, she seems like a very kind, respectful, and appreciative person."

"I trust your judgment, Elizabeth. But I am surprised that Nic's house is being rented already. The fact that you're overseeing it, though, does bring me some comfort. Because I know how much Nic and his home have also meant to you."

"Yes, you're correct," Elizabeth affirmed solemnly. "I will continue to be mindful of how everything goes this week. And if you have any concerns whatsoever, please let me know right away."

"I sure will. But I have a strong sense that everything will go well. If you'd like me to, though, I'd be glad to keep an eye out for Maddie and the home."

"I'd appreciate that. And I certainly hope you get a chance to meet her."

"Me too! And I suppose," Tink admitted, "it's better that the house is being used and appreciated rather than sitting empty, especially during this holiday week."

Still, the elder woman had unspoken reservations about anyone other than Nic and his expected beloved staying in the home. Wasn't this home to have become a cozy nest for those two lovebirds? Never was the plan for it to become a rental place for tourists.

Yet, for Tink, disengaging from the activities next door had proven to be nearly impossible. After being caught peeking out not once but twice, she'd promised herself to stay busy enough that her focus would remain solely in the kitchen. Therefore, Tink had stepped away from the window and even her baking to prepare a light lunch. The curious elder managed to resist temptation long enough to enjoy half a sandwich and a few bites of carrot raisin salad. But when she heard the roar of Elizabeth's car in the adjoining driveway once again, the meal was quickly abandoned, along with all of her good intentions.

Tink had scurried across the kitchen and located two holes in the lace curtain large enough to look out but, hopefully, not be detected. She then watched as Elizabeth made a few trips back and forth from her car into the house with what appeared to be groceries, delicatessen takeaways, French bread, and a large box with something ornamental poking out of the top. As Tink continued to watch with unabated curiosity, she wavered emotionally between immense inquisitiveness and the slightest feelings of shame.

Oh, how I wish I could keep my mind on my own matters. But since I can't, perhaps I can contribute in some way, like bringing a plate of welcoming cookies over there, Tink considered. *My offering may seem meager in comparison to the wonders that clever Elizabeth has produced from inside that tiny car of hers. Still, I feel fairly confident that nothing would quite rival my award-winning cookies.*

So, when at last Elizabeth was seen leaving the house with her briefcase and keys, Tink knew that was the chance to make her move. So, she grabbed the prepared plate of cookies and beelined out the front door.

Now, as they stood outside, Tink listened respectfully to Elizabeth and managed to refrain from interrupting even though she had an unending list of questions.

"Tink," Elizabeth said, "I hope you don't mind that I gave Maddie your phone number. I encouraged her, of course, to call Larry or me first. But in case she's unable to reach one of us, she may need to call you."

"That is absolutely fine," Tink replied agreeably. "I'd be glad to help in any way I can. That's what neighbors are for."

"How very true," Elizabeth acknowledged with a sense of relief. "I'm heading back to the office now. But thank you for your willingness to step in if need be. And I hope you know that you can always reach out to me yourself anytime. Because," she added with a little wink, "that's what friends are for."

"Exactly! And thank you, Elizabeth. But, before you leave," Tink interjected, "may I ask you just one question?"

"Of course."

"I do have a concern," she confided. "I'm confident, however, that you'll be able to put this worried old woman's mind at ease."

"I'll do my best," Elizabeth assured her.

"I hope you don't think I'm being impertinent, but I'm wondering what has become of Nic's personal belongings since his estate has yet to be settled? Are they still in the house?"

"That is an important and understandable question," Elizabeth said in a reassuring manner. "But please don't worry because, shortly after the funeral, Larry and one of the other staff members went to his house and retrieved his files, jewelry, and other valuables. These are secured at the bank. And then, for the past few months, Maria has been methodically packing, labeling, and moving his other personal items into the attic, where they are securely locked. As you know, that large space was recently finished with both air and heat, so it's a clean and safe environment. Maria's really done an excellent job, and only a few of his books are still in the main part of the house."

"I'm so relieved. And I know how very capable Maria is," Tink acknowledged. "She assisted me when the time came to go through Grant's belongings—a task I could have never done alone. I admire her stamina, fortitude, and grace. And had I been assigned the job of going through Nic's possessions, all I would have produced would be an enormous puddle of tears on those new wood floors. And that, my dearest, would not have been acceptable in any home, let alone one that had recently been renovated."

Elizabeth smiled softly and nodded compassionately. For as competent as she typically was, sorting through her deceased friend's effects would have challenged her emotional stability, as well.

"Thank you so much for explaining that to me," Tink offered. "Now, I promise I won't keep you any longer."

"Alright, then, I'll get going since I have a meeting scheduled with Larry. I wish you a wonderful Thanksgiving, Tink!"

"I wish you also a very Happy Thanksgiving! Good gracious," Tink added in a sudden fluster, "now that we've mentioned that, I realize I have another important question for you. Will that make you late for your meeting?"

"No, it won't," Elizabeth affirmed. For as eager as she was to speak with Larry about the future possibilities for the S.O.S. Foundation and Grand-Papa's estate, conversations with this spry elder always seemed to uplift her day.

"Thank goodness. Because I need to ask if Larry has mentioned anything to you about the annual basket deliveries? As you know, for the past several years, he and Nic delivered bountiful food baskets on

Thanksgiving Day to the S.O.S. families in need. And I have always made the pies for dessert. But I haven't heard anything from him yet, and Thanksgiving is only three days away."

"No, he hasn't mentioned this to me either. But when I meet with him today, I'll be glad to ask him since I realize how much those deliveries meant to him and Nic. And I firmly hope that the tradition will continue, along with all of the other foundation's worthy outreach programs."

"So do I! My heart really goes out to Larry and the difficulties he must be having in simply carrying on from day to day. I wish I could do more to help him, but I still struggle some days to find my own strength and courage. But that's enough about that! Just know that I'll be more than happy to bake the pies again this year. I just need to be given the go-ahead."

"I'll definitely discuss this with him today and let you know where we stand as soon as I can."

"That will be so helpful. Thank you, Elizabeth."

"You're very welcome, Tink."

"So, for now, goodbye, Elizabeth. Have a great afternoon," Tink said as she watched the slender woman walk with such style toward her car. Then, as Tink turned to go back home, she suddenly remembered the plate of cookies she'd been holding all along.

"Glory be," she muttered aloud. *After all that fuss, I completely forgot to give Elizabeth the cookies.*

So, once again, in a sing-songy voice, she called out, "Eee-liiiIz-a-beethh, you'll never believe it, but I forgot to give you these homemade cookies. May I tempt you to take them back to the office?"

"Tink, you are so sweet!" Elizabeth exclaimed. "It is never easy for me to say no to any of your delicious treats. But why don't you give them to Maddie instead? That would give you a chance to welcome her to the neighborhood."

"Oh, yes, I like that idea very much!" Tink replied enthusiastically. "Maybe I should wait a little longer before going over so she can get settled in a bit more."

"That sounds perfect. I'm sure she'll enjoy meeting you, and I know how much she'll love your cookies!"

After one more truly final goodbye, Elizabeth climbed into her car and drove away. And as Tink began the walk back, she noticed a lightness in her step.

Chapter 32
Larry

"Is that you, Elizabeth?" Larry hollered from his desk after hearing the front door open. He then heard the familiar click, click, click of her high heels across the floor. But, still, he wanted to be certain who had arrived.

How uncouth, Larry thought critically. He had never been one to yell inside his building. But he didn't feel like getting up, let alone leaving the comforts of his office. *I'll do better the next time*, he asserted, while still remaining firmly planted in his chair.

"Yes, Larry, it's me, " Elizabeth called back. "I'll be there in just a couple of minutes to catch you up on everything."

"Alright," Larry replied, rubbing his eyes in an effort to wake up. Because, for the last hour, he'd alternated between napping and nervously fidgeting with the miniature sailboat. Why did Elizabeth want to talk with him about that commemorative keepsake? And why did she insist on him looking at an old photograph? He already had enough questions in his life. He didn't need more riddles, especially from her.

Dismissing those thoughts, Larry reached inside the upper right drawer to retrieve a small mirror. He wanted to check his appearance to make sure there were no telling signs of napping or crying. Thus, after a few adjustments and pulling a brush just once through his thick hair, he simply sat and waited. But he didn't wait long because Elizabeth soon appeared in the doorway. Still, she hesitated briefly before speaking because she sensed this might not be an easy conversation.

"Everything went well at the house," she stated softly. "The papers are signed, the visitor packet and keys delivered, and the rent's been paid."

"Honestly? Nic's home is rented, and someone will be staying there tonight?" he asked incredulously. "I can't believe how quickly all this has happened. The house wasn't even listed a day ago. But," he muttered, "I guess that's what he really wan… I mean, uh, I guess that's… uh, that's good."

Elizabeth merely nodded and continued, "I made sure that all the necessary supplies were stocked, and, as you requested, I took good care of the renter. I bought her a nice meal from Robertson's Deli, bread and desserts from the bakery, and flowers from Freeman's Nursery."

"Thank you," Larry said with a heavy sigh, realizing just how conflicting those instructions must have been. And he couldn't explain why, and fortunately, she hadn't asked yet for an explanation.

"Speaking of flowers," she continued, "I saw the arrangement on my desk. Where would you like me to put that?"

"Wherever you'd like," he responded bluntly.

"Should I put them in the reception area so more people have a chance to see them?"

"I guess so if that's what you want to do."

"That's fine. I'll just place them on the front table then."

"But, why would you do that?" he asked gruffly. "They're for you."

"What? The flowers are for me?" Elizabeth asked in uttering surprise, remembering that Henry Freeman had mentioned Larry making a recent floral purchase. But never had she considered the possibility that they were for her.

"Yes, I bought them for you," he added sharply, still remembering the cool reception of the potted plant he'd given her a few years back. And this well-intended gesture didn't seem to be going much better.

"I just can't believe it," she stammered, "They're… so…".

"What?" he interjected impatiently, "alive? You don't like them?"

"No. I mean, yes… I mean… I like them very much. They're beautiful! But why are these for me?" she questioned, unable to hide her astonishment.

"Because," he explained, "it's Thanksgiving week. And that's the least I can do to say thanks for all the extra work you've been putting in since, well, you know, since summer."

"I'm really touched, Larry," she responded sincerely. "Thank you so much."

"You're welcome. I'm just relieved to know you like them."

"I love them! The arrangement is absolutely exquisite!" she said honestly while opting to omit the fact that she had just purchased a nearly identical arrangement for Maddie. Instead, she added, "You know, I'm fairly generous with myself. But still, I would never have bought anything this decadent for my home unless I was expecting company or hosting a party. I truly appreciate this lovely gift."

"Well, that's good," he stated, exhaling deeply. "Now, I know you want to discuss something with me. Let's go ahead and begin."

"Actually, as much as I want to explain the significance of that old photograph and how it relates to an idea I have, I feel we need to talk about a more time-sensitive matter first."

Larry immediately became uneasy. He was barely holding up for one conversation, and now he had to brace himself for another one that was even time sensitive?

"Alright," he agreed begrudgingly. "Why don't you go ahead and have a seat?" he suggested, pointing toward the chair across from his desk.

"Sure," Elizabeth responded in disbelief. Because in the many years she'd worked at this company, meetings between Larry and herself had always been brief, and she always stood up—listening, offering suggestions, helping establish work priorities, and then quickly returning to her desk to begin working on the agreed agenda. This had been the routine ever since the beginning of her employment, with the only exception being her initial interview and the first week of training. Nevertheless, Elizabeth complied while still making note of yet another odd request from her boss.

As she gracefully took a seat, Larry glanced out the large window overlooking Center Street. He felt painfully disconnected from the world beyond. Just a few months earlier, he'd walked on that very sidewalk with oblivious contentment. But that comfortable life felt almost lost to him now. His lamenting, however, was interrupted - not by Elizabeth's voice but by the sound of an incoming text. He reached nervously for his phone and read the message in silence.

Slouch...
What Elizabeth has to say
is urgent.
Please give her your full attention.
Thanks much.
N

Larry sat motionless, staring at the words while Elizabeth waited quietly. He then looked up and said, "So, now tell me what's on your mind? You have my, uh... my full attention," he added, quoting the text and quivering.

"Thank you, Larry. I believe this conversation is quite important."

"Yes, I understand," he replied, refraining from adding, "so I've been told."

"Forgive me for being so direct, but do you have plans for Thanksgiving Day?" she inquired.

"No," he answered flatly.

"I'm asking because after I left the rental house, I chatted briefly with Tink Kendleton. She wanted to know about the Thanksgiving basket deliveries for the S.O.S. families and if you would like her to make the pies again this year?"

All Larry managed to produce was a nearly inaudible grunt.

Elizabeth proceeded cautiously with her next words. "I realize that you and Nic established this tradition several years ago and spent the day preparing and delivering the food. And I believe this community outreach is a worthy one to uphold. So, if you would allow me, I would like to help prepare the baskets and even make the deliveries with you."

"But, don't you already have plans for Thanksgiving?" he inquired.

"No, actually, not this year. I'm not traveling, and I have no other commitments."

"But, it's too late anyway," he argued. "Nothing's been done. I haven't called a single family or any of the businesses that usually make donations. It couldn't possibly ..."

"Larry," Elizabeth interrupted respectfully, "today's only Monday. I can start making calls to the families and the businesses right away. There's still plenty of time to pull this together."

"Are you serious?" he asked doubtingly.

"Yes, I am. I would be more than happy to help out. How many households would be involved?" she asked, easing into the conversation.

"We typically gift a Thanksgiving basket to eight families. And we've always rotated the recipients because there are so many in need. Each family receives a fully cooked meal, including turkey, gravy, stuffing, mashed potatoes, side vegetables, rolls, butter, and one of Tink's pies. I have the list of families right here," he gestured, opening a drawer in his desk and pulling out two sheets of paper. "I also have the names of the businesses that have contributed in the past. I printed these out two weeks ago, but that's as far as I got. I just couldn't bring myself to make a single call."

"That's understandable," she said kindly. "Why don't you just give all of it to me, and I'll start the process?" she suggested, extending her hand. "Because you know, when I set my mind to something, I invariably get it done."

"Yes, you do. But are you sure you really want to take this on?" he questioned. "It can be quite an undertaking."

"I'm absolutely positive! Because of my involvement with the S.O.S. camps this past summer, I really care a lot about the young sailors and their families. So, I welcome the chance to help as much as possible and, hopefully, even see some of the sailors again during the deliveries."

"I'd like to see them also," he admitted. "And I did want to make the deliveries this year. I just don't have it in me to do it alone."

"Then let's do it together."

"Alright, let's try," he agreed, handing her the papers. "But, how will I ever thank you for helping with this also?"

"I think the beautiful autumn arrangement you've given me today is thank you enough. Let's call it even. Now, I'd better go get started."

"Wait a minute. What about the discussion regarding that photograph?" he asked, pointing at the old black-and-white image.

"Oh, we'll get to that, I promise," she said, standing up. "But first, I need to tend to this. You must admit, though, the little girl in the picture is pretty darn cute," Elizabeth added with a hearty laugh as she turned to go. "I'll keep you updated on the basket progress," she promised, talking over her shoulder.

"Alright. You do that."

No sooner had she left his office, Larry heard the sound of another incoming text. Without resistance, he read…

Thank you, Mate.
I'm sure Elizabeth will
handle this perfectly.
Now, why don't you go home
and be the Slouch
on the couch?
N

Chapter 33
Maddie

How can I begin to describe this amazing day? Maybe I can't in words. But I've certainly written on my heart the playfulness of the wind, the kindness shown to me by everyone I've met so far, and the uncanny synchronicities that all led me here.

Maddie sat at the wooden kitchen table, nibbling on the last bite of a sumptuous supper and writing in her journal. Everything on her way to Cape Cod had been successful - inspired beyond even her own imagination.

After Elizabeth had left, Maddie realized she hadn't eaten much all day, so she went straight into the kitchen to eat. She opted to dine there in order to watch the golden, late afternoon light streaming through the large paned windows. This also offered her an expansive view of the backyard, including the garden and surrounding ivy-covered stone walls. As well she could also see part of the neighbor's garden and back steps leading to what Maddie guessed might be her kitchen. Still, Maddie decided not to close the privacy shutters just yet since Elizabeth had assured her that the inquisitive neighbor was really a kind, elderly woman.

The delicious meal consisted of soup, salad, and the most perfect French bread. Maddie enjoyed each distinct flavor and the fact that such superb, fresh food had been a generous gift on her first night in Port Saint Smith. She also delighted in the stunning cornucopia centerpiece, filled with chrysanthemums, salmon-colored roses, sunflowers, pussy willows, dried fruits, and autumn leaves. That thoughtful gift served as a most welcoming gift, especially during this week of Thanksgiving.

After a day of travel and a satisfying supper, Maddie felt satiated and also a bit weary. So, she wrote a little more in her journal, cleaned up, and then retreated upstairs. Tea and dessert could come later, but for now, she wanted nothing more than to slip into a hot, restorative bath. The lighting in the bathroom was soft, and the deep spa tub was surrounded by luxurious products - lavender soaking salts, organic oatmeal scrub, and scented soaps in various shapes and fragrances. After months of excitement and a fair amount of worrying, she happily allowed herself to become fully immersed in this tranquil setting. The bubbles, soothing water, and flickering candlelight helped further relax her. And with nowhere else to be and nothing else to consider, she drifted into a sweet state of ineffable peace.

An hour or so later, Maddie returned downstairs, feeling clean and refreshed. She wore her favorite travel pajamas, slippers, and the plush, new cotton bathrobe found hanging in the closet. Upon entering the intimate study, she was immediately enveloped by a sense of serenity and belonging.

Tomorrow, she decided, *I'll light a fire. But tonight, I am content to simply sit in the stillness of this lovely room.*

She curled up comfortably on the loveseat and began writing again in her journal.

I could have never anticipated or even orchestrated the extra-ordinary events that happened today. And what a joy for me to be in this lovely home, in this charming town, and to have already met such good people.

Before I left home, my hope was to have clear insights and signs guiding me to a perfect place on the Cape. I was definitely concerned about not doing enough research or making reservations before my arrival. Yet, everything has unfolded in the most remarkable way. And so little effort has been required on my part other than to trust and continue on as I am being intuitively guided.

The drive to the Cape was easy, and a walk in the woods proved to be the essential turning point. If it weren't for the wind dancing among the leaves, I might never have twirled around and then seen the little mossy sign that pointed the way to Port Saint Smith. Then Shirley, the kind volunteer at the Chamber, did everything she could to help me. And what an incredible coincidence (actually, I know that nothing this good could really be a coincidence) that this home, La Maison Enchantée, *was called in as a rental just as I was deciding where to stay. I rather sense that someone else, in addition to Grandma Anise, has led me here. Because this home already feels so perfect, as though, in some amazing way, it was waiting just for me.*

The realtor also spoiled me beyond belief. Thanks to her, I had a memorably delicious meal and afterward bathed in a spa bath surrounded by sheer luxury. To which I say YES! Even the cornucopia centerpiece Elizabeth gave me is so apropos since this entire experience has already overflowed with blessings.

Based on how well everything has gone so far, I sense that the rest of my holiday week will be just as amazing. Still, I wonder how I'll spend my days? Where will I feel inspired to go? Who else will I meet? And I sure hope to find out who actually invited me to the Cape.

Maddie paused from her writing and glanced at the information packet next to her on the loveseat. Elizabeth had explained most of the contents in detail, including the contact information, local recommendations, and the bike trails. She also told Maddie that in the sizable packet were various brochures from the area. Yet, Maddie was not tempted to study them now. She decided instead that a cup of tea and dessert would be perfect.

The kitchen was dark as she entered the room, so Maddie turned on the lights and closed the window shutters. She then set a kettle of water on the stove to heat and chose a tea from the generous selection provided. Just as the tea kettle began to whistle, though, another sound was heard —a knocking at the backdoor. Turning to see who was there, the face peering through the door's glass panes was easily recognizable. Maddie quickly removed the kettle, turned off the stove, and went to open the door.

"Hello," Maddie said softly.

"Hello," the elderly woman responded in kind. "You must forgive me for showing up unannounced, especially now that I see you are in your pajamas. But I noticed the lights were on and wanted to officially welcome you to our neighborhood. Elizabeth told me you would be staying here. So, I came over to introduce myself. I'm Teresa Kendleton, but please call me Tink. I live at that house over there," she said, pointing in the direction of her home.

Maddie resisted the temptation to say that she knew exactly where Tink lived, having seen her more than once peering out the window. Instead, she smiled and said, "I'm glad to meet you, Tink. I'm Maddie Stuart. Would you like to come in?"

"Oh, no, I wouldn't think of intruding on your first night. But, how kind of you to ask. I just wanted to say a quick hello and bring you a plate of homemade cookies. I love to bake, and these were made with my not-so-secret awarding-winning ingredient—love," Tink stated with sweet enthusiasm.

"I'm sure they're delicious. Thank you so much. And your timing couldn't be any better. I was just about to have some tea and a little dessert."

"Wonderful! Don't you just love it when everything comes together so perfectly?" Tink asked enthusiastically.

"I sure do!" Maddie agreed wholeheartedly.

"But before I say good night," Tink offered, "I do owe you an apology for my impertinent behavior earlier. I think you may have seen me staring out my kitchen window when you first arrived. I know better than to do that, but I got carried away when I saw all of the activity going on over here."

"That's ok. I'm pretty curious, too, and I probably would have reacted the same way," Maddie stated kindly.

"Well, aren't you sweet to say so. But still, I am sorry." Then, with a sigh of relief, Tink asked, "Are you settling in nicely? Is everything going well so far? What do you think about our delightful little town, Port Saint Smith? And what are you planning to do during your visit?"

Before Maddie could begin to answer, however, Tink sighed a second time, saying, "Good gracious, forgive me again. I'm going on and on, and I must remember that you've only just arrived! You're probably very tired."

"I'm alright," Maddie assured the neighbor. For she was enjoying Tink's visit. "Everything's gone really well since I arrived. Usually, when I travel, my plans are literally mapped out well in advance. But I decided to do this trip differently and just go where I felt instinctively guided. And I'm so glad I did. Because now I'm staying in this lovely home in such a sweet town that I'm sure I wouldn't have found on a travel site."

"How wise you are, dear! So often, we create such rigid plans and then miss out on the spontaneity and adventure along the way. As for me, I'm happy to know it's you who's staying here," Tink offered honestly. And, to her own surprise, she added, "This home was always intended to be shared with…well… I mean… designed for… well, meant to be for someone special like you! And I hope your time here will be most enjoyable and memorable in every possible way. But I'm chattering on instead of allowing you to have your evening snack. So, I shall say goodbye."

"Well, thank you so much for coming over. I'm glad we met," Maddie said, already charmed by this unabashed elder. "I hope to see you again."

"I hope so, too! And remember, I'm just across the way if you need anything. I may be an old woman, but I'm not the kind who sits on the porch idly rocking in a chair. I'm almost always cooking or baking or doing some sort of volunteer work in the community. Now that I think of it, a little something else might just show up on your back porch. I'm just saying…" the spry woman offered with a merry wink as she turned to leave.

Maddie giggled aloud and watched as she made her way down the back steps. Unable to resist saying one more thing, Tink called back over her shoulder, "Keep an eye out also for a handsome, red cardinal. He's been hopping around all day! I think he may have been announcing your arrival!"

"I definitely will! I love cardinals."

"I do, too, dear! Goodnight."

"Goodnight! And thank you again for the cookies."

As Tink crossed between the two yards and went up the back steps into her home, Maddie noticed a gentle breeze moving in the cold night air. She stood for a few moments in the doorway, listening to the comforting sound of the wind as it whispered close by and imparted a light caress on her cheek.

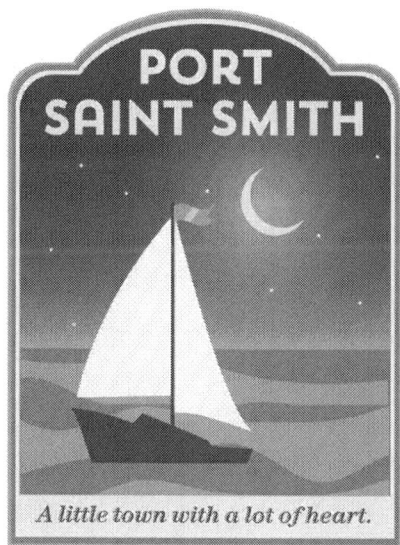

PORT
SAINT SMITH

A little town with a lot of heart.

TUESDAY,
NOVEMBER 22

Chapter 34
Larry

Larry stood on one of the long, wooden docks at the marina. The sun had just risen above the horizon, and the early light shimmered brilliantly across the lapping water. He'd woken unusually early with a sense of lightness he could barely recognize. So, he'd decided to stop at the port on his way to work. Watching the gulls soar effortlessly across the sky and the fishermen heading out in search of the day's catch, he released several long sighs and gratefully breathed in the familiar ting of cold sea air.

To his great relief, Larry felt comforted at the marina as though being greeted by an old friend. For months, he'd avoided coming here unless necessary, afraid to feel betrayed by the very place that had always brought him such happiness. Then, gazing out at his sailboat, *The Great Getaway*, Larry was surprised once more not to be overcome by grief. Since mid-summer, he had scarcely stepped onboard to perform the minimum upkeep, let alone consider sailing anywhere. But today, he stood calmly composed, able to recall the vivid dream he'd had the previous night. The dream conveyed a mighty idea so clearly that reimagining it now was quite effortless. In fact, he even began to feel a sense of hope rising up within him - a feeling all but forgotten in recent months. And because of that, Larry was also immensely relieved that he had not sold his boat.

For the past several weeks, Larry had struggled with deciding whether to keep or sell his boat. If he were to sell it, how best should it be advertised, Larry wondered. Trade magazines covered his desk at home, and his computer was bookmarked with numerous boat listing websites. Yet, he had spoken to no one about this quandary. Since his best friend and only sailing partner had died, who was there for him to talk to anyway? He certainly wasn't going to burden Elizabeth with anything else after all the extra work she'd been doing.

Larry hoped that his pain would be gone when his boat was no longer tethered to the slip at the Port Saint Smith marina. This avid sailor yearned to release the mooring ropes as much as he yearned to release the sorrow associated with Nic's passing.

When Larry's elderly parents died within a few months of each other, he mourned them both in a way that felt quite natural. And fortunately, in the aftermath of their respective funerals, his thoughts never became muddled with confusion or clouded with resentment. Because his parents' passing was predictable and inevitable —they were old, and it was to be expected.

But when Nic died, the natural order of life was deeply disturbed and irrevocably disrupted. Within days, Larry's judgment and reasoning became unclear and uncertain. He couldn't make simple decisions such as which sandwich to order at the deli. And he couldn't imagine ever wanting to take his boat out again.

Larry had first become interested in boating due to Nic's infectious love of the sea and sailing. And Nic had been his only sailing mate. Since the funeral, however, Larry had done everything possible to avoid the boat and anything to do with the marina.

If I can't even climb aboard the darn thing while it's tethered to the dock without feeling nauseous with grief, why not go ahead and sell it, he'd reasoned. *Then I'd be rid of the constant reminder and, hopefully, much of the pain.*

Larry realized, though, that he may never understand how Tink came to advise him against selling *The Great Getaway*. How had she sensed what he was planning to do? And how did she happen to speak to him on the very day he'd decided to begin the ad? He was still bewildered by this uncanny timing. Yet, she was to be credited with stopping him from making what could have been a most regrettable mistake.

Their conversation had taken place just a few days earlier during one of his morning pilgrimages between the coffee shop and his office. Due to the heaviness of his heart, Larry had been avoiding conversation with his fellow townsfolk. He would either offer a quick nod of hello and turn away or, more often, divert his eyes altogether, as though engrossed in something seemingly amazing in a nearby shop window or simply the foliage of the trees or shrubs. But, on that day, Larry was sincerely preoccupied with deciding where to place the advertisement for the boat's sale. Would the tri-county newspaper provide enough coverage, he considered. Or should the notice be listed online for a wider audience?

As he walked, purposefully keeping his glance down, Tink had stepped into stride right alongside him. At first, he did not notice her as she quietly matched his pace. But, once he became aware of her presence, Larry was amazed that this short woman of considerable age was keeping up with him.

Without so much as a hello, she began to speak. "Larry," Tink said in a firm yet comforting voice, "I hope you're not planning to sell that fine sailboat of yours." Larry stopped abruptly and stared at her in complete disbelief. He studied her aged face, looking for clues as to how she could have possibly known. But all he saw was a sweet sparkle in her eyes and the caring expression of a very wise friend. Unnerved by her words and unsure how to respond, he said nothing and resumed walking. And so did she.

"After my beloved Grant died," Tink proceeded, "I wanted nothing more than to sell my house because I couldn't imagine living there without him. Every room echoed the remembrances of our happiness. The entire place began to look like a mausoleum filled with memories and memorabilia, and I felt trapped living alone inside those walls."

"Truthfully," she continued, marching right alongside Larry, who slowed his pace slightly to accommodate her, "I couldn't think of any reason not to sell. You may even remember that I spoke to you about listing my home. But we never discussed it again. Because fortunately, my sister intervened and advised me against it. She strongly recommended that I not make any decisions of consequence for at least one year after Grant's death. That was very hard for me to do because I was so miserable living there surrounded by nothing but sorrow. I wanted to change everything! Still, I promised myself to wait, and somehow I managed to keep that promise. And I will tell you now that I am immensely relieved that I did. Once I saw my way out of the dark haze of grief, I knew that our home was exactly where I belonged. And I am so grateful every day to be in the very place where all our happy memories occurred. I have also watched this same home serve as a perfect setting where new memories continue to be made with my friends, neighbors, and loved ones."

As they reached the front door of Larry's office building, Tink looked directly into his eyes and said, "I hope you'll listen to me, Larry. I have known the unbearable heartbreak of death too many times and can only imagine the pain you must be feeling. While that boat of yours may be a source of great sadness to you now, I sense that it will bring great happiness again, not only to you but to many others as well."

Larry shuddered whenever he remembered that conversation, still unable to comprehend the unfathomable timing of her advice. Even though he'd shared this decision with no one, Tink spoke as though she'd been given the exact information. *How was that possible*? he questioned. *How had she known?* Yet, her message had startled him enough that by afternoon, he vowed to wait one year before deciding whether or not to sell.

Now, as he looked over at the neglected, mighty sloop, his recent dream began to feel like an exciting possibility rather than just another elusive vision that sleep so often brings.

Reflecting back on the details, Larry could see himself again in the midst of a magnificent party taking place along the marina docks. While the rows of boats of varying size and kind bobbed up and down in the water, the multi-colored strands of lights hung between the mast and the bow of his stately sailboat. A welcome banner suspended over the main entrance read The Captain's Supper in majestic letters. He, the captain of *The Great Getaway,* was hosting this grand event to celebrate the triumph of the S.O.S. summer program, as well as something else involving the foundation that, as yet, had not been revealed to him.

The night was clear, and the stars shone brightly in the dream. And the sweetest of winds moved joyously amidst everyone attending the celebration. The party guests included the young sailors and their families, the volunteers and their chosen guests, various city officials, and the business owners who had given their time and resources in a myriad of ways. The children, supervised by a few young adults, were in the clubhouse playing games, eating pizza, and enjoying ice cream sundaes. While outside on the boat deck, there was an impressive feast for the adults, including sumptuous appetizers, roasted seasonal vegetables, entrees of all kinds, and a stunning selection of desserts.

Presently, on this cold November morning, Larry recognized that *The Great Getaway* was the centerpiece of this splendid affair. And the name—The Captain's Supper—was most fitting because he would be creating the menu and preparing much of the feast himself. He could also envision moving amongst the guests who delighted in the outstanding meal and convivial festivities. And all of this was surprisingly easy to imagine because the dream had presented every single detail of the event—the invitations, the decorations, the guest list, and more. So, Larry committed at that moment to keep his boat. For he could see that happier days would possibly come again.

Before going into the office, the now-inspired man lingered just a little longer, surveying the needs of his boat. He planned to come back during the weekend and reestablish the maintenance schedule necessary to maintain this worthy vessel. Even the idea of hosting a party of that magnitude helped him feel that much more encouraged. And although in the dream he had not seen his sailing mate in attendance at The Captain's Supper, Larry was confident that in some way Nic's presence would be onboard.

Chapter 35
Elizabeth

Elizabeth's morning cup of coffee sat on a coaster while the slender fingers of her hand ran softly along the smooth wood of the antique Escritoire. The early sun's rays shone brightly in the room and helped illuminate this treasured piece of furniture—a piece of furniture that had been in the Moreau family for several generations. Elizabeth could fondly remember Grand-Papa sitting at this desk, writing long letters back to his family in France. As a child, she would often tug on his sleeve, eagerly pleading with him to come outside and play. The old man would almost always accommodate her by setting down his pen and joining her for silly games on the grand lawn.

Elizabeth also recalled her father sitting at this same desk, struggling intensely to make the most difficult decisions regarding the family's finances. At the time, she'd felt so powerless and scared but still unable to fully comprehend exactly what the troubles were.

Undoubtedly, this singular piece of furniture stored the varied tales of her family within its intricate cubbies and inlaid wooden drawers. And Elizabeth did her best to focus on the happier times, hoping that by doing so, the pain and disappointment might be healed.

Most mornings, she began sitting at this desk with a cup of hot coffee, a blank piece of paper, and an elegant writing pen. There, she would outline her plans for the day, finding solace, strength, and inspiration by reflecting

184

on the memories of those who had sat there before her. Although Elizabeth was not quite certain what happened to her loved ones after death, she trusted they were not merely looking down and observing her from some abstract place in the sky. She believed, instead, they were often close and assisting in ways she may not fully fathom but nevertheless welcomed and appreciated.

Sipping mindfully on the hot beverage, Elizabeth prepared a strategy for the time-sensitive tasks ahead. There was plenty to do to ensure that the basket deliveries would once again be successful. Fortunately, the day before, she'd managed to speak to five of the eight families and had informed them that this outreach program was being sponsored by the same volunteers and business owners who'd supported their child's S.O.S. sailing camp. And when asked if they would like to receive a complete Thanksgiving dinner on Thursday, all five families gratefully agreed.

Additionally, two of the businesses were also called, and both assured Elizabeth that they would be honored to offer their support again this year. In fact, due to the death of the S.O.S. founder—their fellow citizen and friend—had each said that if any additional provisions were needed, they would gladly provide more. Thus, Elizabeth felt confident that the response of the other businesses would be the same.

Yet, this clever woman had even greater goals for the baskets. *Why not include a few special keepsake gifts, along with the meal?* she determined with a smile. The idea appealed to her greatly, and as she contemplated just what those extras might be, Elizabeth pulled various drawers of the Escritoire open and closed, open and closed. This was also a little game she'd played as a child with Grand-Papa. When he was preoccupied with his correspondence and resolutely resisting her promptings to play outside, Elizabeth would stand on her tippy toes and distract him by fiddling with the drawers. The kindly elder would try to act annoyed, but they both knew he enjoyed her amusing antics. After this cherished heirloom came into her possession, Elizabeth continued to open and close the drawers as a way to relax and remember.

Upon pulling one of the larger center drawers open, Elizabeth noticed a familiar, beloved card made of ocean blue construction paper. She carefully pulled it out and placed it upright in front of her. But before rereading the heartfelt words inside, Elizabeth decided she'd better update Larry on the basket progress so far.

Promptly, she wrote and sent a text:

All is going well! Five families have said yes, and the two businesses have agreed to contribute. I'll contact the remaining families and businesses today and keep you posted.
Glad to be helping.

Elizabeth also knew she needed to talk to Tink soon but felt it was a bit too early to call. So, she decided to shower, get a second cup of coffee, and catch up on other correspondence first. After attending to those, she dialed her number.

"Good morning," Tink chirped cheerfully.

"Good morning, Tink. This is Elizabeth. I hope that I'm not calling too early."

"Gracious no, dear! With so much to do, I woke up even earlier than usual. The curtains are open, the morning light is streaming in, my apron is on, and after a few bites of breakfast, I'll be working feverishly in the kitchen. With all these happy tasks to tend to, there's no time to dilly-dally. Now, tell me, my friend, what can I do for you?"

"First, let me thank you for offering to make the pies once again for the S.O.S. baskets because I'm happy to report that we will definitely be needing them. Larry has given the go-ahead for the deliveries, and I am pushing forward with all the plans. "

"What happy news! I'll start preparing right away," Tink exclaimed.

'I can't begin to imagine what all that entails," Elizabeth responded.

"Oh, nothing much, really. After filling the counters with all the necessary ingredients, I add a little pinch of this, a smattering of that, and a fair amount of elbow grease to roll out those delicious, homemade crusts. Then, the fresh fruit process begins. But it is all such a joy and a pleasure for me, I assure you."

"I believe you," Elizabeth said, "but I'm afraid I'd be all thumbs and elbows if I were to try. Best I stay focused on what I'm good at and leave the baking to the expert."

"So be it, Elizabeth! We each have strengths," Tink concluded.

"I'm just so excited to be helping this year," Elizabeth declared. Then, with a noticeably different tone, she added, "I do have a few concerns,

186

though, that perhaps you could help me resolve. Because, although Larry has agreed to the deliveries and to some of the cooking, I'm handling the rest. And I don't want to overtax him with too many questions."

"You're smart to avoid asking him too much. I'm even surprised he said yes. But I meant what I said about helping in any way I can. So, tell me exactly, what are your concerns?"

"Well, Larry has always cooked the turkeys and made his renowned stuffing. And fortunately, he's committed to doing that again this year. And you know how much he enjoys cooking, so actually, I believe that may be very good for him."

"Let's hope so, Elizabeth!"

"After making more calls and coordinating the remaining donations, I plan to pick up the rolls from the bakery and other items from the grocery store, such as butter, cranberry sauce, mulled cider, sweet tea, and so forth. But, I am at a real loss regarding the side dishes."

"So, you mean the mashed potatoes, candied yams, vegetable casseroles, and so on…is that right?"

"Yes, that's right. I could ask Theo at the deli, but I know he's already so busy this week. Plus, I'd hoped to ask him for a different type of donation. The only other option I have," Elizabeth said with an unintentional, dramatic pause and heavy sigh, "is to attempt to make them myself, which is a rather frightful consideration. I've been known to venture into my kitchen, but only due to the fact that's where my coffee maker is. At least, I'm honest enough to accept my shortcomings, and cooking is most definitely one of them. In fact, I can assure you, there aren't any trophies displayed in my home acknowledging my abilities, and probably never will be!"

Tink laughed and replied, "That may be true, but to your credit, you've already had two highly successful careers. I wouldn't know the first thing about interior design, for example, as evidenced by my own home, which features the same décor as when I moved in decades ago. Accepting the truth about our limitations and then doing our best to excel in our areas of expertise is wise and admirable.

"Now, let's focus back on the side dish dilemma. Allow me just one moment to give that some consideration, please, and I'm sure I'll come up with a suggestion."

"Of course, take your time. I'm appreciative of any suggestions at all," Elizabeth replied with notable gratitude.

The elderly woman could then be heard softly humming a little rhyme, "Fiddle dee da and fiddle dee dee, I wonder what good idea will come to me?"

Elizabeth giggled quietly at Tink's unique and delightful approach to problem-solving. Perhaps she should consider this melodic method the next time logic and reason fail her.

"There is also nothing quite like a little nibble or two," Tink announced, "to help inspire my creativity." That comment was followed by the sound of a loud crunch, which Elizabeth presumed might be a piece of toast or a croissant. She had to stifle another laugh as her admiration for this refreshingly honest friend increased immeasurably.

Soon enough, Tink had encouraging words to say; "I think I've come up with a wonderful solution."

"Really?" Elizabeth asked in relieved surprise. "I just hope you're not planning to do this yourself. I couldn't ask any more of you."

"No, dear, not me. Fortunately, I know my limits. But I will gladly help start the process so that everything gets done promptly. Let me explain. I'm sure you know that, in the past, Nic made every one of the side dishes. And he had such fun cooking for his S.O.S. families. But, what you may not realize is that when this outreach program began, his kitchen was not a particularly familiar place for him, either. Sure, he could prepare a few bachelor basics, but nothing more, really. Yet, his contributions to the baskets were always a triumph. So, what has been a closely guarded secret until now is the fact that I provided him with the initial direction and many of my own recipes.

"During the first years, Nic was terribly afraid he would fail and that his contributions would be a fiasco. So, I suggested that he initially use some of my time-tested dishes, and he agreed. He was such a planner, so we discussed every aspect of the process—canned vs. fresh or frozen ingredients, glass vs. metal, temperatures and times, etc. Nic also wanted to make sure I approved the results. Thus, we began a most precious tradition. While I was in my kitchen baking cookies, fruit, and pot pies, he was in his, making the candied sweet potatoes and other vegetable casseroles. Then, in hopes of winning one other's approval, we started to exchange small samples of each. I would make him a tiny cookie tray and individual mini pies, and he would bring me a plate covered with little tastings of his various dishes. What delicious fun we had enjoying each other's endeavors! But, alas," Tink sighed slowly, "that was then, and this is now. So, let me not get sidetracked by those memories."

Although Elizabeth realized that Tink was not looking for sympathy, she still felt inspired to offer caring words of support, "That must have been very special and fun for both of you."

"Yes," she replied wistfully, "it truly was. But, back to the matters at hand..." Tink then went on to explain her side dish solution to Elizabeth, who exclaimed, "What a great idea!! I think you're a genius and, most definitely, a saint!"

"Let's not go that far!" Tink chuckled. "I could never live up to such a reputation! I am glad, however, that you think the idea may work. And now that we've sorted that issue out, I'm wondering what you're planning to use for the baskets?"

"How did you know that was my other question? You really are amazing! Tink, I'm always taken aback by your willingness and readiness to be supportive and insightful. And so, yes, what *am* I going to do about the baskets? I'm not exactly one of those crafting types who enjoys going into oversized art supply stores. I might have more incentive, however, if there were a fabulous shoe section in there, also!" Elizabeth added with a laugh. "But, either way, if I did venture in, would they have enough of what I need? So, where do you recommend I could find eight large baskets on such short notice?"

"Fear not, you perfectly professional, non-crafting woman. You won't have to look any further than the shelves of my pantry. I have an abundance of trays, buckets, and baskets left over from various guild functions. Last spring, the ladies of the Port Saint Smith Guild hosted a fund-raising event, and we ended up with at least ten extra-large baskets, which I've been storing at my house. I believe they'll be perfect for the Thanksgiving deliveries. Maybe you could come by this afternoon and have a look? I'll be gone later this morning, taking cookies to the Homes for Hounds Rescue Center. But I should be back by one o'clock or so."

"That sounds perfect! I'm so pleased you've solved my other dilemma so quickly. Why don't I plan to come by around two or two-thirty?"

"That'll be great. I'll look forward to seeing you then."

"Alright, Mrs. Kendleton," Elizabeth stated in a mockingly formal voice. "Before we sign off, though, please be advised that I intend to propose to the city that the name of this town be changed to Port Saint Tink in your honor. Because, over the years, you've contributed in so many ways and have touched the lives of countless people and animals with your kindness, generosity, and good deeds!"

"Don't be silly, dear Elizabeth. That would be way too much trouble on account of all the signs, posters, website pages, maps, and printed materials that would need to be corrected. However, maybe the town would simply consider placing a gigantic statue of me right in the center of the park. I'd like to be wearing an apron over my cute, plump tummy and holding a mixing bowl and spoon. Now, that would be much more to my liking," she jested, as both of their homes were filled with the sweet sound of laughter.

Elizabeth wiped happy tears from her eyes and said, "I'll make sure to suggest that at the next council meeting!!! In the meantime, have fun visiting the doggies, and I will see you this afternoon. *Merci beaucoup. Au revoir.*"

"*Au revoir, mademoiselle,*" Tink replied.

Elizabeth then signed off and set the phone down on her desk, feeling extremely encouraged.

The S.O.S. Thanksgiving Basket Benefit is sailing along smoothly, she mused. Glancing directly in front of her, Elizabeth realized that she'd almost forgotten about the sentimental correspondence propped up in the center of her desk. So, she took a moment to study the simplistic, construction-paper greeting card that had been cut in the shape of a sailboat. It appeared to be gliding with ease across gentle waters.

Upon receiving this special note, Elizabeth remembered that even then, as one of the head volunteers at the S.O.S. camps, she wasn't sure who had helped the young sailors create such imaginative thank-you notes for the instructors and volunteers.

How appropriate to come across this today, Elizabeth recognized. For she still loved to read the words, even though they were now committed to heart. This particular card had been given to her by one of her favorite young campers, Trevor. He was a first-time sailor and a bright and caring eight-year-old. And for reasons unknown, an unlikely yet meaningful bond had formed between them. Every day, Trevor would report his progress, and Elizabeth would give him much encouraging support in celebration of his achievements.

Then, during the graduation party at the end of summer, he sought Elizabeth out and proudly presented her with the thick, slightly sticky envelope. After opening the card and reading what was written inside, Elizabeth knelt down and gave Trevor a heartwarming hug. That moment, like his endearing card, she would remember forever. And now, carefully opening it, she read the message once again.

Dear Miss Elizabeth,
You are really, really nice.
I am glad you are my friend.
I Love You,
Trevor

Deeply touched and feeling more clarity of purpose than ever, Elizabeth placed the blue sailboat back up on her desk and began to make the rest of the phone calls. One of the families she hoped to reach today was Trevor's, and she wished, more than anything, that they would accept the donation so she would be able to see her young friend again. With nervous excitement, she dialed their number.

Chapter 36
Maddie

I'm finally here! And I'm just amazed! After months of planning, waiting, and worrying, I'm actually waking up on the Cape and in this most luxurious bed. I slept well and feel so rested. I'm very excited about my first full day in Port Saint Smith. But, before I do anything else, I'm going on the back porch to swing. I just want to sit there, look at the garden, listen to the birds, and simply be. I can't think of a better way to start my vacation.

Maddie set her journal on the nightstand, washed up, and slipped on warm, cozy clothes. Then, with great delight, she descended the stairs. Forgoing even a cup of hot tea, she bundled up in a coat and scarf, opened the kitchen door, and stepped out onto the porch.

The morning was cold and bright. She stretched her arms overhead, breathed in deeply, and felt wonderfully invigorated. For the first time in a long time, she had no agenda other than to enjoy herself. And although Maddie hoped at some point to go for a bike ride and to explore downtown, more than anything, she wanted to let the plans for the week unfold in an easy and inspiring way.

Walking to the end of the porch, Maddie gathered her coat tighter around her and sat on the large swing. As the chains and bench began to rock back and forth, they created a rhythmic creaking, which she found comforting. She also enjoyed the collective song of the birds as tiny starlings, sparrows, and chickadees flitted about the garden, contributing to the morning chorus. Maddie wondered, too, if the cardinal Tink had mentioned would also make an appearance. Then, as if her thought were an invitation, the handsome red bird immediately landed on the porch railing close by.

"Chirp, chirp!" he offered in exuberant greeting.

"Well, good morning to you," Maddie replied, ever so pleased.

Excitedly, the cardinal hopped about for a moment, then flew directly over to Tink's home. There, he landed on her windowsill, hopping up and down again. Maddie smiled in delight, sensing that the bird was acknowledging some kind of connection between herself and Tink. But the curtains in the neighbor's windows were still closed, and the elderly woman was nowhere to be seen. So, the bird lifted off, circled once in the air, and then flew high into the branches of a large tree with one final chirp.

After watching the winged visitor until he was out of sight, Maddie focused once more on the experience of swinging.

I feel so relaxed, she recognized, gently gliding back and forth. *Maybe the only purpose of swinging is to simply let go and be happy.*

The air was still, as were the leaves on the trees. And, moving with gentle ease, Maddie was soon lulled into an even deeper state of relaxation. Eventually, she stopped pushing against the wooden floorboards. Yet, the suspended swing continued to move ever so slightly. Maddie was not startled, however. She just closed her eyes and became even more present in that moment.

Back and forth, back and forth, the bench slowly moved as though being softly pushed.

But how is this happening, she wondered. *What could possibly be causing the swing to continue moving? Unsure but still relaxed, Maddie* opened her eyes only once to look around. Yet, all she saw was the porch, the swing, and nothing more.

After a few more pleasant minutes, the swing came to a soft stop. Maddie eased off the bench and looked around again. Instinctively, she sensed she was not alone but saw no one else there. Unafraid but beginning to feel a bit chilled, she decided to go inside.

The warmth of the house embraced Maddie fully. She immediately removed her scarf and coat, set the kettle on the stove for tea, and then looked through Elizabeth's generous offerings in search of a perfect meal. Before long, she was enjoying a delicious breakfast—organic granola, fresh fruit, and jasmine tea. This was followed by one of Tink's tempting cookies, which was an unexpected treat.

Who says, Maddie mused, *that dessert should only follow lunch or dinner? While I'm on vacation, I may just end all of my breakfasts with some sort of sweet. Why not?* she declared with a guilt-free giggle. And, not needing to be anywhere else, she lingered at the table, enjoying every sip, taste, and indulgence.

After the meal and a quick clean-up, Maddie walked down the hall toward the stairs. Passing the study, though, she paused briefly and looked into the inviting room. The fire was not yet lit, and everything else was just as she remembered, with one exception. On the loveseat, next to the packet Elizabeth had given her, was a small, white envelope. Maddie didn't remember seeing it before and wondered if it had inadvertently fallen out from between the other packet items without her awareness. So, she entered the room to have a closer look.

Perhaps Elizabeth forgot to mention this to me, Maddie reasoned as she picked the envelope up. *It's probably just a standard thank-you note from her company expressing gratitude since I chose to stay in one of their properties. But, obviously, it is intended for me,* she noted, since her name was inscribed on the front. The letters, however, were quite clumsy, as though written by a young child.

Curiously, Maddie turned the envelope over and opened the flap. The silver foil lining and the matching cream-colored note card were of the finest quality. And on the front of the elegant, enclosed card, she did not see the logo of the real estate company, as expected. Instead, there were three initials embossed in dark, navy ink:

NDP

Who is this from? Maddie wondered. *Those aren't Elizabeth's initials, and I don't think they're her boss's either since she referred to him more than once as Larry.* Eagerly, she opened the card and saw several words scrawled with the most peculiar penmanship. The faint handwriting was messy and seemed incongruous on such fine stationery. But rather than being the correspondence of a young child, now she guessed this might have been penned by an elderly or sickly person.

This handwriting, Maddie realized with a gasp, *reminds me of Grandma Anise's just before she died. Since Grandma's hands were so unsteady, forming words on paper became a very difficult task. Maybe the person who wrote this is very sick or even close to death,* Maddie considered. The idea, however, made her quiver, and she began to wonder if the note had been written by the owner of *La Maison Enchantée.*

Elizabeth told me how athletic he was—both a competitive cyclist and avid sailor. What if he can no longer walk upstairs and was forced to move from this beautiful two-story home due to illness? That might explain why a few of his personal belongings are still here.

Maddie decided to do her best to read the note. She carefully looked at each awkward letter and slowly discerned the message.

> *Dearest Maddie,*
> *I welcome you to this home.*
> *May the love here*
> *surround, support, and uplift you.*
> *Yours,*
> *N*

Maddie held the note to her heart, unsure why something so small had touched her so profoundly. Yet it had, and tiny tears filled her eyes. The simple, sweet message gave her such a sense of warmth and acceptance. And Maddie realized that, not since childhood had she felt so at home. Then, as she stood up to leave the room, still clutching the card tightly, a slight draft of sea-scented air wafted through the room.

Chapter 37
Shirley

Shirley bustled around the Chamber of Commerce as though there was something important to do. There wasn't. Still, she was trying to stay busy to avoid stewing over the unwelcome news she'd received the night before.

No one is to blame, Shirley reminded herself with evident disappointment. *But, dahn it, what will I do with myself now?* she fretted while tidying up a stack of brochures for the second time. *I feel deflated right in the midst of this holiday week! And, no doubt, a few visitahs will come into the Chambah today. But tomorrow, I'm surah everyone will be focused on their Thanksgiving preparations. Maybe I'll tackle one of the messier chores that no one else herah likes to do because cleaning is a perfect and productive way for me to take my mind off my woes.*

The Port Saint Smith Chamber of Commerce volunteer walked across the room to survey the fireplace. The hearth could use sweeping, she determined, even if very little time had passed since the last cleaning. She would remove the few burnt ashes, brush the insides thoroughly, and then stack a new pile of logs inside.

And then, wheneveh we do have visitahs, Shirley reasoned, *the fire will burn a little brightah. And that,* she thought with a distressed sigh, *will at least give me something to do. Howevah, I don't need to rush into that task just yet. Perhaps I'll sit down for a few minutes first and have a cup of hot cocoa.*

No sooner had Shirley poured the drink, enjoying the aromatic scent of chocolate, when the sound of the bells above the door heralded an arrival. Without hesitation, she anxiously turned to see who had entered. To her great surprise and delight, she saw her dear friend and neighbor, Tink Kendleton.

"Good mahning, Tink," Shirley called out. "What a wondahful surprise!"

"Good morning, Shirley," Tink replied in an equally cheerfully voice. "I was hoping I would find you here. So, I decided to stop by instead of calling."

"Would you like a cup of cahfee or hot chocolate?" Shirley asked hopefully.

"That's mighty tempting, but I'm on my way to the rescue center to give the doggies their holiday treats."

"I undahstand. And let me just say what a good person you are to even remembah them in the midst of everything else."

"Well, they bring me as much joy as I bring them, so everyone wins!"

"I'm surah. And I'm also surah glad you stopped by today. Not one person has called or come in, and I'm getting rathah restless since I have very little to do."

"Well, that's excellent!" Tink exclaimed to Shirley's utter bewilderment. "Because I have a request that will resolve that situation, which is precisely why I wanted to speak with you."

"Oh, really?" Shirley asked curiously.

"Yes! Help is needed, and I feel there is no one more qualified than you," Tink stated sincerely. "This task requires excellent communication, organization, and follow-up, which describes you 'to a T.' So, unless you have other demanding obligations, I'm hoping that this will keep you busy enough and feeling purposeful."

"That's amazing because I was just wondering what I would do all day. And Tink, you know I'm always glad to be of service."

"I do know that about you, and so many of us are blessed because of that. Now, let me explain what's happening."

"Alrighty," Shirley said resoundingly.

"I'm sure you know that for the past several years, Larry and Nic delivered the Thanksgiving baskets to several S.O.S. families."

"Yes," Shirley replied, "and I know that many of our local busi-nesses contributed the food, that Nic and Larry did the cooking, and you made all of the delicious pies. But I've nevah been directly involved myself."

"And that, I hope," Tink said with a merry wink, "is about to change."

"You don't say?" Shirley squealed. "What is it I could do to help?"

"Well, since our beloved Nic has passed, Larry is not his usual self. No doubt, you are aware of that."

"Oh yes, I surah am," Shirley commented, remembering the strained conversation she'd had recently with Larry on the phone.

"Fortunately, our darling Elizabeth Moreau has volunteered to coordinate the efforts so that this important tradition continues. She's already doing an exceptional job pulling this together, even at the last minute. But more helpers are needed. And I suggested to her that the ladies of the Port Saint Smith Women's Guild might be able to provide the necessary assistance."

"I don't see why not," Shirley agreed readily.

"Right! But I also realize," Tink acknowledged, "that most everyone is already busy with their own holiday plans this week. I'm personally up to my ears in ingredients, which, admittedly, makes me giddy with delight!!" she chuckled. "But, I figured that if just a few of the ladies make an extra side dish or two, we would have enough for every basket."

"I think it's a wondahful idea!" Shirley agreed. "I could easily make a casserole or two myself, and I'm surah that many of the other gals will be glad to contribute as well."

"That's exactly what I had envisioned since our organization is known for truly showing up, especially in times of need. We're not all about pearls and tea parties, now are we? And I thank you, Shirley," Tink continued, "for not hesitating to help out. But I'm also wondering if you would have time to make the calls to organize the efforts?"

"Yah betcha! I'd be glad to. How many dishes will be needed?"

"Well, the plans this year are to deliver eight baskets. Luckily, Larry has agreed to still cook all of the turkeys and his delicious stuffing. Elizabeth is picking up rolls, butter, drinks, and a few other items. She plans to begin assembling the baskets tomorrow night. Then, each family will ideally receive mashed potatoes, candied yams, as well as one or two other side vegetables."

"You can count on me to do this," Shirley confirmed vigorously, "And I wouldn't be surprised if we have this resolved within the hour."

"That sounds great!" Tink proclaimed. "I told Elizabeth that I'd speak to you about this, and she was so relieved and grateful."

"And I am grateful to you, Tink, for asking me. Because this will give me something to do since I have nothing else going on this week."

"What do you mean?" her long-time friend asked in astonishment. "Isn't your cousin arriving soon?"

"No, she's not coming anymore," Shirley bemoaned. "She called last night to let me know she'd fallen and broken her ankle. So, traveling is out of the question."

"I'm so sorry to hear that. I'm sure you're both very disappointed since you always have such fun together when she visits."

"Yes, I've been looking forward to seeing her for weeks. But, now, there will be nothing and no one," Shirley stated dolefully.

"Well, that's not acceptable at all!" Tink quipped. "I'm certain that I have a solution for that problem, too! You simply must come to my house on Thanksgiving Day and share in the holiday feast and festivity."

"Are you surah?" Shirley asked hesitantly.

"Are you kidding? Of course, I'm sure! You know I would love to have you there."

"Oh, Tink, thank you. You're such a good friend."

"And so are you, Shirley. Well, I'm glad that's settled, also. I'd better get on my way, though, to see the dogs so I can be back home when Elizabeth arrives around two. She's coming to see the large baskets left over from the guild's Spring Fling. I think they'll be perfect for the deliveries, and it's just another way the ladies of the guild will be helping out. Plus, I'm very delighted to tell her that you've agreed to organize the side dishes. She'll be thrilled!"

"Tink, we may just need to add "expert problem-solver" to your long list of talents," Shirley teased.

"We just might!" Tink laughed in response. "And I'm glad that Elizabeth is tall enough to retrieve the baskets herself. That way, I won't have to climb up the ladder again. I was rummaging around in the pantry yesterday morning, and, wouldn't you know, the phone rang at that exact moment."

"And guess what?" Shirley asked. "That may have been me calling, but I didn't leave a message."

"If it was you, I'm sorry I couldn't pick up."

"That's alright," Shirley assured her. "I just wanted to talk to you about a lovely young lady who had visited the Chambah. She was on her way to look at Nic's home as a possible rental for the week."

"Are you talking about Maddie Stuart?" Tink inquired.

"Yes, that's her name," Shirley replied happily.

"I met her last night. She seems as sweet as pie, which is a mighty strong statement coming from an award-winning pie baker!" Tink admitted.

"She definitely seems that sweet to me, too. I'm so happy you've already met her."

"Well, I must admit," Tink confessed, "that I had real reservations about someone else staying in Nic's home. But somehow, Maddie seems to fit there."

"I'm so glad to herah that," Shirley said.

"Yes, and I hope to see her again during her stay."

"I would enjoy seeing her again also. Maybe she could join us for Thanksgiving dinnah if she doesn't already have plans," Shirley suggested.

"What a splendid idea! I don't want to seem too pushy. Still, I'd love her to join us. We'll just have to see how the week goes. But I need to be on my way," Tink announced, turning to leave. "Feel free to keep me posted on your S.O.S. progress."

"Okee dokee," Shirley asserted. "I'll be glad to. And thank you again for inviting me to Thanksgiving dinner."

"You're very welcome. Bye-bye."

"Goodbye!"

The bells chimed above the doorway as Tink exited. Then Shirley walked briskly to the office in the back, amazed at how quickly her circumstances had changed.

I'm a dahn lucky woman, she recognized, *and a mighty thankful one too.*

Chapter 38
Stephen

"Hey Maddie, guess who's calling?" the male voice on the recording asked playfully. "I don't want you to have to think too hard since you're on vacation. So here are two clues: 1) I'm your very favorite neighbor, and 2) I'm also the person who spoils your cat while you're away. Or, well, what I really mean is that I'm the person who provides such quality care for Miss Priss in your absence." A light laugh could be heard on the message, and then the caller identified himself.

"This is Stephen, of course. And I decided to send you a recorded message because I was afraid that I might forget something I wanted to say since I have so much to share. Most importantly, though, the finest feline in the world and I want to tell you about our triumphs.

"We are thrilled to report that the pet pram is proving to be a big success! Her Highness and I have ventured out twice, and so far, she hasn't scratched or hissed at anyone. In fact, she actually seems content in her classy, caged confinement. She looks around attentively, listens to all the different sounds, and sniffs intently at the interesting, new smells. Can't you just picture her—such a pretty, privileged pussy cat—being stylishly chauffeured down the sidewalk? She is quite a sight to behold!

"Yesterday afternoon was our first trial outing, and we didn't go too far in case of disaster. Initially, Miss Priss was not pleased about going inside the carrier. She probably thought I was taking her to the vet's office. But once we left the building, she settled down and began to enjoy herself.

"Then today, I took her on my mid-morning walk for coffee, and I certainly didn't want to leave her outside the shop. Fortunately, they weren't very busy, so I was able to bring her right in. After I got my coffee, we went for a stroll in the park. Of course, several people stopped to admire her, and she absolutely adored the attention. And I promise to let you know about any of our future escapades. But, so far, I'm feeling very optimistic.

"I am curious what you've been up to, sweetie, while her Highness and I have been parading around town. Hopefully, you're getting settled in and starting to have some fun. But don't worry about calling me back because I'm sure we'll speak soon. You can update me then on the weather, the wind, and the witch that may be living right next door. Even if I don't want to wait, I will. So, tata, my good friend, from me and you-know-who!"

With the press of a button, the recording ended, and Stephen hit send on his phone. He was pleased to provide Maddie with such an upbeat and informative message.

Next, Stephen began the search within his home once again. He even asked the cat, "Miss Priss, do you know where my sunglasses are? I haven't seen them since we returned from our walk." There were no signs of concern or interest from her as she continued napping.

This is really bothering me, Stephen lamented. *Maybe I left them at the coffee shop amidst all the pet-pram commotion. Because after that, we went to the park, and it was so shady there that I may not have realized I didn't have them on. I guess I'd better go back and see if I left them on the counter,* he decided. *And if not there, I'll need to look in the park.*

Without further hesitation, Stephen pulled the pram out of the hall closet and announced, "Miss Priss, we're venturing forth again with the mission to locate my missing eyewear. Hopefully, the third time out will be a charm.'"

The sleepy cat showed little resistance as Stephen persuaded her into the carrier. He then pushed the pram into the hallway, took the elevator to the ground floor, and stepped out into the bright afternoon.

The walk to the coffee shop was quick, and, like earlier that morning, he did not want to leave her unattended. However, the shop was much more crowded than before. Still, Stephen managed to carefully wedge the stroller between the door and the back of the line. Preoccupied with worries about finding his sunglasses, Stephen didn't take notice of anyone else, including the person standing in front of him.

"What have we here?" the handsome man inquired curiously as he turned to look at the pram.

Jarred back into the present surroundings, Stephen stated proudly, "This cat's given name is Sasha. But, those of us who know and love her well simply call her Miss Priss."

"She's a real beauty. Are you here to buy her a kitty-cat cappuccino, or are you getting something for yourself?" he asked in jest.

"Funny you would say that," Stephen replied, smiling. "Because, when we were here earlier, the barista wanted to give her a little something, but apparently, they only have treats for dogs. Imagine that! Perhaps that will change soon."

"Hopefully, it will, since that only seems fair," the affable man agreed and continued by saying, "I don't remember seeing you here before, and I come fairly often."

"I usually arrive around 10 in the morning to get my coffee," Stephen explained. "But I had to return today because I may have left my sunglasses earlier."

"Did you call to ask if they had them?"

"No. I live so close by, I just decided to walk back."

"Hopefully, they'll have good news for you," he offered optimistically.

"Thanks," Stephen replied, "I hope so too."

"I need my little caffeine boost in the afternoons, which explains why we haven't crossed paths before. I'm Rafael, by the way."

"How nice to meet you, Rafael. My name is Stephen."

As they continued to chat, the line grew shorter until Rafael was at the counter. After placing his order, he stepped aside to wait. Then, Stephen stepped forward and was greatly relieved when the young lady not only remembered him and Miss Priss but had already put his sunglasses safely away in the office. Moments later, she gave them back to the appreciative owner.

"Well, that's fortunate," Rafael commented after Stephen moved away from the counter. "I'm happy for you."

"Thanks. I was worried they wouldn't have them, and we'd have to keep looking."

With a cup in hand, Rafael walked in front of Stephen through the crowd toward the exit. Next, he held the door open so Stephen could push the pram through.

"Would the two of you like to join me while I sip on my coffee?" Rafael asked.

Quite surprised by this unexpected invitation, Stephen couldn't manage to find his voice. But he was able to nod a meek yes in response. So, Rafael found a perfect place for them to sit with the warmth of the sun on their backs and near a large tree where the cat could be entertained by the skittering squirrels and fluttering birds.

With great ease, they proceeded to have an enjoyable conversation about their lives and interests until, at last, Stephen looked at the time.

"Do you realize that we've been here for well over an hour?" he stated in disbelief.

"That's amazing," Rafael responded. "I'd better get back to work, or my crew may get concerned. I'm not one to usually take long breaks, and this is one of our busiest weeks of the year. In fact, I'll be on-site tonight until about 1 a.m., if not later. Which explains the large coffee," he said, raising the cup in salute.

"That's late. What kind of work demands such hours?" Stephen inquired.

"I'm a set designer, and we're in the midst of several large corporate holiday build-outs. The businesses prefer that we work off-hours, which is fine with me. I'm a bit of a night owl anyway."

"So am I," Stephen confessed. "Do you have to work late every night this week?"

"No. We hope to finish around 10 p.m. on Wednesday. Thanksgiving is always a day off, and then we begin again mid-Friday afternoon. The work can be demanding, but I have to admit I love it! Because there are always new challenges, which makes it a lot more fun."

"How interesting! I'd love to hear more about your work, but I know you need to get going."

"Yes, I really do. And I'm guessing it's time for Miss Priss' high tea and toast…?" Rafael chided.

"How did you ever know?" Stephen responded in mock amazement and smiled broadly at the idea of a tiara on Miss Priss's head as she sipped high tea and nibbled on the equivalent of toast for a cat.

"We could meet here again tomorrow if you'd like," Rafael suggested.

"I'd like that. Same time, same place?"

"Perfect. I look forward to seeing you again."

"So, will I," Stephen replied bashfully, surprised at how timid he suddenly felt.

Rafael stood up, looked directly into Stephen's eyes to say goodbye, and then bowed to Miss Priss before walking away. Stephen watched the handsome man's every step until he was out of sight. Then he bent over the pram and whispered excitedly to the cat, "Oh my gosh, Miss Priss, apparently the third time really is a charm!"

Chapter 39
Maddie

The temperature did not seem quite as cold as the day before. Maddie felt confident, therefore, that wearing a turtleneck, jacket, scarf, and a pair of pants designed for sporting activities would be warm enough. She gathered a few essentials—the property key, a small amount of cash, one credit card, a water bottle, and a few snacks, placing them, along with her silenced phone, inside her backpack.

Next, she walked out back and unlocked the garden shed, pleased to find such a sturdy, new woman's bike ready for her use. Designed to be ridden both in town and on the beach, it also had a sturdy Nantucket basket large enough for her backpack.

I can't believe that just yesterday I was at the Chamber of Commerce trying to decide where to stay, she thought. *There were so many great options—the quaint, historic inns, places on the beach... however nothing could have matched the perfection of this location. The house and garden are beautiful and very close to the quaint downtown area. And I can even ride this bike straight to the beach on a trail that's just behind the backyard wall. I'm so glad I was at the Chamber when that call came through. What perfect timing!*

As Maddie turned the bike toward the street, a gentle breeze tickled the chimes in Tink's garden, creating a sweet little melody. Pausing for a moment, she delighted in watching the colorful rods dance merrily on their strings. She noticed, too, that although the curtains in Tink's windows were now open, although there was still no sign of the elderly woman.

Straddling the bike, Maddie began peddling at an easy pace. Her hope was simply to become more familiar with the area. Thus, in lieu of relying on the map, she intended to allow her intuition to guide the way. Trusting her innate instincts this far, had proven most favorable, so she planned on using the same strategy for the remainder of the vacation.

As she rode along, Maddie enjoyed seeing more of the autumn decorations in the yards and on the porches of many homes. Dried, white starfish also perched in several windows while weathervanes shaped like rabbits, roosters, whales, ships, and mermaids spun in response to the whims of the wind.

Maddie also made note of the various colors that the homes were painted. She saw plenty of traditional, white colonial houses with black shutters and red doors. But her favorites were those painted in the soft hues of the sea—misty blues, soft ocean greens, and muted grays. Nearly all of the residences featured cedar shingles, which Maddie recognized as a classic Cape Cod trademark. And many of the home's names were stylishly etched on mounted quarter boards. *Captain's Quarters, The Homesteader, Thistle Dew, Rose Cottage,* and *Swallow's Nest* were some of the residential names she saw along the way. Maddie had read that this maritime tradition dated back hundreds of years when mighty ships would proudly display their given title on carved quarter boards attached to the broad side of the vessel.

For Maddie, the bike ride proved to be immensely pleasurable. With no set itinerary, her sense of leisure increased with each turn of the wheels. She was grateful to be in good health, especially as she began pedaling up a steep slope. And although her speed declined, Maddie successfully reached the top of an impressive hill. There, she stopped to take in the spectacular view below as glorious hills gave way to the majestic sea and tiny boats bobbed in the shimmering waters of Cape Cod Bay.

Eager to see more, Maddie set off again, heading downhill at a good clip. She continued cycling in a few other neighborhoods and circling cautiously through the roundabouts that featured thick displays of holly berries and hostas. Soon enough, Maddie arrived at the center of town, slowing her pace considerably to better appreciate the charming area. She delighted in seeing the friendly chatter of neighbors greeting one another on the sidewalk and in the park, smelling the distinct aroma of roasting coffee, and hearing the church bells ring on the quarter-hour, as well as the faint sound of a tugboat in the nearby harbor.

Port Saint Smith's central park's design featured a thoughtful symmetry, which Maddie observed as she rode around twice. On one end of the expansive lawn was an inviting gazebo that she imagined was used for weddings, musical performances, and old-fashioned puppet shows. On the other end was a family playground with picnic tables, gaming boards, and a washroom. Multiple benches were strategically positioned on every side of the square beneath rows of mature trees. With ample places for conversation, relaxation, performances, play, and wanderings, Maddie felt not only a true sense of appreciation but also a strong sense of grounded belonging.

How extraordinary! Maddie thought. *The very heart of Port Saint Smith seems to be embodied in this park square. The joy here is most evident. And today, I'm just exploring. But tomorrow, I'm excited to come back for some shopping and sightseeing. Maybe I'll also treat myself to a meal at one of the local restaurants.*

In order to experience another part of the community, Maddie steered the bike behind the stores and through a few small alleyways. She saw boxes being delivered to the backdoors of the businesses and prep chefs taking a quick break before the busy lunch crowd appeared. She also watched as an optimistic group of birds sought to find food in and around the trash bins.

As Maddie rode slowly away from the more populated shopping area, she soon came upon the Community Theater of Port Saint Smith. The embossed brass plate near the sidewalk indicated that the historic building dated back to the 1920's. She decided to lean the bike against a tree and walk closer to the beautiful building. Peering inside the old, glass ticket window, she saw several of the posters from past theatrical productions. She also looked at the shadowbox-style display case announcing the upcoming holiday performance, which looked very entertaining.

I wish I could see a show while I'm here, but it looks like nothing is scheduled this week. According to the poster, the next performance begins in two weeks and runs through Christmas Eve. I might like to come back to see that, especially in this beautiful, old historical building.

While musing over that idea, Maddie realized she was getting hungry and needed to consider lunch. For a moment longer, she stood outside the theater contemplating her options.

I could go back to the park and eat a few of the snacks that I brought. Or I could try one of the tempting cafes on Center Street. But I think going back to the house makes the most sense. In the warmth of the kitchen, overlooking the beautiful garden, I can eat some of the delicious food that's already there. Yes! That plan feels perfect.

With her decision made, Maddie drank plenty of water, straddled the bike again, and began the pleasant journey back. The intriguing street names along the way were among many aspects of the town that continued to capture her attention. She noticed roads named for captains and queens, flowers, birds, trees, ponds, and bays. Maddie also recognized the names of some of the indigenous people—Wampanoag, Nauset—who had settled in the area long before the Pilgrims arrived. And she noted several other places of interest... a tiny, turn-of-the-century post office and various places of worship, including churches of different denominations, a synagogue tucked in amidst great pine trees, and a rustic Quaker Meetinghouse.

Only a few more blocks and Maddie was riding down a street that already had a familiar and fond name to her—Windswept Way. With breathy exhilaration, she peddled faster and soon turned into the driveway of *La Maison Enchantée*. Immediately, she saw a car in the next driveway and Tink Kendleton unloading shopping bags from a sizable trunk. Maddie came to a quick stop and called across the way.

"Hi, Tink," Maddie said in a friendly voice.

"Hello there!" Tink responded gleefully as she turned to greet her.

"May I help you with your bags?" Maddie offered earnestly.

"I think I've got everything, but thanks for offering. I just picked up a few extra ingredients at the market," Tink explained, struggling to lift the four bags and an oversized pocketbook.

"I don't mind helping," Maddie countered, quickly putting the kickstand down and walking toward the elderly woman.

"Well, I won't say no twice to your sweet offer," Tink replied with apparent relief as she set the bags back down. "I guess I am a little weary, but maybe that's because it's lunchtime."

She then gestured in the direction of the back porch and asked, "Maddie, if you would please, just set the bags on the back stoop near the door, and I can get them from there. That'll be a big help! And as much as I'd love to invite you in, my kitchen looks like a snowstorm just blew through, what with all the sugar and flour I'm using in my many baking endeavors. But thankfully, progress is well underway for the various cookies, fruit pies, and even my day-before-Thanksgiving pot pies."

"Good for you!" Maddie said with true admiration.

"Yes, the potpie tradition started with my dear friend who…" Tink stopped speaking abruptly, exhaled deeply, and acted as though her full attention was now needed in order to walk up the back steps. She paused a little longer, shrugged her shoulders, and continued, "Well, anyway, a few years ago, I saw how busy my friend was shopping and preparing for his contribution toward the S.O.S. Thanksgiving Basket Benefit. So, I decided to make a delicious pot pie for him and several of my other neighbors, figuring they were all so busy preparing for Thanksgiving that having a homemade supper delivered the day before the holiday would be a welcome gift. Indeed it was, so I've continued this every year on the eve of Thanksgiving. Of course, someone always teases me about doing too much this week, especially at my age. But my heart and kitchen are so full of love that I'm sure I'm the one who always feels the most uplifted."

"That's beautiful," Maddie commented, setting the bags down as instructed.

"I can't help it. We all have our ways of contributing, and this just happens to be mine. Sadly though, I'll have one less pot pie delivery to make this year," she stated solemnly, glancing down instead of over at Nic's home. "Unless," she added brightly, looking back up, "you would allow this sentimental, old woman to bring you one of my piping-hot pot pies for your supper tonight? Everyone else gets theirs tomorrow, but I'm making a small sample batch this afternoon. I promise I won't be a bother to you, either. I would simply leave it on the back porch wrapped tightly in foil around sunset and be on my way."

"Really?" Maddie asked in genuine surprise. "That sounds amazing!"

"I would be delighted to bring you one, my dear!" Tink exclaimed.

"Well, your cookies are so good; I can only imagine how tasty your pot pies must be! I'm happy to accept your offer. Thank you so much, and thanks again for stopping by last night."

"You're most welcome," Tink replied. "I know I'm old-fashioned, but better that than just an old coot with a closed heart."

Maddie nodded in understanding and said, "Yes, I agree. I have a good friend who often teases me about being a 'softy.' But the truth is, I know he is, too."

"Perhaps we all are, Maddie. We just try to hide it for fear of being hurt," Tink remarked thoughtfully. "But, I'd better get myself inside for a bite of lunch and resume my baking, or I'll have some mighty disappointed friends in this neighborhood. Oh, wait. I just had another idea. Speaking of neighbors and friends, if you would really like to taste the best of my cooking, maybe you would join us for Thanksgiving dinner? The table is large, but the group will be rather small. And I realize that you may already have your own plans. I just wouldn't want you to eat alone on the day intended to gather together."

"I actually don't have any plans at this point," Maddie admitted.

"Well, isn't that perfect? Then, let me officially invite you to join a few good folks right here at 'Café Tink,'" she said, laughing and pointing at her house. "Your presence would be most welcome!"

The thought of sharing Thanksgiving at Tink's seemed fantastic to Maddie, for she was already captivated by this delightful woman. Still, she wanted time to think about it and then make an inspired decision.

"I won't pressure you, dear," Tink added, sensing Maddie's hesitation. "But will you please give my invitation real consideration?"

"Yes, I will, and thanks so much for asking me, Tink," Maddie replied respectfully.

"Fair enough. And if you do decide to be my guest, all I ask is that you let me know by tomorrow night. I tend to make a bit of a fuss setting the table and would want to be certain there is a proper place for you."

"I will definitely let you know by then. Besides, I need to return your cookie plate. And let me tell you, Tink, that they are so delicious that I even ate one this morning after my breakfast!" Maddie confessed.

"Oh, you might not be the only one who's done that," Tink said merrily. "What were they thinking when it was decided that cookies should only be consumed later in the day?"

"Right?!" Maddie concurred.

"When you do stop by, though, just come to this kitchen door because that's where I'll be mostly for the next two days. But feel free to run along now and have your lunch or whatever you're planning to do. I can bring the bags inside from here. What a joy to have seen you today, Maddie."

"I'm glad to see you, too. And good luck with all of your cooking and baking!"

"Thank you, my dear! And don't forget to check your porch tonight."

"Oh, I won't forget," Maddie assured her, walking back toward the bike.

Reflecting on her continued and unexpected blessings, Maddie wheeled the bicycle back into the garden shed. *My evening meal,* she thought in amazement, *will again be delivered right to the house. And I've also been invited to a home-cooked Thanksgiving dinner. I can't wait to tell Stephen, who probably imagined I'd be eating cold clam chowder out of the can. I wonder what he'll be doing on Thursday. I just hope he'll have a good Thanksgiving Day.*

Chapter 40
Tink

The knock on the door was firm and confident. Tink was not startled, however, since she was expecting this visitor. Brushing flour from her hands, the busy baker scurried across the kitchen, opened the door, and offered a cheery hello.

"Good afternoon, beautiful lady!"

"Good afternoon, Tink," Elizabeth responded in kind.

"*Entrez s'il vous plaît,*" the elder said to her friend of French heritage. "Bravo to you, too, for remembering to come knocking at the back door," Tink added as Elizabeth stepped inside. "And may I also say you are looking exceptionally radiant today. I'm guessing the S.O.S. basket plans are coming together well."

"They really are!" Elizabeth exclaimed. "I'm so glad I took on this project. I'm finding such satisfaction in organizing this because I can just sense the happiness to be shared on Thanksgiving Day when the deliveries are made."

"You know, dear, I don't believe there is anything comparable to the joy of giving. Just look at me - I'm not exactly red-carpet-ready. But, I'm all smiles because I can already anticipate the enthusiastic responses of everyone on the receiving end of my efforts."

"Yes! That's it exactly!" Elizabeth echoed.

"And to tell you the truth, my friend," Tink admitted, "these past

213

few months have been fairly difficult for me, as I'm sure they have been for many of us. But, when I lose myself in service, joy flutters back to the heart like a bird returning to its nest."

"How right you are," Elizabeth affirmed.

"I've already visited those precious doggies at the Homes for Hounds Rescue Center today, and I'm not sure who was more excited—me or them. Now, I'm moving onto pie baking after picking up a few more ingredients at the market. Donating to the S.O.S. Thanksgiving baskets is always a favorite of mine. And I'm so glad to be working on this annual benefit with you, Elizabeth."

"Thank you, Tink. And you know what I find interesting? For years, I've been involved with the theater, working, quite literally, behind the scenes. I have served on the Board of Directors—including the role of President—and even, on occasion, lent a hand with the sets, props, and costumes. But, the S.O.S. project feels different to me since I'm interacting much more directly with the citizens from our community. Plus, this is helping the same sailors and families that we got to know so well this past summer, which makes it even more special!"

"Yes," Tink agreed, "it is for me too because I'd never met any of the families before. But now, I can actually picture them gathering around to enjoy the meal and then gobbling up my pie."

"Isn't that fun to imagine?" Elizabeth proclaimed. "And I want to mention another important point about this benefit. I'm truly taken aback by the generosity of our fellow townsfolk. Everyone I've spoken to has donated willingly and without hesitation. The contributions are already added up, and I still have more businesses to speak to this afternoon, which is so exciting!"

"How wonderful," Tink acknowledged. "Frequently, I've been in a position to request donations for this charity and that benefit, and I continue to be amazed by the giving spirit of the good folks here in Port Saint Smith. I strongly believe that people are innately good. When offered a chance to give, they almost always come through and often in ways beyond our hopes and expectations."

"I couldn't agree more, and I'd love to tell you what happened this morning at Freeman's Nursery, one of our favorite local businesses. I went in to ask if they would be willing to donate to the baskets as I've requested of many other non-food-related businesses.

"Because what I want to do this year," Elizabeth explained, "is extend the goodwill of Thanksgiving beyond the one day and the one meal. I would like for each family to have a few keepsakes as meaningful reminders long after the food is gone."

"What a lovely idea!" Tink declared.

"Thank you," Elizabeth replied. "I wasn't even sure if the idea would work, but I wanted to at least try.

"So, Ella and Henry Freeman were wonderful when I went in. They were genuinely pleased to participate in the basket benefit. And I'd hoped they would find a little something to give, perhaps a few packets of seeds or the like. But what a privilege for me to watch them walking hand in hand around their nursery, deciding exactly what they wanted to donate. And what did they decide - to give each family a beautiful, large autumn-colored chrysanthemum plant. Plus, each child will receive an herb garden kit, including seeds, soil, and a sizable planter. Tink, this example of generosity was true, not only for them but for all of the other merchants that I've spoken to so far."

"Isn't that uplifting?" Tink commented. "Yet, I'm not surprised. The Freemans are the kind of people who find fulfillment and delight in helping others. And we are fortunate to have many individuals like that in this community. Though, you are the one, Elizabeth, who I personally want to acknowledge for coming up with such a splendid idea. I don't think that any lasting contributions were included before. How ingenious you are to add that to the tradition."

"Thank you," Elizabeth replied humbly. Then, as though she was going to leave, she reached for the doorknob, saying, "Speaking of acknow-ledgments, please stay right there because I have a little something for you."

Next, she stepped outside and retrieved a small gift bag intentionally left on the porch. With sweet anticipation, she returned and extended the bag to Tink, saying, "When I saw this at Freeman's Nursery, I just knew it was meant for you."

"What? You bought something for me?" Tink asked in surprise. "With everything else you've got going on, I can't imagine why you felt inclined to do this also."

"Because, Mrs. Kendleton," Elizabeth explained with a tone of authority, "I felt it was only right to find a way to thank *you* for your unending contributions to our community. So, on behalf of the citizens of Port Saint Smith, I offer this gift as a token of gratitude during this season of Thanksgiving. And," Elizabeth added with a mock, stern voice,

215

"don't even think about saying 'You shouldn't have.' I did it, you deserve it, and that's all there is to say."

"Well, I'm deeply touched by this thoughtful gesture," Tink replied sincerely, plopping down in a nearby chair. She then gestured for her guest to join her at the table. Elizabeth did as requested, watching as Tink stared in wonderment at the gift bag. She then began carefully removing the colored tissue paper. Upon peering inside the bag, Tink became visibly shaken. She looked back up at Elizabeth and asked with unexpected tenderness, "Do you even know how much this particular gift means to me?"

Elizabeth softly replied, "I felt so drawn to the display in the store, and my instincts guided me to this exact design. Did I get it right?"

"You sure did, and I thank you with all my heart, dear friend." Tink pushed herself up to standing and walked across the room, all the while carefully holding the bag in her hand. Elizabeth watched as Tink mindfully hung the stained-glass art piece in the window just above the sink.

Without a word, the elder returned to the table and sat facing the window so she could admire the gift.

"How extraordinary!" Tink exclaimed. "I shared with you earlier that I've had some very sorrowful days since Nic's death. But this past Sunday, I vowed to get on with my life and do my very best to enjoy the holiday season.

"I even had a dream that night in which Nic promised to send me a sign of reassurance," she continued. "That very day, a bird came to visit me. And not just any bird but a bright red cardinal. He landed right there at my kitchen window," she said, pointing, "and I promise, he was tapping to get my attention. I'm certain Nic sent that handsome messenger to me. And now look what you've brought me—a beautiful red cardinal made of stained glass, which is hanging in the very same window where he appeared. How amazing is that?"

"That is amazing! And I swear the cardinal design kept catching my eye. I'm just so pleased to see how happy this makes you!"

"I'm thrilled! I've seen that fancy display at Freeman's Nursery filled with so many beautiful choices—butterflies, flowers, lighthouses, dragonflies, you name it. But for you to be inspired to buy this exact one for me is remarkable. Every day, I will look at it and thank you with all my heart."

"I just knew I couldn't leave the store without buying the cardinal for you," Elizabeth offered. "And now I know why."

"Yes, because I've always watched for signs," Tink confided. "They remind me that our loved ones in spirit are doing well and enjoy sending their love and encouragement in so many different ways. And although we don't talk about this often, I believe most people feel the same way."

Elizabeth smiled and nodded in unspoken agreement.

"So, thank you, dear one, for this gift that serves as yet another sign of reassurance. But," Tink said with a long exhale, "We'd better change the subject, or I may end up in an emotional muddle thinking about Nic, which would not be good, especially with all I intend to accomplish today."

"Alright," Elizabeth readily agreed. Then, with only a slight hesitation, she said, "I do have something else I wish to discuss with you. But we both still have plenty to do today, so I feel it may be wise to delay that conversation."

"Oh, do tell me a little bit so my thoughts can change direction. Would you please?" the elder requested, with an irresistible twinkle in her eyes.

"Alright, if you insist," Elizabeth teased.

"I'd really appreciate that," Tink gratefully responded while placing her hands contentedly in her lap.

Pausing briefly to gather her thoughts, Elizabeth then proceeded, "I'm sure you've come to realize that I am a visionary and a woman of great determination. I mention this because I have an idea, perhaps a very grand idea, that could benefit the S.O.S. Foundation and help guarantee its ongoing success. I'm bursting with excitement at the possibilities and really eager for us to discuss this. So, when we do have a chance to talk, I want to share this vision with you, especially in light of what this could also mean to our beloved Port Saint Smith."

"Oh, Elizabeth, you're mighty clever! You've already taken my mind out of the past and have me eager to know more about the possibilities for the future. Won't you please tell me a teensy bit more?" Tink pleaded. "Just another hint to keep me going until we have more time to talk?"

"Alright. I'll share a little more with you, and then I'll need to get going," Elizabeth answered, sitting back in her chair. "Tink, some of the happiest days of my childhood were spent near the sea. Those memories always seem to stand out more than any others. Ironically, though, I have done very little sailing. Nevertheless, to use a sailing metaphor, I believe

217

there are moments in our lives when the wind catches the sails of our passion, and we are propelled forward almost effortlessly in a new and inspired direction."

"I am not a sailor either," Tink acknowledged. "But, I understand and appreciate that analogy. Because, in my life, I have also had times when the winds of change have carried me forward in an intentional and beneficial way."

"Exactly!" Elizabeth declared. "I was sure you would understand. I share this with you because just a few days ago, I began to sense a very welcome but unexpected shift of this very kind. It felt, and still feels, as though the very wind of change you referenced is clearly guiding me along."

"Oh, how exciting!" Tink exclaimed with a clap of her hands.

"Yes, it really is," Elizabeth agreed. "And remember this past summer how much we enjoyed watching the novice sailors learning to understand and anticipate the shifting winds as they navigated their boats in the port? I was enthralled to see how the wind billowed in their sails, pushing the little boats forward. And now, that same kind of impressive wind seems to be swelling my sails and filling me with a deliberate sense of purpose and drive."

"That's remarkable, Elizabeth."

"And so was the vivid dream I recently had. In it," Elizabeth recounted, "an amazingly detailed concept for helping the S.O.S. Foundation was revealed. I am certain I could not have conceived such a meticulous plan on my own. It's as though the idea was gifted to me. But," she said, pausing, "that is all I dare tell you today since we both have so much left to do. I promise, though, to give you more of the details as soon as time allows."

"That's so intriguing!" I sure wish I didn't have to wait to hear more, though. You are right, however. If we don't attend to those baskets, we may still be sitting here discussing this at supper time. Oh, wait, speaking of supper, that reminds me. I wanted to tell you that I invited the sweet visitor from next door to Thanksgiving dinner. She helped me carry groceries up from the car, and that's when I decided to ask her. I'm not sure if she'll join us or not. But I certainly hope she does."

"How kind of you," Elizabeth commented.

"I wouldn't want her to be all alone on Thanksgiving," Tink acknowledged, "and I think she might enjoy our little group."

"I'm sure she would," Elizabeth agreed.

"And what about you, dear lady? What are your Thanksgiving plans, if I may ask?"

"My only plan, at this point, is to help with the basket deliveries."

"Well, you've got to eat, so why don't you come by after you're finished? Nic always came over after the deliveries, and we all enjoyed hearing about the families and how well everything went."

"I would love that," Elizabeth replied honestly. "Thank you for inviting me. I'll really look forward to that. I just don't know when I'll be arriving," she added hesitantly.

"That's alright. Any time will be fine. And the food will be plentiful, so come hungry," Tink encouraged her. "Now, why don't we make our way into the pantry to look for those baskets? I beg you, though, to ignore all the clutter. This is far from an ideal time for someone as refined as you to be pursuing the pantry."

"I promise that won't bother me," Elizabeth laughed as Tink led the way through the kitchen, laundry room, and into the expansive storage space. After switching on the light, the much shorter of the two women pointed to the top shelf and said, "See that stack of baskets up there on the left? Do you think they're big enough for your needs?"

"I think they'll be perfect!" Elizabeth exclaimed.

"Great! And here is a step stool for you to use," Tink offered. "If you wouldn't mind, just hand them down to me."

After a few minutes, eight large baskets had been retrieved, carried through the kitchen, and stacked neatly by the door.

As Elizabeth prepared to leave, Tink said, "I'm so glad those baskets will be put to good use. Also, I should have the fruit pies ready by late tomorrow afternoon. Would you like me to deliver them to the office? That's where Nic and Larry always assembled the baskets in the previous years."

"Oh, yes, I would be most appreciative if you don't mind," Elizabeth replied. "I still have quite a lot to do in order to put all the pieces of this wonderful Thanksgiving puzzle together. But if you do need a hand, I could always come by and pick them up."

"No, I can manage just fine," Tink affirmed.

"Excellent. Now, please tell me what I can bring for dinner on Thursday. I could attempt to put one of those gooey, green bean casseroles together. You know, the kind with crunchy bits on top. How hard can that be? I could at least try," Elizabeth mumbled with a nervous laugh.

"Fiddlesticks! You're my guest, so you don't need to bring anything. But thank goodness you mentioned green beans because I completely forgot to tell you about the side dishes that are needed for the baskets," Tink said with breathy excitement. "I went by the Chamber of Commerce this morning and spoke to Shirley. And guess what? She is absolutely delighted to be helping out. In fact, she is enlisting the help of several other guild members and will be coordinating everything. She's so happy to be involved, and I'm sure the other ladies will also be glad to pitch in. So you don't need to worry at all. Because when the ladies of the guild get the all-call for help, we show up!" Tink proclaimed proudly.

"Thank you so much, Tink! What a relief!" Elizabeth sighed. "I don't know what I would have done otherwise. Of course, I'll have to thank Shirley also the next time I see her."

"That'll be easy since she'll be here on Thursday, as well. The poor dear had all her holiday plans canceled at the last moment, so she'll be in attendance, as will Charlie and, hopefully, Maddie too. I'm really looking forward to Thanksgiving, especially now that I know you're coming."

"I'm sure it will be a very special gathering. But, I'd better be off and leave you to your baking."

After sweet goodbyes were exchanged, Tink watched from the window in amazement as Elizabeth managed to load all eight baskets into her pint-sized car. The elderly woman stood a moment longer, admiring the new stained-glass cardinal and wondering when she might see the real bird hopping and chirping again on her window sill.

Chapter 41
Larry

I don't recall how long it's been since I was in the kitchen for any length of time, Larry thought to himself. *In the last few months, I've made a few decent meals, but nothing along the lines of my usual culinary endeavors.*

Like a recently injured athlete afraid to resume competition, Larry was concerned that he may have lost his cooking mojo. But since he had committed to making the turkey and stuffing for S.O.S. baskets, he hoped with luck and effort, inspiration would resurface again. Once all the ingredients were assembled, the ovens were preheating, and the aroma of sauteing garlic and onion filled the air, Larry wanted nothing more than to rise, like yeasted bread, to the occasion. Still, this once confident amateur chef felt incredibly awkward in the very place where creativity and gratifying self-expression typically ruled.

No calls, clients, or important transactions had demanded his attention at the office earlier. So, by midafternoon, Larry had locked up and left the building. Most people, he'd reasoned, were either traveling or preparing for their Thanksgiving meal, and he realized that his own preparations needed to get started also. He drove, therefore, directly home, but not to lay on the couch napping or watching T.V. For this was a time-sensitive task, and today was the day it must be done. The herbs and spices in his kitchen required a thorough inventory to determine which needed to be replenished due to insufficient quantities and which needed to be replaced due to expired freshness dates.

The initial inspection of the seasoning supplies proved to be quite cathartic for Larry. Just holding the bottles of Italian herbs—sage, oregano, rosemary—as well as the sea salt and black pepper felt uplifting. As he continued to assess the stock and compose a shopping list, his mind cleared, and his outlook brightened.

Larry realized he'd also been avoiding this essential chore and many others for fear of becoming emotionally overwhelmed. For this kitchen *his* kitchen was steeped in a massive amount of memories. Many delectable, multiple-course meals had been prepared here and enjoyed in the company of his best friend. And because his grief had been such a sorrowful and solitary affair, Larry felt extremely vulnerable just standing in the bright, expansive space. Yet, as he attempted to step aside from his suffering, at least for a little while to be in service to others, Larry's state of mind was quickly improving.

The shopping list is ready, and so am I, he declared with determination. *I may not be operating at peak performance, but I'm going to do my best to accomplish all of this. Thankfully,* Larry acknowledged with a deep sigh, *I'm not in charge of the entire project or even the menu. Elizabeth has stepped in once again where I faltered, and I owe her such a debt of gratitude. But how does one repay this level of dedication and commitment?*

The sound of a text message immediately rattled the pensive man. Since this was still business hours, Larry knew he needed to identify the sender. To his great relief, however, the message was from Elizabeth and not from someone else, especially someone now deceased. Apparently, she wanted him to call when he had a few minutes so she could update him on the basket progress. Seeing as he was already focused on the project, Larry called her right away.

"Hi Larry," Elizabeth answered immediately. "Thanks for giving me a call. Is this a good time to talk?"

"Yes, it is," he replied decisively.

"Well, I'm happy to report that everything is going to plan. I've been busy coordinating the donations, which is why you haven't seen me at the office today."

"That's okay, I understand. I actually locked up and left early, myself, in order to begin the prep in my kitchen. My herbs and spices needed to be assessed because fresh ingredients," he stated with conviction, "are one of the most essential elements to successful cooking."

"That makes good sense," Elizabeth agreed, pleased to hear such clarity in his voice.

"And Elizabeth," he proceeded, "I don't think we've talked about expenses yet. I'm sure you know that Nic established a sizable trust fund for the S.O.S. Foundation. So, whatever costs are incurred will be reimbursed by that fund."

"Yes, I am aware of that and glad to know those funds are in place. However, not one penny has been spent. Everyone I've spoken to has been exceptionally generous because they still believe in the S.O.S. Foundation. They want to see this organization continue and honor the founder as well. But, if there are any expenses," she assured him in an effort not to dwell on Nic's memory, "we'll sort that out later. And I'd like to give you a few other updates."

"Ok, go ahead," Larry agreed, suddenly feeling a bit gutted by the mention of his best friend's name and the reminder of the important role he'd had in this community that still loved him dearly.

"Fortunately," Elizabeth proceeded, "we are all set for baskets and pies, thanks to Tink. And as you might imagine, her kitchen is bustling with all kinds of activities. But she assured me there would not be a mix-up in the ingredients for the canine cookies and the other offerings intended for the Thanksgiving benefit. I told her that was a relief!" Elizabeth chuckled with the hope of humoring Larry. "Then, between Robertson's Deli and the grocery store, all of the food has been provided—appetizers, rolls, butter, the eight turkeys, and so much more. In fact, all of the turkeys are scheduled to be delivered to your home in coolers early tomorrow. Is that good for you?"

"Yes," he said. "That'll be fine."

"I also have a few other surprises lined up to include with the offerings," Elizabeth added with evident excitement. "But some of the very best news, at least for me, is the fact that Shirley Lund is recruiting the guild ladies to prepare all of the side dishes."

"That's helpful," he stated flatly, trying to rally to match her enthusiasm. Because although Larry was impressed with her progress, he was struggling to offer even the most basic words of appreciation. "You're doing a great job. Thank you."

"You're welcome, Larry. I'm glad to be helping. I loved volunteering at the camps this past summer, and I'm so fond now of the children and their families. So, I'm really looking forward to making the deliveries with you on Thursday. I think we're going to have fun."

Larry grumbled audibly, convinced he'd all but forgotten how to have fun.

Then, for the next few minutes, Elizabeth continued the conversation, explaining her plans to assemble as many of the donations as possible the night before at the office. Larry listened politely and agreed with her ideas until she presented him with one final question.

"As you know," she admitted, "my skills in the kitchen are basically limited to making coffee and heating carry-out dishes. That being said, however, I am sincerely offering you my services as a sous chef on Thanksgiving morning. Would you please allow me to assist you in the kitchen with the turkeys and stuffing? I'll arrive as early as you request and promise to quietly and respectfully take direction, even if what you tell me is to get out of the way."

A silence fell between them as Larry considered this unexpected request. He'd always enjoyed sharing his kitchen and culinary knowledge with Nic and had given real consideration to teaching beginner cooking classes in the training room at Robertson's Deli. But could he handle having someone else in his home, especially in his kitchen, at this time? Could he be around someone so alert and yet, unwittingly invading the space that he was only now reclaiming for himself? Feeling pressured and agitated, Larry replied, "I'll need to think about that."

"Ok, I understand," Elizabeth acknowledged. "I'd love to help, but I'll accept your decision, regardless of what it is."

"Thanks," he responded. "I'll let you know tomorrow."

"All right. I hope you have a good evening. And unless there is something else, I'll say goodbye."

"No, that's all. Thanks, Elizabeth. Goodbye," Larry replied, relieved the call was over. He set the phone down and immediately returned to his inventory. For he didn't even want to consider her request. Moments later, however, a familiar sound announced an incoming text. *What now*, he grumbled, guessing Elizabeth needed to tell him one more thing. But when he reached for the phone, Larry saw this message instead:

Let her help, Slouch.
You'll have fun!
Happy cooking.
N

Chapter 42
Maddie

The glow of the fireplace softly lit the cozy room. Maddie curled up on the loveseat and placed the hand-sewn quilt over her legs. On the coffee table in front of her was a cup of herbal tea and the last of Tink's homemade cookies. The relaxed traveler felt content and reflective as she began writing in her journal.

> *I'm pretty weary at the end of my first day of vacation. But I'm also very happy because my experiences so far have really been wonderful! And I continue to be in awe of the remarkable "coincidences" that have happened just since yesterday. More than ever before, I've had clear confirmation that following my intuition will invariably lead to extraordinary outcomes and sweet serendipities. How rewarding to consciously participate in this amazing aspect of life.*
>
> *I began this day by sitting on the back porch swing, watching the sun's early rays illuminate the trees and colorful birds flit joyfully about the garden. Most noticeable was a lively and attentive bright red cardinal that actually perched very close to me on the railing. He even seemed to be singing along with the squeak of the moving swing. But did he notice that the swing was moving without my effort? It was so extraordinary!*

Cardinals are often considered messengers from the other side. So, I wonder if he was intentionally sent to me? I've never noticed that particular bird before. And I don't sense he is coming to me on behalf of Grandma Anise or anyone else who has passed. Yet, it's interesting that he appeared. And maybe he's the same cardinal Tink had mentioned to me. If so, I understand why she's so enamored with this handsome little guy.

After swinging for a while, I went back into the kitchen and had a great breakfast, along with another one of Tink's incredible cookies. Dessert at breakfast seems so indulgent, but isn't this the perfect time for me to stretch the very edges of my ordinary life? That's exactly what I want from this trip—to see and sense far beyond any confines that may be limiting my joy and spontaneity. And I'm sure I burned off any extra calories since I spent the next several hours exploring this town on a new women's bike that had been inexplicably placed in the garden shed. I sure can't understand that, but I'm thrilled it's there. This is another one of the unexpected benefits of staying here.

It just can't be a coincidence that I was guided to Port Saint Smith and this home, La Maison Enchantée. *Everything suits me so perfectly as if someone had planned all of this in expectation of my arrival.*

Touring the area on the bike was exhilarating. I rode high into the hills and saw the most stunning view of the ocean below. I then cycled slower through various neighborhoods and the downtown streets for a different perspective of this beautiful area. And tomorrow, I plan to walk leisurely through downtown. That should be fun!

When I got back, I was so happy to see the neighbor Tink in her driveway. She seems like an exceptional person— friendly and energetic, especially considering her age. I also admire her independent spirit. Because when I offered to help carry her groceries up to the house, she actually said no at first. How many elders are just barely getting by, let alone thriving? She sure is an inspiration to me!

We had a nice chat, and I can't believe it, but she invited me to Thanksgiving dinner! I'm kind of excited because I've been concerned about being alone that day. But I didn't give her an answer yet since I want to think it through a little more. I'm fairly private, and I won't know anyone there, which could be awkward. However, when I consider my options—eating here alone or at a restaurant—neither is appealing. Plus, I genuinely like the idea of celebrating the holiday with Tink and her friends, who I imagine will be just as interesting as she is.

I must remember that the main reason for this getaway was to meet new people, or at least that one special someone who whispered to me on the wind. Maybe he'll even be at Tink's. on Thanksgiving! Wouldn't that be amazing? Either way, I want to welcome experiences that will uplift, inspire, and increase my joy! So, I'll probably accept her invitation tomorrow when I return her cookie plate.

On another note, Stephen left me the cutest message. Apparently, he and Miss Priss are getting along famously as he strolls her around in a fancy pet pram. What a sight that must be! The thought of it makes me so happy for both of them. And I love the fact that they are venturing out while I am also away, having my own adventures. I'm even napping, which is far from typical for me. I actually slept for two hours today after a delicious lunch, thanks to Elizabeth. With nowhere to be, nothing to be done, and all the time that I wanted to relax, I relished every lazy—no, let me rephrase that—every restful moment!

After waking up, I wandered back downstairs and saw that Tink, as promised, had left me a hot pot pie just outside the kitchen door. How lucky am I to receive more delicious food delivered right to my doorstep! When I tell Stephen about all this, he'll probably think I'm making it up! But Tink was so excited when I accepted her offer to bring me this meal—as if I would say no? I did sense, though, a real sadness when she told me there was one less pot pie delivery to be made this year. I'm guessing it was for someone very close to her who maybe moved away.? I just felt, however, it wasn't the right time to ask her who it was.

And now I find myself sitting in this cozy, little study, watching the fire and thinking about the owner. Where is he now, I wonder? This room still feels so vibrant with his essence. And I don't think it's due to the fact his cycling and sailing books are still here. I did put his curious welcome note right in the middle of the mantel because I am touched by his heartfelt words and how embraced I feel in his home.

When Maddie finished writing, she set her journal on the coffee table and, leaning back into the loveseat, gently closed her eyes. The crackling of the fire filled the otherwise silent room. Within minutes, and without so much as a whisper, she began to sense an unmistakable presence near her. This presence, his presence, felt so welcome, yet still so unrecognizable. Was this the one who had invited her to the Cape? Perhaps. Yet, on this hushed night, in this small, quiet room, there was no wind nor an enticing voice. All she felt was a distinctly masculine presence right beside her. With a slight bit of reservation and even trepidation, Maddie leaned back further, wanting to better understand who he was and why he'd chosen to be with her.

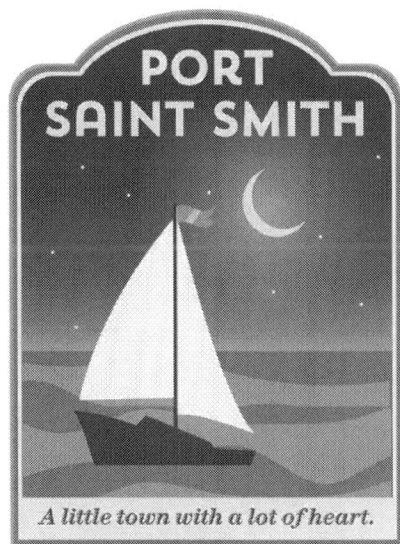

PORT
SAINT SMITH

A little town with a lot of heart.

WEDNESDAY, NOVEMBER 23

Chapter 43
Tink

The hours whirled by in purposeful activity as Tink bustled back and forth in her cheery kitchen. She was also keenly aware that the chime of the old grandfather clock was no longer a painful reminder of another sorrow-filled, empty hour. With purpose came hope, and Tink sensed that the heavy fog of despair that had clouded so many of her days since summer was beginning to dissipate as though being blown away by a determined yet unseen wind.

Earlier in the morning, when she had pulled the heavy drapes open in the parlor, Tink was genuinely happy to see the radiant light streaming in, filtered only by the leaves and branches of the large trees. At last, she was able to welcome the bright sunshine and the promise of a new day.

Presently, as Tink assessed the remaining itinerary, she paused to acknowledge the many achievements from the day before. The industrious elder was extremely pleased with her progress thus far and the monumental amount of cooking and baking already accomplished. Furthermore, she was encouraged by her improved strength and focus. Now, her desire and intention going forward was to maintain that same optimistic outlook and level of productivity and, thus, avoid the painful reminders of the past.

Yesterday had also brought with it a most enjoyable visit from Elizabeth—a woman who consistently impressed and amazed Tink. The

231

vivacious professional, who'd come to pick up baskets for the benefit, had brought with her a thoughtful gift. And not just any little widget or whatnot, but a most timely and truly perfect present.

I'm absolutely astonished, Tink thought as she looked at the stained-glass bird suspended in the large kitchen window. *Of all the many styles Elizabeth could have chosen, she selected this one, stating how strongly she'd felt it was the perfect one for me! How right she was! Because regardless of the frequency of my special, winged messenger's visits, I'll always have that lovely cardinal to look at in my window, which will inevitably remind me of Nic's unfailing love and support from the other side.*

As Tink continued staring at the window, she began to sing a sweet tune, encouraging the cardinal to visit.

"Little birdie, little birdie, I hope you'll come by.
Little birdie, little birdie, please don't be shy.
You bring me a message of hope for my heart,
I welcome your visit and have from the start."

Tink did not see the bird, however, but noticed instead the houseguest from next door walking towards her home. Quickly, the old woman tidied her apron and waited excitedly to hear a *knock, knock*.

"Hellllooo neeighborrr!!" Tink rang out joyfully as she opened the door. "How good to see you this morning!"

"It's good to see you too, Tink," Maddie replied.

"Would you like to come in for a moment since it's rather chilly outside?"

"Sure, that would be nice," Maddie said as she stepped into the warm kitchen.

"Welcome to my home," Tink said proudly. "And as much as I'd like to give you the first-time visitor's traditional tour, I can't today because of my countless cooking commitments. But perhaps you'll allow me to show you around another time? Because, at this moment, as you can see," Tink explained, waving her arms in demonstration, "I am busy making pies and a plethora of other preparations for tomorrow's grand festivities. But that's enough about me. Tell me how you're getting on? I certainly hope that you've been warmly welcomed by everyone in Port Saint Smith. Are you settling in well and sleeping soundly? And most importantly, my dear, are you feeling at home at *La Maison Enchantée*? There is nothing I would like more for you than that."

Maddie was unsure how to respond to Tink's numerous queries, especially since the last one resonated so closely with her own feelings. How could she ever convey to this sincere woman, or almost anyone else, how much that house already felt like home to her? Moreover, what about the company she so often felt there - much like that of a beloved? The presence seemed to sense and understand her far beyond words and logic. Even in the silence, his kindness and devotion spoke straight to her heart.

But was that even possible, Maddie wondered. *And, if so, how could it be explained?*

Before answering, Maddie paused momentarily, composed her thoughts, and then replied, "Everyone has been so kind and helpful since I arrived. I'm settling in beautifully - sleeping soundly and feeling remarkably at home. Also, I'm eating well, maybe a little too well—much thanks to you and Elizabeth. Everything, Tink, has really been better than I could have ever hoped."

"I'm elated to hear that, Maddie. And look," Tink exclaimed, "I got goosebumps on my arms when I heard you say you feel so at home."

"I got them too!" Maddie echoed.

"Well, there you have it!" Tink expressed excitedly, "You're obviously meant to be here because, to me, goosebumps are almost always a confirmation of something truthful being revealed!"

"I agree," Maddie stated enthusiastically.

Then, Tink added, "I'm so pleased that it's *you* staying next door. We all are—Elizabeth, Shirley, and I. And so would anyone else who's had the pleasure of meeting you."

"That's very kind of you to say," Maddie replied with a slight blush. "You have all welcomed me so warmly."

"'Tis our pleasure, dear, I assure you," Tink responded. "Now, tell me, what brings you over to my house? And may I offer you a snack or something to drink? Hot tea? Juice? Or one of our local favorites - coffee milk?"

Maddie smiled warmly at this good-hearted woman's nearly irresistible hospitality.

"No, but thank you. I just had a big breakfast, so I'm still full," she explained.

"I know how that feels," Tink acknowledged mischievously as

she lightly patted her tummy. And looking down momentarily at her midsection, Tink happened to notice the empty plate in Maddie's hand.

"Good gracious, you didn't have to trouble yourself with returning that old plate. I buy them at the pet rescue thrift shop, two for a quarter," she chuckled. "But since you did bring it back, I suppose I'll just have to fill it up again. Unless," Tink suggested with a wink, "you didn't like my cookies. And perhaps, you also found the pot pie to be dry and tasteless. Is that correct?"

"Oh, yes," Maddie responded dolefully, deciding to play along with Tink's silly sense of humor. "The cookies and the pot pie were really quite awful. But, of course, I wasn't planning to say anything. Since you did mention it, though, I think it's better to be honest. I only ate every single bite and crumb, so your feelings wouldn't be hurt."

"How dreadful for you, dear!" Tink quipped. "I'm terribly sorry to have put you through all that. My guess is, then, that you won't want to endure Thanksgiving dinner, either. I wouldn't want you to feel obligated to eat more distasteful food."

"Actually, you're incorrect about that," Maddie declared. "I thought I'd give you one more chance. So, if you'll still have me, I'd like to RSVP yes for tomorrow."

"Oh, Maddie," Tink squealed, "I'm over the moon that you'll be coming!"

Tink's giddiness pleased Maddie immensely, as did hearing the very same term Stephen had used to describe her own happiness about coming to the Cape.

"Thank you for saying yes!" Tink continued. "You've absolutely made my day, and it isn't even lunchtime yet!"

"Thank you for inviting me," Maddie replied. "And, just for the record, I'm sure the food will be amazing! Now, please tell me what you would like me to bring."

"Nothing but your sweet self," Tink assured her.

"Really?" Maddie questioned. "I'd be glad to help contribute toward the meal."

"I won't hear of it," Tink insisted. "You're on vacation, which means all you need to do is enjoy yourself and not fuss over any such nonsense. I have rules in this house," she explained while holding up an imaginary proclamation. "Any guest of mine that happens to be on vacation while attending a holiday function hosted here is henceforth prohibited from contributing in any manner toward the festivities."

"Well, in that case, I wouldn't want to break your rules," Maddie said with a little laugh while also breathing an internal sigh of relief. For although she would have been glad to bring a side dish or the like, she was happy just to come as a guest.

"I'm glad that's resolved," Tink affirmed with finality. "And I assure you, there will be plenty of good food, perhaps some of my best ever."

"I believe that!" Maddie stated. "Everything I've tasted so far of yours has been amazing!"

"Thank you, Maddie. I pride myself on making everything with an extra bit of love, which I consider to be the only necessary ingredient. So then, why don't you plan on coming over around two o'clock tomorrow? We older folks tend to eat on the early side. Any later, and I'm afraid we might just nod off before dessert, which would be most unacceptable!"

"Ok, great, I'll be here at two. And I'd better let you get back to your baking."

"Yes, you're right. I need to get busy. But hopefully, we'll have more time to chat tomorrow. What are your plans for today, if I may ask?"

"I'm going to drive into town to do some shopping, with hopes of finding a special thank-you gift for my friend Stephen, who is taking care of my cat while I'm gone."

"I'm sure you'll find something perfect for him. We have all kinds of shops with a wide array of items, depending on his whims. I'll be curious to know what you find if you care to tell me."

"I'd be happy to," Maddie agreed readily.

"Great! And thank you, again, for stopping by this morning with such good news," Tink replied.

"You're welcome," Maddie responded. "Good luck with all you're doing!"

"Thanks! I'll need it! I'm always glad to have a wee bit of extra luck," Tink affirmed with a twinkle in her eyes. "Now go and enjoy your day, Maddie dear!"

"I sure will! Bye, Tink."

"Bye-bye!"

Tink watched and waved from the open doorway as Maddie returned next door. And although she could not see the cardinal, Tink was sure she could hear his distinct *chirp, chirp, chirp* in a nearby tree.

Once Maddie was out of sight, Tink turned, closed the door, and sat down at the kitchen table. Her intention was not to have a snack, rest from her work, or even read a passage from Nic's journal. No, the wise elder wanted to have a few moments of quiet reflection before resuming her activities.

How understandable for me to feel justified in focusing on my losses and my sorrow, along with the terrible realization of what will be no more. Yet, now, at last, I'm able to recognize once more that every day offers its own reassuring gifts. However small or great they may be, my acceptance of these offerings gives me the opportunity to experience more gratitude than grief.

The simple sight of a ladybug has always brought me delight, Tink reflected. *The stunning vision of a rainbow crossing the sky could never become mundane. And Maddie's brief visit feels like a little gift of joy! Knowing it is the day before Thanksgiving, I'm going to spend the next few minutes being mindful of my blessings.*

I'm grateful, Tink enumerated, *for my good health, which is quite remarkable for my age. I'm grateful for this comfortable home located in such a wonderful town. I'm grateful for the rescue doggies that I can visit almost anytime. I'm grateful to watch boisterous Bailey running around the yard with the children across the street. But, most importantly, I'm grateful to have so many special people in my life—good neighbors, good friends, and even that old bird of a sister of mine, Martha Louise. And somehow, like a cool breeze on an intensely hot day, meeting Maddie has been one of those unexpected gifts. I realize she won't be here long. Nevertheless, she has brought life back into that house, which has brought more joy back into my heart.*

With that thought, Tink turned to look out the window at the home next door that had been shadowed by death for months. She also glanced at the stained-glass cardinal hanging in the very same window. And just below this new gift from Elizabeth, she noticed that the real cardinal had arrived. He was sitting on the window sill looking up as if in admiration of the handsome rendition of his likeness. Adding this winged messenger of hope to her list of gratitudes, Tink placed her hands over her heart and softly said, "I am truly blessed to have so much good in my life."

Chapter 44
Larry

Larry wasn't groggy when he woke up Wednesday morning. This alone was startling since he'd become so intensely familiar with the unfathomable heaviness of his own grief. Rising with even the slightest amount of optimism was an unexpected surprise.

With this lighter outlook, Larry got up, showered, dressed, and headed directly into the kitchen. There, he surveyed the expansive countertops covered with loaves of bread for stuffing, onions, fresh herbs, and countless jars of spices. The scene filled him with excitement. Still, an underlying sense of uneasiness remained. For Elizabeth had asked to help him with the food prep for the basket benefit. That endeavor would begin before dawn tomorrow, which meant she needed to have his answer today.

Larry recognized that Elizabeth's offer was sincere. Nevertheless, it felt very much like an imposition. Until recently, Larry had always welcomed company into his home, delighting in the chance to share his passion for cooking. Various groups of friends, almost always including Nic, would sit, chat, and watch in eager anticipation as the hobbyist chef prepared elaborate, multicourse meals. Sailing, sports, and sauteing were among the many enjoyable topics bantered about. However, ever since Nic's passing, Larry's new habit of isolating made the idea of having anyone else in his home feel nothing short of intrusive.

Despite my efforts to appear to be the same fun-loving yet reliable businessman, Elizabeth, more than anyone else, is aware of my real situation, Larry recognized. *She has seen me struggle to manage the most mundane matters and has willingly taken on additional responsibilities like a true professional. She's also done her best to overlook my frequent sullen moods. I guess I'm afraid that if she's here for any length of time, I won't be able to hold up as well. I may lose my temper or, more likely, what little focus I do have. And it's not like I can escape to the porch to sulk or to the sofa to sleep. At least at work, I have my office door to hide behind. But at home? I would have nowhere to get away.*

When Larry first started receiving text messages addressed to his nickname Slouch, he was forced to realize that his actions, even those assumed to be unseen by anyone else, were, in truth, being witnessed. And not only were his actions being observed, but so were his moods. He was startled to read texts referencing how he actually felt, including the last unsettling communication that had encouraged Larry not to worry about Elizabeth helping in his kitchen. The message indicated he would have more fun. But how could Nic sense any of that? How could that insight be coming from someone no longer considered alive?

Can he truly know what I am thinking or feeling? Does he really grasp how resistant I am to the idea of Elizabeth coming over and 'helping' with her admittedly absentee abilities? Larry pondered this as he began to peel and eat a banana. *Can Nic literally be aware of my emotional state without my saying a word out loud? How can that be remotely possible? Well, regardless, that's too much for me to consider right now,* he decided. So, Larry shoved the remaining banana in his mouth and scored two points by successfully throwing the peel into the trash. He then gathered his belongings and left for work.

After making his usual stop at the bakery for coffee and a breakfast croissant, Larry arrived uncharacteristically late at the office. Without any conscious awareness, he'd sauntered slowly down Center Street, looking in shop windows, contemplating the need for a few more spices, as well as an additional loaf of rye bread to perfect the stuffing. He'd even stopped to chat with one of his neighbors and, for a few brief moments, had immersed himself in the holiday spirit along with many of the other cheerful residents of Port Saint Smith. This was yet another unanticipated but welcome surprise to him.

Larry's mood continued to brighten as he arrived at work and prepared the office for activity. Rather than slump over his desk as had been his habit for months, he sat upright in the large, plush chair and noticed once again the old photograph Elizabeth had left with him. He still had no idea what the significance of it could be. Was she going to call him out on his inappropriate behavior, saying it was only fitting for a child as young as that little girl to act in such a manner? Or perhaps she would cite the old man as a good example of responsible attentiveness, which he knew he owed to his business, if not his entire life. Both hypotheses, Larry realized, were ridiculous, but what other reason could there be?

The frustrated man studied the image and tried to at least determine the location of the photo. Having been in real estate for years, the building did seem slightly familiar. Still, he was unable to identify anything, and wishing to avoid further exasperation, Larry turned the image over and placed it on the far corner of his desk.

Fortunately, Larry's holiday conviviality remained, causing him to have little interest in his work. He idly picked up one of the miniature brass boats and began turning it over in his hands. He was proud of his contribution to the S.O.S. Foundation now, despite his many initial concerns regarding the camps. There was no doubt about the significant difference it had made in the lives of the campers and their families. Every year, numerous thank you cards and emails were received, crediting the organization with higher grades, improved self-esteem, and notably more cooperative behavior. Additionally, the citizens of Port Saint Smith found such joy in helping these underserved youth.

However, Larry was unable to fathom how the organization could successfully continue without Nic's dedicated leadership and direction. Once, when they had been out on the boat, his best friend and sailing mate had spoken to him about the word *endurance*. This, Nic explained, was one interpretation of his last name in Greek. Endurance, constancy, and victory defined the name Paramonos. And all of those characteristics, Larry knew, clearly defined Nic. How tragic then that a man so victorious in nearly every way and so well-loved by the community would succumb to death long before old age.

I can only hope, Larry thought, *that without children to survive him, Nic's foundation would at least live on. But I just don't see how.*

These concerns mingled with Larry's attempts to find any plausible reason to refuse Elizabeth's kitchen assistance. He was not surprised, therefore, to receive a timely text addressing both of these matters.

239

Slouch,
with Elizabeth's
direction and efforts,
the foundation will flourish.
And, regarding her help tomorrow,
just say yes!
You won't regret it.
N

How can he do this? Larry struggled to understand. *In life, I could never lie to Nic. He could always sense when I was worried or upset. And apparently, that hasn't changed, which I find very disconcerting. But perhaps, in time, I may find comfort in that too.*

Larry continued to fidget with the boat as a growing sense of restlessness began to replace his lingering lethargy. Although he couldn't justify leaving work this early, Larry yearned to just walk back out the front door and get caught up in the festive mood of the day again. He even considered just walking back downtown amidst the other bustling shoppers; the idea of which stunned him, since only two days earlier, he'd intentionally walked in the alleyways to avoid those same, jovial people. Yet, being among them earlier this morning had felt good, and even a little fun.

Fun? Larry thought with a jolt. *There's that absurd word again! Well, I'm certainly not having any fun here. So, as the sole proprietor of this company, I declare the office officially closed for the Thanksgiving holiday, and I'm definitely locking up within the hour.*

The next sixty minutes ticked by slowly. Still, there were no calls or visitors, so Larry felt justified in his decision to leave. Like an eager student on the last day of school, he walked briskly toward the exit. As he did, though, his cell phone rang, and Larry paused long enough to identify the caller before deciding whether or not to answer.

"Hello," he said.

"Good morning, Larry. Elizabeth here. I wanted to give you a quick update on my progress. Am I catching you at a good time?"

"Yes, go ahead," he replied.

"I have a few more donations to pick up before arriving at the office. Wait until you see what all there is! The wonderful citizens of our town have been overwhelmingly generous. And even though Tink gave me eight good-sized baskets yesterday, I'm actually concerned they won't be large enough to hold everything. Can you believe that? Don't worry, though; I'll figure it out one way or the other," she assured him, not waiting for an answer. "I'm just grateful you drive such a big truck. We will certainly need it!"

Larry barely mumbled a response before Elizabeth continued speaking, "And whenever we do have a chance to talk about that old photograph, this enormous outpouring of generosity will figure into the conversation. But, with everything else on my agenda today, that discussion will have to wait."

"Alright," Larry replied with a feeble attempt to hide his relief.

"Regarding my schedule," she explained, "I should arrive at the office sometime before one o'clock. Tink will be dropping off the pies later this afternoon, and Shirley has asked all the ladies of the guild to deliver their side dishes by 5 p.m. I plan to pre-assemble the baskets in the conference room tonight, leaving room, of course, for your main contribution tomorrow. I've even had several offers to help me, but I'd rather work alone this year so I can figure it out as I go along. I think it'll be fun! How does that all sound to you?"

Larry was slow to say anything because he was wrestling once again with the word *fun,* which kept showing up in one form or another. Earlier, when he was out, he'd even noticed a sign in the bookstore window announcing an upcoming event. The bold words at the top asked the question, "Looking for more fun this holiday season?" Larry realized that the advertisement may have been up for weeks, but he'd never read it until this morning.

I can only wonder if this is Nic's way of getting my attention until I agree to Elizabeth's request, he speculated. *It certainly feels like his style, as a contractor-builder, quite literally, hammering home a point!*

I'm beginning to believe that, and if so, I'm sure he won't leave me alone until I do give in. I might as well tell her yes right now so I can get on with my day without being badgered incessantly by him or the word fun.

So, in response, Larry said, "Your plans sound good. And I um, well, uh, regarding your offer to help with the cooking tomorrow, I guess it's alright. That is if you can arrive by 6 a.m. I start much earlier, though, in order to guarantee that all the deliveries are completed at a reasonable time for the families."

Mary Hayes

"Of course," Elizabeth agreed with great excitement. "I will ring your doorbell right at 6 a.m., holding a large coffee in my hand and wearing unusually flat shoes on my feet." Then, pausing momentarily, she added in a quieter tone, "Thank you, Larry, for letting me come over. I promise to do whatever I can to be helpful. And fortunately for you, with my inadequate culinary knowledge, you won't have to worry about me making so much as one suggestion regarding the seasoning or anything else for that sake!"

"I'm sure it will all be fine," Larry stated bluntly, not wanting to extend the conversation any longer than necessary. Then, after apprising Elizabeth of his plans to close the office early, he said goodbye and left the building. And although he felt encouraged by her enthusiasm and sincerity, Larry was still not convinced that they would actually have *any fun* tomorrow.

Chapter 45
Maddie

I'm excited to wander around the downtown area, Maddie thought as she walked back from Tink's house. *All the shops, restaurants, and that pretty park are just begging for exploration! But I'm glad I stopped by Tink's first. Her joyful response when I told her I'd be coming to Thanksgiving dinner was so pure. I can really tell that she didn't just invite me because she was worried I'd be alone for the holiday. It's clear that she genuinely wants me to be there. And what a great feeling to be wanted and to also have such a strong confirmation that my decision to attend tomorrow was the right one.*

Maddie gathered her small backpack and bottle of water before getting in her car to drive the short distance to downtown. As she drove, she continued to think about Tink.

I wouldn't feel right walking in without a small gift to show my appreciation, even though Tink was adamant that I shouldn't bring anything for the meal. Since I plan to do some shopping today anyway, I'll keep my eye out for a little something for her. Also, I hope to find a nice present for Stephen to thank him for taking care of "our cat" while I've been gone.

Soon, Maddie was parking the car and slowly strolling down Center Street. With no sense of rush, she gazed into all the windows and casually meandered in and out of several stores. She noticed many quaint touches, including the attractive, carved wooden signs hanging over the shops, which served to advertise the various businesses.

Before long, she wandered into the Beanstalk Bookstore and Cafe, which, according to a framed and faded newspaper article near the entrance, had been founded and run by the same family for over fifty years. Maddie quickly became ensconced within the tidy rows of tall shelves and, for almost an hour, remained happily immersed in the world of paper and printed words. She glanced through various regional cycling magazines and then spent the rest of her time looking at books written by Cape Cod authors with topics ranging from mysteries to romance novels, travel, history, and the area's intriguing local folklore.

Nevertheless, she did not find a compelling gift there for either Tink or Stephen. Nor did she make a purchase for herself, although the temptation was quite real since a particular journal stood out among the others. The cover of this book was unlike any she had chosen before. Typically, Maddie was drawn toward journals featuring floral artwork by botanists or impressionist painters such as Van Gogh or Renoir. Yet, this cover had a stunning watercolor rendering of a bright red male cardinal. The bird was perched on the limb of a lush green pine tree and appeared very present and aware rather than distant or aloof. Still, Maddie reasoned her current journal had just about enough pages to last the week, and, most likely, she had another one at home. Thus, this purchase, however tempting, was not made.

Maddie left the bookstore, walking past a hair salon and old-fashioned barber shop featuring a spinning red and white striped barber pole. She passed a few other shops before entering a clothing boutique offering stylish fall and winter wear. Connected to this store was the Cranberry Cove Gift Shop, showcasing a selection of decorative pillows, luxurious bath items, and a line of gifts that any nautical lover would be proud to own. This ocean-themed display was so attractive that Maddie imagined for a few moments what living near the sea might be like. Would she be happier if she were closer to the sand, the waves, and the salty sea winds? The idea alone filled her with immense joy as she recalled the first briny breeze that welcomed her on Monday when she arrived on Cape Cod. She allowed the memory of that sensation to envelop her again and, in doing so, felt immediately calmer. Recognizing that this sense of inner stillness was a sign of something beneficial, Maddie embraced it even more.

After leaving that shop, she walked next through the door of Robertson's Deli. Here, the mood was noticeably different. No one was ambling about, but instead, the customers were purposefully shopping, most likely to complete their Thanksgiving dinner menu. Additionally, Maddie noticed that regardless of how busy the shoppers and sales staff were, they remained polite and friendly with one another as they filled their bags and buggies. She also realized that this must be the place where Elizabeth purchased the delicious welcome dinner and the gourmet groceries. No wonder it was so crowded on this particular day.

Maddie's intention was just to look around since there was still an abundance of food at the house. Yet there, among the camembert, brioche, and bustling people, she noticed a small container featuring the whimsical face of an exceptionally satisfied cat.

Organic Cape Cod Catnip? Maddie mused. *I'm sure that would delight even the ficklest feline, including my own, finicky Miss Priss. I think I'll buy a tin for her. And why not? Stephen shouldn't be the only one who gets to spoil our beloved cat.*

Maddie looked around a little longer, then carried the tin toward the counter where, after two other sales were rung up, she was greeted by a friendly gentleman.

"Hello! Welcome to Robertson's Deli. Is this your first time in?"

"Yes, it is," Maddie responded, rather surprised and pleased. With so many customers in the store, how impressive that he recognized her as someone new. Perhaps, she thought, unlike the large city where she lived, this town was small enough that he knew all his regular clientele that well.

"I hope you've found everything you need," he stated respectfully.

"Yes, I think so," Maddie replied.

"Did you have any questions I could answer, or was there anything else you were specifically looking for? If so, I'd be glad to assist you."

Because his inquiry seemed so genuine, Maddie decided to ask about a gift for Tink. "Well, I was hoping to find a small hostess gift."

"I may be able to help you with that," he said, stepping out from behind the register. "I'm sure Neal and Suzette can manage the counter for a few minutes on their own. Why don't you tell me about the recipient? What do they like... cheese or wine, perhaps?"

"Actually, I'm not sure since I only met her recently. But I do know she loves to bake."

"Ahh," the man acknowledged thoughtfully. "We have many exceptional items she may enjoy using with her baking. Why don't you follow me?" he suggested as he began adeptly navigating his way through the maze of carts and customers. Then, pausing momentarily, he turned back to her, saying, "By the way, my name is Theo. I am one of the proprietors of Robertson's Deli."

"I'm glad to meet you, Theo. I'm Maddie. I've already tasted some of your food, and it's fantastic."

"I really appreciate your saying so. Our intention is to carry many fine, specialty items, as well as offer truly personalized service," he shared, continuing to walk.

Along the way, Theo pointed out a few clever baking gadgets and unique ingredients, such as crispy caramel bits and a rich mocha mousse sauce. But nothing seemed to catch her attention until he paused in front of an end-of-aisle display.

"Here's a tasty item that sells extremely well year-round and is definitely unique to the area. This is Beach Plum Jelly, and we're lucky to still have it in stock because it's very popular with both visitors and locals alike. What makes this special," he explained, "is the fact that the plums grow on bushes in the sand dunes around Cape Cod. I can assure you also, from personal experience," he admitted with a playful smile, "it is absolutely delicious!"

"Oh, yes, that sounds amazing," Maddie said enthusiastically, for she could easily picture Tink adding the jelly on top of a cookie or spreading it generously on a homemade biscuit. "I think that'll be perfect."

"Excellent. And, since you mentioned this is a present, I'll be glad to put it in one of our signature gift bags with tissue and a nice ribbon at no extra charge. Now, is there anything else I can assist you with?"

"No, I don't think so. But thanks for being so helpful," she replied as they walked back toward the counter.

Before long, Maddie was exiting the deli and feeling pleased with her two purchases. Determined to find one more, she happened to notice an Artist's Co-op close by.

What a beautiful gallery, Maddie thought upon entering. *Stephen loves art, so maybe I'll find something for him here.* She stood momentarily and simply appreciated the wide range of mediums on display. There was jewelry, pottery, weavings, and paintings in oil, watercolor, and acrylic. She then walked leisurely from the front of the gallery to the back, admiring all of the displays and the interesting textures, colors, and styles. Next, she browsed through a small rack of original watercolor paintings by a gifted local artist. Among the many impressive choices, Maddie found a masterful still-life of a ripe pear alongside a cream pitcher. Both were situated on a rustic, wooden table as soft light streamed in from an unseen window. And she decided this would be a wonderful thank-you present for Stephen. He had often commented on his preference for still-life artwork because, as he put it, who doesn't love a pear or peach?

Intrigued by this same artist's paintings, Maddie continued to glance leisurely through the rack. She stopped abruptly, however, and gasped upon seeing a painting like no other. Contrary to the previous softer renderings, this painting featured a dark, stormy seascape. In the center was a small sailboat heeling almost completely to one side as a lone sailor struggled to keep it upright amidst the perilous winds and water. Fear filled the sailor's face, and his fate seemed uncertain. The only hope that appeared was the sight of a faint, nearly angelic figure shrouded in a single ray of light breaking through the dark, ominous clouds.

Maddie could not comprehend why this image was so compelling and yet so incredibly upsetting at the same time. She felt drawn to it as if she were responsible for saving the sailor, which made no sense. Yet, the image shook her emotionally, and she desperately wanted to reach out to him with strength and even love.

Unnerved, Maddie returned the painting to the rack, purchased the gift for Stephen, and quickly went outside. The cold air and a faint breeze immediately helped to calm her back.

Still, why would that piece of art impact her so intensely? Maddie wondered. She'd never known anyone who was a sailor, let alone someone harmed at sea. Maddie decided to go across the street to the park in order to collect herself. Walking along a small path toward the center, she noted the various plants and flowers that graced the walkway. Soon, she sat down at a secluded bench and began to breathe consciously. She repeatedly inhaled very slowly, followed by long, deep restorative exhales. This cathartic exercise and the lovely setting served her well. And Maddie refrained from thinking any more about the troubled sailor in the disturbing seascape.

As peace was restored, Maddie decided that a good meal would be in order. She'd taken note earlier of the charming café adjoining the bookstore and decided to make her way back there. Although the temperature was chilly, she still requested seating in the garden area, just off the main sidewalk.

The hostess guided Maddie through a trellis covered with a beautiful honeysuckle vine to a private table and took her drink order. The chamomile tea came out almost immediately, and Maddie welcomed, warming her hands on the side of the cup as the tea bag steeped inside.

After reading through the menu, Maddie placed an order for a bowl of corn chowder and a side salad. The meal arrived shortly thereafter and was quite delicious. Maddie ate mindfully, enjoying every bite. Then, after finishing, she ordered a decaf cappuccino in lieu of dessert. And since she was in no hurry to go anywhere else, and the setting was soothingly serene, she allowed the feeling of relaxation to permeate through her even more. She closed her eyes, allowing her other senses to become more pronounced as the muffled voices along the sidewalk became less apparent. Instead, she focused on the splashing sound of the nearby fountain.

Soon, a soft, warm breeze began to lightly tickle her face, reminding Maddie of a recent dream. Only two nights earlier, she'd distinctly dreamed about sitting alone at an outdoor café sipping a cappuccino. As she did, a tender wind was softly brushing her cheek as an intriguing voice assured her that she was in loving company. Just as before, the scene repeated itself, and she felt him with her. His presence, accompanied by the wind, was undoubtedly the same presence becoming more familiar and endearing to her with each day.

But who is this that visits me in my dream and also in my awakened state? Maddie marveled. *What a paradox that this strong male presence feels so real and yet so ethereal at the same time. In some ways, he reminds me of others who have passed to the other side. Yet, he is much more alive to me and certainly more alluring. Whoever he is, and whatever this is, I just don't want it to stop.*

Maddie continued to keep her eyes closed and deliberately dismissed her curiosity. She wanted only to revel in his presence. So, when he kissed her delicately on the side of her face, she could do little but accept his tender touch. And next, without uttering a sound, he simply said, "Thank you, my love, for coming to the Cape. Thank you for finding me here."

Chills spread across Maddie's entire body as she murmured breathlessly.

How easily I can feel and hear him! Unlike the imaginings of a dream, I know this is real. I know he is real. And I love being so connected to him.

Then, Maddie heard her name being called softly at first and then again just slightly louder.

"Maddie… Maddie, am I interrupting you?"

But this was not his voice. No, this was a female's voice speaking out loud. Slowly but still quite transfixed, Maddie opened her eyes and saw Elizabeth Moreau standing in front of her.

Chapter 46
Elizabeth

Elizabeth stood patiently just inside the garden cafe, watching Maddie enjoy what appeared to be a sweet moment of bliss as she sat tucked in a little alcove. As an excellent observer of life - situations, settings, and people—she had honed her ability to be keenly aware of everything around her. And, by methodically adhering to this practice, Elizabeth knew she would be best prepared for whatever needed to be done or not done, spoken or not spoken. This skill alone had kept her mind sharp and her innate instincts intact.

Having quietly called Maddie's name twice, Elizabeth now waited and watched for her response. This astute woman knew better than to prod, push, or even pronounce her presence in some obtrusive way. Yet, in that brief time, she was able to surmise that Maddie had most likely dined alone, seeing as there was only one water glass and one place setting at the table. And apparently, shopping had also been part of this visitor's day, as evidenced by the multiple bags on the chair beside her. And considering the besotted expression on Maddie's face, Elizabeth guessed that she might be in the midst of a romantic reverie. For why else would she completely ignore the cooling cappuccino in front of her?

While she stood waiting, Elizabeth recalled when she'd first become aware of her heightened senses. From early childhood on, she could strongly sense and even merge with the very essence and beauty of the natural world around her. Conversely, she could also feel the tension of the adults around her, including the unspoken problems that wouldn't be discussed with someone so young. Nonetheless, this caused her to feel anxious, powerless, and unsafe.

As she got a little older, Elizabeth would often secretly watch through the slates in the kitchen door as her parents discussed difficult situations, most notably their financial troubles. Although she was not old enough to help, she became acutely aware of her capacity for empathy and the intense desire to make a real difference.

Elizabeth could also remember witnessing her grandfather's rapid physical decline, even as his vibrant spirit tried to hide the seriousness of his condition. He adored her so much and went to great lengths not to disappoint her in any way. Elizabeth missed very little, and since she was aware of his deteriorating condition, she found simple ways to help support him without addressing what everyone else refused to discuss with her. Due to his growing weakness, she would often run ahead of him and open the door, pretending it was all a game—her becoming the dutiful servant to the mighty king. And when his failing fingers dropped little things, Elizabeth would act like a joyful yet helpful bird and fly them back to him, all the while tweeting a sweet song.

Although those times were bittersweet, Elizabeth reflected, *I am still grateful for my varied childhood experiences, which afforded me the opportunity to express compassion and strive to better understand what I knew to be true below the surface of the obvious. And those exceptional skills have helped me become a better family member, a loyal friend, and even a successful businesswoman.*

Elizabeth's thoughts, however, were interrupted as Maddie began to stir. Registering the fact that her name had been called, she slowly opened her eyes and offered a whispered hello.

"Hello," Elizabeth replied in kind, keeping her voice soft. "I apologize for interrupting, especially when you seem to be in such a dreamy state. But I didn't want to miss a chance to say hi, either."

"I'm glad you did," Maddie offered sincerely, trying to orient herself.

"I also wanted to make sure that everything is going well at the house. Do you have a few minutes to chat?"

"I sure do," Maddie replied with a smile while lightly shaking her head in an attempt to become more present.

"Great! May I join you at the table?" Elizabeth asked. "It looks like you're here alone."

"Yes, have a seat," Maddie suggested, pointing toward the empty chair across from her. Yet, she had no intention to explain to Elizabeth that she had not, in truth, been entirely alone.

"Thank you," Elizabeth said gratefully, pulling the chair out to be seated. "I've literally been running around all morning, and these aren't exactly what you'd call running shoes," she quipped, quickly removing her high heels. "I've got to rest these feet, if only for a moment. And, if you're not in a hurry, I'd love to order a cup of coffee and hear how your stay in Port Saint Smith has been so far."

"I'm not in a hurry at all," Maddie stated. "So, go ahead and order, and I'll just sip on my cappuccino."

"That sounds perfect," Elizabeth agreed as she adeptly waved a server over. She then ordered a cup of black coffee and asked Maddie if she would like anything else. "Can I treat you to dessert, perhaps?" Elizabeth inquired.

"No, thank you. I'm perfectly content with this," Maddie responded.

"Alright. That'll be all," she informed the server, "thank you."

As soon as they were alone, Elizabeth turned her attention back to Maddie, saying, "You may have noticed that I am a fairly direct woman, and I always strive to be honest. As far as I'm concerned, it's the only way to be. So, that being said," she continued, "I promise, you don't have to say a single word. But, if I were to guess, I'd say that you were thinking about someone extra special when you first walked up. Am I correct? I'm curious because you had the most extraordinary expression on your face. In fact, you still have an amazing glow around you."

"Really?" Maddie asked in amazement.

"Oh yes, it's quite remarkable - almost like there is a presence surrounding you in addition to a radiance emanating from you."

"I'm amazed that you see that," Maddie managed to say.

"I am also. That's really a first for me! Yet, it's so beautiful to be able to see the essence of both of these merging." Before Maddie could comment, however, Elizabeth continued, "I understand, though, if you wish to keep your thoughts and experiences entirely to yourself."

Maddie was not sure what, if anything, to say. Still feeling the tingle of his kiss on her cheek, she was astonished that Elizabeth could see and validate this experience - his very presence surrounding and then

252

blending with hers. Unable to begin to find any words and even a clear explanation, Maddie decided to say nothing. She merely offered a weak smile and a slight shrug of the shoulders, suggesting, "I don't exactly know what to say."

"Well, good for you!" Elizabeth exclaimed with sincere admiration. "I appreciate anyone who can hold their own counsel and not feel obligated to speak simply because someone has asked them to. But if you ever do want to share a confidence with me, I assure you that I am both a compassionate listener and one who regards a private conversation as just that—private and not to be shared with others."

"Thank you, Elizabeth," Maddie replied with relief and the reassurance that if, at some point, she wanted to share, their conversation would remain confidential.

"But tell me this," Elizabeth asserted, clearly redirecting the conversation, "how is everything going at the house? And I'd also love to know about those intriguing shopping bags - unless that's a secret, too," she added playfully.

"There's no secret there," Maddie replied with a little laugh. "As for the house, I don't think I could be more content or comfortable anywhere else. It suits me beyond belief! And you thought of everything - soy-scented candles, luxurious bath items, the plush, cotton bathrobe, etcetera. Oh, and I took the bike out yesterday and had a wonderful time riding it!"

"Excellent! I'm so pleased to hear how happy you are there."

"Yes, I really am. And thank you again for all you've done for me.

"You're very welcome, Maddie. And what about those shopping bags...? I see you've been to Robertson's Deli and, just like me, couldn't leave empty-handed. My purchases, however, usually require a large buggy and wouldn't possibly fit inside a few small bags."

"Believe me, I could have easily bought more. But I'm very pleased with the two things I did buy, which are both gifts. The first one is actually for my cat. I feel a little guilty leaving her behind, even though she's being spoiled beyond words by my good friend, Stephen. So, when I saw the can of organic Cape Cod catnip, I knew she would love it!"

"Oh, what a lucky cat," Elizabeth commented.

"She's definitely not lacking for attention, treats, or affection," Maddie stated. "And fortunately, I had expert help with the second gift. The co-owner, Theo, was kind enough to walk me around the store and made several good suggestions, which was so good of him considering how busy they were."

"That's our Theo! He is always exceptionally helpful, and so is his partner Neil and their adorable store manager, Suzette. For years, they've all guided me wisely and have also created stunning gift baskets for many of my new homeowners. Honestly, I don't know what I would do without them."

"I can see why," Maddie stated. "He didn't hesitate to help me find a great hostess gift, which is for Tink Kendleton, by the way. She's invited me to Thanksgiving dinner tomorrow, and I wanted to bring a little something to show my appreciation."

"And let me guess," Elizabeth declared boldly, "she emphatically insisted you don't bring any food, am I right?"

"You're exactly right!" Maddie concurred.

"Well, you've got to admire that wonderful woman! She knows what she wants and isn't shy about saying so," Elizabeth professed.

"I really do admire her," Maddie admitted, "and I also like her very much - just like you said I would! And you were right about her baking, too! She's already given me a plate of incredibly delicious cookies and a pot pie that's probably the best I've ever had. So, between your generosity and hers, I think I'm more spoiled than my cat!"

"As it should be!" Elizabeth exclaimed. "What's the point of a vacation if it doesn't include carefree days, outings and adventures, extra napping, plenty of shopping, indulging in decadent foods, and," she added with a wee wink, "perhaps, even a little romance, too?"

"Exactly," Maddie agreed, smiling.

Then, for the next few moments, both women sat quietly, enjoying their coffees and the pleasant space between them.

Eventually, Elizabeth said, "You will most likely see me again tomorrow. Tink has invited me to dinner, as well. She insisted that I come by, even though I may arrive later in the day. Larry, the owner of our company, and I are delivering Thanksgiving baskets to several families, and I don't know how long that will take. But Tink assured me I can arrive at any time."

"I'm glad to know you'll be there. I've been a little worried about not knowing anyone else there, besides Tink," Maddie confessed.

"Not to worry. You'll know me, as well as our delightful hostess. And you met Shirley Lund at the Chamber of Commerce, and she'll be there also. I'm sure you'll feel comfortable with whomever else will be in attendance. Almost everyone from this endearing town goes out of their way to be welcoming. They certainly did when I moved here from New York. I felt more embraced by the good folks of Port Saint Smith than maybe anywhere else I've traveled on Earth."

"What a great feeling that must have been," Maddie commented appreciatively.

"It certainly was. And I imagine you will feel the same tomorrow. What's interesting, too, is that in all the years I've lived here," Elizabeth continued, "this will be the first time I've been at Tink's for Thanksgiving. She's invited me several times to her famed feast, but I've always been away during this holiday week. Since work is typically slower during the holidays, I take the opportunity to travel, which I adore! I usually visit good friends in New York or Sedona. And every few years, I'm fortunate to stay with my lifelong friends in Paris and Italy. If I had a sweetheart, which I currently don't, I'm sure we would be traveling together. But this week, I'm very glad to be in town, especially now that I'm involved with such a rewarding project - the S.O.S. Basket Benefit - which is precisely what had me on the run this morning. I'm loving every minute of it, though! I've been wanting a purpose beyond my everyday life, and I think I just may have found it."

"Good for you! Do you want to tell me a little more about it?"

"Certainly. Have you heard about the S.O.S. Foundation yet?" Elizabeth asked.

"No, I haven't," Maddie replied.

"Well, S.O.S. stands for Spirit of Sailing, which is a local foundation that provides sailing lessons for underprivileged youth. For the past several years, these lessons have been held, free of charge, at summer camps in Port Saint Smith's busy little port. The success of these camps has been beyond our imagination and has even brought our community that much closer together.

"This last summer, I began helping with the camps for the first time. In fact, I worked in partnership with Tink, which proved to be a joy-filled experience! And only this week did I step in to help with the basket program.

"Each year," Elizabeth explained, "Thanksgiving meals are delivered to several of the S.O.S. families in need. And I've been coordinating much of the efforts with the merchants by gathering donations and scheduling the deliveries with the families. Tonight, I will begin assembling the large baskets, and tomorrow, Larry and I will make those deliveries."

"You're obviously putting in a lot of time and effort," Maddie acknowledged. "And I'm sure it feels rewarding to be helping with such a worthy cause."

"Yes, it does! And I'm thrilled about how well everything is going! But most importantly, I'm looking forward to seeing the families and the young sailors tomorrow. To my own surprise," Elizabeth admitted vulnerably, "I've missed them very much."

"I imagine you have. Those kinds of endeavors can be life-changing," Maddie stated.

"They really can be," Elizabeth replied reflectively, specifically remembering the valued friendship she and Trevor had established. "Truthfully, though, I feel so honored to be a part of this. And what's even more encouraging is a new idea I'm working on that would greatly benefit the Foundation, as well as safeguard a most important landmark in this area. But I'm not at liberty just now to say anymore," she added, holding her index finger up in front of her lips. "Once I am, however, I assure you that everyone within a hundred-mile radius, if not more, will know all about it! And hopefully, they'll become as excited and committed as I intend to be."

"Wouldn't that be wonderful? I've done quite a bit of volunteering myself and have always found it to be so fulfilling and gratifying. I've also seen firsthand that even if the needs of an organization seem to be insurmountable, the commitment of a dedicated group can achieve almost anything."

"You're absolutely right, Maddie! I've witnessed just this past summer how willingly the citizens of this town rallied when a real need arose. And I have reason to believe they will do so again. Plus, I'm personally ready for the challenge and beyond thrilled about the possibilities," Elizabeth shared with contagious conviction.

"I'm very happy for you," Maddie extolled. "And maybe you could email me the updates when you're ready to make the announcement. Since I already have such an affinity for this town, I would love to stay informed."

"I'd be happy to keep you updated," Elizabeth responded. "But I'm also warning you - I may find a way to get you involved! Or, I may just need an objective listener to offer support and possibly insights."

"I would be glad to help in either way," Maddie assured her.

"Well, thank you, kindly," Elizabeth gratefully responded. "Before I get ahead of myself, however, and overly focused on the new project, this current benefit still needs plenty of attention. So, I'd better get back to the office before our beloved baker, Tink, arrives with her homemade pies. With any luck," Elizabeth added playfully, "she'll bring an extra one for sampling's sake. But, first, I may have just enough time to pop back into Robertson's Deli. You've inspired me to buy Larry a gift for tomorrow morning. I more or less invited myself over to assist him with the cooking, and he agreed, but not without great reservation. Larry's quite an accomplished amateur chef and, undoubtedly, the king of his kitchen. And I think he realizes that this damsel is more often in distress than feeling self-assured when it comes to pots, pans, and poultry! Yet, maybe he'll lower his emotional drawbridge a tad sooner if I arrive with a gourmet gift in hand."

"That sounds like a perfect idea," Maddie commented.

"Thanks! So, I better get to it," Elizabeth announced as she stood to leave. "And thank you again for letting me join you and even interrupt that blissful state of being you were in earlier. You almost looked as if a wistful wind had entranced you," she declared dramatically. "*Au revoir, mademoiselle, á demain*—I'll see you tomorrow."

"Thank you, Elizabeth. I look forward to seeing you tomorrow also and wish you the best of luck with the baskets."

"Thank you so much! Bye for now."

"Bye-bye," Maddie replied.

As she walked in the direction of the deli, Elizabeth concluded, Again, *I cannot help but thinking how much I like Maddie! My gut sense tells me that she's exactly who she appears to be - a caring, compassionate, and conscientious woman. I wonder if she'll ever return to Port Saint Smith? If she did, I could tell her more about my idea for the Foundation, as well as the hidden history of* Beauté Par la Mer. *I would love to share that with her in person. Maybe she'd even be interested in attending the holiday performance at the theater. I'll have to mention that to her before she leaves.*

Just moments later, Elizabeth swung open the door at Robertson's Deli and sought the attention of her good friend and shop proprietor, Theo.

Chapter 47
Stephen

"Oh, thank goodness you answered. I have so much to tell you! I have news, Maddie. *Big* news! But, tell me about you first."

Before Maddie had a chance to reply, however, Stephen continued.

"Is my favorite vagabond having fun on that fancy piece of land protruding into the Atlantic Ocean? And are there any amorous winds wrapping around you? Or are you being bowled over by blustery nor'easters?"

Maddie knew her good friend well enough to recognize he was in an exceptionally good mood. So, rather than chat on about herself, she replied briefly and quickly deferred back to him.

"I'm doing great," Maddie responded. "I just got back to the house from an enjoyable day of shopping and eating in town. The wind has been exceptionally friendly. And although I have good news to share with you also, I'd love to hear yours first!"

"Well, all right, if you insist! But would you like to try to guess why I'm so giddy?"

"Um... ok. Let me think for a moment... so... my guess... you went out for an afternoon stroll with Miss Priss, who was perfectly perched in her prestigious pet pram. Then, all of a sudden, you were surrounded by a film crew asking if they could feature both of you in their upcoming documentary about life in the city. Am I right?"

"No! But, I like your idea, and maybe that'll happen the next time we're out parading through the park. But you were partially right because this does involve Miss Priss and an important outing we went on. Shall I tell you more?"

"Absolutely!" Maddie replied emphatically. "I demand an explanation for all this unprecedented giddiness!"

"I'll surrender, therefore, to your demands. Because I'm just about to burst with excitement if I don't tell you immediately." And without a moment's hesitation, Stephen began to recount what happened the day before. "Well," he said with an evident air of drama, "I couldn't find my sunglasses anywhere, and I looked in every possible place in this apartment. So, guessing I'd inadvertently left them at the coffee shop and hoping they were still there, Miss Priss and I bundled back up and returned to find out. However, when we got there, I was stunned by how busy the shop was. I had no idea how many people drank coffee in the afternoon since I always go in the morning. The line was so long, and the place was unfathomably crowded! But I wasn't about to leave Her Highness outside on the sidewalk. And I can assure you, what I did next was not a popular move! Amidst the crowd of caffeine-craved customers, I pushed the pram right inside. I was at least careful not to bang into anyone. And oh, Maddie… there he was… this gorgeous guy standing in line just in front of us. I'd never seen him before and, believe me, I would have remembered! We're talking magazine-cover handsome. But wait, Maddie, let me ask you something first. Do you even have time to hear all of this? I'm babbling on, and my tale has just begun."

"Are you kidding? Of course I do! What matters to you matters to me—that's our pact. Plus, I'm on vacation, so go right ahead and tell me the full version of the story."

"Okay, excellent. Thanks! Let me try to catch my breath first since I haven't been this ecstatic in a very long time. Alright," Stephen continued in a breathy voice, "there we were in line, Miss Priss and I, waiting ever so conspicuously. And I think he must have sensed how uncomfortable I felt, which is probably why he started speaking to me. Can he believe it? He turned around and said, 'Hi! Your cat is beautiful!' Of course, he immediately noticed Miss Priss's outstanding good looks. But, I was so gobsmacked by him that when he paid her a compliment, I completely failed to mention the fact that she was your cat and not mine. I may have even taken all the credit. Forgive me, Maddie - I hope you're not mad at me."

"Ha! Not at all!" Maddie replied, laughing as she could easily imagine just how brilliantly baffled Stephen must have been.

"Thanks. You're the best of friends. Now, let me proceed. While we were waiting, I told him why I was there. He was so kind and kept chatting with me until the time came for him to place his order. Once Rafael ordered—oh, that's his name, by the way. Isn't it dreamy?" Stephen quipped without waiting for her response. "After he ordered, Rafael stepped aside from the counter, waiting to see if my sunglasses were there. That was so sweet of him, wasn't it?"

"Yes, it really was," Maddie replied.

"Well, I have more good news because the great folks at the coffee shop were holding my sunglasses in the office. What a relief! Then, the next thing I know, this wonderful man and I, and of course, Miss Priss, too, were sitting side-by-side at one of those tiny, little bistro tables out front. While he drank his coffee, we talked with such ease that you'd think we'd known each other for years and not just for a few minutes, randomly standing in line at a coffee shop. Being with him felt so natural and enjoy-able. He's funny, interesting, engaging, and, oh, did I mention gorgeous?"

"You just may have mentioned that already, but not to worry," Maddie said, laughing again.

"Well, facts are facts. Anyway," Stephen continued enthusiastically, "we were together for almost an hour before I realized the time. I needed to get back home to serve her majesty dinner, and he needed to go back to work. Rafael is a set designer, by the way, and apparently, a very successful one. He owns his own company, and, along with his team, they're putting up holiday displays all over the city—in banks, corporations, and at a few high-end hotels."

"That's impressive," Maddie offered.

"I thought so, too, especially since he's obviously talented with visuals and also appreciates artwork, like I do! And you'll never guess what happened next. As we stood up to leave, Rafael said, 'I hope we run into each other again.' And I believe he really meant it. So, I responded with, 'I hope so too'.

"But Maddie, you know, when matters of the heart are involved, I can be surprisingly shy. So, I have no idea where my next words came from because I actually said, 'Why don't we meet here again tomorrow?' How brazen was that?! And he said, ' Let's do it,' which is even more amazing!"

"Stephen, that is amazing! I'm so happy for you! And I'm inclined to remind you that I'm the one who's been telling you to get out and about more often. See what can happen when you do?" she teased him.

"Okayyyy, maybe I'll admit you were right. But then again, maybe I won't, even if you were. But now, let me get to the very, very best part. So, silly me, I could barely sleep last night, and then I spent the better part of the morning trying to figure out what to wear. Finally, the time came for us to meet again. And I'm telling you, we had just as much fun as we did yesterday. We sat and talked effortlessly while Miss Priss received twice the attention.

"Also, at some point in the conversation, I did finally own up to the fact that I was pet-sitting for you, my neighbor and good friend, while you were on holiday at the Cape. He then directly asked me if you and I were more than just friends. Somehow, I managed to stammer out an awkward explanation, saying that you were a girl but certainly not a girlfriend. And that I wasn't the kind of guy who has girlfriends. Fortunately, he not only understood, but he gave me the flirtiest, little knowing wink in response."

"Well, how about that?" Maddie exclaimed.

"How about that?!!" Stephen concurred. "I also said that since you were away, I had no plans for Thanksgiving. I shared with him that my mother had died a few years ago and that you, my best friend, had abandoned me to find adventure and perhaps, even romance on Cape Cod. But, Maddie, I don't blame you one little bit for running off like that. In fact, I'm very proud of you for actually throwing caution to the wind! Or maybe it's the other way around, and it is the wind bringing you a more carefree life. Or both! But, either way, I'll be without your good company this holiday. So, Mr. Handsome must have taken pity on me because can you imagine what he said next?"

"Sure. I think he suggested you spend Thanksgiving Day all alone with that spoiled cat, watching old black-and-white movies and eating take-out food. Am I right?" she jested with a giggle.

"No, you are not right," Stephen sighed in mock exasperation. "He asked me if I would like to spend the day with him."

"He did? Really? How exciting!" Maddie replied in delight.

"Yes, it was very exciting. Except, I said no."

"You did not!" Maddie insisted. "Don't even joke with me about this."

"I'm not joking," Stephen admitted. "I did tell him no, and then I had the nerve to blame it on your cat! I was thrilled, of course, that he asked, but I was just too nervous to say yes. It's been such a long time, Maddie, that I was afraid to mess it all up."

"Oh, Stephen, you wouldn't mess it up! You're a great guy," Maddie said encouragingly.

"Thanks for saying so. And, lucky for me, Rafael must have felt the same way. And he was also perceptive enough to realize that I was making excuses. I think he knew I wanted to say yes. So, he persisted without being too pushy, and at least I wasn't foolish enough to refuse his invitation the second time."

"Well, that's a relief!" Maddie declared. "You had me worried there for a minute."

"I know; I was worried, too! But he really seems like an understanding guy. Plus, he told me that his Thanksgivings are usually very uneventful, as well. His demanding work schedule leading up to the holidays is so intense that Thursday is his only day of rest. But he told me, with the sweetest smile, that he would gladly make an exception from resting this year."

"Yeah, for you, Stephen! And yeah, for him! I'm so happy about your good news."

"Thanks, Maddie. I knew you would be."

"Have the two of you made special plans?"

"Yes, we're just doing something simple, which is fine with me. He asked me to come over in the afternoon and he'll cook dinner for us. Now, as you might imagine, I'm a nervous wreck! Should I bring flowers or a potted plant? Is that too much? Is that too soon? Or should I bring a bottle of wine—even though I don't drink the stuff? And if so, white or red? And what should I wear—casual but not too casual? Is it any wonder that I initially said no? Just making these simple decisions is almost too much for me to handle."

"You underestimate yourself, Stephen. Trust your first instinct to guide you wisely."

"You're right, as always," he sighed in response. "And you must forgive me because I can't talk much longer. He's supposed to call soon to discuss the menu. He wants to know my preferences and if I have any food sensitivities before he goes to the grocery store tonight. But, not to worry, I still want to hear your good news. Can you just tell me the shorter version today? Then, I promise to listen to every little detail the next time we speak. Is that all right?"

"Of course, I understand."

"Thanks, Maddie! Oh, and I do want to say one more thing before you speak. Please don't worry about Miss Priss. You have my word that I will not leave her alone very long. And I will also give her a few extra Thanksgiving treats upon my return."

"I'm sure she'll be fine. I'm not worried at all. I just want you to have a great time."

"I'll make sure of it. Now tell me about you…"

"Well, everything here has been amazing, and everyone has been exceptionally kind. The house where I am staying is beyond beautiful. I know I told you that already, but I swear, it's as if it had been designed specifically for me. I even received a lovely welcome note from the owner. But, Stephen, it was written in the oddest penmanship. Maybe he's in poor health, which might explain why he doesn't live in this two-story house anymore. Because I was told that, at one time, he was a top athlete—an award-winning cyclist and avid sailor. So, I don't know what's become of him. But we can chat about all that later. I'm just certain I'm meant to be right here. And I have, quite honestly, received a cornucopia of blessings, along with a wonderful invitation to a homemade Thanksgiving dinner."

"You have?" Stephen queried, "Is your host good-looking too?"

"No, but she is rather cute and spry for a woman in her eighties. Do you remember my mentioning the elderly woman who lives next door?"

"You mean the wicked woman who was peering out the window when you arrived in your fairytale town?"

"Yes, but, on the contrary, she is anything but wicked. She's kind and generous and even an award-winning baker. And she has invited me to join her and a few of her friends for dinner tomorrow."

"That sounds really nice," Stephen stated. "And I'm relieved I don't have to worry anymore about you eating all by your lonesome. And I can actually hear in your voice how serene you are. Had we known how happy this would make both of us, Miss Priss and I might have shipped you off sooner!"

"I'm sure you would have," she agreed, laughing. "But I do miss you and 'our cat,' and I bought you both presents yesterday."

"Did you? But only one each? Just kidding! You didn't need to buy me anything. But, of course, I'm thrilled you did! Are you going to tell me what it is or at least give me a hint?"

"Nope, I'm certainly not. It's a surprise. You'll just have to wait until I get home."

"You're so thoughtful, Maddie. Oh my, that's Rafael calling me now. I need to hang up. Please forgive me. I don't want to keep him waiting. But, just know how happy I am that we both have such nice plans for Thanksgiving. For this and our good friendship, I'm very grateful. Happy Thanksgiving, Maddie!"

"Happy Thanksgiving, Stephen. Have a great time tomorrow."

"You too, Maddie. Love you big!"

"Love you bigger."

Maddie heard the click of Stephen signing off and then placed the phone on the kitchen table. Sipping slowly on her tea, she reflected further. *I definitely want to tell Stephen about sensing someone else so strongly at the café and also here in this house. But I'm not ready yet. I want to more fully feel all that this is and better understand what he means to me before sharing it with anyone else.*

At that very moment, Maddie noticed a cluster of autumn leaves swirling and dancing just outside the window. *I'm not sure who you are,* she said softly towards the wind. *But I welcome you now more than ever.*

Chapter 48
Maddie

The soothing night sounds blended with the soft creak of the swing, lulling Maddie into an even deeper state of relaxation. Her late afternoon and early evening had been spent enjoying simple activities after the earlier excursion into downtown. A brief but animated conversation with Stephen had been delightful. Writing in her journal resulted in the creation of a short, reflective poem. This was followed by a satisfying, light supper and warm bath.

A wave of immense gratitude washed over Maddie again on this eve of Thanksgiving as she slowed the movement on the swing. She opened her journal to reread the words written a few hours earlier.

The wind's beckoning, I heeded
and thus, came to this place
where I'm filled with wonder,
joy, gratitude, and grace.
The people here are kind
Like friends already to me.
Yet, I sense another strongly
Whom I cannot see.
Alluring and endearing,
his presence is quite real.
But, who is this I welcome?
Who is this I feel?

The poem spoke to the mystery that Maddie could not yet comprehend. Setting the book aside, she began rhythmically swaying back and forth once more, all the while pondering the fact that less than a week earlier, the idea of canceling the trip had been very real. Her main concern had been about feeling isolated and alone during a holiday week. By contrast, though, a rich sense of appreciation and even awe had filled every day since arriving in town. She was truly pleased with what had happened already and excited for what lay ahead in the remaining days on Cape Cod.

Likewise, Maddie was feeling optimistic about attending Tink's Thanksgiving celebration due to the overwhelming enthusiasm of the neighbor coupled with the fact that Elizabeth would also be in attendance. And although this relatively private visitor to Port Saint Smith was still a bit nervous, she remained hopeful about fitting in, savoring a delicious meal, and having a memorably good time.

With that in mind, Maddie looked over towards Tink's home - the setting for tomorrow's festivities. She saw the neighbor standing in the kitchen window, gazing up toward the night sky. Tink was blowing kisses in the direction of the stars and wiping small tears from her eyes. With her shoulders more stooped than usual, Tink turned away from the window, and soon the kitchen went dark.

What a tender moment to witness, Maddie thought. *I doubt Tink was simply wishing upon a star. Maybe she was sending blessings and her love to those she's lost on the other side.*

She and I may both seem to be alone, Maddie continued to reflect, *but, in truth, we really aren't. I'm sure we both have loved ones who have passed, still checking in on us from time to time. Yet, I wonder if Tink believes this, too. And I'm curious to know if she senses their presence or notices the signs of reassurance they are sending? I know how comforting those experiences are to me. And, as much as I'd love to discuss this with her, I don't foresee asking Tink these sensitive questions, at least not tomorrow.*

My own beliefs have certainly been stretched by this amazing presence so often with me. I'm enthralled and fascinated by him. Yet, I don't recognize him, nor do I have a memory of anyone like him. Is he someone I've met before and can't remember? Or is he seeking me out without having ever met me before in this life? I just can't help but wonder, who is he to me?

As Maddie contemplated all of this, a strong breeze kicked up behind her, pushing the porch swing forward. Yet, the wind was not evident anywhere else. For the leaves on the trees were still, and the chimes in Tink's garden hung silent.

Maddie was startled but not afraid, intrigued but not intimidated. For when the wind came close to her but nowhere else, she knew he was also present. Yet, there was no reason to turn around because she understood now that he would not be seen standing behind her.

Then a scene from earlier in the day flashed back to Maddie, as it had two other times just before. So, she decided to focus on that image and further consider its importance and significance.

The scene Maddie recalled had happened upon her return to the house in the afternoon. She'd stood in the driveway for a couple of minutes, admiring the family across the street. The doorway of their home was decorated with a festive fall wreath, while a friendly scarecrow stood flanked by two tall stalks of dried wheat leaning against a bundle of hay. The family of four was playing fetch with their dog in the front yard. Maddie watched as the parents joyfully engaged and encouraged their two young children. Shrill shouts of delight could be heard as the golden retriever, apparently named Bailey, ran back and forth in search of balls thrown in various directions. And though no audible words of hello were exchanged, the entire family smiled and waved at Maddie, who, in return, smiled and waved back.

Even after watching such an endearing sight, though, Maddie had no doubts or misgivings about one of the most important decisions she'd ever made regarding her life. For, at no point in the past had she ever yearned for a traditional family or even children of her own. Yet, having a meaningful love was still her only unfulfilled desire. Thus, sitting on a swing on a cold night in Cape Cod, she realized, at the deepest level, that even that desire need not come in a conventional way.

I am always glad to share in other people's joys—proud moments at graduation, engagements, wedding celebrations, the birth of a new baby, and so on. And rarely have I ever been envious of another's attainments or accomplishments. But, I do desire to be understood, held reassuringly, and loved beyond words.

Just then, the wind behind her began to encircle her completely. She felt and welcomed this understanding embrace, which seemed to answer the very calling of heart. Then, the cool air became still once again, and the swing stopped moving. Without the creaking sound of the metal chains, Maddie could hear more clearly the distinct serenade of night sounds—a choir of chirping crickets, countless frogs croaking, and a lone owl hooting in a nearby tree. The harmony of it all filled her with a serenity that the city had never provided. And Maddie realized that a simple life like this could be a very good one.

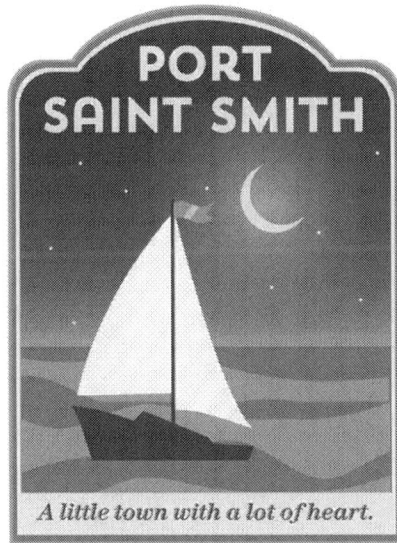

PORT SAINT SMITH

A little town with a lot of heart.

THURSDAY, NOVEMBER 24

Chapter 49
Tink

"Glory be! Today is Thanksgiving Day!" Tink exclaimed aloud, sitting slowly up in bed. Her muscles were stiffer than usual, no doubt from the extra efforts put forth for the various holiday preparations. But that did not deter the elder from planting her feet immediately on the floor. Then, in an attempt to touch her toes, she inhaled, bent forward, and exhaled a boisterous laugh since her hands went no further than her knees.

I'd better stick with cooking and baking, the octogenarian chuckled, *rather than attempting any real efforts at athleticism. Fortunately, my active life helps me stay in pretty good shape. I'm also aware of something else most fortunate - the fact that on this particular morning, I am genuinely thankful to be thankful. I was very afraid,* Tink acknowledged, *that I'd be too melancholy to even think about Thanksgiving, let alone celebrate it. I've been very blessed in my lifetime to enjoy many wonderful gatherings with family and friends. But during the past several years, Nic's presence has made the celebrations in my home that much more meaningful. Without him, I couldn't imagine feeling any joy for the holidays.*

Mercifully, two unexpected surprises have occurred this week - the auspicious arrivals of both the brilliant red cardinal and the sweet visitor next door. The cardinal serves as a significant reminder of Nic's continued love. And dear Maddie, a fine young woman, feels far from the

271

typical Cape Cod tourist. She seems genuinely interested in our history, culture, authentic local fare, and getting to know a few of us quirky townsfolk, which alone speaks to her bravery and good taste!

Just then, the heavy chime of the grandfather clock brought Tink back into the present moment. *Oh my!* she muttered; *this is no time for mental meanderings. The dinner guests will be arriving in a matter of hours, and I still have a considerable amount of work to do. If I don't get a move on, the only things we'll have to eat for this proclaimed feast will be bread, muffins, apple butter, and various pies. Of course, that wouldn't be such a bad menu, would it?*

Tink immediately began scurrying around - freshening up and putting on a cooking frock. En route to the kitchen, though, she stopped briefly in the parlor to open the drapes and officially welcome the day. With happy anticipation, she tugged on the thick cords and delighted in seeing a bright, clear morning. She even rapped on the window, waving hello to her neighbor Adam, who was jogging by with Bailey, faithfully scampering at his side.

Next, Tink marched straight into the kitchen with noted enthusiasm and tied on her favorite apron. While doing so, she peered out the window in hopes of seeing her red-winged friend. But with no sight or sound of him, she settled on appreciating the beautiful cardinal gift that Elizabeth had given her.

Allowing for no other distractions, Tink made a detailed list prioritizing what remained to be done. Prepping the main course, a local, organic, farm-fresh turkey, was on top of the list, followed by making the ginger pumpkin soup, which had become an annual favorite. Four side dishes and a relish tray rounded out the menu, and Tink was determined to accomplish everything in a timely manner.

A joy-filled laugh accompanied the thought of this final intention as Tink recalled her fastidious mother often saying,

"One should never approach cooking
in a higgedly-piggedly way,
or you may stumble throughout
and oft times lose your way.
Order and tidiness need be your friend.
Then a successful outcome
will undoubtedly be yours in the end."

The memory of this little rhyme made her smile all the more as Tink welcomed every happy memory after so many sorrowful weeks and months.

"First things first, however," she declared, opening the large appliance, still referred to in her home as the ice box. *I'll need all my strength and stamina to accomplish this ambitious list, so I'd better begin with a proper breakfast.* After surveying her choices, she retrieved two fresh figs, a cup of yogurt, butter, and creamer. She then started up the ancient percolating coffee pot, and as it began to gurgle, a pumpkin muffin was placed in the toaster oven to warm.

Tink was soon sitting at the kitchen table enjoying a delicious meal. Nic's journal lay close by, and she struggled again to resist the urge to simply read a page or two. *I cannot allow myself the time to look at that now*, she affirmed, stuffing a warm piece of muffin in her mouth. *I honor the life of my dear friend, especially on this day. But I have too much to do to risk being waylaid by regret or grief.*

So, Tink turned her focus back to the stained-glass cardinal, all the while nibbling on this morsel and that. With fervent determination, she finished her breakfast, pushed away from the table, and walked over to the sink. She searched again out the window for the cardinal, hoping he would help give her even more strength. But when he didn't appear, Tink's willpower suddenly collapsed. She grabbed the rooster timer and sat back down at the kitchen table.

I don't think reading a few little words will hurt, she reasoned. *But I know myself well enough that if I do get sidetracked, the old rooster will cluck loud enough to help return my attention to my responsibilities. Because the last thing I need on Thanksgiving Day is a flood of tragic tears.*

Tink set the timer for ten minutes and then randomly opened to the page on which Nic had described the angel he saw in the sailing dream shortly before his death.

The lovely figure floated just above the waves—like an angel, wholly untouched by the raging sea. Her eyes were kind, and her sweet smile comforting. And even amidst the ominous clouds, her auburn hair glistened as though the sun was still shining brightly.

Startled, Tink abruptly closed the book. Sitting in the silence, she contemplated the words and struggled to understand an idea she'd just

273

considered. *Am I reading too much into this?* she wondered. *Is this merely a coincidence? Or could there actually be a connection between this passage in Nic's journal and the lovely visitor staying next door in his home? Nic's description of the angel seems remarkably similar to Maddie. She has such kind eyes, a genuinely warm and sincere smile, and like Elizabeth mentioned the other day, strikingly beautiful auburn hair. Although I don't know her well yet, based on our few exchanges so far, her gentle presence has almost an ethereal feel, like that of the angel.*

No sooner had that thought occurred than a tiny tapping could be heard at the kitchen window. Tink turned to see what was happening. And there, magnificently illuminated in the morning sunlight, was the red cardinal chirping and hopping about. So as not to startle the bird, Tink stood up, and she slowly approached the window. To her amazement and delight, he remained on the windowsill.

"Good morning, my new friend!" Tink offered in greeting. "You're quite active today. And you're as good-looking as I remembered," she added. "I'm sure Maddie would agree. Have you been 'round to see her yet, on this Thanksgiving Day?"

Immediately, the cardinal lifted in flight, flew a purposeful, figure-eight loop between the two homes, and then eagerly returned to the windowsill.

"Well, based on that response and your flight pattern, I'm guessing you have. And aren't you and I lucky to have such a wonderful young lady staying right next door?"

Again, the bird responded with a passionate flutter of his wings. Next, he hopped around in a circle and flew directly over to the porch railing at *La Maison Enchantée,* where he remained.

How amazing, Tink thought. *The cardinal really must be a messenger sent from Nic. He showed up again today, precisely when I began reading Nic's journal. And when I asked about Maddie, he immediately flew over to that porch. Could this all just be a coincidence? I think not,* Tink acknowledged with a knowing smile.

Now, I must get busy and avoid any other interruptions so I can accomplish all of today's full agenda. But still, I can't help but think about the uncanny similarity between Nic's description and Maddie. This has certainly lifted my heart and given me the extra encouragement that I wanted today.

Turning her attention back to the tasks at hand, a good-sized turkey was skillfully seasoned, filled with homemade stuffing, and placed to roast in the oven. Then, the aromatic ginger-pumpkin soup began simmering on the stove while the additional side dishes were readied for serving.

As a reward to herself for accomplishing the most essential aspects of the main course, Tink cheerfully trotted into the dining room to complete the final stage of setting the table. Only twice a year did she afford herself the luxury of such extensive formalities: linen tablecloth with matching napkins, crystal goblets, fine silver cutlery, and a lovely, fresh floral centerpiece—which Henry had delivered the afternoon before.

Thanksgiving was one of the two days that she opted for this type of indulgence since both holidays centered around a celebratory meal. The other special occasion typically took place on the first Sunday in June. For that is when Theresa Isabelle, aka Tink, threw herself a fine soirée. The spirited elder used her birthday as a reason to thank her dearest friends, neighbors, and family for bringing such joy into her life. And while the number of guests on Thanksgiving was usually smaller, lending toward a more intimate gathering, the attendee list for the birthday celebration was extensive and noticeably more diverse.

The early summer soirée, weather allowing, always spilled over into Tink's sizable garden, gaily adorned with fairy lights and hanging lanterns. Party guests meandered among the pale-purple coneflowers, the blush-pink hydrangea, and dreamy lilac wisteria, finding sanctuary on one of the many seats or benches. But some, like her sister Martha Louise, chose to stay indoors. Tink's sister almost always perched in the parlor where only a few guests wandered in, and even fewer stayed. By contrast, though, Aubrey, the outlandish director of the Homes for Hounds Rescue Center, eagerly roamed the garden in colorful, mixed-matched garb, looking for any lost, wounded, or abandoned animals. "One never knows who might be in need of help," she could be heard saying each year as she snooped under bushes and scampered around trees.

Presently, as Tink stood staring at the empty place at the far end of the table, years of memories flooded in. All the more reason, she resolved to create a new seating arrangement to avoid the acute reminder of Nic's absence. For Nic had quite naturally become the welcome guest of honor on these two festive occasions. On Thanksgiving, he would sit at one end of the table and she at the other. At the annual birthday bash, he would mingle among the guests, serving drinks and making sure the success of the night did not fall solely on the aging shoulders of the birthday hostess.

Two evenings earlier, in preparation, Tink had ironed the linens, polished the silver, and hand-washed her mother's china and crystal. While many her age would have delegated those chores to someone else, she found genuine satisfaction in this work. Next, in the silence of the elegant dining room, she would routinely envision her guests eating heartily, enjoying animated conversation, and laughing aloud. Then, on the night before any gathering, she would set an intention that every aspect of the celebration be heartfelt, the meal not only satisfactory but notably delicious, and each guest uplifted by the company of others.

But last night, and for the first time since Nic's passing, Tink had been unable to complete this meaningful tradition. She'd struggled to sense the possibility of any happiness in the room, and all she could imagine was her friends feeling uncomfortably displaced and eating in awkward silence. Yet, she knew this would most likely not happen. Still, without Nic at the table, everything seemed painfully askew. So, Tink had retreated to bed, feeling defeated and overwhelmed.

Fortunately, after a good night's rest, the clarity of a new day enabled her to create a wonderful, new seating arrangement—one that would undoubtedly please each of her dinner guests, as well as herself. With no time left to dawdle and a tangible sense of excitement, Tink began moving around the large table with the near grace of a ballerina. She placed a goblet here and a butter knife there, swishing and swirling as inspiration flowed.

How limited I was, she mused, *to think the hostess must always sit at the head of the table. This is my dinner party, after all, so I don't need to conform to stringent social etiquette any more than I usually do! Therefore, I'm going to sit on the side of the table closest to the kitchen. That will save me a few precious steps, going back and forth. And I will assign my place of honor to this week's special guest, Maddie, so we will all be able to see her sweet face and enjoy her company without undue strain.*

As for Elizabeth, I will ask her to sit at the other honorary place in celebration of her attendance. I'm so grateful to know her better now due to our unforeseen involvement in the S.O.S. summer camps. More than ever before, I admire this woman's incredible organization, dedication, leadership abilities, and impressive capacity for compassion. Plus, I'm fairly sure that only a few individuals know just how gracious she's been in taking on additional responsibilities at Larry's office. Yet, I've never

276

heard her complain or offer a snippet of unseemly gossip nor a shred of boastful bragging about her extra efforts. All this time, she's managed to remain professional while still protecting the privacy of this challenging situation, which is truly admirable.

I must also admit that Elizabeth has me wondering what she wants to talk about. She's so excited, which has me really excited, too! I definitely plan to keep an eye on her in the upcoming months because I sense that she's on the verge of something very big. But this is not the time to think about the future when the present is in need of my full attention.

Now, let's see—where exactly was I? I guess I still need to figure out where to place my good buddy, Charlie—perhaps on Maddie's right? I'm just so glad he's coming again this year. He was always such a reserved person, but that has changed greatly since his wife's passing. I don't know this for a fact, but I suspect he wasn't always the easiest person to live with either—complaining about this and grumbling about that. Yet, everyone knew what a good woman Genevieve was. But when she became ill, Charlie was so overcome with fear and sorrow that he began to soften immediately. The transformation was astonishing to observe, as he quickly shifted from being overly critical to being genuinely kind and even helpful. And so many of us have had the privilege of witnessing this grumpy, old guy become a mindful, generous, and loyal friend.

Charlie's transformation deepened, I believe, in the lonely hours that haunted his life, following Genevieve's death. In her small but well-tended garden, he came to understand and cherish her even more. And he also found there, amidst the towering tomato plants and vining snap peas, the comfort and redemption he desperately needed. At last, Charlie had found a new purpose. For now, he's known throughout the neighborhood for generously sharing the continued bounty of his beloved's garden with his neighbors, fellow citizens, and friends.

Speaking of sharing, Tink decided with a sudden change of thought, *I'm going to place Shirley across from me. She is yet another example of someone who lives and breathes generosity. This good woman greets the Chamber visitors with such sincere enthusiasm, gladly sharing her extensive knowledge of the area with anyone who asks. She also volunteers countless hours for our Ladies' Guild. And as a friend, Shirley has never faltered. She's been as reliable as my grandfather clock and as good-hearted as anyone I've ever met.*

So, that's settled! There will be two people on one side of the table, one person on the other side, and one at each end. But that still creates an imbalance, although I don't expect to invite anyone else at this late hour.

A thought soon occurred to Tink, though. *Perhaps I'll deliberately leave one seat empty like they often do at weddings, except without the placement of a commemorative rose or photographs. This will serve as a gentle reminder of those not physically here anymore, but nevertheless very present in our hearts and in our lives. I like that idea immensely*, she affirmed.

Tink then clasped her hands together with tremendous relief. *Now that I am content with the seating arrangements, I can go back into the kitchen and attend to the remaining preparations for today's festivities.*

Chapter 50
Larry

"Good morning," Larry said with apparent surprise as he opened his front door. "You really did manage to arrive at 5:30 a.m. But, then again, I'm not entirely sure that is actually you."

Larry remained perplexed as he observed the person standing in front of him. For in no way did she resemble his valued employee of many years. Other than the tall stature and the familiar coffee cup in her hand, he could not have guessed this was Elizabeth Moreau. Her signature blonde hair was tucked inside a ball cap, and her wardrobe consisted of a bulky jacket, baggy jeans, and flat sneakers.

"I realize," Elizabeth explained, as she stepped inside, "my appearance may be a bit startling. But, as promised, I came prepared to work. And fortunately, the paparazzi did not manage to snap any unflattering photos of me on the way."

"Well, that's definitely a relief," Larry replied wryly.

"Indeed, it is! And I hope that my punctual arrival in this unflattering, yet utilitarian, outfit conveys the humility and sincerity of my desire to be truly helpful."

"Yes, that is most evident," he replied, still stunned by her uncharacteristic outfit. "I'm sure I've never seen you dressed so, well, uh, so informally. Go ahead and put your jacket on the chair over there in my office," he suggested, pointing, "and then follow me."

Elizabeth did as requested and walked in silence as Larry led the way down the dimly lit hall.

"As you can see," he announced at the entrance of the bright, expansive kitchen, "cooking is well underway. But there is plenty left to do. So, if you would put this apron on, we'll pick up where I left off."

"I'll be glad to," Elizabeth replied. "And I understand that our efforts are time-constrained. But first, I have a little something for you," she said, handing him a Robertson's Deli gift bag.

"What's this?" he asked, trying to hide his irritation. For Larry had structured the morning's agenda in such a finite way that this kind of delay could throw the schedule off.

"It's a gift to show my appreciation of you on Thanksgiving Day. Would you please open it now?"

Reluctantly, Larry took the present, glancing uncomfortably at the time. He quickly removed the tissue paper and, abiding by his meticulous routines in the kitchen, folded it and placed it immediately in a drawer. Next, he pulled out of the bag an attractive wooden box and silently admired the hand-carved container. Then, he opened the hinged lid, revealing five glass bottles, each individually labeled.

"France, Sicily, Hawaii, Cypris, and Bali," he read aloud. "Unrefined salts from around the world. What a wonderful gift," he admitted softly.

"I'm so happy that you're pleased," Elizabeth said, smiling. "I must confess, however, that I had a bit of expert advice. Theo was gracious enough to help me."

"Well, this was an excellent choice, and I will definitely be using them. In fact, I may add a pinch of the French salt to the gravy right now. Thank you, Elizabeth," he added humbly. "That was very thoughtful of you."

"You're very welcome. Now, I'll put that apron on, and we can go straight to work."

"Great," he replied, placing the salt box in the center of the counter.

But as Elizabeth tied the apron around her waist, Larry began shuffling back and forth nervously. Before her arrival, he'd been concerned about what kind of help she would actually be able to offer since Elizabeth had always been so different from his other staff members. She seemed to avoid conversations about the latest cooking trends or a favorite go-to recipe. Nor was she one to bring in leftovers from a meal or homemade desserts to share with the others. She was, however, always glad to treat everyone to a delivered deli lunch or an occasional hot pizza. But cooking anything else, had been out of the question.

When Larry and Nic began the S.O.S. Basket Benefit, the cooking had always been divided up equitably between them. They'd chosen to work independently at their respective homes and, by doing so, had accomplished everything without conflict or constriction of space. And although Larry didn't want to, he couldn't help but compare that situation to now. He'd much rather work alone than have someone getting in his way or standing about awkwardly, unsure what to do. But Elizabeth's offer to help had been genuine; plus, she'd salvaged the whole benefit this year. So, how could he say no? Then he'd received a text message that left little choice but to say yes.

While Larry paced, Elizabeth silently waited for his direction. Finally, he broached the subject.

"Forgive me for asking, but I was, um, well, uh, just wondering how you might describe your prepping skills in the kitchen—you know, chopping, dicing, and um, uh, sautéing?"

Without a moment's hesitation, Elizabeth offered her answer, "In all fairness to you, the one word to describe my abilities would be the French word *rien,* which means "nothing." As much as I love good food, I'm honestly only an expert at eating it. How a good meal gets from the market to the kitchen and onto my plate has simply remained a mystery to me.

"However," she continued, adjusting her apron, "I stand before you, a most humble and willing assistant. I promise that if you explain the basics to me and illustrate precisely how you would like things done, I'll do my very best to learn quickly, follow your instructions exactly, and work as hard as I can."

"Ok then," Larry responded, attempting to hide his misgivings. "Let's begin your lessons."

Turning toward the closest counter where an impressive row of cutlery was laid out, he lifted the smallest knife and, in a slow, deliberate voice, explained, "This, Ms. Moreau, is a santoku knife. It is excellent for chopping. But, like all of my knives, it is extremely sharp. Please use extra care when handling this and any other tools in this kitchen."

"I definitely will," she assured him solemnly.

"Good. Then, I would like you to use this knife for chopping onions, which we'll need plenty of for the remaining batches of stuffing. Let me show you the safest and most effective technique." With incredible patience and an even-tempered voice, Larry demonstrated his preferred method, allowing Elizabeth to ask questions and observe him from all angles.

Elizabeth soon attempted to repeat his movements, but her efforts were cautiously clumsy and unsure. Quite unexpectedly, Larry suddenly felt exceptionally compassionate. For he was witnessing a woman he'd known for a long time show such evident vulnerability. At the office, Elizabeth consistently exuded confidence and professionalism. And during the summer camps, when she'd admitted having no experience working with children ever, she still exhibited a comfortable sense of authority. Yet, her connections with the young sailors felt earnest and sincere. But now, rather than becoming discouraged or defensive as she ineptly grasped the large onion, Elizabeth disarmed Larry by quietly laughing at her own inabilities while still expressing an honest eagerness to learn.

So, once again and with the same amount of patience, Larry demonstrated the technique, and before long, Elizabeth began to perfect that skill along with several others. The amateur chef stood back in amazement as he watched her achieve what had taken him months of practice or considerably longer to attain.

What an outstanding aptitude for learning she has, Larry recognized in silence. *I can see now that she may be able to contribute more to this morning's efforts than I had expected. I'm certain also she could achieve just about anything she sets her mind to.*

Before long, while Larry continued prepping and monitoring the various stages of the turkey's cooking, mounds of onions and celery were chopped, as well as bread toasted and cubed for the stuffing. He then explained the remainder of the morning's itinerary with a strong emphasis on the tight time frame. And as he spoke, Larry felt a clarity within that had been absent for so long. After muddling about for months, he welcomed this sense of clear composure that the cooking and instructing were bringing out in him.

"The goal in the past," he succinctly explained, "was to deliver the meals to each family by or before 2 p.m., and we've always managed to do that. Because I don't have professional-size equipment, there is no way multiple turkeys can be cooked simultaneously. So, I have always gotten up precisely at midnight - the official beginning of Thanksgiving Day—to start cooking. I use the oven and an oversized air fryer - staggering the process accordingly.

"Fortunately, today," he added, knocking on the butcher block island, "all is going to plan so far, which is encouraging."

"That's excellent, Larry, and obviously quite an achievement. And I can imagine, after a full day like this, including the deliveries into the city, you come home and stagger onto that sofa for a proper nap."

"You're absolutely right! I've turned down many enticing dinner invitations for fear I would yawn uncontrollably while resting my elbows on the table as the host or hostess was making a meaningful speech," he confessed with a laugh.

Elizabeth laughed along, saying in agreement, "That would be awkward, not to mention uncouth. And I imagine any host, besides Tink, of course, might take offense at such behavior."

"Yes, they just might," he agreed.

An amiable mood began to permeate the room, along with the aromatic smell of seasonings and sauteing vegetables. Laughter and a sweet lightness filled the spaces that had held only loneliness and grief for many months. And any remaining tension between the two also dissipated like rising steam into cold air.

Side by side, and hour after hour, the two successfully assembled eight main courses under Larry's expert tutelage. Much to his surprise, all aspects of the meal were completed, not only on time but ahead of schedule.

"Well," Elizabeth proclaimed, "I think this is reason enough to celebrate! Do you, by chance, happen to have the ingredients for your famed aperitif on hand?"

"I sure do," Larry affirmed. "Not only do I have all the ingredients, but they are chilled and ready to be served at a moment's notice."

"Wonderful! Then, I am requesting that moment to be right now. I believe we have time for a little impromptu indulgence, don't we?"

"I think we do," Larry readily agreed, glancing quickly at the time.

"Because, let me inform you, Monsieur Walters, I have had the distinct privilege of enjoying sumptuous street foods in Seattle, some of the finest pastries in Paris, and Michelin Star cuisine in New York City. But," she continued with an air of mock arrogance, "I have *never* had anything so delightful or refreshing as your apricot aperitif."

"Really?" Larry asked in disbelief.

"Yes - truly! You served it last year at our holiday party, remember? And everyone loved it and wanted more… including me."

"You're right. They were clamoring for a second glass, which I had not anticipated," he recalled proudly.

"Well, what's not to love?" Elizabeth queried. "The taste is divine, the color is beautiful, and the bubbles add extra fun. Plus, the calories are limited, and it does not require alcohol. So, it can be enjoyed by everyone without guilt. I think you've created a very special beverage, so much so that I am personally volunteering to taste-test it once again today, just to be sure. And then, I promise, we can head out to make the deliveries."

"Alright," he agreed, readily opening the refrigerator. "I like your idea and wouldn't mind having one myself."

Elizabeth looked on with admiration as Larry mindfully blended the chilled, organic apricot juice, imported sparkling water, a hint of sweetener, and a generous amount of fresh lime juice into two glasses. In a matter of minutes, he handed her the drink and said, "Here you are, Elizabeth. Enjoy!"

Before sipping, however, Elizabeth raised her glass to him and said, "I offer a toast to you, Larry, on this Thanksgiving Day. Let us celebrate the success of the S.O.S. Basket Benefit. May these efforts, and those of our amazing friends in this community, bring joy and fulfillment to these precious families. Cheers!"

"Cheers!" Larry echoed sincerely. Then, as they took their first anticipatory taste, Larry discretely looked over the rim of his glass to see Elizabeth's response.

"Well, Larry," she said in an exaggerated tone, "this beverage is even better than I remembered, which is saying a lot. Bravo, my friend, bravo!"

"Thank you, Elizabeth," he replied modestly, looking down. "I appreciate you saying that."

"Of course. You know me to be an honest person, and this is *magnifique!*"

Again, Larry shuffled nervously, modestly turning away. Still, a pleasant silence remained as they slowly savored their drinks.

After completing her beverage, Elizabeth then made a request. "Larry, I'd like to quickly go by my house to change and then meet you at the office in about 30 minutes or less. Would that be alright?"

"Yes, that's fine. I need to load the truck, which I can manage on my own, as well as change, before heading out."

"Great," Elizabeth replied. "And loading all of the donations at the office shouldn't take too long. The food baskets are ready to go, and I'm excited for you to see everything else that has been given."

"Is it really a lot?" he questioned.

"Yes, it actually is," she responded.

"Well, I hope it all fits," he stated nervously. "Now, let me walk you out."

As they left the kitchen, Elizabeth picked up her jacket and paused briefly at the front door.

"Larry, I really am a team player. And I know when I first arrived in Port St. Smith, you had reservations about hiring me. You probably thought I'd be in and out of this little town in less than a year. Fortunately, though, you gave me a chance, for which I remain most grateful. I have a very good life here, and I'm quite happy. I also feel that you and I have formed a strong and respectful working relationship—much like a golfer and their caddy or a pitcher and a catcher. How's that," she asked, as an aside, "for a couple of sports metaphors?"

"That's pretty good," he acknowledged smiling.

"So, I thank you once again for allowing me to help today. I had fun, and you really taught me a lot."

"I'm glad to know that," he sincerely stated.

"And going forward, you can continue to count on me. I don't foresee getting traded to another team anytime soon."

"Well, that's also good to know," he replied, laughing.

"But, before I risk saying something terribly inaccurate like I'll catch that pop fly on the 50-yard line, I shall say goodbye and meet you at the office in just a few minutes."

"Alright. And I, uh," he added hesitantly, "want to thank you, Elizabeth, for coming over today. You really were helpful, and we did have some fun."

"We sure did, Larry. I enjoyed our time together, and I'm glad I could help. See you later."

"Bye."

Elizabeth turned and walked to her car. As Larry began to close the door, a strong gust of wind quickly swept into the house. The blinds rattled in the windows, papers rustled on his desk, and a small, yellow post-it note drifted down and landed at his feet. Larry bent over to pick it up, noticing writing that did not resemble his own. He read the abbreviated message and was forced to lean against a wall as his knees buckled. Still, he made himself look at the note again, and there on the little paper were two words scribbled in barely legible handwriting:

Cheers, Mate!

Chapter 51
Maddie

Maddie woke much later than usual and was surprised to see the time on the bedside clock: 10 a.m. What a joy to indulge in such a long, deep sleep and wake so rested. Since she had no specific plans or obligations other than attending Tink's Thanksgiving gathering, she gave herself permission to move at an unfamiliar yet pleasantly slower pace.

Had this been any other typical holiday morning, Maddie most likely would have gone for an early bike ride and then prepared her contribution for the celebratory meal. Having grown up in rural America, a strong work ethic had been modeled daily. Thus, Maddie tended to be a task-oriented person. Outside of work, cycling, and reading, she dabbled in various crafting projects and modest gardening with indoor potted plants. For she enjoyed the gratification of the creative process itself, as well as the satisfaction of the end results. So today, the novelty of moving about with no prearranged agenda was relaxing, especially in such a conducive setting that encouraged little else. Because, as she and Elizabeth had discussed at the café, what was the purpose of a getaway if the activities and pace did not differ from one's everyday life?

The morning passed with gentle grace. After rising from bed, Maddie eased into a few of her favorite yoga poses and then ate a light breakfast, wisely saving room for the holiday feast to follow. Afterward, she put on her coat and meandered about the frosty garden, enjoying the remains of its evident, bountiful beauty. Just beyond the garden, the arched wooden gateway in the center of the tall, back wall held allure. So, Maddie decided to explore beyond the back of the property. After turning the lock through a series of security numbers, the heavy door stuck slightly for lack of use but finally creaked open to reveal the exceptional beauty of the Piney Grove Trail. The pathway was wide, and the immense pine trees were plentiful. No one could be seen in either direction, so with the curiosity of a child, Maddie ambled alone down the walkway. As she did, the majestic pines began whistling in sweet harmony as a gentle breeze passed through. Without hesitation, she determined to ride the bike in the next two days all the way to the end of the trail to find the ocean.

After walking a little bit further, Maddie turned and circled back to the house. There, she made herself a cup of tea and brought it carefully into the study. Since she had not done much reading yet, the idea of perusing the books on the shelves was inviting. Among the collection were the topics of architecture, cycling, and notable photographs of Cape Cod. But one book captured her attention more than any of the others. It was a large, coffee table-size volume featuring the splendor of New England sailing. Maddie had been sailing only a few times in her life. But she'd always loved how quiet and seemingly effortlessly the sailboat was propelled through the water by the sheer force of the wind. How could something unseen, she wondered, still be so strong and impactful? Yet, when the vessel aligned itself with the direction of the wind, the results could be so impressive.

Wanting to know more, Maddie removed the large book from the shelf and placed it on the table in front of the loveseat. She lit a small fire, settled into her usual cozy place, and then eagerly began looking through the pages. But the written words did not speak to her nearly as much as the crisp, colorful photographs featured on almost every page. She found the contrast of billowing, white sails against the azure blue skies strikingly beautiful. And she noted that the sailors appeared less focused on the destination and more so on the expansive pleasure of the experience.

Page after page, Maddie savored each of the stunning images. Then, as she came to the end of the book, a loose photograph near the back fell out. Instinctively, she went to return it, but curiosity caused her to take a closer look. The photograph seemed fairly recent, and in it, there were two men wearing summer, sailing clothes. They stood side by side in front of a large sailboat moored at a marina. The name painted along the side of the boat read *The Great Getaway*. Maddie looked back and forth at the two men, noting their differences. Fair-haired with broad shoulders, the man on the right was quite tall with his chest out and his large hand resting on the taffrail of the boat. The shorter man on the left had darker features and was toned and tan. His stance was more relaxed yet just as engaging.

Maddie turned the photo over, noting an inscription dated two years earlier. In bold penmanship, it read:

Nic-
Thanks for the sailing lessons and
our many amazing adventures.
You're a stellar mate and great friend,
Slouch

Curious about which man was Nic, presumably the owner of *La Maison Enchantée*, Maddie turned the photograph back over to look at the front. Which of the two men, Maddie wondered, had welcomed her with such a kind note but in an awkward handwriting? Was he the larger man on the right standing proudly in front of the impressive sailboat? Or was he the slighter-built man with an air of quiet confidence and warm, sincere eyes? She puzzled at the realization that both men looked physically active, and neither looked as if they would have the handwriting of an old man. What could have happened? Which of the two men wrote my note? And where was the owner now?

Regardless, Maddie realized that she kept being drawn to the tanned and trim man whose presence seemed so kind and alluring. And as she continued to glance at his image, a soothing warmth came over her entire body. She felt as though she already had a distinct sense of him. But she wasn't sure why or even how that could be possible.

For several moments, Maddie continued holding the photograph and staring at his image. Then she heard the faint ringing sound of a text message coming from upstairs. Although she was reluctant to move from this sweet space, she was concerned that the message might be important. So, Maddie placed the photograph back in the book and returned the book to the shelf. And because she had a strong desire to stay in a peaceful state, she ascended the stairs without hurrying.

Crossing the large room, she checked the time, reminding herself that she would soon need to get ready to go. So, Maddie picked up the phone and read the message from Stephen.

I'm a nervous wreck! How are you?
Oh, and Happy Thanksgiving, Maddie
from me and Miss Priss.
She says, "Meow, Meow!!"

Recognizing that Stephan may want to talk, Maddie decided to call him rather than return his text.

"Happy Thanksgiving, Stephen!"

"Happy Thanksgiving, Maddie," he replied.

"Are you both ok?" she inquired. "And are you a little worried about the day ahead?"

"Well, the good news is Miss Priss is just fine! I'm the one that's been jumping and jittery since dawn!! I'm still trying to figure out what to wear to Rafael's, what to bring to Rafael's, and what to say to Rafael! And as you might have presumed, Miss Priss has been no help to me. She's sleeping soundly, oblivious to all the shirts, slacks, and shoes I've laid out as options. Even when I woke her up to ask for her assistance, she simply sniffed about, hoping there might be a treat for her in the midst of the mess. And that, my friend, is why I reached out to you."

"You're going to be just fine, Stephen," she assured him. "But first, before I help you, I want you to go over to your bay window and look out."

"Alright," he agreed, abiding by her request. "Now what?"

"Ok, go ahead and exhale a long, slow breath, and relax your shoulders as best you can."

"Alright," he said, sighing.

"And please do that one more time, so you'll be a little calmer, making it easier for you to think more clearly."

"One can only hope," he quipped.

"But are you better?" Maddie asked.

"Yes, a little bit. Thanks."

"You're welcome. Are you ready to talk about your clothing options?"

"Please!" he replied.

"Well, Stephen," Maddie proceeded to say, "blue is always a good color for you. So, why don't you wear that favorite blue shirt of yours that you told me is also really comfortable?"

"That was my first inclination, but then I got all befuddled."

"Best to go with your first instinct," she reminded him.

"You're right. I knew that. Okay, so that's resolved. And Rafael asked me to bring a bottle of wine. But should I bring white, or red, or both, or even some champagne?"

"I suggest you bring a white and a red - that way, you're covered. And why not save the champagne for a future date—maybe New Year's Eve?"

"Oh, I love that idea!" Stephen said resoundingly. Why didn't I think of that? Probably because I've been spinning in circles ever since he invited me over. And I'm rather glad that you're not in town to witness my ridiculous behavior."

"Stephen, don't be so hard on yourself. You're such a wonderful person, and obviously, Rafael can see that in you. Just be true to yourself. Because remember, you'll want to be with someone who actually appreciates and supports your awesome, authentic self. So, even if you're befuddled, laugh about it and go on."

"You're right again, Maddie!" he offered in relieved surrender. "Thanks for the encouragement."

"I think you're going to look very handsome and have a great time together!"

"I hope so, and you have fun today, as well!"

"Thanks, Stephen. I need to start getting ready now, though. So, take another deep breath, give Miss Priss a cuddle from me, and know that you have my full support."

"You're the best, Maddie!" Stephen asserted. "I swear, if we *were* living in a storybook fairytale, you would definitely be my Fairy Godmother!"

Maddie laughed and said, "Then I grant your wish—a very romantic and Happy Thanksgiving!"

"And so it shall be! Bye, Maddie!"

"Bye, Stephen!"

With a big smile, Maddie set the phone down and began preparing herself for dinner at Tink's. Before long, she was stepping out the back door, carrying a small gift bag in her hand. For just a moment, she paused to look over at the swing.

Mary Hayes

Did that swing really keep moving back and forth after I stopped pushing it? How could that even be possible unless someone else was pushing?

As she pondered this, the male cardinal landed close by on the porch railing. Maddie quietly crossed the porch so as not to startle him and walked slowly down the back steps. The attentive bird did not flinch or fly away, but instead, he began flying alongside her. He continued this all the way with her until she reached Tink's back porch. Then he flew over to the elder's kitchen window, landing adeptly in the center of the sill. In amazement, Maddie knocked on the back door, astounded at witnessing the cardinal's unusual behavior. She also wondered if there was some kind of connection between the bird, herself, and Tink. But before she could give that any more consideration, the door swung open, and she was warmly welcomed and invited inside.

Chapter 52
Elizabeth

Elizabeth prepared a large thermos of black coffee to go after quickly changing her clothing at home. She didn't recall ever in her life having such a busy Thanksgiving morning. Yet, helping Larry in his kitchen since pre-dawn had been both enjoyable and educational.

I feel so joyful and on point today! Elizabeth acknowledged as she finalized her tasks. *And I'm deeply honored to be helping with the S.O.S. Basket Benefit this year. Even Larry, who was clearly opposed to the idea of making the annual deliveries, seems more engaged now. But what's most exciting for me is the chance to see the children again, especially Trevor. I sure hope he'll be at his house when we arrive and that he'll remember me as fondly as I remember him.*

Before locking up, Elizabeth took a peripheral glance in the mirror, approving her appearance, and in doing so, caught sight of Trevor's handmade sailboat card propped up on the Escritoire. Seeing this, she felt an increased sense of hope and anticipation. She also reflected on the other valued possessions typically stored in that same antique piece of furniture, such as the old black and white photograph she'd given Larry to ponder.

No doubt, he's anxious to be told the meaning of that image. But today will probably not be the best time for that conversation since we have so much else going on. And I can only imagine the myriad of emotions he must be feeling, many of which are probably very difficult to handle. So, I don't want to risk overwhelming him, although I do wonder if he'll be willing to go with me to Beauté Par La Mar *over the holiday weekend. I'd like to explain to him there, amidst the grandeur of the estate, not only the significance of the photograph but also the future vision for the S.O.S. Foundation.*

Realizing the morning was swiftly elapsing, Elizabeth collected her keys and coffee and got into her car. She fired up the engine and backed onto the road, grateful to have a little more time to herself.

I believe the intense grief I felt following Nic's death must have cracked open a nearly imperceivable shell that had been encasing my heart. After a major move, downsizing professionally, adapting to an entirely new town, and two disappointing love affairs, I must have unconsciously placed armor around my vulnerable heart under the pretense of protection. And I can certainly see now how wary I was. But no one wins, especially me if I walk through life emotionally guarded. So, I am resolutely committing, specifically after spending the summer with such sweet children, that I would much rather risk the volatile yet transitory discomfort of pain that may happen, rather than miss out on the greater gifts of good - gifts like the raucous laughter and hugs I shared with Tink, and the other camp volunteers. For if my emotional shield had remained intact, I may not have fully appreciated the unforgettable tenderness of Trevor's friendship, along with the feeling of his small hand in mine. Thus, on this Thanksgiving Day, my sincere intention is to allow my heart to experience the full range of feelings so I do not diminish the love that I can give or the love I can receive.

When I first began working at the S.O.S. camps, Elizabeth recalled as she guided her car through the streets of Port Saint Smith, *I lacked my usual courage, so much so that others could visibly see how nervous I was. That was such an unexpected arena for me that I was often at a loss for words. And when I did speak, I frequently stuttered, which hasn't happened to me since 7th-grade speech class. How odd for that nervous behavior to resurface once again. I also stared out to sea often, unsure of which direction to go when making important decisions. Yet, I understood that in the absence of Nic's decisive leadership, someone needed to step up, and I felt strongly compelled that it was mine to do.*

As her car curved around corners and roundabouts, Elizabeth relished the solitude which allowed her the opportunity to more fully feel the rich awareness of an awakening that had been coming to the surface of her consciousness for the past several weeks.

I am ready now to give more of myself, my time, and my love. Even last summer, I clearly recognized the need to serve in that leadership position. Who else could have fulfilled that pivotal role besides me? Larry was in no state of mind to take that on, and no one else seemed available. Plus, I felt intuitively inspired to say "Yes," even though my mind struggled with just how unqualified I was to lead a children's sailing camp. Yet, that is exactly what I did with Tink's remarkable assistance. And we were, admittedly, a most unlikely duo that actually proved to be a fun and formidable team. While she effectively oversaw the volunteers, I managed the administrative duties - creating the comprehensive schedule of events for each day, for every sailor, and for all of the counselors. I also shopped at the grocery store for the children's snacks and lunch meals, which put me in completely unfamiliar territory. Never before had I purchased mini juice boxes, tiny bags of baby carrots, or packages of individual potato chips. Yet, absolutely everything flowed together beautifully, as though arranged and then sustained by an unseen force of good.

But where I initially failed was in my communications with the campers. Not being a mother nor having spent much time around young children, I had no idea how to relate to them. I was so awkward and insecure, never exactly knowing what to say. I didn't want to talk down to them, nor did I want to ignore them. But what could I offer in conversation that would possibly hold their interest? So, I withdrew, afraid they wouldn't like me.

Thank goodness that precious boy Trevor talked to me during the second week of camp. I still remember standing stiffly against a wall on lunch duty, trying to avoid any eye contact. But, with the true innocence of a child, he came over to me and asked, "Miss Elizabeth, do you like cheese?"

Dumbfounded, I actually had to think for a moment. Then, I stammered an inappropriate answer, saying, "Yes, especially French camembert."

"Camen-what?" he questioned with a puzzled expression. "I don't know what that is, but if you're hungry, you can have some of my cheese. It's really yummy."

The honesty of his words and the kindness of his offer cut straight through my tense walls of trepidation. Rendered helpless, all I could do was nod my head and mumble a meek "Okay, thank you." Trevor immediately brought me a half slice of his bright orange American cheese with the proudest smile. I accepted it, ate it willingly, and fussed profusely at just how yummy it really was. Then, with the common ground of our love for cheese, Trevor and I had the first mutual interest to talk about. Each day following, we found other things to discuss, such as our great appreciation of music and the wind. And that singular connection with him gave me the courage to speak to the other campers, who, to my great surprise, were also engaging and fun to converse with. Soon, I came to understand that by simply showing genuine interest in them, my insecurities quickly dissolved and were replaced with a sense of ease and natural comradery.

Realizing that she'd be arriving at the office in a matter of minutes, Elizabeth pressed on with reflective thoughts, grateful to have had this significant time of contemplation.

The campers are all so special to me now. I could never have imagined embracing the company of juice-sipping, chit-chattering, sailboat-navigating children. How fortunate, though, that I did. And that is just one of the many unexpected blessings to have come out of Nic's tragic passing. My friendship with Tink has also grown much closer because of this shared experience, so I am truly looking forward to being a part of her Thanksgiving celebration this afternoon. And I can't help but wonder what other wonderful happenings may occur when I shift from the pattern of distancing myself due to fear and say "Yes" inspired to inspired direction!

Even this morning in Larry's kitchen, I felt insecure and uncomfortable in such an unfamiliar setting. How could I possibly be of any help to him when I've had such an aversion to cooking? Yet, by all measures—be that cup, spoon, or laughter—my efforts proved to be beneficial, much to both of our astonishment. We had a good time, celebrated our success, and even managed to finish ahead of schedule.

The fact that I'm not traveling during this holiday week is another clear sign that I am right where I need to be, doing exactly what I need to be doing. I could have easily taken off like I typically do—going to New York, wandering through museums, seeing a couple of shows, dining with friends, and so forth. And that would have been predictably pleasant. But I just didn't feel inclined this year to be away, which allowed me to step in at the last minute to coordinate the S.O.S. Basket Benefit. And what a welcome gift to be able to visit the sailors and their families today! I'm just so happy to be planting my feet in the fertile soil of Port Saint Smith for the rest of this holiday season and seeing what other wonders may unfold. Because if this week is any indication of how that will play out, I have great hope for what lies ahead.

Elizabeth's reflections came to a stop as she pulled into the parking lot of the office. Larry was waiting outside, and after a brief discussion regarding the delivery plans, they entered the building together.

"What's all this?" he asked in bewilderment upon seeing several tables covered with both baskets and various other items.

"Oh, just some of the donations provided in the last two days," Elizabeth answered nonchalantly. "Why don't you start bringing those plants and gift bags out to your car while I fill the baskets with the refrigerated food?"

Still baffled, Larry did as requested, dutifully carrying the eight full-size chrysanthemums outside two at a time, then returning for the eight large fall-colored tote bags his associate had filled the night before. As he did so, Elizabeth placed cool packs into the baskets to keep the butter and other necessities chilled.

Nevertheless, Elizabeth could clearly sense her boss's skepticism about fitting everything inside his truck. Since all else had come together so perfectly, she trusted this essential stage of the process would also prove to be successful. So, after the baskets were brought outside, they carefully placed this here and that there and quickly managed to find room for all of it inside the vehicle. Elizabeth just had to hold one of the flowers in her lap, which she was happy to do.

Then, Larry politely closed her passenger car door, and they began the drive west toward Sagamore Bridge.

He was the first to speak. "I'm curious what all we have in the back besides food and flowers. Because, in the past, having enough space in this sizable truck was never a problem. In fact," he added jovially, "your little sport-about car could probably fit inside of this truck."

"I think you're right about that," Elizabeth agreed, laughing, pleased to see the continuation of the morning's morning.

Well," she explained, "I initially reached out to the list of merchants who had donated in the past. Fortunately, all of them agreed to contribute again. Then I thought, why not visit a few of the other shops—at least the ones I personally frequent? They may also want to help out. And did they ever! Five additional store owners gladly contributed, including Betina at the Acorns and Apples Gift Shop - giving each family a lovely set of autumn kitchen towels. The Freemans, of course, generously donated the gorgeous mums. And Theo went above and beyond for us since we are obviously two of his very favorite customers!"

Larry laughed, knowing he couldn't disagree.

"So, I will just warn you now," she continued, "if I'm involved again next year, which I would love to be, there's no telling what all we'll have for the families."

"I can only imagine! If you're in charge again, we'll probably need to add a trailer to the truck's hitch," he quipped playfully.

"What a good idea! Just imagine the possibilities!" Elizabeth agreed. *And that is only a small part of my intentions and aspirations for the S.O.S. Foundation*, she affirmed silently to herself. *But that discussion will have to be at another time. Right now, I'm going to relax and enjoy the drive on this cheerful Thanksgiving morning.*

Chapter 53
Tink

Tink hustled through the kitchen with renewed vigor that she'd feared would take many more months to return. The thrill of having dinner guests, especially Elizabeth and the sweet, unexpected visitor Maddie, caused nearly all of her lingering sorrow to vanish. And as the grandfather clock chimed another passing hour, Tink continued to thoughtfully complete every aspect of the meal.

Two of her invited guests had already arrived, and another was expected soon. Just as she was removing the sweet potato casserole topped with sugared pecans from the oven, a soft knocking sound could be heard. She quickly pulled off the red rooster oven mitts and scurried over to open the back door.

"Happy Thanksgiving, Maddie! Welcome to my home."

"Happy Thanksgiving, Tink," Maddie replied cheerfully.

For the briefest moment, the elder paused, looking directly at this lovely young woman as the sun shone brightly upon her face and hair. There, Tink observed a truly compassionate countenance radiating with grace and kindness. And, in that moment, she recalled the words in Nic's journal:

"Her eyes are kind, and her sweet smile comforting. Even amidst the ominous clouds, her auburn hair glistens as though there is still sunlight."

"Forgive me, dear, for staring. I know that's considered to be rude. But I must ask... has anyone ever said you remind them of an angel?"

Blushing slightly with surprise, Maddie humbly said, "Well, actually, yes, one person did tell me that—my Grandmother Anise."

"Well, she may have been a bit more biased than me. But I dare say we are both correct. Now, please, come in."

Stepping inside, Maddie was immediately greeted by a rich medley of aromas—roasting turkey, simmering gravy, pumpkin bread, and much more. Quite suddenly, she was flooded by a wave of emotions—partially because of the words Tink had just spoken, and also remembering the smell and delight of the many holiday meals she'd spent at her Grandmother Anise's home.

Then, as Tink started to close the door, she noticed the male cardinal flying in circles right outside. "Oh look, Maddie, my cardinal friend is here again today. He's been coming for the past several days to my kitchen window to say hello. Did you happen to notice him?"

"Yes, I sure did," Maddie replied. "I think he even accompanied me here because when I came out of the house, he was perched on the back porch railing as though he'd been waiting for me. And as I started to walk toward your house, he seemed to be flying right beside me. I couldn't believe it!"

"That's remarkable! But I'm not surprised! That bright bird seems very aware of what is going on around here. Maybe he even likes the fact that we're getting to know one another. I'm not sure, but I'd like to think that's true. Either way, let me take your coat now that you're inside my toasty kitchen."

"Thank you," Maddie acknowledged, removing her outerwear. "And this is for you," she stated quietly, extending to the hostess an attractive, monogrammed gift bag tied with raffia ribbon.

"My heavens, what a surprise! But didn't I tell you, my dear, not to bring anything?"

"You did. But I think what you said was not to bring any food for the meal," Maddie explained. "So, this is just a little gift for you as my way of saying thank you for inviting me today."

"Well, that wasn't necessary. But, oh, how sweet of you, and I do love presents! Is it okay if I open it now?" Tink asked with the eagerness of a child.

"Yes, please do," Maddie said with a smile.

"How exciting! After that, I'll take you into the dining room to meet the others."

Tink fussed about the bag's beauty and functionality and then untied the string, removed the garnet-colored tissue paper, and peered inside. "Beach Plum Jelly?! Maddie, you're the dearest! This is my very favorite jelly in the whole world! Now I know you are an angel, and this is just more evidence of that fact. Thank you so much!"

"You're welcome," Maddie replied, smiling. "I'm really glad you like it."

"Like it? I love it enough to suggest we get out a couple of good-sized spoons and sample it this very minute. But I'd better show a little more self-restraint and wait long enough to enjoy it with our Thanksgiving meal. And oh, how delicious this will taste atop a warm biscuit. Don't you agree?"

"Oh yes, that will be perfect!" her guest agreed.

"So that's settled," Tink stated. "I'll be happy to share your thoughtful gift with everyone else, which will just multiply all of our joy!"

And with that, Tink placed the empty gift bag on the kitchen table alongside Nic's journal. She paused briefly in silent gratitude for her past and present blessings. After which, she turned back to Maddie, saying, "Speaking of everyone, let's go say hello to my two friends who've already arrived. You can relax with them at the table while I put the finishing touches on our Thanksgiving feast. And, just so you know, Elizabeth, your realtor, is also coming for dinner, but I'm not exactly sure when she'll be arriving."

"How wonderful that she's coming," Maddie commented.

With a flourish, Tink then exited the kitchen, followed by Maddie. They walked the short distance down the hallway, passed the grandfather clock, and stepped into the large, formal dining room. There, seated on either side of the table, were two contented people amiably sipping on hot, mulled apple cider.

"May I have your attention, please," Tink announced. "I would like to welcome precious Maddie Stuart to my home and introduce her to you first, Charlie."

"How good to meet you," he stated solemnly, rising slowly to standing.

"I'm glad to meet you too, Charlie," Maddie replied to the elderly gentleman.

"Did you know, Maddie, that Charlie lives on this same street, just a few houses down?" the hostess inquired.

"No, I didn't know that," she answered.

"Yes, all three of us have been neighbors for many years, for which I feel most fortunate. And I'll make note of the fact that Charlie and I consume a fair amount of calories in my kitchen on a Saturday night. Though, at our age, calories are of little concern. Am I right, old man?"

"They are of no concern at all," he stated bluntly as a sizable cracker topped with cheddar cheese teetered between his hand and mouth.

"Charlie, maybe I can persuade you to tell Maddie about your garden, as well as our mutual adoration of fresh fruit pie. We used to play cards as an excuse to get together for dessert. However, we're both terrible card players, so that old codger and I now just sit around and tell stories about the good ol' days. We don't exactly discuss the days of horse and buggy, but we do talk about the local five-and-dime store, the awkwardness of school dances, and the hopes of going steady way back then. Yet, the main purpose for our time together is simply to taste a variety of seasonal, homemade pies—blueberry, rhubarb, pumpkin, apple, and so forth."

Charlie nodded silently while still smiling in agreement.

Next, Tink turned to her right.

"And speaking of sweets—I believe you have already met sweet and good-hearted Shirley Lund."

"She certainly has," Shirley interjected before Maddie had a chance to reply. "I helped her find a wondahful place to stay that just happens to be right next door to yah house."

"Indeed, you did!" Tink concurred joyfully. "And look at all of us today gathering together. Maddie is not only acquainting herself with our town but also with some of us colorful locals. How lucky are we?"

"Lucky indeed!" Shirley replied as Charlie nodded again affirmatively.

"Now, young lady," Tink proclaimed, pointing a large wooden spoon toward an empty chair, "I've set a place for you there at the end of the table since you're one of our celebrated guests. Please make yourself comfortable while I go back into the kitchen to put this spoon to better use. Dinner will be served very soon, my friends, and hopefully, Elizabeth—our other guest of honor—will be arriving shortly."

As she turned to go, Tink added, "Shirley, can I count on you and Charlie to keep the conversation lively?"

"Yah betcha," Shirley asserted.

"Wonderful!" And with that, Tink trotted cheerfully out of the room.

Chapter 54
Maddie

While her Thanksgiving guests exchanged convivial conversation in the dining room, Tink completed the meal preparations in the kitchen. The joyful woman moved about with excitement and soon had the first large platter of food ready to serve. With a slight bit of fanfare, she marched into the dining room and placed it in the center of the extensive buffet table. Immediately, she returned to the kitchen, and for the next several minutes, the holiday hostess paraded back and forth with more platters, plates, and abundant bowls of food - each time to the audible sound of approving "oohs" and "aahs."

When everything had, at last, been brought out, Tink stood behind her chair at the table and said, "Welcome again to my home, dear ones, on this Thanksgiving Day. As you know, Elizabeth Moreau is also an expected guest. But, since she is helping Larry with the S.O.S. basket deliveries, her arrival time is uncertain. So, we are going to proceed. Before eating, however, I would like to take a moment to offer a few simple words of gratitude and acknowledgment."

Looking briefly at each of her guests, Tink then professed, "I feel truly blessed to be sharing this meal and this day with each of you. And I wish to extend a heartfelt thanks to Maddie, our honored guest of honor. Let me applaud you," she continued, turning toward the youngest person at the table, "for the courage you've shown in being here today. From

303

what I understand, you had no guidebook or trusted colleague recommending Port Saint Smith as a must-visit place. Yet, you bravely ventured outside your known world to join us in ours. And we are all the better for it. My hope, therefore, is that your willingness to explore the unfamiliar will be rewarded beyond even your own imagination. May we all be bountifully blessed by the unexpected and grateful for our blessings in their many forms.

"Furthermore, in remembrance of those who are no longer seated here amongst us, one empty chair remains at this table. I believe in truth that they are not really gone and that their presence is still with us in more ways than we could possibly imag…" Without warning, though, Tink's voice cracked, and she struggled not to cry. Instead, she made herself focus more intently on the compassionate faces looking toward her. After a deep exhale, she managed to steady herself and begin to speak again. "When we encourage and welcome them, I believe that their essence will become even closer. So, may we never doubt that a meaningful relationship can be experienced with anyone on the other side."

Suddenly, the back door flew open as a mighty gust of wind swept in. It swirled briskly around the kitchen, pushed its way down the hallway, and swiftly entered the dining room.

"Good gracious," Tink exclaimed. "How did that happen? I'd better go see what's going on."

"I hope everything's alright," Shirley gasped nervously.

"Do you need any help?" Charlie inquired.

"No. But thank you. I'm sure everything's fine."

As Tink exited the room, Maddie became acutely aware that an unseen presence had just entered, along with the wind. While the other dinner guests waited for the return of their hostess, Maddie unmistakably felt someone sit in the empty chair to her left. *Does anyone else notice what's going on?* she wondered, looking around surreptitiously. But Charlie focused only on the empty plate in front of him while Shirley glanced anxiously in every direction except at the once-empty chair.

Tink soon bustled back into the room, offering a sensible explanation. "Well, in all the years of living in this house, I don't recall anything like that ever happening before. My guess is that with all the excitement of Maddie's arrival, escorted by our cardinal friend, I must not have closed the back door properly. So, the wind decided to make its way into this room, just like an invited guest."

Maddie said nothing but recognized the remarkable truth in her statement.

"To me," Shirley asserted, "the wind seemed to insist on joining us. I swear I even felt it circling around the room at least once and then stopping suddenly. Did you feel that also, Maddie?"

"Kind of, yes," Maddie replied softly, hoping she wouldn't be asked any more questions.

Apparently, everyone else only sensed the gust of wind entering and swirling around the room, Maddie thought. *But I'm guessing I'm the only one who realizes the chair beside me is no longer empty. I believe it is now occupied by the same endearing male essence that has visited me often since I arrived on the Cape.*

"I want all of you to know," Tink announced, "the door is now properly closed, and the wind seems to have calmed down. So, tell me, friends, where did I leave off in my little speech?"

"I think you were about to say cheers or amen or something to that effect so we could all start eating," Charlie suggested mirthfully.

"How right you are," Tink agreed with a little wink. "Thus, in conclusion, let us all be mindful of and grateful for our many blessings— both those expected and unexpected, seen and unseen. And so it is!"

"And so it is!" they all echoed back in expectant unison.

"Now, please take your plates over to the buffet," Tink encouraged, "and help yourselves to as much of anything as you wish. This meal was made for you with lots of love. So, enjoy!"

One by one, Tink's dinner guests stood up, walked to the extensive side table, and filled their plates with an abundance of sumptuous food. Once seated again and the first few satisfying bites taken, everyone spoke effusive words of praise.

"You've outdone yahself again," Shirley declared.

"Yes, this is very tasty," Charlie affirmed.

"Amazing" is about all Maddie could say as she took in the feast before her, the kind people around her, and the compelling companion beside her.

"I'm so glad you're all pleased," Tink stated sincerely with a slight bow of her head.

"We surah are, and we're all so fortunate to be herah," Shirley said. "Maddie, I don't think you or Charlie know this, but I was supposed to do my own entertaining today," she explained. "My cousin was planning to visit this week, but she broke her ankle a few days ago, so she couldn't come. Shortly aftah I found out, Tink stopped by the Chambah of Commerce fah a chat. When she realized my plans had been canceled, she invited me to attend this Thanksgiving dinnah rather than stay home and reorganize my linen closet, which is probably what I would have done. And that is no way to spend a holiday. What good fortune to have such a loyal friend, wouldn't yah say?"

"Yes, it certainly is," Maddie agreed. "I'm grateful to also have been invited," she said, smiling sweetly at the hostess.

"Me too," Charlie mumbled with a mouth full of mashed potatoes.

"Tink definitely has a way of bringing people togethah," Shirley offered sincerely. "You may think you've come to Tink's parties for the superb food and a bit of fun. And that's all true. But we'll probably leave having also formed deepah friendships too. Like the old expression says, 'the proof is in the puddin'. But in Tink's case, the proof of her goodness is in the pies, cookies, cakes, and good friends she has gathered over time. "

Tink listened to these words of acknowledgment but said nothing. She busied up instead, smearing butter and a generous dollop of Beach Plum jelly on a biscuit.

"Even aftah all these years," Shirley continued, "I am lucky to call Tink my good friend. But, when I first moved to Port Saint Smith and was introduced to her, I was rathah taken aback by her name. What kind of a grown woman would have such a quirky name, I wondered. Our precious Theresa Kendleton, that's who! And do you happen to know how she got her nickname, Maddie?"

"No, I don't," Maddie replied.

"May I tell her, Tink?" Shirley asked hopefully.

"Of course, you may," Tink agreed.

"Thank you! Well, what I understand is that as a newborn baby, Tink was christened Theresa Marie. Her fathah took pride in telling everyone she'd arrived with such a luminous spirit and a twinkle in her eyes. So, he began calling her Twinkle, Twinkle Little Star, like the song. Then, her youngah sister, Isabelle, was born, and when she began to talk, she couldn't say Twinkle, Twinkle. All she could do was point with her plump, little hand and say Tink Tink. Of course, everyone delighted in this variation of her name, and before long, they all began calling her Tink, a name which obviously stuck," Shirley said in conclusion. She then asked, "Did I get the story right, Tink Tink?"

"You sure did," the elder replied enthusiastically. "I think you may even tell it better than I do."

"Thanks!" Shirley replied gleefully.

"And if I may say so," Charlie interjected, "time has not diminished her twinkling spirit."

"How right you are, Charlie!" Shirley chimed in. "Tink really is our local shining star—brightening up the dark corners of our lives wherever and whenever needed."

"Well, that's all very nice, and I appreciate your good words," Tink murmured humbly. "But, perhaps we can find other things to talk about now besides me."

"Alrighty. Let's talk about our special guest," Shirley suggested readily. "Maddie, would you tell us how yah stay in Port Saint Smith has been so fah?"

"I'd be glad to," Maddie stated, pausing from her meal. My visit here has been incredible! I'm enjoying myself more than I'd even hoped," she admitted.

"How wondahful! And are you pleased with yah lodgings next door?"

"Absolutely," Maddie affirmed, "Thank you again, Shirley. I really appreciate all your assistance in finding such a perfect place for me to stay. And the map you drew for me has been very handy."

"I'm just glad I could be of help," Shirley responded brightly.

"We all know that home was designed for someone very special like you," Tink added.

"Well, I'm very grateful to be there because it is so conducive to peace there," Maddie shared. And as those words were spoken, she felt a tender touch brushing across the top of her hand.

Chapter 55
Elizabeth

Tink was so deeply immersed in Thanksgiving conversation, casserole, and roasted carrots that she didn't hear the knock on the back door. Elizabeth took the liberty, therefore, to enter on her own and call out from the kitchen.

"Hello...? Tink...? It's me, Elizabeth."

"Oh, Elizabeth, hello!" Tink called back from the dining room, scrambling to her feet. "Come on in."

Elizabeth crossed the large kitchen, walked down the hall, and entered the room with a friendly greeting to all, "Happy Thanksgiving!"

"Happy Thanksgiving," everyone warmly responded as Tink hurried over to welcome her last arriving guest.

"We're all so happy to see you and hope you're not too weary from the deliveries."

"Not at all. I actually feel energized. And oh my, Tink," Elizabeth declared as she glanced around the room, "I feel as though I've just stepped into an elegant scene from a classic movie. The food all looks sumptuous, and the room is simply stunning!"

"That means a lot coming from someone with such notably refined taste. I do find great joy in entertaining my cherished friends. And here you are, arriving at the perfect time! We've just started to eat. So, please, make yourself a plate of food and be seated. I've reserved the other place of honor for you," Tink explained, pointing excitedly toward the chair opposite Maddie at the far end of the table. "Since this is your first holiday meal in my home, I wanted you to feel truly welcome and celebrated."

"Thank you, Tink. That is very thoughtful! And I will gratefully take you up on the invitation to serve myself. I realized on my drive over that we didn't stop to eat all day. So, admittedly, I am rather hungry."

"Perfect. There's plenty of food, including ample leftovers for Larry, which is my way of thanking him for his efforts each year with the basket deliveries. I imagine he's stretched out on the couch, too tired to attend anyone's Thanksgiving gathering. But still, I'd love for him to share in our holiday feast."

After picking up the plate at the head setting, Elizabeth ambled over to the bountiful buffet. There, she helped herself to a smidgen of this and a sampling of that. No sooner was she settled in her seat than Shirley burst out with questions.

"How did the deliveries go, Elizabeth? Were therah enough side dishes fah each family? I sure hope therah were! And was it wondahful seeing the children again? I'm so eagah to hear everything. We all want to know how everything went, right Tink?"

"Yes, we're very excited to hear about the deliveries," Tink agreed. "But why don't we let Elizabeth have a little something to eat first?"

"Of course," Shirley acknowledged. "You're right, Tink. Please forgive me, Elizabeth."

"It's perfectly fine," Elizabeth stated agreeably, politely placing her fork on the rim of the plate. "I'd be happy to share about our day."

"Gosh, no," Shirley insisted. "You go ahead and enjoy this amazing meal. Besides, I just remembered something important I need to mention to you in case I fahget. Why don't I talk while you begin to eat?"

"Alright," Elizabeth agreed, quietly relieved, with the fork readily back in her hand.

"There's a good chance you'll be hearing from a man named Jake Harrison. Actually, that would be Doctor Jake Harrison. I received a call from him yestahday at the Chambah, asking several excellent questions about our community. I guess he liked the answers because he then requested a referral for a real estate agent. I gave him your name first, as I typically do. But I also gave him information for a couple other realtors out of fairness. I'm surah you understand. Oh, and he did mention something about bringing his son to visit the area during Christmas break. He's a widower, and apparently, he's considering relocating at the first of the year. But that's all I know. So, in case he does call, and I sense he will, I wanted you to be prepared."

"How considerate of you, Shirley. And I really appreciate the recommendation," Elizabeth stated. "I hope they do visit, as I'd be more than happy to show them just how special Port Saint Smith truly is."

"Our amazing little town certainly has room fah two more good people, if not more," Shirley added with a persuasive smile directed toward Maddie.

Maddie bashfully returned the smile, noticing once again an endearing touch on her hand.

"And whenevah yah ready, Elizabeth, we're all still anxious to hear about the deliveries. But no rush," Shirley said with an innocent shrug of the shoulders.

"But before you do that," Tink interjected, speaking slower than usual to allow this late arriving guest a little more time to eat, "I wanted you to also know, Elizabeth, that after we're all done with dinner and dessert, I'll be putting together a sizable feast for Larry. I've done this every Thanksgiving since the S.O.S. basket deliveries began. But seeing as my regular courier won't be able to help this year, would you mind driving it over to Larry's house on your way home? Is that asking too much after such a long day?"

"Not at all—I'd be more than happy to," Elizabeth acknowledged.

"Much appreciated, I assure you," Tink responded, relieved that those arrangements had been made.

"And speaking of deliveries," Elizabeth graciously said as a segue, looking around the table at four expectant faces, "let me not keep you waiting any longer." Delicately wiping her mouth with the napkin, she continued, "I'm extremely pleased to report that every aspect of this year's deliveries came together quite miraculously. And yes, Shirley, every single basket had a plentiful amount of side dishes—much thanks to you and the ever-so-resourceful ladies of the guild. I thank you so much for stepping in at the last minute with such a willing attitude. Your efforts contributed greatly to the overall success!"

"What wicked good news!" Shirley squealed with delight. "I was so happy to be of help this year, and I know Tink always is, too!"

"And, speaking of Tink," Elizabeth added, "your name came up in conversation at least twice today. One of the children's grandmothers, who is probably close to your youthful age, inquired if the homemade pie was baked, and I quote, 'by that fabled woman named Tink Kendleton. Although I haven't met her myself, I sure hope to one day since her pie baking is legendary 'round these parts.'"

"Imagine that?" Tink replied with an impish smile. "And how did Larry do today?" she inquired next.

"He did really well," Elizabeth assured her. "He smiled a lot and seemed to sincerely enjoy the interactions with the children and their families. He even laughed along with me at my feeble attempts to help in the kitchen. I learned a lot from him because my basic skills were non-existent to begin with. He's a very good teacher."

"That is such wonderful news," Tink responded with evident relief.

"Yes, and I believe he was really proud to continue this worthy outreach program and glad to be reminded of the positive impact it has on our community and the S.O.S. families."

"What a blessing," Tink said. "And I know this has taken a lot of effort on your part, Elizabeth. So I commend you for taking charge this year, especially since, well… uh," But Tink stopped speaking abruptly and busied herself, instead by spooning more Beach Plum jelly onto a biscuit already laden with butter.

"I was honored to help," Elizabeth affirmed.

"Me too! And I'm definitely willing to help again next year," Shirley declared. "It was fun and purposeful, which, to me, is the best! And with more time to plan, there's no telling what the guild members will be able to provide in the future."

"Exactly!" Elizabeth replied. "Larry even said we may need a trailer if the contributions exceed those we had today. And he may be right!"

Then, even Charlie expressed an interest in donating jars of his homemade pickles and tomatoes. "All I need is the go-ahead, and I'll begin prepping in the spring."

"Consider this the go-ahead," Elizabeth acknowledged with a broad smile.

In silent admiration, Maddie watched as members of this endearing community willingly offered their time and talents in support of those in need. *I would love to help, too,* she thought, *if I were to be here again during Thanksgiving week. How extraordinary to feel a part of such a giving group of dedicated citizens.*

Everyone then returned to contented eating and a palpable, close-knit comradery. Wisely though, as the lull of full stomachs began to set in, the sage hostess announced, "Often at my dinner parties, I suggest a topic of discussion while the meal is settling and the coffee to accompany dessert is brewing. Today, I feel inspired for us to share with each other one of our favorite childhood memories. It can be anything that you wish. But perhaps the focus can be on something that may have helped you better appreciate the very wonder of this life. However, if you feel at all uncomfortable, sharing is never required," Tink added in a reassuring tone.

"Also, for the sake of time, I may briefly respond after each person shares. But, I do ask that you refrain from also commenting at this point. Otherwise, we may still be here tomorrow for brunch, which I'm not actually opposed to, except for the fact that I have a commitment to gift wrap at the bookstore in order to raise funds for the Homes for Hounds Rescue Center. So, unless someone objects, I'll go first and will talk slowly, giving each of you a little longer to decide what you might want to say." And with that, Tink began.

"As a wee child, I experienced such joy in observing nature. My mother would often find me plopped down in the midst of our garden, studying the structure of a flower, the flight pattern of a bee, or the interweaving of a vine. I would collect fallen acorns, pine cones, and feathers to study later in my room. And I have never ceased to find inspiration in the vast and intricate tapestry of life itself. Look at us, for example. We come from different places and backgrounds. Yet, we are gathered here today in a supportive formation of friendship, which is so beautiful. And what about all that exists around us in the unseen realm? That fascinates me also. For are we the only ones present here at this moment? Or are we joined as well by the angelic realm and our loved ones in spirit? That topic, however, I will save for another celebration. So, in closing, my childhood served as the notable beginning of my boundless curiosity, my adoration and admiration of nature, and the gathering of good things and good people together. Now, that's enough about me. Who would like to speak next?"

Shirley quickly looked around the table and then eagerly replied, "I'll go next if that's alright?"

"Absolutely, go right ahead," Tink encouraged.

"My dollies!" Shirley blurted out. "I loved playing with my dolls. I would line them all up in a neat row and teach them their numbahs, lettahs, and colahs. The dolls, of course, were not very interactive. But to

312

me, as a child, they were well-behaved. Unlike my cat, who I tried to teach one day. He let me know immediately that he had no interest in sitting down to learn anything. But my dollies were good students, and I can see now that is exactly where my love fah teaching began. And for ovah fahty years, I was an educator. And that career was, for me, so remarkably rewarding. I made so many lasting friendships and feel that I contributed to my students' lives in significant ways. And that's my story," Shirley concluded.

"Thank you, Shirley. How precious for us to know where it all began," Tink commented. "Plus, I have personally witnessed the positive influence you've had on many of your students and can attest to your triumph as a teacher."

"Thank you kindly, Tink," Shirley replied modestly.

"You're most welcome." And before the conversation could veer off topic, the hostess quickly turned her attention toward another guest in hopes she would feel comfortable enough to share. "Maddie, would you care to say anything?"

"Yes, I would, thank you." After a small pause, Maddie proceeded, "For me, it was always fireflies. I loved to watch them twinkling on and off in the meadows at night. I even used to believe, and perhaps, still do, that they were magical in some way—like tiny fairies coming out from the woods to dance under the evening stars."

"How sweet, my dear," Tink commented kindly. "To me, fireflies definitely have a little mystery and magic. When we stay open to the wonder around us that is not always easy to explain logically, we undoubtedly can experience even more of what intrigues and engages us. And that can certainly add a more meaningful and exciting dimension to our lives."

As Maddie nodded in agreement, she once more felt the soft squeeze of her hand. Her heart fluttered in eager response and the knowledge that she was receiving such a tender yet clandestine touch.

"Thank you for sharing with us, Maddie," Tink said sincerely.

"You're welcome," Maddie replied in kind.

Ever so gently, Tink then inquired, "Charlie, will you please indulge us with a childhood story? I'm sure you have a few tales to tell."

At first, the elderly man squirmed uncomfortably in his chair, and Tink feared he might refuse. Still, she waited hopefully in silence, and after further hesitation, he did speak up.

"When I was a boy," Charlie began, "probably around eight years old, I had a friend at school who invited me for a playday at his family's country home. I was thrilled because this was such a big outing. Having grown up in an area that was called the poor side of the tracks, I'd never been anywhere special before. Oh, how I remember my mother scrubbing me cleaner than usual that day and insisting I wear my best outfit. She also lectured me about good behavior, insisting that I do whatever his parents told me to. I don't know if I was more excited or more nervous when they finally came to pick me up in their big, fancy car."

Abruptly, Charlie stopped speaking as if reconsidering the idea of saying anything at all. Yet, no one pressured him while they awaited his next words. With a deep sigh of resignation, he continued speaking.

"My friend's father drove carefully out of town and through back roads, some of which I'd never seen before. All the while, his mother made light conversation about school, what we'd eat for lunch, and so on. I thought we'd never get there. But, at last, the left turn indicator clicked loudly as the speed of the car slowed down. And Timothy—that was my friend's name—poked me as we turned onto their road. A bit further on, Timothy pointed out an enormous estate just before their own. Immediately, I was captivated by the massive iron gates protecting the entrance and two long rows of tall trees lining the driveway. I had never seen anything like that in my whole life. I craned my neck as long as possible until it went out of sight. We drove just a little way further before pulling into their driveway, which was quite grand in its own right. Theirs was a Colonial-style home with white columns, rocking chairs, and a manicured lawn. His father parked on the circular drive, and we all got out of the car and went inside to eat a big meal that had been prepared by the help."

Charlie paused again, afraid he was being too long-winded or possibly even boring. But Tink, sensing his concern, nodded in encouragement as if to say, "Go on, please, we're all really listening."

"Well, then," he said, clearing his throat, "after lunch, which was a mighty feast for a humble boy like me, Timothy begged his parents to let us go outside and play. With his mother's cautionary permission and his father's insistence that we do not venture into the woods, we finally left the house.

"I must add," he then stated frankly, "for reasons I have yet to figure out, the next part of this memory has come to my mind so often lately, which is odd since I hadn't thought about this event in years. Anyway," he said, shaking his head in bewilderment, "despite his parent's clear instructions, Timothy marched straight into the woods saying, 'Remember when we saw the big, iron gates? I want to show you the enchanted castle way behind those gates. I know the shortcut through the woods.' I was stunned. I didn't want to go against his parents' rules because I didn't want to get in trouble with either them or my mother. But I followed along anyway, too nervous to be left alone and excited to see a real castle. Then Timothy led us expertly along an unmarked path, and although I was really afraid, I didn't want to miss out on the adventure."

Maddie listened attentively, as did the others, while the hand that had been embracing hers clasped even tighter.

"Having grown up in such a small part of town, I was unfamiliar with this kind of woodsy terrain," Charlie admitted. "But, I did my best to keep up, scrambled awkwardly over the thick roots and fallen limbs. And just as we were approaching a clearing, I saw a tall, silhouetted figure standing boldly against the bright sky beyond. I was terrified and certain we were trespassing as a stern voice bellowed out, 'Who goes there?'

"I was shaking so badly that I didn't take another step further. But Timothy insisted that everything was alright and that we should proceed. Reluctantly, I moved just a little closer to the ominous figure. And what happened next, I swear I'll never forget...

"The tall man laughed aloud and replaced his stern voice with a kind tone, saying, 'Timothy, my young friend, how good of you to come! Who, may I ask, has traveled the wooded path with you today?'

"I was still in shock when my friend introduced me to this man - a man who proved to be one of the most exceptional people I have ever met. I tried to stop trembling as he pulled a bag of macadamia nuts from his pocket, inviting us to have a few. Apparently, he'd been feeding them to the squirrels and snacking on them himself, which he illustrated by popping one into his mouth. Next, he asked if we wanted to have a walk around his property. Immediately, we both said yes, and off we went— the enigmatic man with his long, walking stick and us eagerly trailing behind. The castle, as Timothy had called it, was indeed grand, but we only saw it from the outside. And not far behind it was the most beautiful view of the ocean. I was enchanted. Yet, the most memorable part of the whole experience was the man's exceptional presence. He seemed larger

315

than life, almost like a benevolent character out of a fairytale. I've never forgotten him. And I only shared this story once with my wife and never with my mother for reasons you'd understand," Charlie recounted. "How odd then," he said in closing, "that this kindly man has come to my mind so often lately."

A hush filled the room as everyone sat transfixed by Charlie's evocative childhood memory. But no one was more moved than Elizabeth, who, Tink noticed, was holding back tears. Rather than pressure her in any way, the wise hostess spoke up quickly.

"Thank you, Charlie. That was a wonderful tale you told! And I realize that it's Elizabeth's turn now. However, I believe this would be the perfect time for dessert and coffee. Let's enjoy that first, and then, if she feels up to saying anything, we'll all be glad to listen. And if not, that's certainly understandable because she must be rather tired."

With a slight tilt of her head, Elizabeth acknowledged her friend's thoughtfulness and sensitivity. And she gladly supported Tink's suggestion.

"I think having dessert now is a good idea," Elizabeth managed to say. "And I will most likely pass on sharing today, but promise to participate the next time we all get together."

"As you wish, my friend," Tink replied agreeably, rising from her chair. "Shirley, would you mind giving me a hand in the kitchen?"

"I'd be glad to," Shirley readily answered.

And with that, the two women left the room, and the other three guests all welcomed a chance for contemplative silence.

Chapter 56
Larry

Larry was stretched out on the couch in the same position that had rightfully earned him the nickname Slouch. The S.O.S. basket deliveries had been extremely successful, and after returning home, he'd showered and immediately laid down for a lengthy nap. Upon awakening, he noticed that the T.V. was silently showing the fourth quarter of a lopsided football game. Rather than switch on the sound, he continued lying in the silence and thinking about this first Thanksgiving following Nic's death. Yet, the exhausted and vulnerable man was not sure he could handle even the slightest amount of reflection without becoming emotionally overwhelmed. He had a little strength left and was also acutely aware of the intense feelings that had been circling around and within him for days like a fierce nor'easter. Worst case scenario, Larry reasoned, he could always turn the T.V. volume back up and lose himself in one of the many football games featured today.

Much like the interlacing weave of the cornucopia basket he'd purchased for Elizabeth, Larry realized all his recent Thanksgivings had been intrinsically woven with activities involving Nic. The planning, cooking, and delivering of each S.O.S. basket was now integrated into the very fiber of this holiday. With the recognition of that fact, Larry was relieved to be lying down as his stomach lurched, and his head felt woozy. He was numb from fatigue and the private struggle of coming to terms with the incomprehensible communications from Nic.

The days leading up to the holiday had been filled with gut-wrenching dread and confusion. Larry had wanted to completely ignore the basket delivery tradition because he couldn't imagine the possibility of proceeding without his best friend's help. Fortunately, Elizabeth had bravely broached the sensitive subject with him. Even so, when she'd brought it up, Larry had done his best to persuade her that it was too late for an undertaking of that magnitude, especially so close to Thanksgiving. But, she hadn't accepted his excuses, and only after promising to do almost everything herself, had he reluctantly agreed.

However, when Elizabeth had asked to assist him in the kitchen on Thanksgiving morning, Larry thought she'd gone too far. She usually was such a perceptive person; sympathetic to his needs and, even lately, to his erratic moods. Why couldn't she see then that he wanted to be left alone? But, once again, he'd begrudgingly given in, not only to appease his top associate, but more importantly, to avoid further prodding in the form of repeated texts.

But how can that be possible? How can I be receiving messages from someone buried in the local cemetery? Larry questioned solemnly, crossing his arms over his sizable chest. *Or is that an indication of sheer madness, as I have often feared? How can Nic write to me in any form - be it text or a piece of paper? Yet, I'm sure he won't be stopping by later today, as he did in the past, with Tink's generous Thanksgiving leftovers. Nor will he be sitting across from me in that chair and teasing me for lying about like a lazy sloth. So, is it even fair for me to feel betrayed by his absence, when he is the one who lost his life? Maybe not! But, fair or not, I'm the one left behind, and he, wherever he is, probably has it pretty easy right now.*

I must admit, though, Larry continued to reflect, *that today was a perfect reminder of Nic's unwavering commitment to helping others. The deliveries felt different from when he and I made them together. But still, everything proceeded like clockwork. Elizabeth and I were well-received by everyone, and I even laughed a few times, which felt good. And although I'm very familiar with her capabilities, Elizabeth managed to impress me again with efforts regarding this endeavor. She shined through it all. Plus, we worked well together in the kitchen, which says a lot for a territorial chef like me. But, beyond all that, seeing the kind expressions of gratitude on the families' faces reminded me once again why we do all of this, and it is admittedly worth every effort.*

Larry continued to lay motionless as thoughts about the day passed

through his mind, and feelings long ignored began to surface from the depths of his heart. He no longer had the strength to avoid those emotions. So, he watched like a passive observer as one outstanding memory from the day replayed in his mind.

"Five of the houses are in the same area, and the last two are a bit further to the north," Elizabeth had explained, as he'd driven his truck across the Sagamore Bridge. "I know you said we won't stay long at any of the homes, which will allow the families plenty of time for their holiday celebrations. So, I will follow your lead as to when to say our goodbyes. Plus, I told Tink I wasn't sure when I would arrive for dinner, and she was completely fine with that. And Larry," she'd added with a notable softening in her voice, "thank you again for letting me be involved, even with the cooking. This has meant so much to me."

"You're welcome, Elizabeth," he'd replied. "Thank you for all you've done to pull this together at the last minute, including your help this morning. I doubt I would have managed nearly as well if you hadn't been there to assist."

"My pleasure—truly!" Elizabeth exclaimed. "And who knew that chopping and dicing would be on the list of my latent skills to be realized? Because I'd more or less given up on having any skills in the kitchen, at all."

A comfortable silence then replaced the conversation as they continued driving north. After the first two deliveries were made to enthusiastic receptions, an easy rhythm was established. Elizabeth would walk ahead to the door with a pot of chrysanthemums in one arm, a large gift bag in the other, and a radiant smile on her face. Larry stood slightly behind her, holding the food basket as his associate rang the doorbell. Soon, they would be greeted by the young sailors and their family members, many of whom were familiar to them from the summer camp.

One after another, successful drop-offs were made as the emptiness created by the absence of each basket in the truck was filled with joy. Then, quite unexpectedly, as they approached the very last house, Larry watched as Elizabeth became noticeably nervous. Her hands were clenched tightly, and she stared uneasily out the window. Unsure whether to say anything or not, Larry decided to remain in bewildered silence.

319

Unlike any of the other stops, after they parked, Elizabeth remained seated as though unable to move. Larry finally asked if she was alright.

"I'm not really sure. I, um, well, uh, this is Trevor's house," an unrecognizably timid voice stammered. "I think you might recall who he is?"

"Yes, I know who you're talking about," he replied, wondering why that was of any consequence.

"Well, we befriended one another at summer camp," she explained, "and I've really been looking forward to seeing him again - apparently more than I even realized. When I spoke to his grandmother earlier this week to coordinate the delivery, I didn't mention that I would be coming. Now I'm afraid he may not be here. Or, worse, he may be here, and not remember me as fondly as I remember him. And that," she admitted with a heavy sigh, "would be so upsetting."

Unfamiliar with Elizabeth showing this kind of vulnerability, Larry could barely speak. Still, he offered a few words, "Well, let's just go find out."

Together, they walked up the short path, donations in hand, and Elizabeth hesitantly knocked on the door. Soon enough, they were warmly greeted by two people - Trevor's grandmother, Delphine, and his father, Michael. Elizabeth managed to wear a brave smile as she gave Delphine the plant and gift bag. Michael spoke sincere words of appreciation as he took the basket from Larry and turned to carry it into the kitchen. All the while, Larry could visibly see the strain on Elizabeth's face.

After graciously receiving the items, Delphine looked directly into Elizabeth's pained eyes and said, "Besides our sincere gratitude, there is one more thing I want to share with you, Elizabeth." And with that, from behind her back, came young Trevor.

"Surprise!" he exclaimed with his hands waving fervently in the air. And before Elizabeth could even express her immense joy, the eager boy rushed toward her, saying, "Miss Elizabeth, you're here! I knew you were coming to see me. I just knew it!"

Everyone watched in awe as he wrapped his thin arms around her. For several moments, he clung to her, and she to him, without a word being spoken. And the only one witnessing the small tears streaking down the side of Elizabeth's face was Larry.

Then, with just as much enthusiasm, Trevor let go and said to Delphine, "See, Grandma, I told you she was coming. I knew she would be here today."

Elizabeth remained speechless, as Delphine nodded and smiled in acknowledgment. Trevor then turned to go back inside, asking, "Please don't leave, Miss Elizabeth, ok? Wait here for me. I'll be right back." With no reservation, Elizabeth stood completely still, waiting for his return, as Larry watched in fascination, genuinely pleased for his colleague.

While the young boy ran into the house, his grandmother confided, "Trevor was so excited about seeing you. But, I told him not to get his hopes up in case you weren't the one making the delivery. He insisted though, that you would be coming."

"That's incredible," is all Elizabeth could utter in response.

The boy soon returned, carefully holding a large piece of paper in his hands.

"I drew this yesterday," he shared, handing it proudly to Elizabeth.

"How wonderful! I'm excited to see it," she responded sincerely, taking the sheet of paper from him. After looking at it, everyone could now see her inability to hold back tears.

While discreetly trying to wipe her face dry, she asked him in a quivering voice, "Is this a drawing of us today?"

"Yes, you're right! It's a drawing of us," Trevor affirmed enthusiastically. "But, that shouldn't make you sad."

"Oh, I'm not sad, Trevor," she assured him. "These are happy tears." After gently wiping her eyes once more, Elizabeth held up the paper so the others could see it.

In the background of the artwork was a small, simplistic house. Standing at the front door were two people who clearly resembled his grandmother and father. On the left side of the paper was a larger figure that looked uncannily like Larry. He stood in front of a truck in the exact color of his own. And in the front yard was a tall, stick-figure woman wearing a blouse, skirt, and fancy shoes. At her side was a boy in casual clothes wearing a sailor hat and holding her hand. The boy and the lady both had big smiles as they stood next to each other. The only unrecognizable aspects of the sketch were the blue wavy lines that appeared across the sky.

"May I point everything out in my picture?" Trevor asked.

"I would love you to do that," she replied.

"That's you and me," he announced proudly, pointing at the two prominent figures in the front yard. "And that's Grandma and Daddy. And over there is Mr. Walters and his truck."

"I'm just amazed, Trevor," she stated, unable to say anything further.

"And see those blue squiggles in the sky?" he asked. "Do you know what that is?"

"No, actually, I don't. Would you tell me, please?"

"That's the wind. But it was kinda hard to draw since it's invisible."

"I think you did quite well. And is there a reason that you drew so much wind?" she inquired.

"Yes, because I think that the wind helped bring you here," he explained. "Not like you were a kite or a bird or something, but kinda like it was pushing you to the house to come be with us."

"That's fascinating," Elizabeth remarked, remembering the significance of the wind in her own prophetic dream.

"May I ask you another question?"

"Yes," he replied innocently.

"You've drawn us all in the picture, even me. But how did you really know that I was coming today?"

"Because I saw you in my dream. First, the wind was blowing all around our house," he illustrated with his arms waving overhead. "Not in a scary way, but in a sorta friendly way. Then you came to the door with all kinds of stuff - flowers and food and presents."

"What he is telling you is true," Delphine confirmed. "Yesterday morning, he shared his dream with me, including the most important part that you would definitely be one of the people bringing our Thanksgiving dinner. I kept telling him that it was a nice dream, but it might not happen. But he insisted and went back into his room to draw every detail in that picture."

"I'm just stunned," Elizabeth expressed, and then looking only at Trevor, she added, "and I'm so lucky we're friends."

"We're very good friends," he exclaimed emphatically. "And do you really like my picture?"

"I like it *very* much! I think it's remarkable!"

"Good, because I made it for you."

"You did?" she asked in astonishment.

"Yes, so you can remember us being together today."

"Oh, Trevor, that is so kind of you. Thank you. I'm going to keep it right next to the sailboat card you made for me at camp."

"That's a great idea!" he exclaimed.

Then, Delphine spoke up again, "We realize that you and Larry may need to get on your way, although you're more than welcome to come in and have dinner with us."

"How kind of you to ask. Perhaps another time," Elizabeth replied warmly.

"Well, thank you for everything you've given us, but most importantly, for coming here today."

"You're so welcome. I'm delighted to see you all."

"And Trevor is hoping to go back to camp next summer," his father added, "if that's possible."

Elizabeth glanced over at Larry for assurance, but he remained silent. So, she said, "We are hoping that the camps will continue next year. And, if so, we will gladly welcome this fine sailor again."

With that, Trevor wrapped his arms around Elizabeth once more, and she heartily returned his embrace.

"I hope to see you soon," she said.

"Me too!" he replied joyously.

As Elizabeth and I left, Larry continued to ruminate about the unusual details of their last basket delivery, *I was too dumbstruck and tired to say anything to the family other than Happy Thanksgiving. But once we began the drive back, I kept wondering how Trevor could have possibly known we were coming. Clearly, that was Elizabeth in his artwork, and I guess he drew me also but with a rather sizable paunch— something that I may need to address in the New Year. And I just can't help but wonder if Nic had a part in this? He showed me the Captain's Supper in a dream, and there was a noticeable breeze. Did he also show Trevor in his dream that we would be coming to his home? Was that Nic stirring things up once again, as indicated by the foretelling swirls of wind?*

I'm not sure, but I don't really want to think about this anymore, Larry concluded with a humph sound. *At least Elizabeth was quiet as we headed back to town. I was so relieved not to have to talk. Only once did I look over to see a most serene smile on her face.*

However, just a few minutes before we pulled into the office parking lot, Elizabeth did speak up. I was so afraid she would want to discuss Trevor's picture and the significance of his dream. I certainly didn't want to have to comment on that, since I'm still wrestling with my own dream and its meaning. I was also concerned that she would want to discuss the future of the S.O.S. camps since that came up in conversation with Trevor's family. Either way, I knew I shouldn't deny her request.

"Larry, may I ask you something," she'd inquired meekly.

"Alright," was the reluctant response heard.

"Thanks. I want you to know first, however, that I will never forget this Thanksgiving. It may be the happiest one I've ever had."

"That's good. Everything went well for which you are to be fully credited," Larry acknowledged.

"Fortunately, everything did go well," she concurred and then added, "I do have a request for you though. Would you be willing to look at a property with me on Saturday?"

"Sure. I can do that," he agreed, relieved by such a simple request. "But we're taking my truck and not that miniature car of yours."

"That's fine," she agreed with a laugh. "I was hoping to go tomorrow, but a front is being forecast for our area with strong winds and rain."

"Oh, really?' he asked. "Thanks for letting me know. Why don't we just close the office for the next few days? We could both use some time off."

"I think that's a great idea! And I'd be glad to take any forwarded calls that do come in," Elizabeth offered.

"Alright. Thanks. I had considered working on the boat tomorrow since I haven't done anything there, well, since, uh… since a while ago. But, anyway, I can do that on Sunday. What time do you want to go on Saturday?"

"Could we meet at the office around 9 a.m.?" she asked.

"Ok, let's plan on that," Larry replied.

"That sounds good. Thank you again, Larry. Oh, and please bring the old photograph with you, too," she requested.

Remembering that part of the conversation, Larry sunk down even further into the couch. He wondered what that picture had to do with seeing a property in the area. Too exhausted to give it any more consideration, he nodded off to sleep once more.

Chapter 57
Maddie

Maddie was filled with a deep sense of gratitude when she said goodbye to Tink. The time at her neighbor's home had been exceptionally enjoyable, and now her arms were filled with containers of delicious leftovers from their Thanksgiving meal. Although Maddie had willingly offered to stay and help with the cleanup, all she'd been allowed to do was give the weary hostess a hug and her heartfelt thanks. And, in that moment of parting, they both recognized the unexpected blessing of a sweet connection between them.

As Maddie walked back towards *La Maison Enchantée* in the twilight hour, she was aware of Tink's attentiveness as she stood on the threshold of the kitchen doorway. Maddie turned, therefore, and waved goodnight, one last time, before going inside. After the food was put away, though, Maddie realized she was not ready for the day to end. So, rather than settle in for the evening, she buttoned up her coat, pulled a scarf around her neck, and walked back outside.

The fading light cast long golden rays across the yard, and the azure blue sky created a dramatic backdrop to the dark silhouette of tall trees. After many hours spent inside her neighbor's warm home filled with laughter and camaraderie, Maddie welcomed the quiet of evening, as well as the crisp, cold air.

With no particular destination in mind, she walked in the opposite direction from her earlier bike route into downtown. The stroll was pleasant, and within minutes, Maddie noticed a house she guessed to be Charlie's. A solitary rocker rested alone on the front porch, amidst an impressive array of thriving plants. And just off to the side was an old, red wagon filled with a few empty glass jars. A small trail of smoke rose up from the chimney, and she imagined the elder gentleman settling in for the night in front of the fire.

Maddie proceeded for another three blocks, then turned right onto a more heavily traveled road. After walking a little distance further, and with almost no other traffic in sight, she became aware of a car slowing down beside her. She continued on, but became a bit concerned when it failed to pass. The car then pulled slightly ahead, coming to a full stop. Not until the passenger window lowered, however, did she realize the person driving the car was Elizabeth Moreau.

"Hello there," Elizabeth said quietly, perceiving that this visitor was in a more relaxed state than when they'd said their goodbyes at Tink's home, just a short while ago. "It's a lovely evening, isn't it?"

"Oh, hi, Elizabeth," Maddie replied, relieved as well as pleased to see her. "Yes, it's such a nice evening."

"How good to see you. I'm just getting back from Larry's, where I delivered the food that Tink had prepared for him," Elizabeth shared. "I placed it in a cooler by the door without ringing the bell, as he'd requested. Then I sent a quick text encouraging him to bring it inside before a family of raccoons decided this generous holiday meal was intended for them. But after that, I was just a bit too restless to go home. And I'm guessing you felt the same?"

"Yes, the night just felt too inviting to stay inside."

"Right? I often go for a drive in the evening if I'm feeling a little stirred up. The movement of the car, and change of scenery seem to clear my head and relax me," Elizabeth explained, as she checked the rear mirror to make sure her car wasn't blocking the road.

"That's one of the main reasons I enjoy cycling so much," Maddie offered. "I can quickly release whatever's on my mind and become fully immersed in the setting around me. Then I invariably return home refreshed and renewed."

"Exactly," Elizabeth agreed. "I've tried meditating many times and even attended a few classes with the hopes of becoming adept at sitting in the silence. Well, let me tell you, I failed miserably every time, and that's admitting a lot for a high achiever like myself. But, put me in a competent car swerving through a few challenging turns or picking up speed on a safe, straight away, and I'm good to go!" she asserted, tapping on the steering wheel. "I guess we all have to find what works best for us, wouldn't you say?"

"Definitely! Whether that's driving, cycling, yoga, baking, or whatever," Maddie affirmed wholeheartedly. "And it may be in ways that seem unconventional to others, but still work for us."

"Well said, Maddie. I'm so glad I saw you tonight. I always enjoy when we have a chance to talk," Elizabeth acknowledged. "Oh, and I didn't get a chance to ask earlier, but Larry specifically wanted to know during our deliveries today, if everything is still going well for you at *La Maison Enchantée*. I told him that, as far as I know, you're really enjoying your stay there."

"I really am. The home feels perfect in ways I can't even explain. And you, Tink, and Shirley have all made me feel so welcome."

"I'm glad to know that. And I must tell you, Ms. Maddie Stuart, you are quite the talk of the town!" Elizabeth added with a broad smile. "Well, perhaps not the entire town. But those who have met you are especially fond of you already."

"That's so nice of you to say!" Maddie replied modestly. "I've loved meeting everyone, and feel so embraced by all the kindness. But I do have a question about the home. Is there any chance that the owner could come by while I'm there so I can thank him personally?"

Taken aback by this request, Elizabeth was at a rare loss for words. When she and Maddie had initially discussed the rental paperwork, divulging such personal information did not feel appropriate. Since Maddie was now becoming acquainted with some of Nic's neighbors and closest friends, however, keeping his death a secret no longer seemed right, especially at this moment. But did *she* have to be the one to inform Maddie of Nic's recent passing? Elizabeth hoped not.

"Well, I uh," Elizabeth stuttered hesitantly, "I can appreciate your desire to speak to him, but um,…" She stopped abruptly then, as the headlights of an approaching car became visible in the rearview mirror. Because she was only marginally pulled over on the shoulder of the road, Elizabeth continued by saying, "Forgive me, Maddie, but I'd better move the car. My good friend's home is just three houses further up the street, and he won't mind me pulling into his driveway. Can we continue our conversation there?"

"Of course. I'll catch right up with you," Maddie replied, as Elizabeth shifted into drive and pulled forward.

During her short walk, Maddie became aware of a light breeze lifting several fall leaves into the air, causing them to swirl and dance in a delightful circle. Even as she proceeded along the sidewalk, they continued to spin playfully around her. And though the wind afforded no words, Maddie distinctly felt his engaging presence—the same intriguing companion that had been visiting her for days now.

Once Maddie reached the waiting car, Elizabeth began to speak. "I apologize for the interruption, Maddie. You were asking about the owner of *La Maison Enchantée,* but, unfortunately, he won't be able to stop by the house. However, I'm sure, if he knew you were staying in his home, he'd be very pleased to have such a lovely person there."

Just then, before a reply could even be given, a stronger gust of wind swirled autumn leaves entirely around Maddie once more, and then carried a single leaf into the open window of Elizabeth's car. The amber leaf fluttered briefly about before settling on a piece of paper lying in the passenger seat.

"Look at this beautiful gift of nature that just drifted into my car," Elizabeth said, holding it up in admiration, and releasing a slight sigh of relief, thankful for the distraction. For admitting the truth of her dear friend's passing felt too vulnerable, and she feared the words might be accompanied by an unwelcome rush of emotions. So, Elizabeth skillfully guided the conversation in a different direction.

"How fascinating that this stunning leaf landed right on top of a flyer for an event I wanted to mention to you."

"That is amazing," Maddie replied, as they both momentarily wondered in silence if the wind had purposefully played a part in that occurrence.

"Maddie," Elizabeth then inquired, "is there any chance you would consider returning to Port Saint Smith before the end of the year? There's going to be a delightful holiday production at the theater, and I'd love to treat you as my guest to see the performance. I'm on the board of directors and have very good seats, and you would, of course, be my guest. I think we'd have fun. Or, if you'd prefer to attend with someone else, perhaps someone special in your life, I could arrange tickets for the two of you to go to the show as my gift. Don't forget, I noticed that dreamy look in your eyes at the café, so maybe that's a better suggestion," she said with a little wink. "Either way, I think you'd really enjoy seeing it, but I won't insist on an answer now."

"I love the idea of coming back here, and since I'm ever so single, I would definitely be coming alone. Going to the theater is one of my favorite things to do," Maddie stated, recalling the old box office window she'd noticed in town during her bike ride. "Thank you for inviting me."

"You're most welcome," Elizabeth replied. "I'm glad I had another chance to talk to you."

"Me too," Maddie agreed. "I think we would have a good time together."

"Yes! And just so you know, I'm someone who really values time with my friends. If I'm dating someone," Elizabeth explained, "or even if Mr. Wonderful moved in right next door, I still won't change my plans. I've always welcomed a healthy balance of time with both my friends and significant other."

"I'm that way too," Maddie affirmed.

"I'm not surprised. Oh, and speaking of romance, who knows," Elizabeth wistfully added, taking in a long breath of cool, crisp air, "maybe this glorious wind will bring an unexpected love into both our lives. I'm certainly open to that, and maybe you are too."

Goosebumps immediately covered Maddie's arms as she softly replied, "I most certainly am."

"Excellent! Well, let's plan to stay in touch—you've got my contact information. Just reach out if you decide to visit again. And, of course, I'll arrange it so that you can stay at the same house for the same rate. To be honest with you, I can't imagine anyone else staying there."

"Oh, that would be wonderful! Thank you so much," Maddie replied with excitement. "I just need to confirm my work schedule, but since I still have plenty of vacation days to use, before the end of the year, that shouldn't be a problem."

"Great! Just give me a few days' notice, if you can," Elizabeth requested.

"I sure will."

"And Maddie, don't you just love when serendipity happens?" Elizabeth asked cheerfully. "I had wanted to talk with you about this performance, but didn't get a chance earlier today. Then I see you out for an evening walk just as I'm going out for a drive. That, to me, is more than just an accident. And what about the autumn leaf fluttering inside my car and landing exactly on the flyer, I wanted to show you? I realize fall days can be quite blustery, but lately, when the wind is blowing, I feel as if a distinct message is also being sent. Do you know what I mean?" she asked curiously, seeking assurance in Maddie's eyes.

"Yes, I definitely do," Maddie affirmed while managing to conceal just how true that statement was to her.

"I personally cherish these experiences," Elizabeth shared. "And maybe I'm thinking more about this right now because it's the time of year when we celebrate our friends and family. But perhaps there is more to it than that. Maybe an angel is offering us their encouragement or someone on the other side is sending these various signs and assisting us with these fortuitous interactions.

Maddie stood in awe of Elizabeth's admission, realizing that even this tender and telling conversation was another validation of her own significant experiences with the wind.

"My Grand-Papa," Elizabeth continued reflectively, "used to tell me that the stars are really our ancestors shining their love down on us. But I'd like to think they are much closer than that. "Then, with a light laugh, she asked, "Am I talking nonsense, Maddie? Has the rich Thanksgiving meal, and fatigue gone straight to my head or, more likely, to my heart?"

"No, not at all. I was very close to my grandmother and have been thinking about her more than usual this week. I believe she is often nearby and finding ways to reassurance me."

"Precisely," Elizabeth stated. "I'm humbled by how often I miss my Grand-Papa, even after all these years. I don't sense him around me very often, but I do think he's still helping me navigate through this fascinating pilgrimage of life. And maybe, just maybe, there are others who are also with us in significant ways."

"I think you're right. We probably have more love and encouragement than we could possibly realize," Maddie agreed.

"And more is almost always better, I like to say," Elizabeth concluded, "especially when it comes to good food, friendships, and matters of the heart."

Then, for a few moments, the two women silently watched the stars twinkled in the sky above and as a serene breeze swirled softly about them.

"Well, Maddie, I believe the long day is catching up with me. My morning started exceptionally early, and while this has been a wonderful day, I think it best that I say *bonne nuit*, good night. May your dreams be pleasant, and your next few days here as sweet as you. And don't forget what I said about the theater. Come back to town, and I'll show you the high life here!"

"That sounds great! I'll do my best to return soon, and we'll kick it up in Port Saint Smith!" Maddie added with a laugh.

"I can only imagine what the neighbors will say when they see us out gallivanting around," Elizabeth stated with delight. "My guess is they'll probably join right in! Anyway, I hope to see you again soon."

"Thank you, Elizabeth, and good night. As my Grandma Anise used to say, 'May you sleep the sleep that angels keep,'" she offered with a tender smile.

"And so it is," Elizabeth cooed.

After Maddie waved goodbye, her thoughts focused on the conversations she'd had with Elizabeth and how comfortable they'd felt. She had not enjoyed a close female friend since her best friend Silvia moved back home to help care for her aging parents.

Acquaintances aren't so hard to come by, Maddie recognized. *But a good friend, who really understands me and shares many of my interests is not as easily found. So, I'm really excited that Elizabeth has invited me to spend more time with her. She seems like an interesting woman who also enjoys travel, theater, and girl talk over coffee. And here is yet another amazing opportunity this adventure is providing that I would have never expected.*

Maddie also noted that she had an uncanny kinship with Tink, a kindly woman who reminded her in many ways of Grandma Anise. She could easily imagine spending more time with this delightful elder, indulging in some of her homemade sweets while hearing stories about this town, its people, and Tink's long and interesting life.

I have to laugh thinking about Stephen's fear that Tink was the evil witch in this fairytale. She actually seems to be an exceptionally kind person. The stories her friends shared over dinner revealed a lot about her—a wise woman who has selflessly helped her neighbors, friends, and this community for decades. What a gift that she happens to live right next to the house where I'm staying.

Interestingly, the more I know about this town, the more at home I feel here. My life in the city has been good, but honestly, never really great. I've never felt fully rooted there. But even in this short time in Port

Saint Smith, I've sensed that genuinely caring about one another seems to be the norm. And that's the kind of place I've always longed to live in.

But what about love? Maddie wondered as she slowly rounded a corner, heading back toward the house. *The few boyfriends I've had so far have been good guys. Two of them were quite handsome and nice enough. And there was great chemistry with another guy, but little else. Still, not one of them understood me to the extent I know I deserve, or to the depth that I desire. I've waited years for that rich sense of connection which I believe can exist between two beings—the sense of oneness that transcends the physical. Because without that connection, sharing a beer at a game, eating fancy dinners out, or random moments of intimacy, just hasn't been enough. And since I'm comfortable on my own, I don't want to settle for less. And that can not be wrong.*

So, maybe this time away is showing me a different kind of love, a love that is not mentioned in the traditional storybooks. Maybe there exists a kind of relationship that doesn't follow the usual fairytale format. But what would that look like? And would that work for me? I don't know. What I do know, though, is that when he is around me, I feel so alive, so connected, and so deeply fulfilled. His words somehow speak straight to my soul. His soft touch on my hand and kisses upon my cheek, show me that he knows what I want and what I need without my asking.

And he is no more a scary ghost than Tink is a wicked witch. Although I can't see him, I feel him in ways I never imagined. I want to know so much more about him. But what is his name? And will he continue to be an important presence with me?

As Maddie pondered these questions, she felt the warm embrace of her hand and the scent of the salty sea surrounding her. And, in that moment, Maddie had the unspoken assurance she was no longer walking alone back to *La Maison Enchantée.*

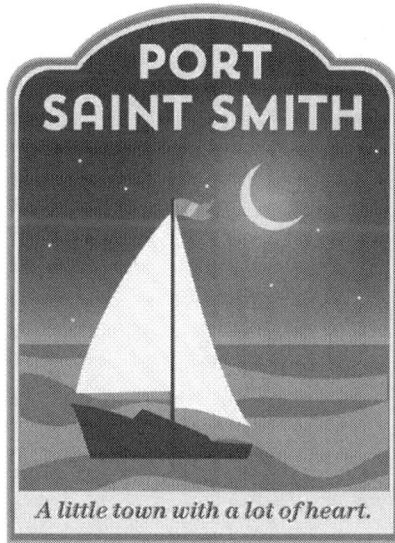

PORT
SAINT SMITH

A little town with a lot of heart.

FRIDAY,
NOVEMBER 25

Chapter 58
Tink

Tink Kendleton plodded down the hall into the parlor, wrapped in a thick robe and sensible slippers. Although her mood was light, her body felt very heavy after four consecutive days of non-stop activity. The holiday week was winding down, and only one volunteer commitment remained. And although weariness was definitely catching up with the aged woman, she had no intention of canceling her plans. Nor was Tink going to miss out on greeting the morning, as she had every day since the beginning of Thanksgiving week.

I may not be hopping about like a spring chicken. But, at least I'm moving forward, even if the pace is more on par with that of an ancient tortoise.

Tugging firmly on the drapery cords, Tink witnessed what had been predicted for the day's weather. Windswept Way, and most likely all of Port Saint Smith, was not only shrouded in a dense, gray mist but also blessed with an ample amount of rain. Still, she stood in silent appreciation as the earth received the necessary wet nourishment.

On every other rainy day during the past several months, Tink had sat immobilized in the dimly lit parlor. The gloomy weather outside had served to compound the same gloomy mood she'd been feeling inside. But on this Friday, following such a joy-filled Thanksgiving Day, the downpour of rain was providing a refreshing cleansing for the earth, as well as, for her. With an open willingness, Tink allowed it to symbolically wash away much of her residual sorrow. And with that release, she recognized that even more space would be cleared for serenity, laughter, joy, and love.

The past few days had been a whirlwind of activity—baking cookies, fruit and pot pies; and hosting a lavish Thanksgiving feast. Everything had gone well and she felt good about her accomplishments. But, more importantly, was the fact that her guests had enjoyed not only the delicious food, but also each other's company. Maddie fit in beautifully with others, and energetic Elizabeth arrived just as the meal was being served. And from that moment on, a congenial rhythm of chatting and chewing convened.

But what about that curious occurrence, Tink questioned, *when the back door blew wide open and a tenacious wind swept quickly down the hallway. It then burst into the dining room as though insisting on joining our little gathering. I immediately went to secure the door and, upon returning, could feel a noticeable shift in the room—as though something significant that had been missing before was now present.*

For the next hour or so, we enjoyed the bountiful food and the blessing of one another's company. Following the meal, I suggested that we each share a cherished childhood memory. Shirley's sweet story about her 'student' dolls was so endearing and clearly foretold her decades-long career as a tenderhearted teacher. I was also very pleased that Maddie felt comfortable enough to share. She reminded us all about one of nature's simple wonders - the mystical sight of twinkling fireflies on a warm summer's night. Next, Charlie told us a fascinating tale of adventure when, as a boy, he met a very intriguing man at the edge of the woods—a man who keeps coming to his mind, and for no evident reason. And curiously, Elizabeth was very moved by his story. Perhaps it reminded her of a similar childhood experience. I don't know. But I do hope that the tenderness of her tears was due to happy memories, and not those associated with sorrow.

The chime of the grandfather clock reminded Tink to return to the present moment. Briefly, she considered what the day ahead would hold. Wrapping presents for charity was a newer tradition, yet a most rewarding one for her. With all the shoppers out and about over the holiday weekend, a good amount of money was typically donated to several local charities, including the Homes for Hounds. But Tink had concerns about any sizable donations being given this day due to the inclement weather. Regardless, she would still be there doing her best to make the presents look pretty. And as she walked out of the parlor, Tink reflected on what her good friends might be doing on this rainy Friday.

I'm certain that Shirley, as the head volunteer at the Chamber of Commerce, will be opening the building soon, if she has not already. Undoubtedly, she's hoping, as well, that the rain won't discourage visitors from stopping in, so she can share her enthusiasm and knowledge of the area.

As for Charlie, Tink contemplated, *I can easily envision him diligently studying the forecast for the weekend. He finds such satisfaction in evaluating how the weather will impact his small but treasured patch of earth. While the rain soaks the ground, he will most likely be spending time soaking up information about the next tomato variety he plans to introduce in the spring. The only foreseeable challenge to this day's agenda could be the fact that his eyes close so often, as he has admitted to frequent, spontaneous napping.*

What about my buddy Larry? Tink continued to wonder. *I hope after yesterday's charitable endeavors, his mood is lifted, and some of his emotional heaviness has been left behind, like my smaller waistline after all of this celebratory eating. I'm glad I was able to send over part of our Thanksgiving meal along with a note of thanks to him. He deserves congratulations for continuing this monumental task, especially in light of such a devastating loss. So, I wanted to convey that my thoughts are with him, and that his efforts are indeed making a real difference.*

Elizabeth mentioned plans for a quiet morning, writing thank you notes to everyone who contributed toward the success of the S.O.S. Basket Benefit. I told her that sending one to me would not be necessary, in hopes that would give her a few more moments to rest. But she did mention the possibility of stopping by to see me at the Beanstalk Bookstore and Cafe and I hope she does! I always delight in her good company.

And our dear Maddie said she would most likely be enjoying some quiet time. Good for her! She's a working woman who deserves to be lazy every once in a while. So, on this particularly cold and wet day, I imagine she'll be glad to stay in and rest, read, or whatever brings her joy. I sure hope, however, to see her again whether by chance or invitation. Mmmm... I have an idea...perhaps she'd be interested in joining Charlie and me for a warm piece of pie tomorrow night. I'll think on that a little more. But right now, I'd better think about getting dressed, or I'll be quite a sight in the bookshop wrapping presents in my fuzzy bathrobe and slippers!

With that whimsical image in mind, Tink began preparing herself to leave. She dressed in a warm, wool skirt and oversized sweater and then made her way into the kitchen. There, she enjoyed a breakfast of oatmeal and an egg, while the handsome cardinal serenaded her with a merry tune.

After eating, Tink went to the hall closet and pulled out a well-worn trench coat, rather than her more stylish London Fog. She also grabbed her sturdy, green galoshes. Never one to be burdened by fashion expectations, Tink laughed to herself, *I look as if I'm about to slog around the misty moors of Ireland in this ensemble. All that needs to be added to this outfit is a plaid kerchief tied around my neck.*

Tink then sat down in a kitchen chair to put on the rubber footwear, still wondering if she'd made a big mistake way back when. *My dear Grant always wanted to add a mudroom just off the kitchen. But that would have meant giving up some of my beloved garden, which, at the time, felt completely inconceivable. But on rainy days like this, I know he is smiling at me—not in a smug sort of way, but with a touch of mirth, acknowledging the beneficial buffer that a small anteroom would have provided between the mud and mess and my kitchen floor.*

"Oh, well, Grant," Tink said aloud, trusting that her late husband would hear her, "as much as I'd like to say 'you were right,' I still can't do it. I have only myself to blame for the muck that invariably gets tracked into this room. Fortunately, I know you can't be mad or even disappointed in me since negative feelings don't exist where you are. In fact, you must also have a better appreciation for that which matters most to me, especially the beauty of the outside world. No doubt, you understand more fully now that I just couldn't forgo any part of my garden in order to avoid some of life's little messes. And isn't that what this elaborate existence is all about anyway? Without the rain, the plants would whither. Without the tears, we might not be able to release the many pains of the past. So, the mess is, quite literally, an integral part of the healing and our return to wholeness."

After months of grieving in near isolation, Tink realized, *I have a renewed appreciation of my friends, and the pleasure of giving back to our community. And thank goodness, hope is also quickly returning.*

Now, I feel ready to shake off the dried mud from my boots, and get on with the joyous journey of this life.

With a big humph, she rose to standing and gathered her belongings—a large pocketbook, her faithful umbrella, two muffins, an apple, and an antiquated, red and black checkered thermos filled with coffee milk. Then, between bouts of rain, Tink hurried to her car with the promise to stomp in at least one puddle for fun, upon returning home.

As she put the vehicle in reverse, and began carefully backing down the wet driveway, Tink thought with a broad smile, *maybe I'll see a glorious sign of love from Grant today, like a rainbow. That would please me immensely, but not surprise me at all.*

Chapter 59
Maddie

Maddie burrowed deeper under the covers, lulled by the constant drumming of rain upon the roof and against the windows. The night before, she had decided to let the natural elements dictate the day, and was grateful, therefore, to stay inside rather than brace herself against the stormy weather outside. Rarely upon waking was Maddie able to drift back to sleep. But, on this morning, she'd already done so twice, noting how remarkably at ease she felt in this bedroom and in this home. With little awareness of the time, several hours ticked by. And only when she felt the urge to rise, did she do so. Moving ever so slowly, she wrapped a light blanket around herself and walked over to the window seat. There, she curled up against several large, comfy pillows, admiring the misty image before her and the random splats of water journeying down the windowpane like purposeful, little rivulets.

How lovely, she thought, *the glass is so wet with those streaks of rain that the scene in the garden below reminds me of impressionistic artwork. The blurring and blending of colors could almost pass for one of Claude Monet's prized lily pond paintings.*

Entranced, Maddie leaned back further in the window nook, wistfully gazing outside. With no plans to be made, and no work to be done, she willingly suspended her usual attentiveness and simply observed the unpredictable path of the raindrops as they wove their way down the glass. One after another, she followed the droplets to the end and then gazed once more at the setting below. Much like the loose brush strokes of an impressionistic painting, the outside world continued to soften into a masterpiece as Maddie's inner world also softened, and the tranquility she felt became like art itself.

In those gentle moments of sweet silence, Maddie sensed that her life was shifting away from the comfortable, yet confined patterns of familiarity. She offered no resistance to this important change, and like the raindrops allowing the course to present itself rather than forcing the outcome, she too accepted the unpredictability of what lay ahead.

Maddie remained in the window nook for quite a while. When she did at last rise, she slowly stepped into the adjoining room. There, in continued silence, Maddie mindfully lit candles, drew a bath, and eased her body down into the warm water. The cedar scent of bath salts filled her nostrils, as little bubbles gently popped against her skin. And the fractured reflection of the flickering candle flames upon the water furthered the feeling of living within an ever-evolving piece of artwork.

In the serene setting, Maddie became even more untethered to anything except the present moment. She began to experience the purest sense of herself—that part not limited to the physical, but expanding into the unseen realm of life itself. And in that spacious state of being, Maddie embraced an integration of change happening in the most organic and yet tender of ways. No words were needed to recognize this transformation occurring on all levels. And she allowed herself to slip deeper into the water and into a richer state of acceptance and awareness.

Only the expectation of Stephen's promised call in the late afternoon kept Maddie remotely aware of the time. With the slightest reluctance, she even-tually got out of the tub and dried off. She then tied a thick cotton robe around her waist and, with slippers on her feet, went downstairs into the kitchen.

Soon, the tea kettle was singing the song of steam, and boiling water was being poured over a suspended tea bag inside a mug. As the tea steeped, Maddie padded about attending only to that which brought her pleasure. And because her much-anticipated beach outing was scheduled for early the next morning, she also began to ready some of the supplies— a small beach blanket, travel thermos, a satchel for collecting a few natural treasures, and a sampling of snacks.

Maddie then reviewed the map that was in her welcome packet. The path to the shore appeared to be short and direct—perhaps a twenty-five-minute or less bike ride. According to Elizabeth, the Piney Grove Trail ended at a small public beach that was not often used. Expectation built within her as everything was looking favorable for this adventure, including the weather report, which predicted that the rain would end hours before dawn, making way for a cold but sunny day.

As Maddie concluded the preparations, her phone began to ring. She saw who the caller was, retrieved her cup of tea, and sat down at the kitchen table. Looking out upon the rain-soaked garden and accepting the fact that the day's tender silence would now be suspended, she answered the call, eager to hear her good friend's updates.

"Hello," she offered in a quiet, melodic voice.

"Hello, Maddie! Did I wake you up? You sound a little sleepy," Stephen inquired.

"No, I'm awake. I've just been having the most pleasant and quiet day imaginable. You would barely recognize this version of me."

"Well, good for you! I'm so glad to hear you're relaxing! That's a perfect use of your time away."

"Thank you," she responded.

"And I'm pleased you got my text last night and are able to speak today. Lucky me!" Stephen said exuberantly. "I'm not sure I can even handle all of this excitement. And I do promise to be a more attentive listener this time because I want to keep my word. So… what would you like to tell me?"

Maddie was slow to respond since describing her day in words would not be easy. "Well," she offered, "I made an earnest attempt to imitate Miss Priss today, and have come to realize just how enviable the life of that privileged cat really is!"

"You're telling me! She has lived up to her title of 'Your Highness' to the extent that her status is now even more elevated since being chauffeured around in her royal carriage. When you return, I am sure you'll notice she's more radiant than ever. Speaking of which, when are you coming back?"

"I'll be back on Sunday afternoon, and once I get settled in, I'll text you about coming to pick up our beloved cat."

"Better yet, why don't you just get settled in and then come by for our usual Sunday meal if you're feeling up to it."

"That would be wonderful. Thanks, Stephen. I'm sure we'll have one or two little things to chat about."

"Just maybe," he teased back. "I'm guessing we could probably talk into the wee hours and still not fully catch up."

"No doubt! But I really want to hear about your Thanksgiving Day. I'm in such a quiet mood; I'd rather be a good listener. And then on Sunday, I'll tell you more about my travels, if that's ok."

"Sure. That's fine. I did want to hear about your Thanksgiving, but we can wait if you wish."

"Yes, let's do that. I'll just say, though, that my holiday was really wonderful. But I don't want to wait any longer to hear how your day with Rafael was."

"Well, alright... I guess we can go ahead and discuss that did-it-really-happen-dreamy-day with him," he said in a sing-songy voice.

"Great!" she said emphatically.

"I'm sure you remember when I first met you, and I said I wouldn't be the least bit surprised if you and I became friends. That wasn't just an idea I had, but a very strong sense I had that day. I mention this because... I'm getting such a similar feeling regarding Rafael. I can actually see us enjoying the Christmas holidays together—walking downtown and looking at the lights, drinking cocoa with tiny marshmallows in front of his fireplace, and even celebrating New Year's Eve together in some grand way. And the best part is the fact that we are so comfortable with one another—laughing, loving, and sharing the wonder of it all with such ease.

"And that's how yesterday was for us. Rafael was an excellent host, and, for the record, he's also a marvelous cook. After I got over my initial shyness, which was rather awkward for both of us, we blended together beautifully. My hard edges gave way to soft smiles and sweet giggles. And our togetherness felt as though we were merging—as though transported out of the ordinary into some idealist setting. We could have been on board in my favorite painting—Renoir's Luncheon of the Boating Party—experiencing a sense of ease while taking in the richness of it all. Do you know what I mean?" Stephen asked earnestly.

"I really do. More than I could ever say," Maddie admitted, as goosebumps appeared on her arms. For here was another reference to an impressionistic painting on the very same day she'd felt transformed by the soft, blending colors. *And weren't the artists of that genre strongly*

343

ridiculed for their original approach? Maddie recalled suddenly. *Their courage to paint in a controversial style caused them to be denied display at the exhibitions. Yet, some of these same paintings are considered today to be the most valuable in the world. Those artists,* she recognized, *were very brave to defy such deep-rooted tradition. And I will also be that brave if I choose to live and love in a way that may not be fully understood or accepted by others.*

"Maddie, we both felt safe enough to be authentic with each other," Stephen continued reflectively. "And how glorious is that?"

"It's the best!" Maddie concurred, honestly.

"That being said, of course, I'm just a messy mush of a man right now! But in the best of ways, I assure you!"

Maddie laughed and said, "I love hearing you this happy! I think it's about time your life had joyous chaos and disorder!"

"I guess so! This morning, I couldn't even remember which drawer my socks were in, if that tells you anything."

"That probably sums it up perfectly."

"Indeed! And Rafael said he'd call tonight, and we are going to make plans to see one another again tomorrow. I have a feeling my bachelorhood could be coming to an end!"

"For which we will both celebrate!" Maddie asserted.

"Yes, we will! But I can tell you're still feeling very quiet, my dear Maddie. So, unless you say otherwise, I'm going to let you go. Please be careful coming home, and know that Miss Priss and I have both really missed you a lot. I hope your week away has been wonderful and that the romantic winds of change may be shifting in your life, as well."

"I think they may be. And, thanks, Stephen, for everything. But mostly for being my very good friend."

"Ditto, Maddie. We love you. Tata!"

"Tata, Stephen. I love both of you, too!"

Maddie set the phone down, took a small sip of tea, and watched in appreciative silence as a few late-day rays of light burst through the darkening sky.

Chapter 60
Elizabeth

A strong gust of wind thrust Elizabeth through the doorway of the Beanstalk Bookstore and Cafe. Fortunately, a small alcove at the entrance offered a reprieve from the storm, as well as a place to regroup. And although a sizable umbrella had somewhat helped shield her, a fair amount of rain still left its impression.

I've never been one to mind getting a little wet, Elizabeth mused as she slipped off her raincoat and hung it on a metal peg. *I rather like a good downpour since it affords me the opportunity to be unapologetically barefoot.* She then removed her wet shoes and placed them alongside the umbrella, now resting in a designated stand.

Next, Elizabeth peeked carefully around the corner in hopes of surprising her friend. However, the immediate greeting clearly indicated that her presence had already been detected.

"Hellooo, Elizabeth!! What a brave soul you are scampering about in this tempestuous weather. You told me that you might stop by, and glory be, here you are!"

"Yes, here I am in all my damp glory! And I'm very glad to see that you're still here," Elizabeth stated sincerely.

"Have you come to do some holiday shopping? If so, I can help wrap your gifts," Tink asked.

"No, actually, I was just hoping to talk to you for a few minutes. But if you're busy, I understand. I know you have work to do."

"What work?" Tink quipped. "The rain is keeping almost everyone away. I've only wrapped two gifts so far, which won't raise much money for charity. Hopefully, tomorrow will be different after the sun reappears. I imagine then that the shoppers will return to town then."

"I'm sure you're right about that," Elizabeth agreed. "I decided to reschedule my outdoor plans for today since tomorrow's forecast looked much more promising."

"That was a good idea," Tink stated.

"Indeed. So, tell me, Tink, how are you doing after such a busy day yesterday?"

"I'm doing well, especially for such an old gal! I will admit, though, I'm glad to have only signed up for the half-day shift. In the past, I've volunteered to wrap gifts for the full day. But these crooked fingers of mine are not nearly as adept at folding neat corners and making fiddly bows as they once were. So, the patrons will probably be better served by the younger volunteers," she added with willing acceptance. "And since it's been so slow, I even had time to mosey around the store a bit, which was fun. I'm not much of a shopper. But I did find a sweet gift for Maddie, which I plan to give her before she leaves town."

"How kind of you! I had a feeling the two of you would get along well. Oh, and speaking of Maddie, I happened to see her again last night after I took the food over to Larry's. She'd gone out for a walk. So, I pulled the car over for a few minutes, and we had a nice chat. And guess what I did?"

"Do tell..." Tink requested.

"I invited her to come back and attend the holiday show at the theater with me," Elizabeth explained.

"What a splendid idea!" Tink said. "Leave it to you to think of something so clever. I would be delighted if she came back! She's such a lovely young woman who seems to fit here so well already. Plus, having both of you at my dinner table yesterday was such a blessing. I'm so pleased that you were able to attend."

"So was I! And what an incredible meal you prepared! Everything was delicious! I have no idea how you managed to do all that in such an exquisite way and all on your own! That's mighty impressive, Mrs. Kendleton!" Elizabeth sincerely stated.

"Thank you for saying so, my dear. I've had just a few years of practice," Tink replied with a wink.

"Well, after helping Larry in the kitchen for a couple of hours, I have a much greater appreciation of what goes into such an elaborate meal. Thanks again for including me. I really had a wonderful time."

"You're most welcome," Tink replied. "Preparing food for my friends is one of my greatest passions, and we owe it to ourselves to recognize and express those passions so that our lives sparkle with joy.

"But let's talk about you now that the wind has officially escorted you right through that front door," Tink suggested, pointing toward the bookstore entrance. "How are *you* doing today?"

"I'm doing great! In fact, my passion and purpose are exactly what I want to talk to you about. I've felt so alive this week coordinating the S.O.S. Basket Benefit. Seeking the donations, assembling the baskets, and then assisting Larry with the food prep was so rewarding and fun for me. But, more than anything, spending time with the S.O.S. families during the deliveries was meaningful beyond words. I'm sure you understand."

"Oh, yes, I definitely do," Tink replied.

"And now I find myself at such an intriguing turning point in my life—as though a new vitality is moving through me, like a restorative breeze brushing away the old and replacing it with innovative ideas that will require my fully focused efforts and energy."

"How exciting, Elizabeth!" Tink exclaimed.

"Yes, I'm very excited! Helping out at the camps this past summer also served as an important reminder of how much I want to, need to really, be in service to our community at an even greater level. The theater is well on its way to lasting success after the fundraiser and renovation. So, my philanthropic attention can be turned elsewhere. Which is where *you* come in."

"Oh, really?!" the elder asked enthusiastically. "I'm certainly intrigued!"

"I was hoping you would be," Elizabeth declared.

"Why don't you come sit here at the wrapping table so we can chat?" Tink suggested, pointing toward a modest folding chair beside her. "If a customer does come in and wants something wrapped, I'll just stand right up and do it."

"That sounds perfect. And I'd be glad to lend a hand. Maybe learning to properly wrap a present rather than depending on gift bags or the kindness of my merchants will be another skill I can acquire."

"Continuing to learn, I've always said, is a great way to guarantee vitality and longevity. Look at me - I'm eager right now to learn all about your idea!"

"Excellent," Elizabeth said as she settled into the small area behind the table. "But, as much as I'm excited to tell you about the idea for the S.O.S. Foundation's future, I feel inclined to share some related background information with you first."

"Alright. I'm ready to hear whatever it is you want to say."

"Thank you, Tink. Because I'm sure you noticed yesterday how moved I was by the conversation at the end of the meal. How ingenious that was, by the way, to ask us to share a meaningful childhood memory— Shirley's dolls all lined up listening to her lessons and Maddie's lovely meadows filled with fireflies."

"Yes, both of those memories were truly delightful to hear," Tink agreed. "I have included themed conversations at my last few gatherings, and I go with whatever topic feels inspired at the time."

"Well, that definitely added a lot to the celebration and brought us all a little closer together, I believe."

"I think you're right," Tink replied sincerely.

"But when Charlie was captivating us with his boyhood adventure, I became quite emotional," Elizabeth confessed.

"I did notice that, Elizabeth, which is exactly why I suggested right then that we pause right then for coffee and dessert," Tink explained.

"Thank you so much for your thoughtfulness," Elizabeth acknowledged. "I knew you sensed my struggle without saying anything aloud to the others. And honestly, I don't think I could have spoken about my childhood memories without bursting into tears."

"I understand," the wise woman offered with a kindly pat on her friend's hand. "Well, actually," Tink candidly continued, "I don't understand what was upsetting you, but that's none of my business unless you wish to tell me. We can go on talking about the weather or the upcoming holiday performance or anything else if you prefer. I am not one to pry."

Elizabeth paused in reflection, hesitant to respond. She was exceptionally nervous about revealing her long-held secret. Yet, she realized in order to accomplish the grand scheme of securing the S.O.S. Foundation, as well as saving *Beauté Par la Mer*, the facts about her past involving that property needed to be told. And there was no one better to share this with first than this trusted, old friend and town sage, Tink.

"No, I must speak now," Elizabeth professed, "while the momentum of this past week is pushing me forward like that blustery wind that ushered me inside a few minutes ago. I might waver in the courage to say what needs to be said, but I don't lack the clarity or conviction about the importance or timeliness of the project. Still, this brings up such tender feelings in me. But I vowed to myself that the days of guarding my heart are over."

"That takes real courage, Elizabeth," Tink affirmed. "Living bravely with an open heart, despite disappointments, pains, and heartbreak, is the only true way to live if we really want the rewards of joy, love, and meaningful connections. So, I thank you with all my heart for putting your trust in me. And I promise to honor and hold sacred whatever you are about to tell me."

"Thank you, Tink. I know I can trust you completely," Elizabeth stammered as tears welled up in her eyes. She wiped them dry and then did her best to begin speaking. "I think you know that I grew up in rural New York. And then, in my early twenties, I moved to Manhattan, where I lived all of my adult life until I came here."

"I've enjoyed everything that city had to offer—the museums, theater, fashion, fine dining, etcetera," Elizabeth explained as Tink listened attentively. "Thus, the move to Port Saint Smith was a considerable adjustment for a fast-paced, metropolitan woman like me."

"Yes, and to be honest," Tink admitted, "as much as I admired your spunk from the start, I worried that this place would not offer you enough to stay happy. Even your incentive for coming to this town was never really clear to me, although the incredible citizens alone could tempt anyone to want to relocate here," Tink teased with an endearing laugh. "But you stayed, and you seem to have made a good life for yourself. You've contributed a lot to the community, and many of us feel very blessed to call you our friend."

"That's so sweet of you to say, Tink. And I am the one blessed to be living here. But you are right. I never told anyone why I moved to Port Saint Smith. I didn't intend to keep it a secret, but the timing to share that information never felt quite right. Even now, when I have good reason, I still feel so vulnerable."

Tink nodded in silent understanding as Elizabeth continued to speak.

"So, before I lose my nerve, let me ask you this," Elizabeth inquired softly, clearing her voice. "Do you recall the, um, the man… that, uh, Charlie told us he met on his walk in the woods?"

"Yes, certainly. He described him as a jovial character, almost bigger than life. But perhaps that was because Charlie was just a wee boy at the time."

"No, what Charlie told us about that man is all true —he had the most joyous spirit of anyone I've ever known. He was profoundly kind and immensely generous. And he always maintained a deep love and appreciation for his family and for life itself. I know that to be true because…," Elizabeth's voice faltered, "because I loved that man very much."

"You knew that man?" Tink queried.

"Yes, that man Charlie described was my grandfather."

"You mean the man Charlie spoke about reminded you of your grandfather?" she asked, confused and seeking clarification.

"No, I'm sure that he was talking about my father's father, my beloved Grand-Papa."

"Really?" Tink questioned incredulously.

"Yes, I spent many a summer in those very woods and at his seaside estate just on the outskirts of Port Saint Smith."

"I had no idea, Elizabeth," Tink stated with unmistakable surprise. In response, Elizabeth offered the slightest shrug of her shoulders and a palpable yet unspoken apology.

The significance of the words lingered between them, and when Tink spoke again, she did so in a quieter manner. "I must admit, Elizabeth, you are a woman of many mysteries."

"While that may have been true in the past, I intend to be much more open in the future," Elizabeth stated solemnly. "For the connection between my grandfather's property and the S.O.S. Foundation is coming together in ways I could have never dreamed or envisioned on my own. And I don't think it's any coincidence that Charlie told us yesterday about the intriguing man he met in his youth. To me, that was an important sign of confirmation."

But before Tink could say anything further or ask one of her many inevitable questions, the conversation came to an abrupt stop as a mighty burst of wind swept a tall man in a soaked trench coat through the front door. He stood bewildered at the entrance, holding a plastic deli bag and looking around as though trying to find something or someone. When at last he turned in their direction, both Elizabeth and Tink recognized him to be their good friend, Theo Robertson.

"Hello, Tink! Hello, Elizabeth!" he said, obviously pleased to see them.

"Hello, Theo," they answered in unison.

"I'm so glad to find you here," Theo exclaimed. "I was told someone would be wrapping presents at the bookstore today. Is that true?" he asked urgently.

"Yes," Elizabeth replied quickly since Tink was still stunned by her recent revelation. "And all of the money will be donated to local charities."

"Wonderful! Are you busy right now?" he asked.

"No, not at all," Elizabeth responded. "We were just sitting here having an engaging conversation."

"Okay, because I'm hoping you can help me out. A good customer came into the deli moments ago, bought these ten boxes of local lavender honey, and would like them wrapped within the hour before she gets on a plane for Europe. Would it be possible for you to wrap these right now? I'm sorry to even ask, especially since we usually place gifts like this in our beautiful, signature bags. But she requested they be wrapped with paper instead to better fit inside her luggage. We're so busy today, but I told her I'd see what I could do. And that's when Suzette told me about the wrapping station set up here."

Elizabeth stood up immediately, saying, "I think we can do that, Theo. Tink and I can work together and, no doubt, have them wrapped within the hour. Don't you agree, Tink?" she asked with an encouraging smile.

Tink murmured a soft yes as her thoughts continued swirling around Elizabeth's surprising revelation. For Tink was wondering if she'd ever met Elizabeth's grandfather in all of her years living in Port Saint Smith? Intrigued by that idea, the elder continued to explore the archives of her memory as the conversation between Elizabeth and Theo continued.

"I would be so grateful if you could take care of that for me," Theo responded with apparent relief. "Fortunately, the boxes are not very big. And, of course, I'll be making a generous donation."

"We'll get started right away," Elizabeth assured him as Theo handed her the bag filled with honey.

"I can't thank you enough," he said emphatically. "Shall I plan to come back in an hour?"

"That'll be perfect," Elizabeth agreed. "We'll see you then."

"Bye," was all Tink could say as she pushed herself to standing.

And as soon as Theo had left, Elizabeth said in reassurance, "Please don't worry, my good friend. We'll continue this conversation very soon.

I have more to share with you about my Grand-Papa, his property, and how this all now comes into play with the S.O.S. Foundation. But we'd better get started on the wrapping since I'm a novice and may work slowly. Where do we begin?"

Tink abandoned her thoughts in order to demonstrate to Elizabeth the basics of wrapping a gift. And together, they began cutting, taping, and adorning the ten boxes of sweet, local, lavender honey.

Chapter 61
Larry

"Don't even think about it," the frustrated man growled aloud as he paced back and forth in his living room. The dreary weather, complete with ominous clouds, intense rain, and sporadic booming thunder, was not helping Larry's mood. "Just leave me alone…at least for one day!" With no one evident in the room to argue back, the ranting continued. "I've done everything you've asked of me. I listed your home exactly when you requested, and it was rented within the hour. How could that happen especially during the off-season? My years in real estate have shown me how unlikely that is. Then you insisted a bike—specifically a new woman's bike—be purchased and placed at the property. And who rented your spacious home? Not a family, not a couple, not even an elderly old man writing his memoir. No—a single female rented *La Maison Enchantée,* and I'm told she is an avid bike rider. How did you know this? And how did you know this in advance?

"Also, after weeks of procrastination and refusing to make any tangible plans, I reluctantly agreed to the S.O.S. basket deliveries. I also begrudgingly allowed Elizabeth to help me in the kitchen. And why did I do that? Not because I wanted to, but because you, the dead man looming somewhere in the ethers, encouraged me to do it in a text. I suppose you want me to admit now, that it was a good idea. Well, it was, but I won't admit it. I'll show you I can be just as stubborn as you. And, to be fully honest, I believe your willful stubbornness most likely contributed to your death."

Larry pounded his fist on the edge of his desk and stormed back and forth between his home office, the foyer, and the living room. Occasionally, the clap of thunder accompanied his outpouring of emotions, serving as a resounding backdrop to his personal drama.

"And look at me! Just look at me! I'm talking out loud in a home where I live alone! And who am I talking to? The walls? A figment of my imagination? A ghost? Or maybe, just maybe, my best friend who apparently thinks provoking me is some kind of fun!? You've even sent me messages in response to my thoughts, so I imagine you can definitely hear me now, especially since I'm raising my voice like a lunatic."

With that, Larry flopped down in the enormous chair behind his desk. He was exhausted from everything, including the Thanksgiving cooking marathon, followed by the eight deliveries in the city with Elizabeth. Watching sports today held little interest, and he wasn't even hungry, which spoke volumes. Fortunately, the office was closed, and Elizabeth was fielding calls so he wouldn't have to deal with the outside world when his inner world was in such chaos.

After the powerful double punch of shock and grief following Nic's death, Larry had somehow managed to keep going while still striving to give the appearance that he was fine. But today, with no obligations, he wanted to be left absolutely alone—to answer to no one, especially this insistent, yet suspicious, version of Nic.

"Obviously, you can hear me whether I'm ranting out loud or merely thinking to myself," Larry muttered beneath his breath. "And tomorrow, I've got to show up for Elizabeth. I can't afford to put her off. So, give me some space today. No requests, no sideline cheering, nothing! Is that clear?"

The shower Larry had taken earlier in the day had done little else than functionally clean him. It had not, as he'd hoped, left him feeling relaxed or refreshed. He'd then put on clean but sloppy clothes and lay on the couch. But, before long, he stood up again, discontent there or anywhere else. He was not comfortable on the couch, in the kitchen, in his bedroom, or on the porch, which was too wet and cold anyway for consideration. Going into town was not a viable option either due to the foul weather or the likelihood of running into one of those cheerful townsfolk swept up in the joy of the season. So, other than napping once,

Larry had prowled anxiously from room to room for hours before this latest pause in his office.

"I've done some investigation, you know," he asserted with his elbows on the desk propping up his weary head. "More than one sleepless night lately has been spent reading about this sort of phenomenon." And with no more ability to speak aloud, Larry's words shifted into silent thoughts intended for Nic.

I've researched websites and read excerpts from books on the subject. And apparently, a significant number of people, especially those grieving, report all kinds of unusual experiences. Birds appearing at noteworthy times, lamps flickering, fans spinning, while electronics and phones are being manipulated. I don't get it, though. It all seems impossible and illogical. Yet, I haven't made any of this up. You've definitely sent me texts and even a written note.

Interestingly, too, you were always the clever one with gadgets— much more so than I was. So why should I be surprised you're communicating like that? I guess you figured it would be a great way to get my attention, and clearly, you're right. Besides, we always texted each other to confirm appointments or finalize who was bringing what on our sailing excursions. How absurd then for me to think that would change after you died!

According to numerous testimonials and dedicated research, some of the more common signs sent from departed ones are white feathers and rainbows. Knowing me, I would have stepped right over that feather, oblivious to its meaning. Or I would have written off a double rainbow on the anniversary of my mother's passing, as nothing more than water prisms in the sky mixed with sunlight and rain. And if my lights had flickered, I would have checked the wires or, if need be, called an electrician. No problem. But astute you sent text messages addressed to Slouch, and there is no denying the significance of that!

So, explain this to me, Nic. Why is it that you were always so good at figuring out problems and fixing things, but you didn't take the time to fix yourself? The renovation of your house became your only priority, and I do commend you on a job well done. Your home is exquisite. But this obsession did not serve you in the end. Sadly, I have come to believe your death most likely could have been prevented. I tried to get you to take just an afternoon off for sailing, or slowdown in some other way. So did Tink, who was desperately worried about you. We both were. But you kept telling us not to worry. *"I'll be alright,"* you insisted. *"It's just the flu or something. I'll shake it off. I always do."* That's what you wanted us to believe, and we were so accustomed to your indomitable spirit conquering almost anything, that we didn't push back hard enough. Nothing seemed to stand in the way of you achieving your intended dreams and goals.

The fact that you believed your love would also soon arrive made no sense to me. But I went along with you, since you rarely faltered in your understanding of life's direction. Both literally on the boat and in your everyday experiences, you seemed to instinctively sense which way the winds of change would blow. Except for the one critical time you willfully overlooked. Why didn't you just stop and take better care of yourself? And I kept reasoning that your symptoms were not that uncommon and what harm could possibly come to you? Obviously, I should have overridden your arguments, for once, and insisted that you get help. My guilt for not having done so will most likely stay with me for the rest of my life. Because the doctors said had they seen you just a day or two sooner, your life could have been spared. So, why didn't I insist? And I can only imagine that Tink has her own share of guilt for not getting you medical help much sooner. I'll never ask her, though. We both could have intervened. Yet, we failed you and thus, failed ourselves.

But who dies like that? Apparently, people do, including that famous puppeteer—you know, the green frog guy. According to what I learned, he'd been feeling ill for several days but ignored all the telltale signs of something more serious. Like you, he was so committed to his work and projects that, despite the concerns of family and friends, he pushed on. And when he finally did seek help, it was too late. Nothing at all could be done to save him.

Nic, when you came into the office to finalize the unforeseeable changes to your will, you looked like a disheveled old man. You were hunched over, coughing, and shaking. I'd never seen you like that before, and neither had Elizabeth, who served as the witness to your legal documents. We were both keenly aware of your odd behavior. But we dismissed it as your being preoccupied with the renovation. How could I have known that would be the last time I'd see you alive? And maybe your illness did start out as a cold or the flu. However, by the time Tink finally convinced you to go to the hospital because you were too weak to say no, the infection had already ravaged your body like a wildfire consuming dry *brush. Your organs were actively shutting down, and no medical intervention could stop the progress. Bacterial pneumonia was the final diagnosis, and the result of this advanced infection was your death.*

But who cares what they call it? You were a careless idiot. Ironically, though, you were never careless with anything else in your life—not with your work, friendships, athleticism, sailing, or the S.O.S. Foundation. This one time however, made all the difference. And we were the ones left behind to suffer, and as for me - I'm exhausted. So, leave me alone today, Nic. You've tested my strength enough, and you were always the stronger one.

Still, I can't figure out why you made the sudden change to your will? Did you have a premonition about your death? You must have, although you never mentioned it to me. You were always upfront with me, as your legal counsel and best friend, about any of the decisions regarding your estate. Yet, the provisions you set up for your home are bewildering, and you never offered an explanation. I do hope that at some point, I will come to understand your decision. Maybe I'll ask Elizbeth for her thoughts. She's typically so rational, yet insightful about such matters. And I'm certainly not! But, I've asked enough of her these past few months, so I'd better wait. Besides, Elizabeth has her own matters to discuss with me, as evidenced by her request to look at a property together tomorrow. And I don't mind helping her, especially with all she's done recently. Still, I'm not managing well as it is, and I hope she just wants a simple opinion from me and nothing more. My guess is that she's feeling cramped or bored in her townhouse and is thinking about buying a home for herself. Maybe the property is on the water since she said it was related to the little commemorative sailboat I was holding in my hand. What else could it be? And I imagine that old photograph is tied in somehow. If it is, though, I haven't the slightest idea how.

With hurt and frustration that had not to date been fully recognized, Larry allowed himself to express these emotions in the privacy of his home. But the anger, confusion, and vulnerability were wearing on him. So, as mid-afternoon gave way to evening, he decided to rise up, both literally and figuratively, to do something constructive with what remained of the day. He also hoped to reconnect with the familiar version of himself before this unfathomable loss began along with the revolving ferris wheel of uncertainty.

Perhaps making a basic French roux will distract me from all of

357

this, he considered. *I've always enjoyed making a thick stock for the basis of a homemade soup. Plus, Tink gave me an ample amount of leftovers so, I could return the favor to her in the form of a tasty vegetable, turkey soup.*

With this in mind, Larry pushed in his office chair. In doing so, he noticed a sheet of paper askew on his desk's typically tidy surface. He despised disorder, especially in the work area. And he assumed this paper had been displaced when he banged his fist down, moments ago. With no other thought than to return it to its rightful place, he picked it up to determine where it belonged. One side was blank, but on the other side were a few scrawled words as if written by a little child. Larry could barely decipher the message, but when he did, his anger, guilt, and frustration instantly gave way to another torrent of tears. As he wept and his body shook, the only response he managed to convey was, "Alright, Nic. Alright."

Still holding the paper in his unsteady hands, Larry reread the note once more.

Slouch, my life was far better because of you.
Regret nothing.
I am the one who is sorry, and must ask your forgiveness.
I was the lucky one to call you my best friend and mate.

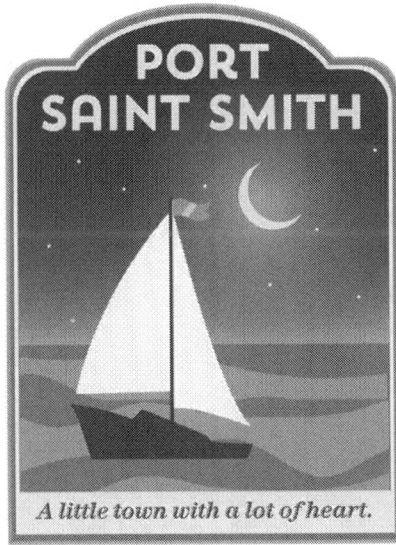

PORT SAINT SMITH

A little town with a lot of heart.

SATURDAY,
NOVEMBER 26

Chapter 62
Maddie

In the soft lighting of the study, Maddie slowly opened her eyes and looked around. *Why,* she questioned with a slight stretch, *am I waking up here on the loveseat rather than upstairs in the bed?* She also noticed that the antique quilt often used during the week was now neatly folded in half and laid across her. The last Maddie recalled, it had been loosely draped around her shoulders. Had she placed it there herself and with such perfection? That was most unlikely.

What time is it? she wondered, squinting in the direction of the mantel. Maddie could barely see the clock but thought that it read 4:30 a.m. *How am I able to read the time, though? Why is there any light in the room if it's hours before dawn?* Yet, there in the hearth, a small fire continued to burn—a blaze that should have gone out hours ago.

When I first settled into the study during the early evening, Maddie remembered, *I stacked only three small logs on the grate. But, flames still flicker, providing the warm hues of yellow, orange, and red. How is that possible?* she marveled in disbelief.

Pulling the quilt all around her, Maddie gradually sat up and saw too that a pillow had been placed under her head—the same pillow that had always been positioned in the sway of the wingback chair across the room. And this was a pillow she had never used during her stay in this home. *How did it get there? Could someone have put it under my head as I fell asleep?* she pondered.

Maddie soon became aware of another scent lingering in the room besides that of the burning wood. It was a pungent, salty sea smell that she'd noticed more than once during her time on the Cape. Eagerly, she breathed in deeply, enjoying how it seemed to calm and even caress her. And then memories of the most amazing evening she could have ever imagined came flooding back.

Oh my... I am starting to remember now. Was it even real, though? Did that really happen? I know it must have happened because I can still feel the warmth and intensity of his presence with me, Maddie recognized as she rubbed her skin, recalling the sensation of him so very near.

I need to record, as best I can, exactly what occurred last night. But what did occur? The feelings continue to be so strong. So, I'm hoping by writing, I'll be better able to remember the details. Because I must remember, Maddie decided determinedly, *before I start to believe that it was simply a dream... which, most definitely, it was not!*

Maddie reached for her journal lying on the coffee table. She pulled the pen from the spiral center and turned to the back of the book. Only one empty page remained before the entire journal would be filled.

Like an artist with their paints, brushes, and canvas, writing had always been a creative and cathartic way for Maddie to observe, reflect, and then process her experiences and emotions. She needed only to sit in silence, and begin the writing process which would allow the remnants to resurface.

With pen in hand, Maddie sighed gently, and without undue pressure or overt expectation, she started to journal.

November 25

Yesterday was a remarkable day of letting myself flow through the hours as I felt guided in each moment. Like the water drops traveling down the wet glass, I released all agendas and mindfully meandered at the most serene pace. I haven't done that very often, but I found it to be incredibly insightful. The experience also put me in a most heightened state of being for the remainder of the evening. But can I slip into that awareness again right now in order to re-experience last night's events when he was here? I hope so because he was definitely here with me. This I know with all my heart.

With another relaxed inhale and deep exhale, Maddie adjusted her position and continued to commit everything to paper as best she could.

The storm was intense, and I was glad to be in the safety of this cozy room. Heavy rains pounded on the roof for hours while thunder rang out, and brilliant bolts of lightning illuminated the sky. Eventually, though, as late day gave way to nightfall, the storm eased off, and just a light drizzle of rain continued. Swiftly, a woosh of warm air circled the room, and I then felt him beside me. But I was not afraid. Quite the contrary. I was pleased more than ever before that he had come to be with me. And I was ready for whatever he wanted to share.

Did I hear a noise? Did I actually hear the woosh of movement in the room when he arrived? No, I don't believe so. Nor could I hear any other sound from him. But I could feel his light touch upon my skin. Slowly... softly...and so inviting. I welcomed him completely, recognizing I only needed to receive.

Instantly, we joined in an amazing place of togetherness—one that transcends any language except that of the heart. Yet, it was not like two becoming one. No, because I remained fully aware of myself and was, at the same time, fully aware of him. But the space between us merged and became non-existent. We blended in a way where division does not exist. And we felt a love that was undoubtedly, the connection of our souls. But was it really love? Yet, what else could it have been? For in the perfection of that moment, the desire or need for anything else did not exist. We were wholly together, and everything outside of that slipped out of my consciousness. There was only us in the purest, sweetest, most satisfying sense of the word.

The sensations I felt with him were utterly unfamiliar to me. Tender, trusting, and exhilarating. I always believed this kind of connection was possible. But I gave up trying with anyone else, because I wanted to be understood without having to explain myself. And he knew exactly where to find my soul without asking and how to fill my heart without effort. And we lingered in that timeless moment, suspended in blissful union.

Maddie felt flush remembering how the energy had pulsated between them. Her body yearned for more, while her mind began to question…

>How can I feel so drawn to him when I can't even see him? And how can we connect so completely, when I don't even know who he is? I want to trust this. I want to trust him. But how can I, when I don't understand what's happening?
>
>Still, I know everything is different now. Everything! Like the raindrops willingly flowing down the panes of glass without a plan, or fear of what may become of them, I must trust what I know to be real, even if my reasoning mind can't make sense of it all. I really want to suspend my doubts, and go where love beckons. And I hope that before long, I will at least know who he is… this one who touches my soul.

Chapter 63
Shirley

Shirley barely felt the cold as she walked along the path from her car toward the front entrance to the Chamber of Commerce. A contented warmth emanated from within her, keeping away the chill of this crisp, autumn day. Next, as she reached for the keys in her pocketbook, she heard the light beep of a car horn. Turning toward the sound, she was delighted to see Elizabeth driving by slowly and waving hello.

"Good mahning," Shirley called back excitedly, realizing though that her words would not be heard through the closed windows. But, Shirley knew that her greeting would be seen and appreciated. As the car gradually progressed down Center Street, the congenial volunteer continued to watch and wave until Elizabeth pulled into the parking lot of Walters Real Estate and Investment. Only then did Shirley turn back to the path and proceed up the walkway.

What a wondahful surprise for Elizabeth to wave hello to me today, Shirley thought appreciatively. *Ovah the years, I have seen her around town and also at various functions, and we've always treated each other respectfully. But we've never exactly been what I would call friends. Howevah, maybe that will change now that we've shared such a special time together at Tink's and both of us helped out with the S.O.S. Basket Benefit for the first time. I would surah like that. I've always admired her, and, like the school principal once said about me, I believe she is a woman of true merit.*

365

Shirley continued up the stone steps toward the entrance. A sizable set of keys clanked and jangled as she located the proper one and fitted it into the lock. Soon, the cheery chimes overhead were welcoming her inside. But instead of walking directly back to the office, as was her usual routine, she meandered over to the fireplace.

I feel different today—so lighthearted, as though a carefree breeze has lifted my spirit. I feel within me a pleasant sense of fulfillment where an emptiness dwelt before. Without even realizing it, I must have been afraid that my life would have no worth after I retired from teaching. Because what good would I be to anyone, if I wasn't a teacher anymore? So, I busied up both here and at home with tasks like cleaning this fireplace a ridiculous number of times. And now I can clearly see there are othah activities to become involved with, like the S.O.S. Basket Benefit. That's a much bettah choice than staying preoccupied with busy work, which doesn't improve my life or anyone else's. I want to spend more time with my friends and enjoy more quiet moments by myself. Because, in the end, how immaculate does this fireplace really need to be?

So, in this very moment, I'm going to do something vastly different for me. Since the Chambah doesn't officially open for an hour, I'm going to pull the rocking chair closah to the hearth, light a small fire, and sip slowly on a delicious cup of hot cocoa.

After making that unprecedented decision, Shirley hung up her coat, placed her pocketbook in a nearby cupboard, and gathered a few logs. Soon, the fireplace was illuminated with a small but gratifying blaze. Next, she poured hot water into a large cup, stirred in a packet of cocoa mix, and topped it with a few indulgent marshmallows. She then sat down in the rocker—puzzled, but not at all unpleased, with herself.

How unlike me to relax at the start of a day! Yet, I have no desire to rush around this mahning. The few chores I do have can easily wait while I try to figure out this unusual mood I'm in. Maybe this is all due to eating so much rich food yestahday. I doubt that, though, because I'm not feeling sluggish or lazy. I just want to sit quietly and think… and I wondah if it's from sharing our childhood memories at the Thanksgiving dinnah table. The stories were so tendah that I can still sense a connection between us today. Maybe Elizabeth and the others can, too. I surah hope so! Because that's what tragedy can do to a community. In the aftermath of grief following Nic's death, the need to be togethah becomes that much more important.

Our friendships are the little dingy boats that help carry us through the rough seas of life and loss. For all we know, someone else could be missing at that same table next year. I don't want to live with regret, and I'm certain that Tink and the others don't want to eithah. So, taking time to share our support and stories can provide a heck of a lot of comfort and hope for us all.

The cup of cocoa went mostly untended as Shirley continued to reflect on these thoughts in welcome quiet and solitude. Rarely had she paused to assess her emotions or the course of her life. But, allowing herself to do so now felt especially good.

I sense that something within me is letting go and being released. Not in a worrisome way, like I'm losing my mental marbles. Heaven forbid! No, this is more like my hands finally relaxing aftah clutching several bags too tightly and for too long. I betcha I've been trying to control outcomes for fear that I wouldn't do or be enough. But that's surah tiring and not at all wise.

I was very disappointed after my cousin told me she wasn't coming to visit. I'd created a schedule of activities for us that would have been enjoyable. I can also admit, though, that our time togethah would have been very similah to those of the past—nice, but lacking anything new or enriching. Howevah, the afternoon spent at Tink's was so precious. We ate and laughed and teased and talked in ways that sparked my heart back to life. I needed that! Perhaps we all did.

When I was quite young, I was so eagah to explore and experience everything and to find friends with whom to share my adventures. I was always very happy! That time in my life was followed by decades of teaching—years filled with the energy and boundless curiosity of the many students in my classroom. Now, it seems I've created a retired life built on safety and routine. How very predictable, dull, and lacking in spontaneity. Well, I say no more—that's not for me! I'll be dahned if I'm going to let that continue. There is too much life left to live, and I'm lucky to have the good health and time to do it! I might just join that senior hiking group that's been posted on the bulletin board for eons. I've passed by it so often with the idea that 'maybe one day'... When did I think that day would come? Well, maybe that day is today!

And aftah talking about my dollies during suppah, I see how those little lessons set up a career in teaching. I don't think I've admitted to myself how much I've missed teaching—not so much the lessons or even

367

the planning but the days surrounded by the lively, children. I enjoy volunteering at the Chambah, but so few youngsters come in, and those who do are expected to be on their best behavior. So, I wondah if there is another way to get more directly involved with some children without the full responsibility of teaching?

Pondering these thoughts, while ignoring her usual agenda, proved to be very insightful for Shirley. As she continued to consider the possibilities, she rocked back and forth, enjoying the creaking sound of the chair against the old wood floor. The woodsy scent of the burning logs gently swirled around her, and as it did, Shirley released a series of long, slow sighs.

I'm satisfied with my life, but is that enough? No, not really. I want to hear the boisterous laughter of children again and be around their playful, innocent ways. How wicked good would that be?!

I realize that the S.O.S. Foundation's purpose is to provide opportunities for underserved children, Shirley considered, *and I've always wanted to be involved with that cause. I just didn't see how I could fit in. I'm no sailor—that's for surah. Plus, I've had plenty else to do in our community, or so I told myself.*

Howevah, stepping in this week to assist with the Thanksgiving baskets was not just okee dokee for me. I absolutely loved it! So, now I'm wondahing if there is something I could do to help the campers more directly next summer. Maybe I could be a greeter on the first day or even a lunchroom helper? Or I could oversee the inevitable Lost and Found Department. That would be great! And I wouldn't have to worry about coverage at the Chambah. There are plenty of other volunteers who could step up. Beatrice asked me again recently if she could lend a hand. But first, I would need to let go of the idea that no one will do it as well as I do. Because, even if that is true, she thought with a merry laugh, *I'm certainly not irreplaceable. And the thought of working with children again would be worth the risk of finding just how very true that is!*

Immersed in the possibilities of this exciting form of service with children, Shirley didn't notice how the increased draft in the room further ignited the fire in front of her. And as the flames flickered stronger, so did her hope for the coming year. Because Shirley certainly understood that given the opportunity, the spirit of service within her would soon shine even brighter like the fire in the hearth before her.

Chapter 64
Elizabeth

Larry's vehicle was the only one in the parking lot of the real estate office when Elizabeth pulled in. She parked her car in the usual place, walked over to his truck, and gave Larry a friendly hello. After receiving a quiet but sincere good morning in return and confirming he had the old photograph, Elizabeth climbed in and asked Larry to head east out of town. He immediately started up the engine and began driving in that direction.

The pleasant camaraderie that had existed between them during the Thanksgiving Day cooking and deliveries remained, so they both felt comfortable in companionable silence. Elizabeth was also grateful Larry had not yet inquired about where they were going or why.

I feel strongly that if this bold idea is going to work, the property must speak for itself, Elizabeth thought resolutely. *The setting is ideal for the sailors, and the pairing of the property and the chateau is a brilliant idea. My deepest hope, therefore, is that Larry will not only sense the immense value of the land but also embrace the merit of transforming* Beauté Par la Mer *into the S.O.S. Foundation's forever home. His support is essential to this success. Not only because Larry was Nic's best friend and business partner, he is also the executor of his estate and the legal representative of the S.O.S. Foundation.*

My concern, however, is his unpredictable behavior. The upbeat

369

and ambitious businessman I've known for years is now often daunted by simply performing his routine daily tasks. So, I'm worried that he could become overwhelmed just considering the inherent challenges required of such an enormous undertaking. Either way, I will know soon enough, she recognized, releasing a silent, little sigh.

As they drove further out of Port Saint Smith proper, the streets began to narrow. Winding turns gave way to long, rural roads, and only once did Larry look over at Elizabeth for the assurance they were heading in the right direction. She nodded yes. But still, he seemed puzzled, no doubt reasoning that most of the newer neighborhoods on the outskirts of town were to the west, but they were clearly going east, parallel to the coast.

After about twenty minutes, Elizabeth instructed Larry to turn left onto a dirt road. They passed a few secluded homes, and then, in a near whisper, she asked, "Please drive a little slower. We're almost there." Again, Larry followed her direction. Yet, Elizabeth could see a strained expression come across his face and his jaw muscles clench tight. But he did not ask any questions, and she chose not to explain anything just yet.

"That's it," Elizabeth blurted out eagerly, pointing toward a gated entrance. "Turn in there, please."

Larry glanced over again anxiously, but Elizabeth encouraged him to continue on through the bent and rusted wrought-iron gates. As the truck came to a stop just on the other side, Elizabeth carefully took the photograph in hand and climbed out of the truck.

Bewildered, Larry got out also and looked around skeptically. Overgrown hedges, thick brambles, and densely interwoven vines comprised most of the landscaping. Only two rows of tall trees lining the drive gave any indication of what may lay beyond the entrance.

"I know this doesn't look promising, but believe me when I say this is a very special place," Elizabeth offered at last. "And I'm bringing along the photograph so I can show you the significance. Let's begin the walk in," she suggested, thrilled to finally be sharing her beloved *Beauté Par la Mer* with someone in her life. And not with just anyone but with the one person whose approval mattered the most.

"I never did understand the significance of that picture," Larry grumbled in a low voice.

"That's ok. I'll explain everything to you today," she stated warmly.

The crunch of the gravel below their feet was the only sound heard as they began down the drive. As Elizabeth led the way, small rays of light pierced through the dense canopy of Beech tree leaves overhead. Eventually, they turned onto a worn path, much of which was covered with thick, green moss. The pathway meandered under a sagging, wooden trellis burdened with an unkempt wisteria vine and through the remains of a once formal garden. Very little beauty remained, so Elizabeth felt no reason to linger. Thus, they forged on until finally, just past a stone wall, the chateau came into view.

Although Elizabeth could easily remember its days of glory, the façade of the grand structure, now fully exposed in the bright sunlight, revealed countless cracks, crevices, and sinking corners. Turning her head subtly to observe Larry's expression, she saw his large shoulders slump and his head shake back and forth in disbelief.

"Please," she encouraged him, "before I tell you the reason why we're here, there is one more view I want to show you."

Larry shrugged submissively and followed Elizabeth once more. Although her preference as a child would have been to traipse barefoot on the lawn, she feared that a more direct route would be too difficult due to the exceptionally tall weeds and the muddy terrain from the previous day's storm. So, Elizabeth carefully proceeded along the obstructed path, which wound around behind the residence. Within minutes, they stepped out from the large shadow created by the chateau to behold a spectacular view of the Atlantic Ocean. Only then did Elizabeth notice a hint of joy returning to Larry's face as he witnessed the sun sparkling and playing upon the waves.

How could anyone deny such exquisite beauty? Elizabeth reflected in awe. *This natural expanse of undeveloped oceanfront is both stunning and serene. Even Larry seems to be feeling a comforting sense of peace in this place.*

Together, they stood and gazed for quite some time in restorative reverence as the ocean lapped faithfully against the rocks along the shoreline.

However, when she could no longer restrain her excitement, Elizabeth requested that Larry follow her back to the front of the residence. With noted reluctance, he complied, all the while looking back toward the sea, until it was no longer in sight. Only when they stood in the exact location where the original photo had been taken did Elizabeth stop and begin to speak.

"Larry, would you look at the photograph again, please," she urged him. "And compare it to what you see before you."

"Alright," he agreed.

Elizabeth watched closely as Larry's eyes searched back and forth between the photo and the depleted structure before him. Then, slowly, recognition began to register as he realized the pristine residence featured in the old black and white photograph was the same as the shabby one barely standing erect just a few yards away.

"I'm guessing this picture was taken right here, but a long time ago…?"

"Yes, it was. The name of this chateau is *Beauté Par la Mer,* which translates as Beauty by the Sea. At one time, as you can see, this place was a true beauty. Now, would you like to guess who the people are in the photograph? Or should I just tell you?"

"Just go ahead and tell me," he replied.

"The man in the photo was the owner of the chateau. He was a very kind and generous man."

"Ok. And who is the child?" Larry inquired.

"The young girl is his beloved granddaughter who spent many summer days visiting her Grand-Papa here."

"And you're telling me all of this because…?"

"Because I knew that man very well. His name was Maurice Gerard Moreau."

"That's your last name," Larry stated directly.

"Yes, it is. We have the same name because that little girl is…" and with that, Elizabeth paused and recreated the same happy expression as the child."

"Is that you, Elizabeth?" Larry asked in surprise.

"Yes, it is!" she uttered joyfully, feeling the fulfillment of finally being able to share this long-held secret with him.

"Wow," was all he could manage to say.

"I was about eight years old when that photograph was taken. Some of the happiest days of my childhood were spent right here—running around the grounds, splashing in the ocean, climbing the rocks, and scampering in and out of every room, which my Grand-Papa not only allowed, but encouraged."

Again, Larry could only stammer out the single word, "Incredible."

"Staying here at *Beauté Par la Mer* with my Grand-Papa was like living in a castle with a benevolent, old king."

"I guess I'm uh… happy for you…?" he mumbled in a barely audible voice.

"Thank you, Larry. And please know that I'd always planned to tell you about my past on the Cape. Even during my initial interview, I almost said something to you then. But I didn't want you to think I was a some privileged person who simply summered on the Cape and wouldn't be willing to put in a hard day's work."

"That was probably smart thinking on your part," Larry replied with a slight smile.

"And truth be told, after I'd established myself as a worthy employee, I came into your office more than once with the intention of telling you about my childhood adventures just outside of Port Saint Smith. Obviously, though, I never did. I wanted both you and Nic to know everything but somehow I justified my silence with the fact that you were always so busy with development projects, client meetings, or off on a well-deserved day of sailing. And the longer I lived in Port Saint Smith, the more difficult it became for me to open up about my past."

Larry offered no response but instead scuffed insistently at an indistinguishable spot on the ground.

"You may even recall," she continued, "I'd requested a private meeting with you and Nic at the beginning of summer. We had scheduled the appointment for the following Tuesday because I no longer wanted to carry the burden of this secret. I think you may have even been concerned that I was going to resign and return to my career as an interior designer since I'd had such fun helping Nic redecorate his home. But then, Nic fell ill and... I... I... just didn't have the heart to bring it up to you again."

At that very moment, a soft, cool breeze was felt on what had been an otherwise calm day. It swirled slowly between them just once and then eased away.

Aware of how unsettled Larry was becoming, Elizabeth still remained composed and gently resumed the conversation.

"I am so pleased to finally be telling you all of this. And Larry, I realize, this is a lot to take in. I do feel strongly, however, that the time for action is now. *Beauté Par la Mer* was a wonderful place for me as a child, and I know it can be a very special place again."

"I can appreciate your enthusiasm better now that I understand this was your grandfather's home," Larry stated. "And you have worked hard, Elizabeth, to create successful careers in New York and again here at the firm. You're certainly one of the most capable people I have ever met, and I'm sure you can achieve just about anything you set your mind to. Nevertheless, most people would be overwhelmed with a project of this magnitude."

"Well, I'd be lying if I said I wasn't intimidated, even though I can clearly envision all that *Beauté Par la Mer* can become. Yet, I'm ready and willing to take it all on. Knowing it is far greater than what I can do alone, though, I knew it was time to speak to you."

"Me?" he asked, taken aback. "What do I have to do with any of this?"

"I couldn't begin the process of a purchase, let alone the transformation, without your go-ahead."

"Why ever not?" he questioned. "I mean, I can't blame you for wanting all of this. The ocean view alone is one-of-a-kind. Still, it's a lot for one person. But you certainly don't need my approval of your choices. You've never requested that of me before."

"Oh no, that's not it at all," Elizabeth exclaimed. "Obviously, with all the excitement of showing you the estate, I got ahead of myself! Forgive me, Larry."

"For what?" he inquired impatiently.

"For failing to tell you exactly why I think this property should be purchased and, if at all possible, very soon. I assure you, though, it is not for me!"

"Who is it for then?" he demanded.

"Let me just say that although Grand-Papa's estate is truly beloved by me, I don't think its purpose is to become any one person's private residence or a developer's dream purchase to be divided up into luxury condominiums. I feel strongly that it has been waiting for quite a long time for just the right owner and a much greater purpose."

"And that would be…?"

"Do you remember this past Monday when you were holding one of the commemorative brass sailboats, and I mentioned that I wanted to talk with you about it?"

"Yes, I remember."

"Great. Because Larry, you, more than anyone else, know how hard Nic worked to envision and establish the S.O.S camps for underserved youth. And the camps have been a true triumph, not only for the children, but for so many of us here in Port Saint Smith. Despite real limitations such as having to use the town's busy marina for the sailing lessons and

374

no dedicated office space to run the organization, each year the camps have been more successful than the last. And this," she said, pointing toward the chateau and the sea, "is how we can ensure that Nic's worthy vision continues for years to come—by transforming this land and home into the permanent location for the Spirit of Sailing Foundation."

"Really?" he questioned doubtfully, looking around again at the disheveled surroundings and decrepit building.

"Yes," Elizabeth stated with conviction. "The residence could be restored and repurposed for meeting rooms, sailing classes, a sizable lunchroom, administration offices, and more. And the grounds would become a wonderful place for so many activities—outdoor games, picnics, and maybe early evening campfires and roasted s'mores. We would also build a dock and boat house, and that stunning expanse of the sea would become the most amazing setting where the children could learn to sail in much calmer and safer waters than the Port Saint Smith Marina."

Larry looked down again at the ground and said nothing.

"I realize that the foundation has some money in reserve. Nevertheless, I'm sure additional fundraising would be necessary."

"Undoubtedly," he stated. "The cost of the land alone could be excessive."

"You're right, and I understand this is an ambitious goal. All I'm asking now is that you consider the possibility of this project. Then you have my word - I will do all the rest. Together with the citizens of this wonderful town, we can safeguard the future of the foundation and truly honor its dedicated founder. Because I believe more than words could ever say, Nic would really want this."

Larry couldn't hear anymore. He shook his head and raised his hand to request that she stop speaking. Then he turned his back on her and began walking towards the sea.

Elizabeth knew better than to follow him. If Larry was going to be able to offer any support, it would have to come from him authentically. She would not plead, coerce, or use guilt to convince him. But she was greatly concerned whether he would even be able to envision all of the possibilities in his compromised state. Could he look beyond the dismal condition of the house to imagine the children learning in the classroom and laughing in the lunchroom? And could he picture the colorful sails of the small boats navigated by the earnest sailors bobbing along in the waters just off the shoreline? Larry well knew the joy of learning to sail. But could he suspend his own grief long enough to help ensure this life-changing experience for the children?

As these thoughts crossed her mind, the soft breeze returned, tickling the edges of the photograph in her hand. Elizabeth held on tighter and waited for Larry's return.

After a considerable amount of time had passed, she saw Larry walking back in her direction. His body language, she feared, was indicative of his mindset. His glance remained down, and his hands were in his pockets as he approached. Once he stopped, he shuffled nervously back and forth—a behavior she had never witnessed in him until recently. Uncertainty… avoidance…confusion. And still, she waited for him to speak.

"I will tell you, Elizabeth, I just don't get it. I mean, I understand the merit of purchasing any oceanfront land on Cape Cod, and this setting is admittedly exceptional. But the house is probably beyond repair. And, if it could be repaired, the requirements of that are just inconceivable to me—the fundraising, the permits, the unforeseeable repairs, the delays, the liabilities, and more. I could go on and on. I just feel it is entirely unrealistic."

"I understand," Elizabeth managed to say faintly. Feeling deeply disheartened, she did her best to fight back tears.

Larry then pulled his phone out of his pocket and looked at the screen.

Maybe he's going to take a few pictures, Elizabeth thought, *and give this idea further consideration. I refuse to give up hope, at least not yet.*

But rather than hold his phone up to take a picture, Larry seemed to fumble awkwardly in search of a text message. He scrolled down anxiously, and Elizabeth thought she heard him say, "Fine. I'll tell her," as though speaking to someone else. Still, she waited without comment until finally, Larry looked up, cleared his throat, and said,

"I swear I don't get it, Elizabeth. Not at all. I think it's too much for any of us to take on. But, regardless of my concerns, I give you my full support. Because," he paused, his voice quivering slightly, "you are absolutely right. This is exactly what Nic would want."

Chapter 65
Tink

The knock on the back door came just as the old grandfather clock chimed half past six on this Saturday night. With much excitement, Tink rose from the kitchen chair and hurried to greet her visitor.

"Maddie, you're here! I'm so glad you found my little note on your porch. Please come in."

Maddie entered the cheery kitchen as Tink continued speaking, "I guess taping the note to a large takeaway container filled with homemade muffins made it easier to find?"

"Yes," Maddie replied with an appreciative smile, "That was very helpful of you!"

"Thanks! I just didn't want you to miss it. And, I'd like you to know, there are a total of six muffins to take home—one for each of the five upcoming workdays and one more to share with your friend Stephen."

"How thoughtful of you, Tink. I was planning to brag about your amazing baking to Stephen anyway. But now he'll be able to taste for himself and know that I'm not exaggerating at all. So, thank you."

"You're very welcome, my dear. I'd set a few muffins aside also for that ol' coot Charlie Kelly. I think I mentioned before that we've had that long-standing tradition ever since his good wife passed away that he comes around on a Saturday night to enjoy some fresh fruit pie. His wife was a fine baker too, so I didn't want him to go without. And I'll tell you what—he and I can do some real damage to a pie in one evening. But Charlie called me this morning to say that he wasn't feeling up to coming over. He mumbled something about still being full from Thanksgiving."

"I can understand that," Maddie affirmed. "I've been eating fairly light myself ever since that incredible meal, which, by the way, I think was one of the most delicious and enjoyable Thanksgivings I've ever had."

"Isn't that nice of you to say?" Tink replied with a faint blush

"I just wished you'd let me stay and help with some of the cleanup."

"Fiddlesticks! You're here on vacation, so I couldn't possibly ask that of you. If, however, you're still coming over for meals in a few years—which is a lovely thought—I may consider accepting your help then."

"Fair enough," Maddie replied sweetly.

"I must tell you, though, Maddie, that having your presence at the table really did my heart much good. Thank you for indulging us with your delightful company. And I was so hoping we'd have a bit more time together, and, by gosh, here you are!"

"Ah, thanks. I was hoping to see you again, also!"

"Excellent. Now, may I talk you into a nice piece of warm pie and perhaps a few candied pecans? I made the most tasty pecans earlier this week but forgot to put them out on Thanksgiving. And they are just too good not to share!" she insisted.

"Well, as you mentioned, I am on vacation. So maybe a little more indulgence is justifiable."

"Indeed it is!! That's the right attitude, my dear! And just one more reason why I like you so much, Maddie Stuart. Now, go on and have a seat, if you would please," the hostess requested, pointing toward the kitchen table, "and I'll get us something to drink. Would you like hot tea? I have many flavors to choose from. Or you could have a coffee milk, plain milk, or something else?"

"Hot tea sounds great, but I am curious to know—what exactly is coffee milk?"

"I'd be glad to tell you. Because when I first moved here, I couldn't understand many of the local traditions. For instance," Tink explained," if you order a milkshake around here, don't expect to be given one of those thick, creamy beverages made with ice cream. Nope. You'll just get milk and flavored syrup. And speaking of ice cream, if you'd like some of those colorful, little sprinkles on top, you need to ask for Jimmies. And don't get me started on what a fluff-a-nutter is… besides, of course, delicious."

Maddie laughed at Tink's entertaining commentary.

"So, when I make a coffee milk, a very popular local drink, it all begins with a large glass of cold milk - be it from a cow or almonds or oats. And then I add my own coffee syrup to flavor and sweeten. I don't use the store-bought syrup, however. I prefer my own, which is made with decaf. That way, I can enjoy this divine beverage anytime, even at night."

"That sounds delicious."

"So why don't I make you a small glass of coffee milk along with your hot tea so you can try it?"

"That's a great idea. Thanks!"

"And while I am busy doing that, why don't you tell me what you've been up to since I saw you last. I'd love to hear about everything - or at least the parts you wish to share," Tink added with a tiny wink.

Maddie had plenty to talk about, but her mind was still preoccupied with the events of the evening before, which she did not plan to divulge to Tink or anyone else just yet. For she could barely put into thoughts or words for herself what had actually happened.

Fortunately, the hostess offered another topic of discussion. "Oh, and one other thing," Tink interjected, before Maddie had time to respond, "I never had a chance to ask you on Thanksgiving if you were able to find a nice present for Stephen. I'd love to hear what you found for him, if you did."

Maddie opted to just touch lightly on her activities of the last two days and then move on to the topic of Stephen's gift. "As you know, yesterday was very rainy! So, I indulged in a blissfully lazy day of self-care—naps, a long, hot bath, and simply gazing out the bedroom window at the garden below."

"How perfectly delightful! Good for you!"

"Yes! It was wonderful! And today, I rode the bike on the beautiful Piney Grove Trail all the way to the beach. It was pretty cold, but I still had a great time. The wind, the waves, the wildlife and the salty air all made for a very enjoyable outing. I can understand now, more than ever, why people come to the Cape for vacation or even to live."

"It makes sense, doesn't it? Having grown up near Chicago, I was quite reluctant to relocate here after my marriage. But with each passing year, I have come to love the Cape more and more. And I'm sure you will, too, if you decide to come back."

Maddie nodded in agreement, and then continued speaking, "In answer to your question about Stephen, I did find a lovely gift for him. Stephen's mother was an avid art collector, and she instilled in him a true appreciation for art. His home is filled with paintings, sculptures, tapestries, and ceramics of all kinds. So I went into the art co-op and bought him an original still-life watercolor by a very talented, local artist. I imagine he will hang it either in his dining room along with a few other impressive still-life paintings or maybe in the kitchen since the subject matter is a pear and a vase on a wooden table."

"That sounds beautiful, Maddie! I'm sure he'll appreciate such a thoughtful gift. And I'll tell you something…I tend to really like people who like art. They're usually fun to be around, more accepting of others, and willing to give themselves permission to actually color outside the lines of life."

"That is certainly true about him," Maddie commented. "He's very funny, and we are always laughing about something. He's also proven to be one of my most loyal friends."

"What a blessing! There is nothing like the gift of a true friendship. Oh, and speaking of gifts, I might just have a little something for you!"

"Really?" Maddie asked in surprise.

"Yes. I saw it yesterday when I was volunteering at the bookstore."

"You were volunteering yesterday? I thought for sure you would be resting after such a busy week."

"I probably should have been, but I'd already given my word. I will admit, though, that I was a bit of a muddy mess when I showed up in my green galoshes and faded plaid umbrella. Plus, the rain kept nearly everyone away. But that gave me time to wander around the store, which was enjoyable since they have so many wonderful things!"

"Yes, I went there this week and could have walked away with bags full of great finds."

"I believe that. So then, you'll be happy to know that's where I found the wee treasure for you. I wasn't exactly looking, but once I saw it, I knew I had to buy it! And I've learned to listen to, and follow the promptings of my intuition. That's always wise, don't you think?"

"Oh yes, that is wise," Maddie concurred.

"So, now the important question is, shall I give it to you right away or wait until after we've had dessert?"

"Whatever you'd prefer is fine with me," Maddie said agreeably.

"Then let's not wait! I've got it right here in the pantry."

Immediately, Tink went to retrieve the present and eagerly handed it to Maddie.

"What pretty wrapping!" Maddie exclaimed.

"Isn't it, though? And I did it myself, which is even more amazing! Let me explain. Not that long ago, my wrapping skills were so awful that the ladies of the Port Saint Smith Guild politely suggested that I no longer offer my services as a gift wrapper for charity. Perhaps, they said, my talents could be better put to use in the kitchen or the garden or just about anywhere else. But I was determined to learn since on the particular day I volunteer each year, all of the funds go to the Homes for Hounds Rescue Center, which is so dear to my heart. So, I practiced endlessly at home with old scraps of paper and different size boxes. And before long, I got much better, to the extent that several of the ladies in the guild were actually impressed, and that's no small achievement. I may not win any awards for this accomplishment, but I am proud of myself for not accepting defeat."

"Well, this looks expertly wrapped! As my grandmother would often say, 'It's almost too pretty to open.' But I'm excited to see what it is, so here goes!"

"I hope you'll like it," the elder said.

Maddie smiled and carefully undid the bow and enough tape to pull a book out. She turned it over, and tiny tears filled her eyes as she was astonished to see the cover. For here was yet another affirming sign in the form of this thoughtful present. Since, just a few days earlier, she had considered buying this very journal for herself.

"What do you think, Maddie?" Tink asked tenderly.

"I love it. I absolutely love the cover and the fact that it's a journal. It's so perfect. And do you know that I keep journals?"

"No, but I guessed you were the type of person who would find value in that kind of reflective writing."

"Yes, I really do. I write in my journal almost every day. And, believe it or not, I was tempted to buy this exact book the other day when I saw it at the bookstore. I think the watercolor rendition of the cardinal is gorgeous, and I couldn't stop looking at it. But I wasn't really shopping for myself that day, and I still had a few pages left in my current journal. But guess what? Those pages are full now, so your timing couldn't be any better."

"I'm just tickled that you're pleased! I believe that the heart will give us insightful messages that our minds may not fully understand. And trusting those messages can be really hard sometimes. But when we do, joy is often one of the many amazing rewards we will receive. And my heart clearly told me that this journal was meant for you."

"Well, I couldn't be happier about it, Tink, especially since it is a gift from you!"

"Thank you for saying that, Maddie. And you know what I find very interesting?' Tink inquired. The handsome cardinal that has been flitting back and forth between us all week arrived on the very same day you did. I don't think that is a coincidence at all. In fact, I believe he was sent as a messenger of love and to help welcome you to our neighborhood."

"What a sweet thought," Maddie murmured.

"Yes. And now that you've mentioned sweets… perhaps it's time we had dessert," Tink announced with a light clap of her hands. "But first, tell me what you think of the coffee milk, and please be honest."

"I think it's delicious!"

"Well, Maddie, as I suspected, you do fit in so well here, and your approval of that fine beverage is just one more indication. If you want more, let me know. Otherwise, I'm going to get our desserts now."

"I'm fine for right now. But can I help you with anything?"

"No, but thanks for asking. Why don't you just sit and relax and tell me stories about your cat or whatever else comes to mind."

And so Maddie proceeded to tell Tink about Miss Priss - how old she was, how she got her current name, and a few of her many antics.

"Miss Priss sounds like my kind of cat! "Tink quipped as she served up sugared pecans, pumpkin pie, and pleasantries. Before long, the two women were enjoying not only their drinks and dessert but also a comfortable connection like dear friends.

Once their bellies were full and their plates empty, however, Tink began to feel weary.

"My heavens, dear Maddie, exhaustion seems to have suddenly caught up with me."

"That's understandable. Why don't I help you clean up and then get going?" Maddie suggested, ready to clear her plate and leave.

"No, I'm not that tired. It's just that I had hoped to show you around the house a little. I wanted you to see the parlor where I keep a few of my most meaningful photographs. And I would have insisted, of course, that we stop to admire my famed trophy case filled with awards, certificates, trophies, and ribbons from many years of baking. But, I can tell I don't have the strength any longer."

"Really, Tink, I've had a lovely visit, but I should probably let you rest."

"No, please, I'm not asking you to leave. Can we just sit and talk a little longer?"

"Of course, I'd be glad to," Maddie replied sincerely. "Can I get you anything?"

"No, but again, thank you for asking. I guess after all I've done this week, my body is letting me know it's had about enough."

"My body would let me know that too, I'm sure, if I'd done all that I know you've done this week. Let's see… you made and delivered dozens of canine cookies for the dogs at the rescue center. You baked eight pies with homemade crusts for the basket benefit. You brought me a plate of just-out-of-the-oven cookies. And the next day, you delivered a hot pot pie - something you mentioned many of your other neighbors would also receive. You hosted a formal Thanksgiving dinner with every imaginable course—all of which was indescribably delicious. And now you tell me you drove in the rain to volunteer at the bookstore yesterday, wrapping gifts for charity. Have I missed anything?" Maddie asked wryly.

"Well, um," Tink considered with a giggle, "I don't think so. And when you list it all together like that, I must admit it does sound rather ambitious for a woman my age."

"Just slightly ambitious," Maddie teased in reply. "And what is your age exactly, if I may be so bold to ask?"

"I am a youthful, eighty-six-year-old," the old woman boasted, attempting to sit up straighter to emphasize her point.

"Eighty-six years old? I had no idea!"

"Most people don't. And every once in a while, I do feel my age, if not even older. But it is grief that has been the biggest thief of my vitality lately. Much more than anything else."

"I'm so sorry. Do you want to talk about it?" Maddie asked compassionately.

"I guess I do because one of my dearest friends died recently and most unexpectedly. He was so young and active—always sailing and cycling. Many in the area also considered him to be one of the finest builders, as well as one of the most generous and heartfelt philanthropists. But, more than anything, he was like a son to me."

"Oh, Tink, I am really so sorry. I had no idea," Maddie said softly.

"His death has been one of the hardest things I've ever endured in my life. And I am a strong woman. I will heal, though, and truly, having you here this week has helped lift my mood considerably. So thank you again for choosing to spend time with this old bird," she offered humbly.

"I've enjoyed spending time with you!"

"Aren't we lucky…" Tink commented and then went on to ask in a much more vulnerable tone, "May I show you just one photograph of him? It's tucked inside his journal."

"Yes, of course, I'd love to see it," Maddie replied kindly.

With quivering hands, the elder reached for the book, which lay near the end of the kitchen table. She turned to the last page and pulled the photo out. But before showing it to Maddie, she spoke of him again. "This good man was a friend to everyone. He was sensitive, caring, and insightful. Yet, in his own lifetime, he never found his true love, even though just months before his passing, he believed with certainty they would be together soon."

Goosebumps covered Maddie's arms as she heard these words. Tink then turned the image around, saying, "This is him. Isn't he handsome?"

Maddie gasped as a wave of shock rippled throughout her body. She had seen this man's picture before. He was one of the two men standing in front of the boat in the photograph that had fallen out of the sailing book. He was the ruggedly handsome one she had immediately been drawn to.

"Who is he, Tink? What is that man's name?" Maddie asked, instantly shaken.

"His name is Nic. Nicolas Paramonos. You're staying in his home."

"What?" Maddie asked incredulously.

"Yes, that was Nic's home that he'd just finished renovating before his death."

"The owner of the house is dead? But he, uh,…," Maddie stammered, "… he wrote me a welcome note. I mean, uh, I thought he did. Maybe I was mistaken," she added, shaking her head.

"I'm so sorry to tell you like this. I thought you may have already known."

"No, uh, I didn't. But that's alright," Maddie affirmed in an attempt to reassure Tink. "It's just that I had, uh… I'd hoped to meet him."

"And I'm sure he would have loved to have met you. He knew his beloved was coming soon…he was certain of that. And here you are now, just months following his death, fitting the very description of the woman he described in his journal."

"I'm not sure what to say," Maddie stuttered, trying hard to hide just how stunned she truly was. She'd had no idea the owner was dead, nor who had been visiting her from the other side. These two seemingly disjointed facts swirled around in the air like autumn leaves caught up in an unexpected breeze.

For a few moments, nothing else was said. Then, when Tink looked over at Maddie, she could clearly see that the sparkle in her lovely eyes had gone out like a candle flame extinguished by a mighty gust of wind.

"I'm so sorry to burden you with this tonight," Tink apologized.

"No, it's alright. I understand. I know how important it is to share when our hearts are heavy," Maddie assured her.

"Yes, it is extremely important. So, thank you, my dear, for listening with such compassion. And, if I may, Maddie, I'd like to share an amazing realization that came to me when I was clearing the linens from the dining room table. Do you remember the wind that insisted on making its way into the room on Thanksgiving Day?"

"Yes, I remember," Maddie replied.

"I think that had something to do with Nic. He always loved the wind! After a day of sailing, he would go to great lengths explaining to me which direction the wind had been coming from, how many knots it was moving in, and how eagerly the sails responded to the wind's direction, which always brought him such great joy. And I didn't recognize it at the time because I was so flustered that the door had blown open. But I believe now that was Nic's way of saying he wanted to join us at the table. Does that make any sense? Or does that sound crazy to you?"

"I think it makes perfect sense," Maddie admitted readily.

"Did you feel the wind in the room that day?" Tink inquired.

"Absolutely," Maddie replied, remembering precisely how the wind had circled the room and then settled in beside her. And she also well remembered the tender touch on her hand under the table. Was that Nic who had so tenderly touched her? Was it the owner of *La Maison Enchantée* who'd been coming to her all along? Was he the one who'd invited her to come to the Cape shortly after his death? Maddie's strength was quickly seeping out of her body as her mind raced to find answers to so many compelling questions.

"Maddie…," Tink said gently, almost calling her back from her thoughts, "You look tired now, also. I just hope this conversation hasn't exhausted you."

"No, but I think you may be right. I'm probably a bit weary after the bike ride to the beach and a fairly busy week," she explained.

"We've both had a full week, and I guess we need to call it a night. But may I ask you just one more question before you go?"

"Of course."

"Do you think you will ever come back to Port Saint Smith?"

"Yes, I hope so. I mean, I'm actually thinking about that already. I can't imagine not coming back here, to be honest."

"Oh, that makes me very happy!"

"Yes, I've been very happy here myself. I feel so… at home. And Elizabeth has even invited me to go to the holiday show at the theater with her."

"Well, wouldn't that be wonderful? I'm sure you would enjoy seeing one of their amazing shows together. And, if you did return, do you think I could talk you into some homemade cookies and a little visit with me also?"

"Definitely, I would love that! If I come back, seeing you will be one of the highlights."

"Ah, how sweet of you. You really are a love, Maddie. And hopefully, I will feel up to showing you around a little bit more when you do return. I'll have to save up my strength. But I can't guarantee that my home will be decorated this year for the holidays. Nic always helped me with that."

"I could help you," Maddie offered without hesitation.

"I couldn't ask that of you. You're a busy working gal, and any time here should be devoted to rest, relaxation, and fun."

"I think we would have fun decorating together."

"Well, I don't put much up anymore. Just a little tree, a stocking, and a few holiday knick-knacks here and there."

"Let's plan on it. I have plenty of earned vacation time to use. I just need to check my work schedule to see when exactly I can come back."

"Really, Maddie, you'll come back to visit and help me decorate?"

"Absolutely, you have my word," Maddie truthfully replied, looking directly into Tink's hopeful eyes.

"Oh, Maddie," Tink responded, gently touching her new friend's hand. "How did you ever end up here? You're like an angel that floated in on an ocean breeze."

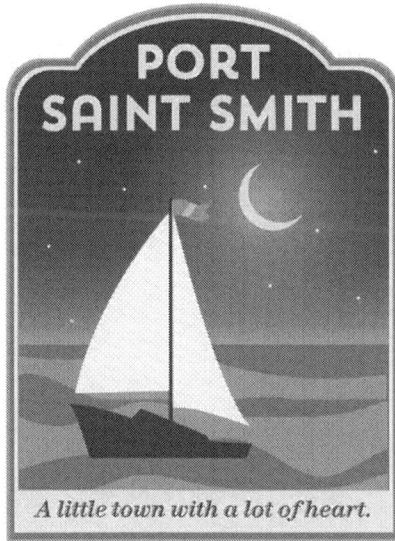

PORT
SAINT SMITH

A little town with a lot of heart.

SUNDAY,
NOVEMBER 27

Chapter 66
Maddie

As Maddie closed the door behind her, the clicking sound of the lock felt finite. She was exhausted because sleep on her last night of vacation had not come easy. And now she was locking up the rental home and feeling the heaviness of departure. Only a few days earlier, she'd stood at this same doorway with a tremendous sense of promise and excitement. For finally, she had arrived right here after being clearly guided to the charming town of Port Saint Smith and then again to this amazing home whose very name spoke of intrigue—*La Maison Enchantée*. Maddie's week on the Cape had been beyond wonderful—everything she'd hoped for and that which she had not even dared to consider. She had seen the sights, bought the gifts, and enjoyed the local cuisine like most tourists. But that is not why she had come to this destination. No, Maddie had come to find the one who had beckoned her there. But had she found him? Did she know for sure who had invited her to the Cape? These questions and other concerns had kept her awake until the wee hours before dawn. As she stood on the threshold of the back porch, Maddie recognized how sad she really was to say goodbye. But to what exactly?

Am I sad to say goodbye to this house? she wondered. *Am I sad to say goodbye to the kind neighbor next door? And to the town of Port Saint Smith? Or am I sad to say goodbye to him? Am I saying goodbye to him? Am I having to say goodbye to someone I never met in life—someone being grieved by so many in this quaint town? Am I also grieving someone without ever having known him? And is that even possible? I'm just so confused! And I don't know what will happen next, which is my biggest fear.*

Without the answers she sought, Maddie paused before leaving to simply look around and take everything in one last time. Her eyes glanced over toward the end of the long porch.

I'll miss the swing and the creaking sound it makes every time I rock back and forth. I'll miss the garden and the different views I've enjoyed from the porch, the kitchen, and the bay window in the bedroom. I'll miss this beautiful house and how it has supported me in ways I never imagined a home could. I'll miss the cardinal who visited often and even flew beside me as I walked to Tink's home on Thanksgiving Day.

But more than anything, I'm afraid I won't have a connection with Nic ever again. I'm worried how much I'll miss him. For isn't that who I've felt so close to me? Isn't it Nic Paramonos who invited me here and has been the devoted presence ever since I arrived? If so, that means the man I have been sensing is really dead. Yet, he wrote me a welcome note, rocked me on the swing, kissed me on the cheek, and so much more. How can this be the end of our time together? Will he come back to my apartment, or will he stay here? For he has already become so vitally important to me. I just can't imagine my life without him.

With no present sense of him for reassurance, Maddie reluctantly stepped away from the back door. As she did, a small cluster of autumn leaves began swirling just above her feet. She looked down to watch the colorful spinning and, in doing so, saw that the doormat had subtle words woven into the fiber. Why hadn't she noticed that before? Quietly, she read the words once to herself, and then again, she read them out loud.

"You are home."

Slowly, a sweet smile spread across her face as Maddie embraced the significance of that statement. She gathered her belongings with a vow in her heart to return to this home, his home, and return soon. And she hoped, more than anything, this would not be the end of their story.

PORT SAINT SMITH

A little town with a lot of heart.

A Note From The Author

Dear Reader,

I am truly happy that this book, *Enchanted Winds* -- my first novel, found its way to you! And I thank you most sincerely for taking the time to read it. My hope is that the journey to Port Saint Smith has been a most enjoyable one as you've gotten to know Maddie, Stephen, Tink, Larry, Elizabeth and the other endearing characters. You may also be wondering now what will happen when Maddie returns to her apartment? Will Nic be there for her? Or must she return to Port Saint Smith in order to connect with him again? Well, plans for the next book are well underway.

Enchanted Winds, I do feel strongly, was gifted to me. One day the story gently appeared in my imagination... an unexpected spark of inspiration and there they were—Maddie chatting with Stephen as he fawned over Miss Priss; and Tink generously offering both her sweet cookies and sage advice to her friends in Port Saint Smith. I immediately welcomed them all! And in the years since they first arrived, I have remained faithful to the telling of their story. However, my intensive (aka slow!) writing style, full time work, and overall active life precluded me from completing this novel any sooner. Yet, I have also come to believe in the divine timing of it all—that regardless of my personal goals and aspirations, this story is coming out into the world at the exact right moment.

For the past twenty-five years, I have worked as an Intuitive Counselor and Medium. What a privilege to offer guidance, beneficial insights and meaningful connections with those on the other side. This was not, however, anything I had ever planned to do. Yet, my abilities evolved in the most natural and organic of ways. Unlike many in my profession, I am completely self-taught. Thus, I was able to forge new methods that I believe are helping to usher in a fresh approach to this line of work. And this is not an easy profession seeing as the majority of the work centers around difficulties, heartbreak, and death. Yet, I consider it an honor to serve in this capacity and strive to always remain respectful and gratitude.

Over the years, I have witnessed so many individuals riddled with guilt after their loved one dies. I have seen many also harboring great fear of what awaits their deceased in the great beyond. And nearly everyone I encounter longs to have any signs, connections or visitations of reassurance from those that have transitioned. What an immense honor, therefore, for me to help facilitate these meaningful connections so that my client can know with certainly that their loved one are not only doing well but wish to maintain their relationship beyond the grave. With no exception, I feel with all my heart that our loved ones are there for us— visiting in dreams, sending messages in whimsical and wonderful ways and offering the constancy of their presence.

My own search for answers came following my mother's tragic death when I was a very young and naive teenager. Throughout her life, I watched this sensitive and caring woman struggle greatly and I could not bare the thought of her struggling any more after death. Yet, I was told by many well-intended people such things as … God obviously needs her more than you do. Even the minister at our church, where we had been faithfully attending for years, told me that he did not think my mother went to heaven. I was but a grieving child devastated by these statements. Thus, in the face of such incomprehensible statements, I had to know the truth! Because none of that made sense to me. So, I began an intensive, self-guided journey in the hopes of understanding what does happen when our loved ones die. For years, I read books, spoke to many, traveled to hear experts speak, and then eventually stepped boldly into this work. And, since then, I have heard countless stories that clearly affirm what I wanted to believe was true way back then.

Perhaps you have also struggled with the shock and/or grief of losing someone dear to you. Maybe you have feared that you will never see or sense them again. Or you are terrified that they are not doing well, wherever they may be. My years of research, along with my work in this field, has taught me so much. I strongly now believe that all souls go to the light and there they will have a full life review to best come to terms with how they lived their lifetime. And there, on the other side, they exist in the most wonderful state of being—a state that I refer to as the "perfected soul state". What heaven for them—quite literally! And I also believe that they want to continue a relationship with us. You may actually hear or sense them. You may have the visitation of a cardinal, butterfly or ladybug. Or you may receive written messages in the most surprisingly ways. My mother sends me hearts almost every day; while my father, who was mostly absent in my upbringing, speaks to me often and has even helped me become a better cook in the kitchen. (A story I will gladly share at another time).

So let me say to you in closing. My wish for you is …

The steady assurance that your loved ones are present with you whenever your heart misses or longs for them.

A clear connection with your inner wisdom, along with a childlike sense of wonder in recognizing the reassuring signs of confirmation along the way.

An ever-growing awareness of that which brings you peace, purpose and joy.

The continued confidence and courage to move in a direction of true inspiration.

And the willingness to receive so much love and support from those both in both the seen and the unseen world.

May it be so.

I hope that reading *Enchanted Winds* has served as a real inspiration to you and that we stay in touch.

I send you great kindness,
Mary

Acknowledgments

Along the path of this novel's long and winding journey to completion, I have had many friends, family members, and colleagues offer their support, encouragement, and worthy insights. I offer my heartfelt thanks to all of you who helped in various ways, kept believing, and continued holding up the lantern of hope to light the way. Bless you all!

And specifically, I wish to thank the following:

Kristen Tame, a most exceptionally amazing woman, has faithfully assisted me in the editing of this book for the last two years. I am honored to have had her excellent collaborative efforts! For Kristen brought to this project not only her passion but also her boundless creativity and impressive vision for what this book, along with the characters and town, could be. She truly envisioned the world of the book and helped it come alive through her comprehensive editing and brilliant graphics. Her contributions have gone far beyond my expectations! This beautiful woman's radiant presence has truly blessed my life and this project.

Silmar Sanchez, my endearing friend, has been involved with this novel since its very inception. She has listened with a compassionate heart to every aspect of this endeavor and contributed in ways both seen and unseen. Then, just weeks before final publication, she swooped in like the unassuming superhero that she is to help infuse the final manuscript with her lovely light of wisdom. Every day, I am blessed by the sweet gift of her presence in my life.

Kelli Hastings, a wise and lovely woman, gave the gift of the final read-through. Kelli's keen eye pointed the way for a number of significant changes that truly helped refine the manuscript. With gratitude, I thank her for her noteworthy contributions.

Jerry Hitt, who is my sweetheart and helpmate in life. He has cooked delicious dinners, done the dishes, tended to the cats, and much more so that I could keep tapping away at all hours of the morning and night. Jerry also committed numerous hours to reading aloud the early version of the manuscript so that I could better hear the areas that still needed work. Thank you for your belief in me and for all your love.

Forrest Hardy, my dear son, has offered me his encouragement and support through the years in so many aspects of my life, including my website and this book. I am inspired by his courage and commitment to better his own life, for which I hope his honorable efforts will be richly rewarded.

Resources

Sandra Champlain is the author of the #1 international best-selling book "We Don't Die - A Skeptic's Discovery of Life After Death" and host of "We Don't Die Radio" and "Shades of the Afterlife" with over 550 combined episodes. I had the privilege of meeting Sandra in 2019 at a We Don't Die event she sponsored in Orlando and again at the IANDS international conference in Philadelphia, where she was a keynote speaker. I must say, therefore, what a genuinely wonderful person she is! And I have found great joy in watching her become a highly recognized and sincerely revered voice on the topic of the afterlife. Sandra organizes online medium classes, courses, demonstrations, and the non-denominational weekly "Sunday Gathering." Sandra is a highly respected author, speaker, and entrepreneur who is committed to making a difference in the lives of others. And because of the sincerity of her efforts and ongoing commitment to bringing comfort to the bereaved and such exceptional teachings and information to the public regarding the other side, a percentage of all Enchanted Winds book sales will be donated to the W.D.D. Patreon account to help support these worthy efforts.

> **Website:** https://www.wedontdie.com/
> **Facebook:** https://www.facebook.com/sandrachamplain
> **YouTube: We Don't Die Radio:** https://bit.ly/WeDontDieRadio YouTube
> **Shades of the Afterlife Podcast:** https://bit.ly/ShadesoftheAfterlife
> **Patreon:** https://www.patreon.com/wedontdieradio

Sonia Rinaldi is a kind and unassuming Brazilian researcher who consistently presents evidence of an afterlife via various research and processes of Instrumental Transcommunication (ITC). Her groundbreaking studies are not only influencing thought leaders and other researchers around the world, but they are also bringing comfort to countless individuals. I was fortunate enough to meet Sonia when she came to America for the first time in 2019. And to meet Sonia Rinaldi is to simply love Sonia! I have such strong regard for her decades-long and transformative research and am certain that her remarkable research will leave a lasting mark on this field of discovery. I also recommend her award-winning film directed by the very talented producer/filmmaker Robert Lyon. ***Rinaldi: Instrumental Transcommunication to the Other Side.*** The film is available on Amazon.

Reading Recommendations

Hello from Heaven! by Bill Guggenheim & Judy Guggenheim

How to Survive the Loss of a Love by Melba Colgrove, Harold H. Bloomfield, & Peter McWilliams

Through the Darkness by Janet Nohavek with Suzanne Giesemann

Grieving as the Path to Healing

After experiencing the loss of someone, or something "near & dear", grieving is an essential, yet natural healing process that is vital to undergo in order to return to a state of peace and well-being. However, grieving differs for each individual in duration, manner and form. Nevertheless, there are several components to grief that are common to all who have experienced it. With its many phases and characteristics, the grieving period will move through various stages. Yet, the stages may appear simultaneously—overlapping one another and/or out of sequence, which would not delay or impede the healing.

In the late 1960's, a Swiss psychiatrist, working with terminally ill patients, Elizabeth Kübler-Ross wrote an invaluable book entitled, "On Death & Dying". In her book, she mapped out the various phases that invariably people go through, during their time of sorrow. While observing their grieving process, she identified five distinct stages and listed them in the order in which they appeared: #1. **denial**, #2. **anger**, #3. **bargaining**, #4. **depression**, and #5. **acceptance**. Her research in identifying the 5 stages ultimately became the definitive protocol for all who worked with dying patients and their families. Her book was also the origin and inspiration for the establishment of all hospice organizations.

During the first stage of grieving, the **denial** stage, individuals may have strong thoughts of disbelief such as *"This can't be really happening. This cannot be possible!"* After coming to terms with the reality of the event, the 2nd stage, **anger,** typically shows up. Initially, anger can take the form of irritation at the slightest stimulus, but it may also quickly escalate to rage & even acts of violence, if awareness and supportive help are not readily available. Along with feelings of anger, guilt can also be experienced due to the concern about having done or not done something.

The third stage, **bargaining**, is a form of child-like behavior such requesting a miracle from the Creator. *"God, if you would let me have one more day with him, I will start praying again every morning."* The fourth stage, **depression**, can be felt as hopelessness, defeat, numbness or immobility. Depression often occurs simultaneously with the three previous stages.

Acceptance, the final stage, is coming to terms at last with the reality of the loss and all that it encompasses. Thus, after this last stage is reached by those who allow themselves to surrender to the grieving process, a feeling of peace, hope and even optimism for the future will return.

Reverend Silmar Sanchez
Ordained, All-Faith Minister
Hospice Chaplain

About the Author

Mary Hayes is a compassionate and well-respected Intuitive Counselor and Medium with over twenty-five years of experience. Serving clients from across the U.S. and internationally, she consistently offers clear and insightful guidance and meaningful connections with those on the other side. Mary's first book, *Express Your YES!,* teaches her simple yet effective technique for readily accessing intuition. Born just outside Boston, Massachusetts, she now resides on a small island near Mount Dora, Florida, with her two adorable cats and her supportive sweetheart, Jerry.

Book 2 is forthcoming, but in the meantime, feel free to visit her website and subscribe to her newsletter. And if you loved the book, please leave a review on Amazon!

www.maryhayes.org

Made in United States
Orlando, FL
10 November 2023